THE CRACKED SLIPPER

The Cracked Slipper

The Cracked Slipper Series, Book 1

Stephanie Alexander

Second edition printed November 2019

Cover and Distribution by Bublish, Inc.

ISBN: 978-1-64704-020-8 (eBook)
ISBN: 978-1-64704-021-5 (paperback)

To my children, Eliza, Harper, and Cyrus

Cinderella and the prince
Lived, they say, happily ever after,
Like two dolls in a museum case…
Their darling smiles plastered on for eternity…
That story.

— Anne Sexton

And graven in diamonds in letters plain,
There is written her fair neck round about,
Noli me tangere, for Caesar's I am.

— Sir Thomas Wyatt

PROLOGUE

ESCAPE

IN A BALLROOM PACKED with those who live their lives governed by strict decorum, a harried woman elbowing her way through the crowd attracts considerable attention. This is doubly true when the woman in question has been on the arm of the crown prince for most of the evening. She does not bother excusing herself. She plows on regardless of who blocks her path, be it a strapping soldier or a frail grandmother. Her corset is a tight fist around her chest, and she fights for a clean breath through a hundred conflicting perfumes and the scent of burning candles. The spell is slipping through her hands. She trips over pieces of tulle dangling from her petticoats and is jerked backwards as others step on what trails behind. It seems inevitable she will be left standing in the middle of the ballroom in her servant's rags.

The tide of her luck changes as the very person who seeks to prevent her from leaving unwittingly allows her escape. Trumpets blare, but the poor buglers are so suddenly and unexpectedly called upon that their normally synchronized fanfare becomes the braying of a troupe of confused donkeys. Callers bedecked in the royal colors of purple and green shout commands through golden megaphones.

"Fall back! Make way for Prince Gregory! Make way for the prince!"

Like hundreds of trained dogs the assembled guests retreat to the far sides of the ballroom. She finds herself alone in a wide aisle, a stranded bride in the heart of a great chapel. Prince Gregory jogs toward her, followed by assorted friends and advisers. The king himself huffs along at the end of the procession. Apprentice magicians check their enchantments. Fireballs hover with subdued crackling above the guests' heads, and giant butterflies freeze mid-flutter. The musicians grind to a halt, but the room hums with chatter and expectation.

"Wait!" calls Gregory. "Please, stop."

She hesitates, pulled by his insistent voice and crestfallen face, and in those few seconds the delicately embroidered sleeve of her silver gown slips over her shoulder. She hoists her skirts and sprints the last hundred or so steps.

The whispering crowd heaves a collective gasp that explodes into an uproar. She can no longer hear Gregory, but the voices of the callers ring out.

"Guards! Do not let her pass!"

The soldiers manning the entrance bumble about, not knowing who they're after in the milling throng of full silk skirts and polished black boots. She blows past them, a silver blur. Once through the archway she still has to maneuver a flight of stairs, cross the cavernous expanse of the Great Hall, pass the next set of guards at the two-story wooden doors, and descend another flight of stairs. She must find her coach, with its driver and six white horses that, upon close examination, bear a distinct resemblance to a parrot and a half-dozen goats. Most daunting, the two Unicorn Guards in full war regalia standing sentry at the head of the drive.

I'll never make it, she thinks.

She does not slow down when she reaches the first staircase and has no chance of recovery. Her right heel strikes the edge of the second slick marble stair, and her leg shoots out from under her. She crashes to her bottom and slides down the rest of the steps. Her dress hikes up past her knees as the marble flies past in alternating stripes of black and white. Both elbows scrape along behind her, but her attempts to stop only succeed in turning herself sideways. Her right slipper flies off and a sharp pain slices through her left foot as it bangs off the banister. By the time she comes to a rest at the base of the staircase she is looking up the way she came. She pushes her petticoats out of her face.

She has no time for humiliation, and jumps to her feet. Her shoe sits halfway up the staircase, too far away to retrieve. She reaches under her skirt and yanks off the other one. She is used to running barefoot.

And here she will be remembered, a thousand times, a million times, until the tumble down the stairs is forgotten and she flees with perfect poise and grace in one unbroken glass shoe. Few will know her as she is now. Just an unnamed girl, disappearing into the night, clutching a cracked slipper.

PART I

CHAPTER I

CONCILIATORY SENTIMENTS

IN THE DAYS OF Eleanor Brice's childhood her teacher had high hopes for her, perhaps a calling to magic. Unfortunately, Eleanor showed herself to be decidedly unenchanted at an early age. No matter how Rosemary cajoled, she could not draw one spark from Eleanor's skinny arms, or pull one spell out of her perpetually tousled blond head. Odd eyes or not, strange signs be damned, Eleanor would not be a witch. So, after her father's death and her stepmother's inheritance of the family estate, Eleanor became a maid. So she remained until age eighteen, when she became the most envied woman in the kingdom of Cartheigh.

Three days after the Second Sunday Ball and her unexpected change in fortune, Eleanor returned to the Brice House to collect her few belongings. She climbed from the elegant white carriage and wrapped her arms around herself, uncomfortably aware of the bare skin above her tight bodice. She greeted the liveried carriage horses. They bowed, the plumes between their ears waving like purple cattails on a marsh breeze, and nickered their respects.

"Mistress Brice. M'lady, m'lady, m'lady."

The soldiers fell back as she passed, a line of stiff, uniformed dominoes. Eleanor smiled at them, but not a one met her eyes. She lifted the skirts of her pale pink afternoon gown and stepped over a few puddles. It seemed the cobblestone drive had lengthened by several miles in the two days she'd been gone. Her wounded foot throbbed in her leather shoes, and she longed for the comfort of her glass slippers. She climbed the steps of her father's house and found the Fire-iron door unlocked, so she opened it.

"Hello?" Her voice bounced off the crystal chandelier, with its missing candles in need of replacing, and floated up the spiral staircase.

"They're hiding."

Eleanor started at the familiar warbling voice. She glared at the red and blue parrot perched on a disintegrating trellis.

"Chou, you mustn't creep up on me like that."

Chou Chou shook himself. "Is it my fault I blend with the roses? Besides, you're as jittery as a thirsty drunk on a fasting day." The parrot lit on her shoulder and whispered in her ear. "You were born to be the lady of this house, even if you've served in it for years."

"Mother Imogene and Sylvia would disagree with you."

"Dragons teeth, darling, it wouldn't be the first time." Eleanor jumped when Chou opened his beak. "*Go sit in a tree where you belong! Eleanor, find my parasol or I shall brain you with my lace hanky!*"

Eleanor laughed through her nerves and pinched his beak. "Why, Mother Imogene, red feathers do suit you. You sound just like Chou Chou, and I know you two are such good friends."

She closed the door behind her, shutting out her guardians' awkward reverence. Long-dead relations peered down at her from the walls, as if they did not recognize the young woman who had wiped their painted faces and dusted their gilded frames for the past eight years.

She walked through the front hall, the sound of her shoes sharp, muffled, sharp as she crossed planks then rugs then planks again. Out of old habit, she gave wide berth to the decorative table below the chandelier. A crude sculpture, two intertwined roses carved into a lump of raw ashwood, sat in the middle of the luminous Fire-iron tabletop, like an ugly bonnet atop an elegant coiffure. Years ago she'd accidentally knocked the statue onto the floor with her clumsy ten-year-old fingers. Mother Imogene had beat Eleanor until blood ran from the child's nose. It stained her gray dusting cloth the purplish color of her bruised face. She'd never touched Imogene's statue again, nor forgotten the shock of her stepmother's enraged protection of such a seemingly trivial knick-knack. The statue remained perpetually and mysteriously dust-free, so Eleanor could only assume Mother Imogene looked after it herself.

Eleanor ran her fingers along the walls, with their wide vertical stripes. Blue, green, gray, repeat. She peered into the empty sitting room. The shadows announced afternoon tea with their long faces, but no one had laid out biscuits or folded the napkins.

"Perhaps you're right, Chou," she said to the bird on her shoulder. "Maybe they are hiding."

The swish of petticoats behind her proved him wrong. She turned, Chou Chou's red wings flapping around her head, and faced her stepmother.

Imogene Easton Brice descended the spiral staircase in that stiff way Eleanor had always hated, where her head did not move except as one with the rest of her body. According to the lady herself, Imogene was known for her beautiful dancing when she first arrived at court. Even at near forty years of age she was clearly beautiful, with her dark shiny hair and delicate features, but Eleanor could never imagine anyone so stiff as a wonderful dancer.

Imogene's daughters, Margaret and Sylvia, trailed behind her. Their matching red and gold pinstriped gowns against the equally stripy walls made Eleanor's eyes want to cross. The three women stopped before Eleanor, their silk skirts bumping up against one another in a discomfited receiving line. Margaret stood between her mother and sister like the cracked cup in a mismatched tea set. Sylvia, at seventeen the younger sister by two years, was a replica of her mother from her eyes to her hair to her nose in the air. Margaret, on the other hand, had her late father's frizzy brownish hair, and his pinched face. *Just-like-that-miserable-drunk*, Imogene often said.

Margaret joined Imogene in a deep curtsy and held the pose. Sylvia curtsied, but kept her eyes pinned on the floor. Eleanor could practically see the heat rising off her head. She had a brief picture of Sylvia bursting into flames in the front hall. If she did so, Eleanor would make no move to put her out.

Eleanor was unsure of how to proceed. "Stand up, please."

The three women straightened. Eleanor still looked down on them, as she towered over each one by several heads. Imogene did a quick sweep of the pink gown, but her gaze lingered on the Fire-iron and diamond necklace resting on Eleanor's chest. Her white hands clenched one another. Eleanor did not trust them, even folded demurely before her stepmother's tiny waist. She was aware of her own hair hanging down her back. She'd always worn it twisted up off her neck while she worked, and this afternoon it felt like a blond banner of rebellion. Margaret's mouth twitched a wordless hello, but still Sylvia did not look up. The silence stretched on.

"Did you want to speak with me?" Eleanor asked.

"Welcome home, my lady," said Imogene. "Happy rumors have reached us. Are they true?"

"Yes. Prince Gregory has proposed." Margaret gasped and covered her mouth. Eleanor went on. "We're to be married in two weeks."

"Our deepest congratulations."

Sylvia muttered something that sounded like *dragonshit*.

"Pardon?" said Chou. He hopped onto Eleanor's head. His talons clenched in her hair.

"Yes—pardon," said Imogene, with a glance at her younger daughter. "Your pardon, lady, if I've ever appeared...harsh. You must know I carried your best intentions in my heart."

"Indeed," said Eleanor.

The impartial reply seemed to encourage Imogene. "Of course. Your father's lack of decorum—and the influence of those conjuring oddballs—"

"You mean the witches of Afar Creek Abbey?"

Imogene nodded. "Your father allowed Rosemary too much sway over you. After he passed on, HighGod bless him, I—I hoped to teach you to be a lady."

"Many girls find the path to ladyship by starving, freezing, and emptying chamber pots," said Chou.

Imogene flushed an ugly red.

"Frequent beatings only encourage only good posture. Long sessions locked in a broom closet lead to the most elegant manners. Lye soap has a wonderful effect on the hands—"

"Peace, Chou," said Eleanor.

"Please," Imogene said, "would you put in a good word at court for your stepsisters, if only for the sake of Margaret? I know you're fond of her. Perhaps you would even have a place for her in your chambers, if it's not too much."

Chou let out an outraged squawk, but Eleanor shushed him again. "Your apology means nothing to me," she said to Imogene. "I won't deny Sylvia a place at court, because I will not embarrass the prince or the king by joining in petty behavior. I will prove those connected with the Brice name are worthy of their association. Sylvia will have to secure her own place, and I hope she has the brains to do so without humiliating us. As for Margaret…"At the sound of her name Margaret smiled weakly.

"I've not forgotten your past kindness. I'll think on your request to join my ladies."

"It's as much as we could expect," said Imogene.

Chou seethed in her ear, but Eleanor dropped a shallow curtsy. Her stepfamily had to follow her. Chou left her shoulder and fluttered about the front hall. He hissed and dropped a pat of bird shit on the floor.

Eleanor called over her shoulder as she walked down the kitchen passageway. "I believe I left a mop on the porch."

Eleanor and Chou met no smell of baking bread as they wandered through the kitchen. No shrill laughter or scathing reprimands. Something built in Eleanor's chest as she ducked low-hanging pots and baskets, and the Brice House held its breath. She stepped into the rear courtyard, and the stones let out a sigh of dust and chicken feathers and flapping laundry.

Eleanor exhaled with them. Eight years of checking her opinions, and suffering for the ones that would not be suppressed. She remembered her stepmother's snidely given refusal to allow her to attend the Second Sunday Ball, despite her noble birth and King Casper's royal decree. *A donkey can't be a unicorn, girl, even with a golden horn.*

Gregory's face swam before her mind and she shivered. She thought of the teasing spark in his light brown eyes. His ring-laden hand gripping hers.

Oh, Mother Imogene, I shall never listen to you again.

She squinted into the HighAutumn sunlight after the house's gloom. Chou flew ahead of her, over two acres of patchy dirt and grass, toward the outbuildings lining the edge of the estate. Eleanor's steps were light, the damage done by the cracked slipper forgotten. She hummed the tune from her first dance with Gregory.

She'd only seen him once since the king's chief magician had delivered her to Eclatant Palace, the great Fire-iron castle of the Desmarais kings. Surely he would visit her today, and carriage traffic would be heavy in downtown Maliana. She did not feel like wasting time with idle conversation so she avoided the pens of the more intelligent animals, like the goats and pigs, because she knew they would ask nosy questions (she avoided the pigs in general anyway, as did most people, because it was hard to befriend an animal that would inevitably end up on your plate). Instead she cut past the chicken house, where the inhabitants were consumed only with scratching and pecking each other. She swept past the sheep, who followed her along the fence line bawling "BAAAARLEY, BAAAARLEY," at the top of their lungs. Luckily as soon as she disappeared behind a shed they forgot she had been there and settled back into their usual wooly stupor.

Chou stopped to harass the goats. They met him at the fence with a chorus of bleating complaints. The parrot strutted along the fence rail. "You should be honored! How many goats can say they pulled the carriage of a future Desmarais princess?"

The goats were unimpressed. "Corn? Where'sa corn? Sore feet. Oh, woes-me. Corn?"

Chou's head feathers went spiky with irritation. Eleanor left him to his squabbling and entered the wood-planked barn. She climbed into the hayloft. The ladder creaked under her weight, and the woman beside Eleanor's tiny bed turned at the sound. Eleanor smiled into Rosemary's well-loved face. The dark eyes and hooked nose, the straight white hair falling bluntly to her chin. Not a soft face, but one that brought Eleanor comfort.

"Dear girl," said Rosemary. Something lumpy squashed between them when they embraced. The battered burlap sack blended with Rosemary's simple gray witch's dress.

"Mother Imogene didn't find it in eight years," said Eleanor, as she took the bag from her teacher. "Yet here it is in your hands."

The witch shrugged her thin shoulders. "There is much of both of us inside."

Eleanor emptied a jumble of books and papers and charcoal pencils onto the bed. Titles and subjects jumped out at her. Algebra. *Carthean Poets of the Last Age*. Theology. *Fire-iron Tariffs of the Second Century*. *The Great Bond: Unicorns and the Desmarais Kings*.

She held up the last, the thickest of the lot, and then picked up another volume in her other hand. The gold lettering on the smaller book read *The Most Special Friendship*. A green dragon and a white unicorn cavorted under a happy yellow sun on the cover. "You didn't miss a lesson, from picture books to great theses."

Rosemary flipped through a pile of yellowing essays written in varying stages of a childish hand. She held one before her. "*Every citizen of Cartheigh should remember the importance of the Great Bond, for without it the Svelyans would be at our doors again*. You were quite the young patriot."

Eleanor took Rosemary's hand. Her voice caught in her throat. "How can I begin to thank you? If not for you—"

"Hush, now," said Rosemary, as she always did whenever Eleanor tried to show her appreciation for Rosemary's years of dedication. "Your stepmother did not see fit to educate her own daughters. Your own father, HighGod bless him, would have dismissed me before your thirteenth birthday."

"I know, but—"

"I've taught wellborn girls for eighty years, Eleanor. I did as you mother would have wanted." Rosemary touched Eleanor's cheek.

Eleanor stepped away and shuffled around the room. She pulled a tattered red horse blanket from her bed. She draped it over her shoulder, but not before pressing her nose into the rough wool. The smell of her father's gelding was long gone, but the habit stayed with her.

"I'm sorry," said Rosemary. "How forgetful of me."

"No pardon needed," said Eleanor, as she tucked her mother's music box under her other arm. Even in the long gone days before her father's death, Eleanor rarely spoke of Leticia Brice. Such ruminations only served to remind everyone that Eleanor herself had been the instrument of her mother's demise. She peeked inside the music box at Leticia's antique Fire-iron hair comb. The comb always seemed too precious to touch, like the martyr's relics in the chapel.

She glanced at Rosemary, who rung her hands at the un-paned window. Rosemary had always encouraged Eleanor to speak her mind.

Eleanor's mouth set in a stubborn line. Rosemary would hear her gratitude, whether she wanted to or not.

"I would thank you for sending me to the ball," said Eleanor. "If you hadn't appeared in the garden—"

Rosemary spun around, a wide smile on her face. "I'm sure it was lovely, darling."

Eleanor's brow wrinkled as Rosemary disappeared down the ladder.

The Hundred Heralds Street wove through most of Maliana on its way to Eclatant Palace. The grandest homes were furthest from the noise and smells of Smithwick Square. The Brice family was unimportant in the complicated hierarchy of the privileged, and their wealth from the self-made smarts of recent memory, so the Brice House was closer to the heart of town. Once through the gates, the white carriage rattled along for only half a mile before the elegant stone manors and their spacious grounds were replaced by wooden-walled, thatched roofed shops of all kinds; milliners, cobblers, bakeries, and butchers. Townsfolk lined the streets. Their gawking and jostling along the edge of the roadway slowed the royal procession to a limping crawl.

Chou did not join Eleanor and Rosemary in the coach until they reached Smithwick Square. He tapped on the window and Eleanor opened it a crack. He squeezed his way inside, collapsed on the seat, and rolled onto his back. His scaly feet pointed at the ceiling.

"Water, please," he said.

Eleanor poked him. "Sit up, you're shedding feathers all over the royal seat cushions."

"Where have you been, Chou?" asked Rosemary.

"Spying, of course," said Eleanor. She offered him a drink from her water flask.

"For your benefit," Chou said between gulps.

"Darling Chou, you're my eyes and ears."

Chou shook himself and paced the cushion. "I clung to the front door and peered through the letter slot, you know. A difficult grip, but a fine vantage point."

Eleanor and Rosemary murmured admiration.

"So, at first it was just la-di-da. Imogene telling Sylvia she must show respect. Sylvia cursing. *Dragonshit!*" Chou did not just repeat Sylvia's favorite profanity. His voice became hers, with all its prissy spite. "Then it got interesting. Perhaps I should just repeat it?"

"Yes, please do," said Eleanor.

Chou opened his mouth and Eleanor felt as if she herself were standing outside the door with her ear pressed to the letter slot.

Sylvia: "*To think I just bowed down to that bitch in her borrowed fancies! I think I'm going to be sick!*"

Imogene, harried: "*Will the king let him do it? He's only twenty-one, after all. Childhood, for a man. And everyone of worth in the city in an uproar about it.*"

Sylvia: "*It's absurd! He can't marry her. He just can't! She's so—so skinny and so damnably tall. Like an alley cat on stilts.*"

Margaret's tentative voice entered the conversation. "*She has lovely hair, Syl...and her face...if you'd just look—*"

"*She has devil eyes, Margaret. Everyone's always said so! And she can't dance—*"

Imogene again. "*She out-danced you on Second Sunday, and you've had years of lessons!*"

"*That's not fair, Mother. She was mysterious...he only wanted her because no one knew who she was. I can't believe we didn't see through that silly spell of Rosemary's!*"

"*If you'd used the skills I've taught you, no spell would have mattered.*" Chou increased Imogene's anger and volume with each word. "*A colossal waste of years of planning.*"

"*I'll go to the palace myself. I'll tell everyone the truth about her. She's no lady—*"

Chou interrupted himself. "Imogene slapped Sylvia across the face."

"No!" said Eleanor.

Chou nodded and went on.

Imogene again: *"Don't you understand the position we're in? If things continue as they are, Eleanor Brice will be princess, and someday queen, and we've made her life rather unpleasant over the last eight years, if you don't recall. One word from her and we could lose everything. This house, our income. We could be banished!"*

Margaret: *"Mother, I don't think Eleanor would be so vengeful. Perhaps we could put all our past animosity behind us."*

Imogene: *"Ha! Margaret, you're a bigger fool than you look. Better that HighGod had sent me Eleanor for a daughter and condemned you to the hayloft. As for you, Sylvia, it is of the utmost importance you marry as soon as possible, while her position is not yet cold Fire-iron."*

Sylvia: *"Marry? I just came out."*

Imogene: *"No matter, there's no time for being choosy or flittering away at parties with silly boys. We must find you a powerful match, and soon. In fact, I already have someone in mind."*

"I'm sorry to say that's the end," said Chou in his own warble. "They retired to the sitting room. No mention of the lucky gentleman who's caught Imogene's fancy."

"We'll find out eventually, I suppose," said Eleanor.

"One fact is clear," said Chou. "While Sylvia may have an eye for a fancy gown, Margaret is a better judge of a lovely face."

Eleanor kissed his silky brow and leaned her forehead against the window. Margaret's conciliatory sentiments held some appeal, but apparently Imogene had no such notions. Eleanor watched the colorful people of her city going about their daily business. The bubble of confidence that had filled her chest at her father's house was suddenly made of granite. "Thank you, Chou. Enlightening, as always."

CHAPTER 2

EASY CONVERSATION

HUNDRED HERALDS WOUND PAST the church where the Desmarais family and their closest allies worshipped, Humility Chapel. After passing a Fire-iron statue of the last Malian king, the road gradually steepened. First Maliana Covey, where the most powerful magicians in the kingdom studied and conjured, was the last structure before the palace itself. As the Covey gate came into view Eleanor's gown suddenly seemed constricting and to her horror she started sweating. She opened the window and hoped the afternoon air would calm her nerves. The coach passed under the massive arched gate in the stone wall surrounding the palace.

She wondered if she'd ever be able to stop gawking at the largest building constructed of pure Fire-iron in the world. Eclatant glowed in the HighAutumn sunlight, its sweeping arches and buttresses melting one into the other. The national flag, a purple banner emblazoned with a white unicorn and a green dragon, hung from every window. The carriage stopped on the marble driveway across from a life-sized statue of King Caleb Desmarais astride the originator of the Great Bond and namesake of the palace, the legendary unicorn stallion Eclatant.

Four soldiers dressed in Fire-iron war regalia sat sentry, each mounted on a living unicorn, at the bottom of a steep staircase. Eleanor had spent her whole life reading about unicorns, but like most Cartheans, she had rarely seen one in the flesh. They were huge; a draft horse would appear a pony in either one's shadow. The stallion closest to the coach had a coat so white it was almost blue, the color of a sheet of long frozen ice. Each muscle was clearly defined under his skin and his mane hung past his arched neck in loose curls. His forelock hung down his long, surprisingly delicate face, and split around the silver horn erupting out of his forehead like a sword. His thick hide made armor unnecessary and he wore only a carved leather saddle and a rein looped over his muzzle. He stood still, except to swish his long, tasseled tail.

Eleanor's heart banged against her ribcage as she took the footman's hand. She lit on the white marble and looked up at the two-story doors. She imagined Sylvia standing behind her, whispering about alley cats and devil eyes.

Wheels ground into motion and Eleanor waved as the coach set off in the direction of Afar Creek Abbey. She fought the urge to grasp the door handle and beg Rosemary to stay. She touched Chou's scaly foot on her shoulder as she started toward the stairs.

A white wall stopped her. "Afraid."

The unicorn's long face eclipsed her view of the rest of the world. She could have counted the curved eyelashes framing his dark eyes. His rider yanked at his rein, trying to move him back in line with his fellows.

"What?" she said, as Chou scurried down her back. He trembled between her shoulder blades.

It was clearer this time. "Do not be afraid." The unicorn's breath was like a warm glove caressing her neck. "We are here for your protection."

Eleanor didn't know how to respond, so she tried good manners. "Thank you. I do appreciate it."

The unicorn nodded his great head and returned to his duties.

Two lavishly dressed young women greeted Eleanor at the top of the stairs. The first girl, curly-haired and roly-poly, squealed and showered Eleanor with kisses. The other girl, thin with dark blond hair and the brown eyes of a hungry doe in winter, gently pulled her friend away.

The curly one, Anne Iris Smithwick, started chattering at once. She was Gregory's cousin (*On his mother's side. Smithwick as in the square, dearest.*), and she had heard all about Eleanor from her brother, Brian. He had been flattering (*Just the prettiest thing he's ever seen, and that's saying a lot!*). The other girl was Eliza Horn Harper, (*Yes, only seventeen and already married!*) and they had been ladies-in-waiting to Gregory's sister, the late Princess Matilda (*Poor dear darling Matilda! Died in childbirth, you know, but we don't talk about it.*). Now it would be their job to show Eleanor to her new chamber (*You'll just love it, Matilda had exquisite taste.*) and help her settle in (*My peal earbobs would look just lovely on Eleanor, don't you think, Liza dear?*)

Anne Iris didn't give Eleanor the opportunity to say much as they led her through the palace to Matilda's chamber. She could scarcely digest the fact that frizzy, plump Anne Iris was sibling to the dashing Brian Smithwick, whom Eleanor had met briefly at Second Sunday and had mistaken for the prince himself. Eliza finally suggested Eleanor might appreciate a bit of privacy.

Once they left Eleanor stood in the middle of the room. Her index finger drifted to her mouth. "I thought last night's guest room luxurious...but...shall we live *here*, Chou?" she asked the bird on her shoulder. She did not think Chou Chou had ever gone so long in silence while awake. "Were we not recently residing in a hayloft?"

"I don't know what to say, darling. Perhaps HighGod is playing a joke on us." He quickly recovered his wits. "If that is the case, I hope the punch line is years away."

Eleanor laughed and exhaled. She cautiously explored the large bedroom. She admired its tasteful furnishings; the four-poster bed hung with pale blue silk curtains, the graceful mahogany wardrobe and dressing table. There were intricacies in each piece, beadwork, embroidery, carvings; all so delicate nothing felt overdone. The sitting area, with its comfortable furniture and a brightly painted writing desk, faced a picture window overlooking the main garden. Chou paced Matilda's bookshelves. "What titles, Chou?" she asked.

"M'lady?"

Eleanor jumped at the soft voice. "Damn!" She spun around, her hand pressed to her chest. As her breathing slowed blood crept into her cheeks. A chambermaid stood beside the bed. Her mouth hung open and a pitcher dangled precariously from her hands.

"Pardon...you startled me," said Eleanor.

"No, Mistress, pardon me," whispered the maid. She crept closer and held up the pitcher. "We filled your bath."

Eleanor smiled at her. "Thank you. And I do apologize. My nerves are in a state."

The maid curtsied and brushed past Eleanor. Eleanor followed her to the bathing room. "Might I help you?"

The maid shook her head, her eyes on the tiles. As she poured some pink creamy concoction into the water Eleanor opened one of the glass doors on the apothecary cabinet. She examined some of the tiny bottles and lumps of soap. Lavender, cherry blossom, vanilla, sageflower.

The maid emptied her pitcher and stood with her hands folded before her. Her position was eerily reminiscent of Sylvia's tense deference, save her curly blonde hair and crooked teeth.

"You may go," Eleanor finally said.

"Your gown, m'lady."

"Oh—oh yes. Of course." Without assistance she would be trapped in this dress, a cheese in a tough rind. Eleanor held her arms out to her sides, and the maid flitted around unhooking clasps and buttons like a drab bird pecking at scarecrow. Eleanor had done her fair share of unbuttoning gowns, and the irony of such attention did not escape her. She focused on the maid's face. The woman's breath smelled of cornmeal. "Do you live here?" Eleanor blurted out.

The maid nodded.

"It's very grand," said Eleanor. "Will you be here every day?"

The woman shook her head. Her brown eyes flitted from Eleanor's forehead to her ears to her chin. She cleared her throat. "No, Mistress. You'll be choosin' a proper lady's maid."

"Oh." *What makes a proper maid?* She bit her lip.

"I'll be here today, though. Tomorrow I return to town to visit with my family."

"Do you have children?"

The woman nodded. "Two boys, Mistress."

Eleanor reached in the pocket of her gown. The chief magician had given her a small bag of coins before she left for her father's house, but the soldiers had never let her get within twenty paces of the populace. The idea of one who had never held a penny in her hand doling out alms had seemed ludicrous, but now she saw an opportunity. She handed the bag to the maid. "For your boys."

The maid looked at the bag of coins as if it might blow raspberries at her. "I can't."

"Please," said Eleanor. "Take it."

The maid slid the bag into her own pocket, her eyes on Eleanor's chest. "Bless you, Mistress."

The maid took her leave, her face hidden behind an armful of lace and silk, and Eleanor stepped into the steaming water. A blush leaked from her hairline to her toenails, so her fair skin rather blended with pinkish water.

She closed her eyes and inhaled the scent of moonberries. The maid's avoidance of her gaze shouldn't have bothered her. *Freak. Devil.* People had always whispered about her eyes. They were large and well spaced, framed with thick lashes and delicate brows, and colored the soft blue of a late summer sky. Then a sudden aberration put the whole flawless picture off. A reddish-brown, rather crescent-shaped smudge obscured most of the iris of her left eye, as if the artist had decided halfway through to change the painting and then abandoned the project. *A bad sign. Evil spirits.*

Eleanor had vague memories of Rosemary's hope that the flaw in her eye might be a magical sign. A tiny Eleanor often sat on the witch's lap and flipped through picture books. By the time she reached age four she could recite the tale of the Great Bond. King Caleb Desmarais, the Dragon Mines of the North County; giant green lizards and unicorns and invading Svelyan armies. Eleanor held them all in her head like her own treasured memories. Sometimes Rosemary asked Eleanor to turn the pages without touching them, but when Eleanor tried nothing happened. She could answer all of Rosemary's questions, but she could not perform the simplest magic.

Eleanor's own father, Cyril Brice, chose to treat his odd little girl with absent affection. He died before his hopes of turning her into a proper lady could come to fruition under the tutelage of his second wife, the self-declared authority on all things feminine. Only Rosemary looked at Eleanor and saw goodness and smarts over a runaway mouth and knobby knees and highly inappropriate eye color.

After Imogene dismissed Rosemary from Eleanor's life, she kept the sole company of her stepfamily for eight years. Before attending the Second Sunday Ball she'd not had a conversation with anyone of the masculine persuasion, other than Chou Chou, who being a bird did not exactly count. No one saw her.

That is, until Gregory Desmarais met her eyes across a crowded dance floor.

Two hours later she waited for him in a new gown, this one gold brocade, her hair heavy and damp against her bare shoulders. Chou flitted from the mantel to her head to the bed posters. Her mother's music box plinked out its mournful tune from Matilda's dressing table. The delicate sound was too loud in the bedroom, like a bugle call in a library. Eleanor lay a handkerchief over the cracked slipper and Leticia's hair comb and shut the lid. The music box settled into miffed silence.

"He's coming," she said as she paced the room, "I'm sure we shall dine together tonight."

Chou's head waved like a clock pendulum. He opened his beak, no doubt to agree that Gregory would most certainly, without a doubt, arrive at any second, when the maid announced the long anticipated visitor.

Eleanor straightened her skirts. "I told you," she whispered.

Chou shook his tailfeathers in what could only be described as a display of birdie lewdness. "I'll leave you, my dear."

Eleanor giggled as he disappeared out the open window. The door opened and Gregory strode into the room. Her eyes darted over his thick auburn hair and strong chin. His features were not delicate, but that did not detract from the robust energy evident in his broad shoulders and powerful frame. He pounded across his late sister's fringed rugs and lifted Eleanor off her feet. "Sweetheart!"

She thought her heart would burst at that endearment. He set her down, and kissed her hands. She didn't have to look far to meet his eyes, as he was not much taller than her. "Gregory," she said, because in that moment she could think of nothing else.

He led her to the couch. "How do you find your chamber? Are you comfortable?"

She nodded. "Yes, very."

He touched her hair, and then turned her face toward his. "You certainly look well."

Between the gold gown and the heat in her face she surely resembled an exuberantly stoked fire. She studied the green piping on the sleeves of his purple tunic. *I danced with him all night. Same man, different fancy room.* She thought of their easy, wine-induced flirtation at the ball. She decided to reclaim it, albeit a less inebriated version.

"Am I making you nervous?" he asked.

"I must say this is the first time I've ever sat on a couch with a prince."

"Well, you're making quite a go of it."

"Am I? In all honestly, I've haven't sat on a couch with anyone in years. I'm moving up the ranks quite quickly."

Gregory raised his eyebrows. "Some would call it improper, to go from dancing to sitting in such a short acquaintance."

"I have to make up for lost time." She laughed, and he joined her.

"What can I bring you?" he said. "Sewing needles? Stationery?"

"No, thank you."

"I want you to be happy. What shall you do in this pretty room?"

"When I'm at leisure I read. I enjoy studying and writing essays." She pointed at the bookshelves. "It seems your sister shared my interest."

"Matilda?" He laughed again. "I'm sure every one of those is a book of dress patterns, or love ballads. She was an expert at embroidery, singing, and correspondence, like every other lady I know."

"I'm afraid I excel at none of those. Although I have recently discovered a love of dancing." *All that time Imogene spent teaching Sylvia to be coy, and yet honesty works just as well.*

Gregory edged closer. "What do you read? Poetry?"

"I do love poetry, but I also find history and the old literature fascinating, and the study of the earth."

He raised his eyebrows again. This time they nearly melted into his red hair.

Eleanor's ricocheting confidence took another swan dive. She changed the subject. "A ball does not make for easy conversation. Tell me, how does a prince spend his time?"

He seemed to forget about her odd scholarly bent as he talked about himself. He became quite animated as he discussed his love of hunting and fishing, of long rides and tournaments. He told her he spent as much time as he could in the Paladine Stables with the unicorns. The great beasts enthralled him, and he involved himself in all aspects of their care and the herd's complex breeding program.

Eleanor listened carefully and nodded when she thought he expected it. Perhaps he realized he was going on at length. He brought her back into the conversation by asking if she enjoyed riding. "As a child I enjoyed it very much, but since my father's death the opportunities have been few and far between. My father had a saddle horse, but he was sold many years ago. He was a lovely animal."

"Bloodstock?"

His interest encouraged her. She nodded. "He was a black gelding. Called High Noon. My father wanted to call him Midnight, but my mother said all black horses were called Midnight and this one needed something more original. So High Noon he became."

Gregory chuckled.

"He was fast, and so clever. Almost like a bird. He came up lame and threw my father. It was an accident, but Papa's neck broke in the fall. I was ten years old, and the constable brought them home—" Eleanor's throat constricted at the memory of her strong, tall Papa draped across High Noon's back like a sack of grain. "My stepmother sold him to one of my father's friends. He called out to me, when they took him away… but I couldn't…I didn't…that's all I have left of him." She pointed at the tattered red blanket on the edge of Matilda's elegant bed.

"It must have been quite a loss." He kissed her nose.

"Well…it is fortunate that we can understand each other's pain. My father, and—" She spit out the words. "—my mother. You mother gone, just four years ago…and then your sister last spring."

"This is a time for joyful thoughts, sweetheart." He raked both hands through his hair, and then pulled her to her feet. "Anne Iris and Eliza will join you for dinner. You'll have a fine meal in your new chamber."

"Aren't you hungry?"

He grinned. "Always. One of many things you'll learn about me."

At that moment the chambermaid announced Anne Iris and Eliza. Gregory blew kisses and took his leave, and Eleanor realized he'd never told her where or when he'd take his own supper.

Anne Iris flounced over to the couch. "Have you any wine, Eleanor, dearest? I'm parched."

"I don't know, honestly."

Eliza sat just as primly as Anne Iris had flopped. "HighGod, Anne Iris. How would the poor girl know the whereabouts of the liquor cabinet? I'm sure she's yet to find the tooth scrub."

Anne Iris crossed her arms across her ample bosom. "Priorities, ladies. Number one, chamber pot. Number two, spirits."

"Number three," said Eliza. "A handkerchief to cover your mouth."

Eleanor snorted into her hand, Gregory's abrupt disappearance momentarily forgotten.

"So," said Anne Iris. "Are you ready for tomorrow?"

"What's tomorrow?" asked Eleanor.

"Let's see," said Eliza. "You're to attend chapel, and then two lunches."

"How can I attend two lunches?"

"Don't eat at the first. Just stir your soup. And then a game of lawn bolls with the Svelyan and Kellish ambassadors."

"Wear something red, if you have it," said Anne Iris. "They like red."

Is there anything red in that wardrobe?

"...an embroidery circle, and then afternoon tea. Then dinner in the Grand Ballroom."

"I'm not known for my embroidery."

Eliza patted Eleanor's knee. "Neither is Anne Iris, darling. She only attends so she can chat up the sisters of eligible men."

CHAPTER 3

AN ODD START

AT THIS TIME OF year there were at least a hundred people living at Eclatant Palace, not including the legions of servants, soldiers, chefs, maids and gardeners. Some were resident courtiers—advisers, magicians, ambassadors, or close friends of the royal family. A constant rotation of young, unmarried aristocrats sampled the excitement of court and perused potential marriage partners. While most of the more settled gentry spent the majority of their time at their townhouses or country estates, they too would descend on the palace to attend an event, ask a favor of the king, or settle a dispute. Eclatant had to be prepared at all times to feed, house and entertain anyone of worth who made an appearance. The court was the heart of the kingdom, a showpiece of the power and sophistication of the Desmarais family, and the envy of the surrounding countries. King Casper Desmarais had spent years, and piles of gold and Fire-iron, perfecting an image of graceful prosperity.

Anne Iris and Eliza took it upon themselves to teach Eleanor the ins and outs of palace life, for they had both lived at Eclatant for several years. They casually explained protocols without making Eleanor feel too much like a country cousin. Chou Chou, of course, adapted to their new home within hours. He settled himself on his new Fire-iron perch and promptly issued commands to the servants.

When Eleanor opened her eyes each morning she stared in wonder at the delicate blue silk curtains floating between the four carved posters of her bed. One day blurred into the next, a parade of dinners and picnics filled with countless introductions to a stream of ladies and gentlemen of various ranks, families and towns. It did not take long for Eleanor to notice the welcoming sentiments behind their toothy smiles never touched their eyes, which tended to crawl over her person like a thousand bees collecting pollen. Anne Iris and Eliza whispered names over her shoulder, reminding her how one was related to the other. Without them she would have despaired of being able to place anyone.

About a week after depositing Eleanor and Chou Chou in his sister's former rooms, Gregory decided to it was high time Eclatant hosted a jousting tournament.

"Has it been some time since the last one?" Eleanor asked Anne Iris.

Anne Iris nodded. "Ten days. Gregory doesn't fancy getting out of practice."

So Eleanor joined the crowd of ladies lining the jousting pitch on a cloudless, breezy Friday morning. With every jolt of wind her hair floated around her face like blond spider webs. It stuck in her eyes and she subtly spit out strands that crept into her mouth. Gregory always complimented her hair, and she still enjoyed the relaxed weight of it against her shoulders, but she made a mental note to check the weather before completing her toilette in the future.

Eclatant Palace loomed behind the pitch, an observant stone steward. King Casper, an older, heavier version of Gregory, sat on a Fire-iron throne twenty paces to Eleanor's right. She glanced at the king, but he seemed formed from the unyielding rock of his palace and his chair. He watched the pitch with his arms crossed over his thick chest and sporadically licked his red mustache.

Eleanor returned her attention to the tournament. The LowWinter sun had some heat left in it, but she shivered anyway. The men rubbed linseed oil on their armor, and the smell overrode the last gasps of a few fading rosebushes. Thick grass tickled Eleanor's ankles under her petticoats. She slipped one stocking foot from her shoe and rubbed her toes in the green carpet.

"Put your shoe on," whispered a voice in her ear.

She turned to face a grinning Brian Smithwick, Anne Iris's debonair brother. His wore a tunic of olive that complimented the green in his hazel eyes. She smiled back at him. He'd asked her for her first dance at Second Sunday, so he was for all intents her oldest friend at Eclatant.

"I shall do nothing of the sort, sir," she said. "Shoes are indeed overrated."

"Even glass slippers?" he asked. He brushed his dark blond hair out of his eyes.

Someone cleared his throat over Brian's shoulder. Eleanor said hello to Raoul Delano, another of Gregory's closest mates. She detected a blush through Raoul's swarthy complexion, and he stuttered out something like a polite response. Unsurprising, as Raoul had done little more than stare at Eleanor with his dark spaniel's eyes during her every interaction with him.

"You're due to mount up, Smithy," he said to Brian.

Brian bowed with a flourish, which incited Eleanor to curtsy and Anne Iris to roll her eyes. The court callers announced Gregory, and the chattering crowd fell silent. Eleanor's breath caught in her throat as Gregory rode onto the pitch. He sat astride a blindingly white unicorn stallion, the largest Eleanor has seen in her limited experience. He wore his fighting armor, solid Fire-iron from neck to toe. Sunlight struck the iron and reflected the colorful costumes of the observing courtiers. He resembled a human rainbow.

The unicorn tossed his head and jigged sideways. Eleanor could not have imagined a more beautiful creature, or a more beautiful man on his back. The sharp outline of his jaw against the armor's equally straight edge. The easy way he sat in the saddle with the rein in one hand and his wooden lance balanced effortlessly on his hip. When his unicorn stopped before her she curtsied.

"My lady," he said.

Anne Iris nudged her, and she pulled a piece of purple lace from the pocket of her gown. As she tied it on the end of his lance she vacillated between euphoria and mortification, for she could feel a hundred eyes upon her and sensed nearly as many voices dissecting her. Gregory turned the unicorn and trotted toward his opponent. Eleanor swiped a glass of wine from a passing servant's tray and took a long gulp.

Eliza raised her eyebrows. "Take care. You're not accustomed."

That fact became painfully obvious as the joust continued. Throughout the match Eleanor cheered loudly for Gregory. She denounced his opponent's lance-wielding prowess, although as she'd never before witnessed a match she could hardly be considered an expert. She heckled the steward. When the other man finally tumbled from his mount Eleanor whooped and ran onto the pitch.

Gregory didn't seem to mind the lack of propriety. He leapt to the ground and met her halfway. A bead of sweat dripped from his auburn hair onto her nose when he kissed her full on the mouth. She heard the gasps of the watching ladies, but by then she'd finished a second glass of wine.

"Eleanor," Eliza whispered as she rejoined the twittering women on the sidelines. "Maybe you shouldn't—"

"Have I broken a law?" Eleanor glared over her shoulder at a wall of swishing fans and wagging eyebrows. She raised her voice. "Some decree banning women from the jousting pitch?"

Gregory wrapped his arms around her waist. His armor was cold against her back. "If you have I shall declare the law null and void."

Anne Iris laughed, but Eliza bit her lip. Eleanor glanced at the Fireiron throne. King Casper had taken his leave. Gregory kissed her hand and returned to his mount, and within half an hour Eleanor rejoined Chou Chou in her chamber to await the next event.

The next morning, of course, she woke with a headache and clammy stomach. The headache was the result of the wine. The tight feeling in her belly was the result of remorse. Her dreams had barely faded before she was reviewing every hour of the previous day in her mind, trying to identify the conversations in which she had said the right and wrong thing.

Maybe Eliza was right. Maybe she shouldn't.

Gregory did not call for Eleanor the next day, but the king's chief magician did. He asked her to wait for him after morning chapel to discuss plans for the wedding. As the worshipers dispersed Eleanor tried to pray, but she could not remember the meditations of her childhood. She gave up and watched the Godsmen tidying up lost handkerchiefs and forgotten prayer books. Even the slap of their soft-soled sandals echoed in the chapel's sharp angles.

Although it was the house of worship for the most important people in the land, Humility Chapel lived up to its name. It was a rectangular brick building filled with rows of backless wooden benches sitting on dark green limestone. A simple stone altar, covered in fresh flowers, stood at the far end of the main chamber. There were no paintings or statues, no idols or adornments of any kind. The windows, for the most part, were small and simple. One large window set into the softly arching ceiling saved it from being dreary by raining sunlight on the bright altar blooms. Humility Chapel was not so different from hundreds of other chapels spread throughout Cartheigh, albeit a bit larger.

The people of Cartheigh and the surrounding kingdoms held a deep belief in the HighGod, but there was little dogma in their religion. Most people stopped by their local chapel a few times a week to pray and tithe, but their churches were loosely connected and the clergy held no real power. The chapels were a vital part of the life of the kingdom, but the personal nature of it all kept the Godsmen from great influence and took away the need for grandiose worship houses. Ezra Oliver stood beside the altar with a thick ledger in one hand. She thought of First Maliana Covey, the second largest building in Maliana, and therefore in all of Cartheigh. In this day and age, the magicians held sway over both power and elaborate buildings.

Ezra Oliver turned in her direction, as if she'd shouted the words rather than thought them. He joined her on the first bench, a slight man with a broad, flat nose and a receding chin. He wore a dark gray tunic and the flattened square hat of First Covey. He smiled at her. His teeth were yellow, but at one hundred and five years of age she had to credit him for having teeth at all.

Eleanor had read about Ezra Oliver for years. Her mind spun with questions for him, from his thoughts on Carthean-Svelyan relations to the latest trends in dragon husbandry. Oliver, however, seemed inclined toward conversation of the matrimonial sort.

"LowAutumn the seventh, in the year Desmarais Three Hundred and Three," he said, as if Eleanor had forgotten her own birthday. He sounded like he had a clothespin attached to his nose. "Your star patron is the Virgin. Blue Hydrangeas. Prince Gregory's is the Lion. Yellow roses."

"That sounds lovely—"

"Speculative rubbish, surely, but it is tradition. Your father is dead, so King Casper will escort you down the aisle."

His abruptness startled Eleanor, but she'd been known to forego pleasantries herself. She reciprocated. "I'd prefer Rosemary of Afar Creek Abbey, if possible."

"A witch? I'm sorry, Mistress Brice, but it won't do for a woman to give you away."

Eleanor smiled. "I've known her as long as I would have known my father, had HighGod not called him on."

Oliver looked up from his notes. "She was your tutor, was she not?"

"Yes, since before I can remember. After my father's death my stepmother claimed she could no longer afford to pay Rosemary. Rosemary didn't care about payment, but Mother Imogene banned her from my father's house anyway."

"How did she come to send you to Second Sunday, if you'd not seen her in years?"

Eleanor began talking, and for the first time since her arrival at Eclatant the whole story came out. How she'd hidden in her room for two weeks after her father's death, with only Chou Chou for company. How Mother Imogene banged on the door and cursed her and finally called Rosemary to the Brice House in the hope of avoiding a battering ram. Rosemary had knelt before Eleanor and promised to hide lessons for her each month in a hollow tree by the front gate. Books, essay, questions to make her think. She made Eleanor swear she'd keep up with it on her own. Make her poor departed mother proud.

She told Eleanor she must stay in the Brice House, never leave, for no matter how bad it seemed within those walls it would be much worse out on the streets. Eleanor could still hear Rosemary's voice whispering in her ear as she clutched at the witch's neck.

Eighty years of bright girls…eighty years of lost potential…I cannot deliver you from your pain…it is not possible, no matter how we both wish it…but I can deliver you from the ignorance of propriety…I will give you what I could not give your mother…

"I begged Rosemary to take me with her, but she couldn't. Still, she didn't forget me. She never missed a month," Eleanor said. "Not in eight years. The lessons…her letters…everything to me."

Oliver's expression did not change as Eleanor rambled on. He didn't interrupt her, or change the subject. Eleanor trailed off and he spoke. "The witches are known for their dedication to desperate cases."

Eleanor nodded. "The sick…the poor of the city—"

"But still, this Rosemary went beyond the call of duty, magical or not. It's unusual. I'm sure you know witches and magicians don't have husbands and wives and children. We live for our talents and our work. Yet she treated you more like—" He seemed to have difficulty understanding his own speculations. "—family. A…how would you say it? A loved one."

"She told me the elder witches warn the youngsters of the dangers of loving ordinary people."

Oliver nodded. "Young magicians hear the same message. It is difficult to watch the ones you love grow up and grow old while you stay the same."

"Rosemary called it good advice, but said she'd always had trouble following it. I think she loves all her students."

"Interesting. And then she appeared at your father's house and conjured you off to the ball? Gown, slippers, the lot?"

"Yes. She was so nervous that night. I would almost have said afraid. The magic taxed her. She's a teacher, not a true conjurer. The spell wore of at midnight. I panicked and fled."

"I didn't believe it myself when you asked to try the glass slipper. But the fit…and Gregory had no trouble recognizing you, rags and dirt and all. I've never seen His Highness so adamant about anything."

"Don't forget goat hair and pumpkin guts, Mister Oliver," said Eleanor. Her own bravado amazed her. "I was a sorry sight, even by servants' standards."

The magician chuckled. "You silenced the High Council's grumbling with that cracked slipper. No one could doubt your honesty." He shook his head. "A former chambermaid with a broken shoe. An odd start…now, your stepmother. She'll be included by name in the proclamation—"

"That won't be necessary. We've never gotten on, you see."

"That was easily surmised. An old grudge?"

Eleanor took a moment, her mind reaching back over years of grudges for the first one. "I'm not certain, sir. She never took to me… from the time my father married her, a few months before he died…you see, when she arrived at the house, with her daughters and her groom—"

"Her groom? You mean a pageboy?"

"No. It was a groom, a proper grown man. Close to my father's age. Odd, I suppose, since she had no horses of her own and we had only my father's riding horse, High Noon…but he left our service within weeks. Anyway, when Imogene first arrived she ignored me. After my father's death, she let her true feelings be known."

"Brave child, to continue studying with Rosemary, even at the risk of Mrs. Brice's rage."

"She would have raged had I remained ignorant or not. " Eleanor touched Oliver's arm. "I want to do well here, Mister Oliver. I've worked hard, for years. Every night. Rosemary left no topic untouched. I hope I can put my learning to good use. Help my husband…and my kingdom. However I may be needed."

Oliver stared at her hand on his sleeve. She blushed and returned it to her lap.

He cleared his throat and returned to business. "I'll keep that in mind, Mistress Brice. Perhaps we can be of mutual assistance. Now, as I was saying, King Casper will escort you down the aisle…"

That afternoon Eleanor attended a baby viewing in the Grand Ballroom. She'd wondered why the event would necessitate such space, but the child in question was a new cousin of Eliza's husband. Apparently every respectable female person in Maliana had been honored with an invitation to coo over the latest Harper offspring. Eleanor met at least a twenty new Harpers and Smithwicks, as well as several Smithwick-Harpers and a Harper-Smithwick.

She spent the first half hour wandering aimlessly with Chou Chou on her shoulder. Her neck stiffened as she gazed at the vaulted ceiling, covered in paintings of men and women, unicorns and dragons, stars and clouds and the sun and moon. Thick golden pillars lined the exterior, and at least fifty candelabras hung from the ceiling on thick brass chains. Larger-than-life oil paintings of famous citizens of the realm adorned the walls, not just royalty but magicians and even several well-known witches. She read the engraved descriptions at the corner of each painting and smiled as she connected the somber faces with her history lessons.

She stopped several times to watch the apprentice magicians, who were amusing the guest with magical delights ranging from sputtering fireballs to live butterfly displays. At each corner of the long, rectangular room an enchanted fountain hovered just above the heads of the tallest ladies. Each sprayed up gouts of water, but somehow never a drop landed on a delicately coiffed head. The walls of the ballroom, made of Fire-iron and interspersed with large rectangular windows, set off the swirl of pastel gowns. Eleanor felt as if she were inside a spectacular garden.

"You should converse with someone other than me, darling," Chou said in her ear. "One can only admire the décor for so long."

"You know me too well, Chou." She didn't see Anne Iris or Eliza, although it was difficult to discern who was who, as most every person appeared to be presenting Eleanor with her back.

She decided to visit with the new baby, as he could hardly find fault with her. As she crossed the ballroom a familiar trilling laughter, the last sound Eleanor wanted to hear, rang out over the chatter and bubbling fountains.

"HighGod in a tree," said Chou. "What is *she* doing here?"

A troupe of exquisitely garbed young women stood around Sylvia Easton like flowers following the sun. Sylvia wore an ivory gown that matched her milky complexion, from her lovely face to her ample cleavage. Tiny as Sylvia was, for a moment Eleanor could see no one but her stepsister in the cavernous ballroom.

Eleanor must have stood out herself, a lone woman of substantial height with a glaringly red parrot perched on her shoulder. Sylvia glided toward Eleanor as if the marble floor had turned to ice. She slipped her arm through Eleanor's. "Sister," she said. "Where have you been hiding?"

"I'm going to pay my respects to the child."

"Go home!" hissed Chou, with no hint of his usual jocularity.

"Master Parrot, we must learn to be civil with one another. You shall be seeing more of me."

Eleanor smiled, determined to keep her dignity. After the disastrous joust she refused to give the women additional ingredients for their stew of speculation. "Shall you come to court, sister?"

Sylvia returned Eleanor's benevolent expression. "I *shall*. Once I'm married I'm sure we will see each other daily!"

"How thrilling!" said Eleanor, with a face like softened butter.

"Thrilling!" repeated Chou, his feathers standing on end. They poked Eleanor's ear. "Positively exhilarating!"

"And who shall you marry?" Eleanor asked.

Sylvia sighed. "Mother has not yet told me his name. She's still handling the particulars, but she promises I'll be pleased." For a moment Sylvia's grin faltered. She shook her hair and set her shoulders. "He'll be a catch of course. Perhaps Brian Smithwick. Or maybe Mister Dorian Finley. He's soon to return to court. I've heard he's the most handsome man in Cartheigh."

"I've heard the same," said Eleanor.

Sylvia had somehow steered Eleanor toward a knot of women young enough to be beautiful but old enough to be condescending. The worst kind, in Eleanor's experience.

"Lady Pellerbee told me the most interesting story about her new draperies," said Sylvia. "It seems her seamstress edged them with yellow beads instead of gold. Can you believe it?"

The women watched Eleanor as if her opinion of curtains would directly determine her suitability to mother the next heir to the throne. "I have no interest in draperies, Lady Pellerbee," she said, "so I can add nothing to this conversation."

Eleanor detached her arm from Sylvia's. She curtsied and went in search of the tiny guest of honor.

"Not the most tactful exit," said Chou.

The party dragged on for another two hours. Eleanor watched Sylvia as she made the rounds of each cluster of women. She chatted with ladies ancient and unmarried and everyone in between. The guests finally dispersed when the baby began shrieking in exhaustion. Eleanor had a wild urge to join him. She retired to her chamber with Chou Chou and a gnawing hope for a visit from Gregory.

Every day increased her irritation at how little time she spent with her fiancé. She had been at Eclatant for nearly two weeks, and could count on her fingers the number of hours she had been in his company. When she did see him, they were usually surrounded by at least fifty people. He would pop into her chambers to check on her and kiss her cheek, but then he was off. Sometimes it was a meeting with his father or an ambassador or some such person, but more often it was a pheasant shoot, or a long ride, or unicorn training. As the wedding drew closer, and the weight of her new position bore down on her, she longed for just one evening alone with him. Perhaps he could offer some advice, or just some reassurance. She'd have to corner him soon, for according to Anne Iris, once his friend Mister Finley returned to Eclatant she'd be lucky to see him at all.

CHAPTER 4

How Hot and Cold He Blows

Dorian Finley's relative handsomeness was somewhat debatable, for such a trait is subject to personal caprice. While most ladies of his acquaintance showed their opinions to be decidedly thus, Dorian found women to be an inanely changeable lot. He supposed some found his temperament wanting. He was, however, universally acknowledged as the Cartheigh's most skilled swordsman. He'd likely passed more hours of his life with a sword in his hand than he had with a fork. Such skills had served him well through seven years in the Carthean army, but they did him no good in ministering to babies.

These tiny Fire-iron scissors were defeating him. He turned his newborn niece's pink hands this way and that, but he couldn't find a good angle. Her fingernails were obscenely tiny.

He looked up at his sister. "I can't, Anne Clara. My hands are too big. I'm afraid she'll never hold a quill if I keep this up."

Anne Clara laughed, and Dorian smiled at the sound. A week after giving birth to her twin girls she was still pale, but the past two days he'd seen hints of a return to her usual sunny practicality. She managed the new babies and her toddler son like a kinder, gentler version of the mine bosses Dorian served with in North Country. Dorian was glad he had come home, and did not regret missing the hullabaloo of the Second Sunday Ball. After a frightening delivery the safety of both Anne Clara and the babies had hung in a tender balance for five interminable days, but now it seemed all would be well.

He crossed the room with the baby cradled in his arms. She was so floppy he feared he might drop her, but then she seemed so fragile he also feared he might squash her. He handed her off to his dark haired sister in the tall four-poster bed. Once in her mother's plump arms she started to squirm and squeak. Dorian walked to the window while Anne Clara adjusted herself to nurse. He heard her whispering nonsense words to her daughter as she coaxed her into position. He looked out over Lake Brandling. His sister's house faced the town of Harper's Crossing, and he could see the town dock and the steeple of Holy Triumph Chapel. The view from his childhood home, Floodgate Manor, was nothing but thick trees. The perspective on this side of the lake differed, but the smells and sounds were the same. A fishy tang in the air. The gabble of the lakegulls.

The Lake District was always a relief after the dry heat of Maliana and the constant drip of the North Country. Still, after four months at Eclatant and over three weeks in Harper's Crossing, Dorian itched to head north. Something about the barren landscape radiating around the Dragon Mines like ripples on a muddy pond always stirred a sense of longing in him. He'd spent the better part of the last seven years traipsing over the mountains and scribbling poetry in a series of ever more tattered ledgers. He knew it was rubbish, but it never stopped him. For years he'd been searching for a word to rhyme with *damp*. He'd tried umpteen variations around *camp*, but it always sounded too trite.

He watched the skiffs on the lake, blue and yellow and red sails like mobile lake lilies. *Boat...moat*, he thought. There could be a poem in there somewhere. *Oar...shore...whore?*

"...often wonder what you're thinking. When you go all silent and staring," Anne Clara was saying.

Paddles and hookers, sister, said a sniggering voice in Dorian's mind. *Sculling and strumpets.*

It was a reply for Gregory, or one of his sergeants, not Anne Clara. He'd overextended this visit, no doubt. Best be heading back to Maliana before such a response slipped his tongue. Anne Clara might faint from shock, and the witches would not approve of post-birth swooning.

A knock on Anne Clara's bedroom door saved them both. Once Dorian saw she was covered he opened it. Anne Clara's butler handed him a note on thick green paper.

"Another message from Gregory?" Anne Clara asked.

Dorian nodded. The army had called him away from Eclatant many times over the course of his six-year friendship with Gregory. Dorian never had one note of correspondence, but these past two weeks Gregory's missives came in a deluge.

He unfolded the note. "I can't believe it."

"Has he actually set a date?" asked Anne Clara.

Dorian nodded again. "In one week. I thought he would come to his senses. Change his mind. You know how hot and cold he blows."

He sat in a lacy pink and lavender chair beside the bed and absently rocked his other baby niece's cradle with his foot. His brow wrinkled. "I can't get my mind around the idea of Gregory as anyone's husband."

Anne Clara reached over her daughter's covered head. She tried to grab a note on the carved Fire-iron table next to the bed but she couldn't reach it. She pointed and Dorian gave it to her.

"I've had letters from Maliana as well," she said. "This just arrived. Cousin Abigail says everyone is up in arms about this girl. Eleanor Brice. I would think she'd get some sympathy. It sounds like she's had a hard row."

"Sympathy?" Dorian asked. "One would think, but every family of quality in this kingdom has been imagining their daughter or cousin or favorite aunt as Gregory's bride since the day he was born. They'll never forgive some girl who has actually had her hands in a chamber pot for stealing him."

"Poor thing."

"She'd better be a quick study, for her own good."

"It sounds like she is. I have it here she's highly educated." Anne Clara explained Eleanor Brice's unique educational history.

Dorian felt a twinge of interest. "Gregory never mentioned that part. He described her hair, her skin, her odd eyes, even her…" He remembered his company and cleared his throat. "Anyway, he never mentioned her education."

To his relief Anne Clara moved on. "Her odd eyes," she said. "You should feel sympathy for her in that case. Perhaps you two can discuss ways to avoid eye contact over a goblet of wine or a game of lawn bolls."

"I don't avoid eye contact. Not since I was a child."

"I'm just teasing you, Dor."

He returned to the window and watched the black water again. Anne Clara spoke from behind him.

"Now that your great partner in mischief is settling down maybe you will too," she said. "You are twenty-four, brother."

"Not likely any time soon."

Dorian knew of his own reputation. Women came to him easily, one after the other, each one just as beautiful and vapid as the last. Eclatant provided a constant stream of pretty smiles and tiny waistlines. A pleasant, if mindless distraction.

Part of him envied his sister's peaceful existence here in the Crossing. Dorian cared little for Eclatant's endless social maneuvering. Palace life held one great appeal for him. For as long as he could read he'd been enthralled by the complex workings of the government, the daily decisions affecting the lives of thousands of people. He stood where he had always wanted to stand, on the very pulse of the crown, and could not imagine the woman who would make him want to abandon that fascination for the life of a country gentleman. Besides, he couldn't be a country gentleman these days if his life depended on it. He had no money.

"You'll have to detach yourself from the Council table someday. When you do find someone she will be a lucky lady indeed," said Anne Clara.

"You flatter me. She will have to put up with my arrogance and boorish sense of humor."

Anne Clara smiled. "As I said, a fortunate woman."

The first baby finished nursing just as the second one started fussing. Dorian kissed Anne Clara's cheek, called for the nursemaid to assist her, and went to gather his belongings. He mused as he pulled out two leather saddlebags stamped with the Desmarais crest.

Leave it to Gregory to choose a bride whose suspect background was no doubt adding gray to the king's hair. Gregory's closet friends were an eclectic bunch. There were the predictable ones like his cousin Brian Smithwick, but Dorian got by on an old name and his own merit, and Raoul Delano was not even a true Carthean. He was the son of an immigrant, a famous Talessee jeweler. Gregory hardly hobnobbed with the stable boys, but he did love a bit of a hard case. It was one of his many quirky charms. The king appreciated none of them, but maybe marriage would help Gregory grow up. Force him into the potential Dorian knew was there.

Dorian threw his clothes and books into the bags. He had no time for folding and wrapping. Gregory insisted he return to the palace in time for the Engagement Ball. When Gregory insisted, Dorian, like everyone else, heeded his call.

Eleanor asked Gregory to dine with her in her chambers on the eve of their Engagement Ball. He seemed to find it an odd request, but she cajoled until he agreed. When Eleanor came out of her dressing room that evening she found a small formally set table in the sitting area, a fire crackling cheerfully in the fireplace, and several servers quietly laying out food and pouring wine. To her pleasure Gregory stood beside the table, a goblet in his hand, waiting for her. He pulled out her chair.

"You look lovely, sweetheart," he said. She had chosen the dark green gown hoping he would appreciate the nod to the family colors. She was not disappointed. "Our green suits you."

"Thank you," she said, with a warm smile. "I admit I'm surprised to see you here. You're always the last one to arrive at any party."

He eased her chair toward the table and sat down across from her. "You know I love to make an entrance, but Dorian is meeting me here at eight o'clock. We're heading into town for the evening to celebrate the engagement and his return. I don't want to miss dessert."

Her smile froze on her lips. It was half-past six. "Well, let's start then, shall we?"

The first course arrived, a soup of parsley and carrots. Eleanor and Gregory made small talk. She could not quite get past the servants. They appeared constantly at her side to refill her water glass or offer her another slice of bread. She struggled for a topic of substance, one not too personal.

"I heard Sir Foust saying the Svelyans are thinking of withdrawing their ambassador. Are tensions rising again?"

Gregory set down his fork. "Where did you hear that?"

"I was standing near him the other night at the dinner in honor of—"

"The Svelyans are merely sending a new ambassador because Paul Roffi is nearing eighty and ready for retirement. Regardless, why are you listening to gossip?"

"I'm sorry, I didn't know. I was just interested."

He reached across the table and squeezed her hand. "Don't worry yourself about such things, sweetheart. It's enough for you to prepare for the wedding and learn your duties."

They sank into silence again. The servants brought the main course, broiled pencil trout from the Clarity River, dressed with tiny potatoes. Eleanor picked up a fork, hopefully the correct one. Her thoughts flitted from one safe topic to the next. She pushed the fish around her plate and tried again.

"How is the breeding this year?"

The effect was immediate. Gregory always became animated when talk turned to unicorns. "Fabulous! I think we will have a crop of four or five foals this year if all the mares carry to term. Tricky stuff, unicorn pregnancy. Even with those tiny first horns the delivery can be dangerous to the mother."

"That makes sense," she said, with genuine interest. "Gregory, would you take me to the Paladine sometime?"

"Of course! Once the wedding and the honeymoon are passed we'll spend some time in the stables. You've already met Vigor, my stallion. He's the finest in the herd, or at least I think so. My father might argue his mount Fortune is superior, but I guess we're all partial. As a member of the royal family you'll have the chance to earn a unicorn of your own."

"Really?" asked Eleanor. She'd had no idea.

"Yes, really," he said. "You know all the unicorns in the Paladine belong to the Desmarais family, and in turn to the crown and the kingdom. We do—how shall I say it—lend them out to certain people. High-ranking nobles or war heroes, for the most part, and sometimes close friends. That person is then wholly responsible for the animal, and the penalties are steep if harm comes to it. It's rare, because unicorns are mystical and nearly impossible to hurt, but when my father was a boy a mare drowned while in the keeping of one of my grandfather's generals. The man hanged the next day."

Eleanor's eyebrows came together. "Perhaps I'll stick to horses."

He laughed. "You'll be fine. I'll help you. The only women allowed a unicorn are members of the Desmarais family, and not many of them are approved. Unicorns are not like horses. Just because you can ride doesn't mean you can master one."

"As of now I can't even ride. It's been almost eight years, remember?"

"Yes, and we will have to get you back on a horse first. But I think you have what it takes. My sister Matilda was a great unicorn handler."

He drained his wine glass. His compliment warmed her, but she could sense his grief for his sister.

"I wish I had known her." She reached across the table to take his hand this time.

"Yes, well, it is a sad thing." He set down his napkin. "Look at the time, I guess I'll have to skip dessert after all."

"But it's only half-past seven. I'd like to meet Dorian. You said he was coming here."

"Did I? I might as well save him coming up all those steps. You'll meet him tomorrow."

"Gregory, I want to talk with you about something." She kept from taking his arm by wringing her hands.

"Yes?"

Her agitation grew as he put on his overcoat. "I'm afraid I'm not doing well at all these events…I never know what to say…I don't think anyone likes me."

She wished she could pull the words in again, like a child sucking pear juice through a reed straw.

He chuckled. "No one likes you? Poor Eleanor! Of course they like you. I've not heard a cross word." He kissed her roughly and her lips were raw as he drew away from her. "You're beautiful and sweet and kind, how could anyone dislike you?"

He took his leave, off to sample whatever delights the darkened city of Maliana could provide that she could not. She waved away the dessert and sat in a squashy chair by the fire. She tucked her feet underneath her and listened as the servants cleared the remnants of the meal. She had dismissed Anne Iris and Eliza for the evening, and appreciated the solitude. In a bit she would retire to her dressing room and the chambermaids would help her into her nightdress. Chou Chou also waited for her, but she could not quite face his cheerful, chattering questions just yet.

How could anyone dislike her? He had asked.

How indeed.

CHAPTER 5

A SPLENDID PARTY

THE PAST THREE HUNDRED years or so had been peaceful ones in Cartheigh. The military engaged mostly in protecting the Dragon Mines, regulating the skirmishes between other countries, or keeping order during the occasional plague. The nobility had, as is often the case, reaped the greatest benefits of three centuries of good fortune. As a group they prided themselves on their sophistication, worldliness, and enjoyment of the finer things. Carthean literature, art, music, and dance were universally admired. Along with love of music and dance, and wealth and idle time, came an appreciation of a good party. The court at Eclatant did nothing on a small scale, and the national holidays were no exception.

There were four Fests, one each season, all falling in the mid-months. First came the Awakening, at the beginning of the year in the month of MidSpring, followed by the Waxing in MidSummer, the Harvest in MidAutumn, and finally the Waning, usually held in MidWinter. To Eleanor's unease, the Waning Fest had been moved forward several weeks this year to coincide with Prince Gregory's nuptials. The excitement would begin with the Engagement Ball and end with the Wedding Ceremony and Celebration.

In long-gone years Fests had been one-day, community or family affairs, and for most common people they still were. At Eclatant, however, each holiday included a week of parties, contests, plays, and concerts. The palace reached full capacity, and those who could not secure lodging on the grounds invaded the townhouses of their friends and relatives.

Happily, Gregory did not mind if Chou Chou accompanied Eleanor to most events, as he often brought along his own gray falcon, Thunderhead. Many people brought feathered companions, and at every party the servants erected an elaborately carved roost in a corner. Dozens of parrots, ravens, hawks and falcons would congregate and chat amongst themselves while daintily nibbling chocolate crackers. The birds swooped about, lighting on the chandeliers for a good view before dropping in on their masters and mistresses to share gossip. Gregory sometimes even brought his two favorite hunting hounds. They wandered in and out of guests' legs, asking politely for food and drooling. The older courtiers found the dogs to be in very poor taste, but of course no one said a word. They simply dropped tidbits and hastily moved on, before their shoes were covered in slobber.

So here Eleanor stood on Gregory's arm, in an alcove off the Grand Ballroom, waiting to enter the Engagement Ball. Chou Chou sat her right shoulder. She couldn't see the crowd, but the thrum of conversation drifted around the corner. As the moments ticked on, her dress assumed the weight of three gowns and she feared her stays were cutting off blood flow to her head. The gown was thick eggplant colored velvet, embroidered with heavy amethysts. She prayed she would not start sweating.

Chou Chou whispered advice in her ear. "Imagine them all naked, even the fat ones."

The trumpets sounded promptly at seven. The royal callers introduced King Casper, and then the highest-ranking advisors, starting with Ezra Oliver. Gregory wagged his eyebrows at her and stole a quick kiss. As always, his grin lifted her spirits.

"His Royal Highness, Prince Gregory, and Mistress Eleanor Brice. May HighGod bless the Kingdom of Cartheigh!"

Eleanor held her head high as they entered the ballroom. The crown cheered wildly. Whether they approved of her personally or not, everyone in attendance embraced the glamour of the ball and the spirit of the Fest. Eleanor smiled and waved. She was one of them, part of the spectacle, proud of her country.

Chou Chou flew off as she and Gregory danced a long, slow waltz. As he led her around the dance floor the assembled crowd *ooohed* and *aaahed*. His hand felt firm and right on her back. When the song ended they bowed to each other. Chou landed again on her bare shoulder as the crowd pressed in. Everyone wanted a chance to compliment the future princess. He flapped his wings in her defense.

"Peace, Chou, you needn't stay here all night. You'll be squashed."

He spoke into her ear to be heard over the crowd. "I think they have all accepted you're staying around. They can't scare you off."

She cupped her hand over his head. "If you really want to watch after me, go see what you can see." He winked and flew off to the party roost.

She turned her attention to the chattering people around her. She and Gregory made their way to the far side of the ballroom where the most important guests were assembled near the thrones. On the way she was introduced to new faces, said hello to those she could remember, and admired the decorations. The magicians had outdone themselves again. Along with the usual fountains, fireballs and performing apprentices, the entire length of the ceiling swirled with giant purple, green and gold ribbons. They folded in and out on themselves in complex geometric patterns, like a child's kaleidoscope.

As they reached the end of the ballroom the crowd thinned, and they no longer had to shout to be heard. Gregory led her toward a knot of men and women gathered on the dais beside the two thrones. She waved to Brian Smithwick, and Anne Iris and Eliza, but she did not recognize the other young women. One man, tall with dark hair, had his back to her.

"Dorian!" Gregory cried. "Dorian, my friend, come meet my bride!"

The dark-haired man turned. He was indeed tall, taller than even Brian. Somehow the lack of frippery on his simple cream tunic called attention to his broad shoulders and narrow waist. Eleanor supposed he would be described as wiry. He had a light, agile look about him that made Gregory seem stocky and verging on pudgy in comparison. He wore his hair shorter than most of the other young men, and she remembered hearing he had been a soldier. She registered a strong jaw and fair skin, but all was forgotten when she got to his eyes.

They were the palest green, nearly colorless. She could almost see his pupils changing size as the magician's fireballs danced overhead. His absurdly long eyelashes could have had a feminine effect if the rest of him had not exuded masculinity. She was put in mind of paintings she had seen of the *j'aguas*, the great yellow-eyed black cats roaming the forests of the kingdom of Talesse.

For once she knew how her own oddly colored eyes affected people. She blushed as she realized she was staring.

Gregory clapped Dorian on the shoulder. "Dorian Finley, meet Eleanor Brice. Eleanor, my dearest friend, Dorian Finley."

She curtsied, and he took the three steps down to her level. She still had to look up at him. "I'm so glad I'm finally meeting you, Dorian. I've heard so much about you."

He bowed. "And I you, Mistress Brice. Rumors of your beauty reached me even in the Lake District. I'm sorry I could not be here sooner, but I had family obligations."

"If you had been here you might have stolen her away," Gregory said. "A great one for the ladies is my friend Dorian."

"You know I leave the new girls to you, Your Highness," said Dorian. "I like a bit of a challenge, and you need to catch them young and naïve."

His disrespect shocked Eleanor, but it bothered no one else. Everyone, including Gregory himself, laughed. The unfamiliar women were particularly amused. They covered their mouths and giggled, and one tapped Dorian's arm with her fan.

Eleanor's temper flared. "Better to be young and naïve than old, arrogant and jaded, Mister Finley," she said.

Dorian turned to her and raised one dark brow. "Peace, Mistress Brice," he said. "How heartless of you to think my carriage over the hill at age twenty-four. I'll forgive the insult if you honor me with a dance."

She started to decline but to her irritation Gregory answered for her. "Fabulous idea," he said.

Before she knew it she was on Dorian Finley's arm, heading for the dance floor. She hoped for a reel so they wouldn't have to talk, but it was another waltz. As they took a few wordless turns around the room Eleanor could tell he was a flawless dancer. She noted the prominent veins lacing his forearms. His hands were rougher than Gregory's, with big, square knuckles. She shook off the blush that once again threatened to creep up her chest. She tried to focus on being angry with him.

"I am sorry," he said in the slow, drawling accent of the east. "I must've sounded like an ass. I forget not everyone appreciates my jests."

His frank apology surprised her. Her defensiveness abruptly drained away. "Accepted. It was a bad start, but I suppose it would be difficult if I hated you, being that you are my future husband's best friend."

"That would be inconvenient," he said, with a gravelly laugh. "I've heard more of your story since I returned. I would love to speak with you about it sometime. Amazing, really."

"Not so much," she said. "It was not idyllic, but I had a roof over my head, and my parrot, and a great friend who stood by me."

"You mean the witch who educated you."

"Yes. I like to think as bad as my situation was, if I'd had a more conventional upbringing my studies would have stopped years ago. I'd be a better dancer, but I'd rather have other talents."

His smiled again. "Well, first, you are a fine dancer. And I think it's wonderful you kept studying through your difficulties. I wish more women did the same. It would certainly improve the dinner conversation at Eclatant. I'd hoped my sister would continue, but my brother thought it a waste of money."

His response pleased her. "I'd say you are a rarity, Dorian, most men are of the mindset of your brother."

"Like Gregory."

"Gregory did choose me, after all, so he can't be completely opposed to educated women," she said, treading lightly.

His tawny eyes held hers, and a few beats of the music passed with no words. "I suppose he isn't. And he has chosen well."

This time she couldn't stop the rising color. He changed the subject. "How do you find court?"

"Exhausting," she blurted out.

"I know what you mean."

"Do you? It's just… a bit odd for me. I've been alone most of my life. I feel like everyone talks and says nothing, but then they are silent and speak volumes. I admire those who are at ease. I hope I don't sound ungrateful, believe me, sir, I'm not…Sometimes I can't believe my good fortune…maybe I'm still in shock," she finished with a laugh.

"I know, don't explain yourself. There's many a night I'd rather be reading by the fire. Most at court think I'm dreadfully unfriendly, but I've learned not to care. I keep my allegiances few. Everyone here wants something from you, and the closer you are to the prince the worse it is. Be careful, Eleanor."

She paused for a moment in search of a response.

Dorian cleared his throat, and she thought she saw a hint of color in his own cheeks. "Listen to me," he said. "We should be talking about the weather and here I am going on."

"On the contrary, I appreciate your honesty. It's a rare thing in this place."

"And I yours. As Gregory's wife, you can count on my loyalty. I think you will make a fine princess."

The song ended but Dorian did not release her immediately. Her own hand did not leave his hard shoulder. She stepped away and he let go with a soft apology. She took his arm and he led her to her waiting fiancé. The world had seemed so right tonight, and now something about her dance with Dorian Finley wobbled it again.

As the party wound down Dorian found himself distinctly drunk. Although he was sure no one else could tell, it bothered him anyway. Perhaps he had overdone it after a month of relative sobriety at his sister's house.

He blamed his wandering eyes on the inebriation. He watched Eleanor Brice's pale, slim form as she floated through the crowd, her gown a stamp of Desmarais purple. Since she was taller than any of the other women, and many of the men, it was easy to follow her bright blond hair. Her features flowed, one to the other, from her slender arms to her elegant neck. Her vaulting pale brows led to a long nose and delicately flared nostrils. She had none of the round softness so worshipped in Carthean women. She seemed to him rather like a lonely lily in a bed of pansies.

He wasn't in the mood to dance, so he ignored the ladies who casually sidled up to him as the orchestra shifted from one tune to the next. Gregory's obvious happiness heartened him, although he wondered why his friend didn't spend more of the evening with the source of his joy. On more than one occasion Dorian noticed Eleanor standing alone. She would hug herself and her blue and brown eyes would flick from one passing face to the other. He smiled at her, hoping to bring her some comfort. She always smiled back.

He shook his head at the warm feeling in his chest. He needed some water or he faced the first hangover he'd had since a storied North

Country drink-off between himself, two sergeants and a Kellish whore. He said a quick goodnight to Gregory and made for one of the side doorways.

"Mister Finley." An unfamiliar voice called to him from behind a statue of one of Gregory's grandfathers.

He peered around the statue. A young woman peeked from behind a marble shield carved with an ornate *D*. He would have to call her beautiful, with her big blue eyes, upswept blonde hair, and bee-stung lips. She looked vaguely familiar, and he thought her name was Katherine something.

"Mister Finley," she said again. She reached out for his hand and pulled him into the shadows. "Or, might I call you Dorian?"

"If you must."

She rambled on about the party for a few minutes and he listened half-heartedly. She finally went where he already knew she was going. "...so thrilling! Can you feel my excitement?"

She laid his hand on her bosom, and slid it down to the lace neckline of her gown. Her chest rose and fell, and her quick pulse beat under the warm, firm skin.

"I can," he said.

She looked up at him and he caught a flash of her pink tongue. "I don't know if I can make it back to my room on my own, sir," she said. "Would you consider assisting me?"

"I'd never forgive myself if you got lost."

She smiled, and he followed her down the passageway.

That night Anne Iris and Eliza helped Eleanor undress. As she stepped out of the heavy purple gown she rubbed her stiff shoulders. "Velvet, never again," she said.

Chou Chou spoke up from his perch. "You must wear velvet at least once during the Waning Fest. Everyone does."

"Since when is a parrot a fashion expert?" Anne Iris asked.

"Since I made your acquaintance, Mistress Smithwick, as you are widely known as the most fashionable lady at Eclatant." He bobbed his head up and down chivalrously.

"You do go on," said Anne Iris, but Eleanor knew both her friends were fond of Chou. All the treats they brought him swelled his belly along with his head.

They lounged on Eleanor's bed in their nightgowns and caught up on the Engagement Ball. Eliza and Anne Iris agreed Eleanor had been a great success.

"You were radiant, dear. Gregory could not have been prouder," said Eliza. "You did not look nervous at all."

"Do I usually?" Eleanor teased. Eliza stuttered clarifications until Eleanor thumped her gently with a pillow. "Thank you, I actually enjoyed it. It was a splendid party. Just as I hoped."

Not completely true, said a voice in her mind. She casually mentioned the topic, or person, that had flitted in and out of her thoughts all night, distracting her from what should have been a sort of victory celebration.

"Tell me about Dorian Finley."

"Oh, Dorian," said Anne Iris. "I watched you dancing with him. He's quite a piece, isn't he?"

Eleanor ignored the question. "How is he related to Gregory?"

"He's not," said Eliza. "The Finleys are an old family from Harper's Crossing. The senior Mister Finley drowned in the lake in front of his own house, and Dorian's brother took control of the family finances. Everyone says they don't get on."

"Apparently his brother withdrew him from Academy early and forced him into the Army. Perhaps he hoped Dorian would be eaten by a dragon or skewered by a rogue Svelyan knight." Anne Iris shivered at the thought, a wide grin plastered on her face.

Eliza threw a stale parrot cracker at her. "Anyway, Dorian gets by on a small stipend and his soldier's salary."

"How did he become so close to the prince?" asked Eleanor.

"He visited the palace six years ago with General Clayborne," Eliza said. "At the time Gregory was fifteen and completely wild, so the king thought it would be good for him to have a companion, an older brother of sorts. The king liked him, and more importantly Gregory took to him right away."

"Hero worship from the start," said Anne Iris with a shake of her head. "So here he is, six years later, one of the most important people at court. It's rather hilarious!"

"Hilarious, yes," said Eleanor, uncomfortably aware that she, too, came here at the price's whim. "What is it Gregory finds so appealing about him?"

Anne Iris leaned toward her. Her eyes were like saucers. "Oh, sweetheart, you have no idea. Dorian Finley is, well, how can I explain it?"

"He's the man any man would want to be," said Eliza.

Anne Iris nodded. "He's an amazing unicorn handler and huntsman. His military commanders sing his praises to the rafters."

"Everyone respects him, because he is known to be widely read on every topic imaginable," said Eliza. "Even the king has come to value his opinion. Gregory rarely makes a move without discussing it with Dorian."

"And of course…" Anne Iris paused dramatically. "He is just plain gorgeous."

Eleanor picked at the coverlet. "I didn't really notice."

"Oh, please," Anne Iris guffawed. "Just because you're marrying Gregory doesn't mean you've gone blind. All the women at court lust after him, married or not. Now that Gregory has left the market, Dorian Finley is the most desired man at Eclatant."

Eliza cut in. "He's probably always been more desired. Gregory just had one over him by being the prince."

Anne Iris dropped her voice to a whisper. "I've heard he takes different lovers all the time, but no one can hold his attention for more than a few weeks. He's supposed to be quite…" She fanned herself. "… skilled."

Eliza rolled her eyes. "Please, Anne Iris, spare us your mooning."

"Don't let Eliza fool you, Eleanor. She only pretends to be a prude. She and Patrick-Clark are known for their undying passion!"

Eleanor stifled a giggle. Eliza's husband, Patrick-Clark Harper, was a short, slight man who wore a seeing glass and spent most of his time in the country. He was kind, and not unattractive, but Eleanor had trouble imagining him filled with undying passion.

"My passion is of no concern!" said Eliza.

"You're right. Mister Finley's passion is far more interesting." Anne Iris collapsed on the bed. She clutched a lace pillow and writhed against it. Eliza pursed her lips. Eleanor wondered if Eliza felt true offense until she saw the corners of her mouth twitching.

"I'm all hot just thinking about it. Chou Chou, bring me some water!" called Anne Iris.

Chou raised his head from under his wing, blinking sleepily. He glided to the bed. "Aren't you girls asleep yet?" he asked.

"No," said Eliza. "Anne Iris is just scandalizing us as usual. But it is true, Eleanor, Dorian Finley is sought after by the women at court. Whether it's because of his friendship with the prince or his other endowments…" Anne Irish swooned again."…one can't really be sure. It's rare, I'll give you that, for noblewomen to desperately chase after a second son with nothing but a soldier's salary."

Eleanor tucked all this information away, adding it to her conversation with Dorian this evening. To her irritation, it made him more fascinating.

"Speaking of chasing men," said Chou, "Sylvia Easton has caught one with quite a lot of money. Imogene wanted her to make a powerful match, and she did."

"Who, Chou?" asked Eleanor, eager to finally uncover the identity of Sylvia's mysterious suitor.

"Hector Fleetwood, Duke of Harveston."

Anne Iris gagged, and even Eliza made a face.

"That's like courting your great-grandpa!" said Anne Iris.

"It doesn't surprise me, really," said Eleanor. "Sylvia would do just about anything for a lifetime of fancy dresses."

"You don't understand," said Eliza. "Hector Fleetwood is ancient. Near seventy. He's a horrible old leach, always grabbing at any woman within reach."

Chou hopped into Eleanor's lap. He flapped his wings and a red feather poked Eleanor in the eye. "They were married just yesterday, in a private ceremony. Apparently the duke prefers quiet affairs these days. Imogene said she would beat you down the aisle. She meant it."

He dropped his voice and Eleanor leaned back on her elbows to make space for his performance. "I passed a few words with Margaret over a glass of wine and some crackers," said Chou. "She said Sylvia has been sobbing herself dry in bed for a week. She refused to eat anything, or even meet the duke before the wedding. Imogene had to drag her to the chapel."

"I can't say I blame her," said Eliza, and even Eleanor felt a prick of sympathy.

Chou went on. "An old raven who has been around the palace forever told me the Fleetwoods are not as showy or as numerous as the Smithwicks, but they hold real power. Harveston is the second most important city in Cartheigh, and they control it. Sylvia is now a duchess. If that old man's performance matches his perversion and he plants a son in her belly she'll be the mother of the next duke."

Eleanor rubbed her forehead. The thought of Sylvia at the helm of one of the most powerful families in Cartheigh, with a vast fortune behind her, was far from comforting. At the moment, however, the other vaguely confusing thoughts circling her head seemed more pressing.

She claimed exhaustion from the party and sent the other girls and the parrot off to bed.

I'm marrying the man I love in five days.

She tossed and turned. She even put a pillow over her head, but Dorian Finley's pale eyes would not leave her alone.

CHAPTER 6

A FINE TRIBUTE TO CARTHEIGH

THE NEXT DAY ELEANOR sought an audience with the one person who always calmed her nerves. She met Rosemary at First Maliana Covey, as she did not have time for the trip across Maliana to Afar Creek Abbey. Two soldiers escorted her down Eclatant's kitchen corridor, through a non-descript doorway, and into a narrow, torch lit passageway. Eleanor stooped to avoid her head brushing the dirt ceiling. By the time they emerged onto the grounds of First Covey she was on the verge of claustrophobic panic. She stepped through another doorway, this one covered in moss and dangling ivy.

They walked through a terraced garden full of boxwoods carved into impossibly intricate images of frolicking woodland animals. Glowing spheres, like giant soap bubbles, hovered and spun slowly at strategic spots. The water in several fountains flowed backwards. It leapt out of the pool and into the basins. Statues of dragons and unicorns stood on pedestals, and as Eleanor passed they whinnied or spit fire. The buildings themselves were stone, and larger than any Eleanor had ever seen other than the palace itself. Wrought in large, plain letters over the main entrance was a message.

MEN OF GREAT POWER TO AID POWERFUL MEN

It made sense. Magicians were out in the world far more than witches. While some stayed in the Coveys as teachers and scholars, far more worked for wealthy patrons, the government, or the army. Magicians served as security forces, advisers, entertainers, or any combination of the three. The most powerful served the royal family, and those who could not find work elsewhere ended up as street peddlers, and in a few cases, assassins.

Once inside, she paused to take in huge Fire-iron statues of famous magicians, kings and war heroes. Tapestries, some nearly a story tall and woven with gold thread, depicted the history of the Covey and the kingdom. The polished marble floor could have been brought over from the palace. Young men clustered together, chatting and comparing notes. She peered through open double doors into a space that rivaled Eclatant's Grand Ballroom in width and breadth. Ladders the height of oak trees lay against the floor-to-ceiling bookshelves. A familiar voice echoed off the library's white and gold walls.

Rosemary sat on a small stool with her knees fairly brushing her chin. A semicircle of young magicians fanned out before her. Some watched her aptly, some fiddled with the fringe on their gray magicians' tunics. A few shot sparks at one another. "Today we will talk about Caleb Desmarais," said Rosemary, "the first Desmarais king, and how he joined forces with the unicorns to bring peace and prosperity to Cartheigh three hundred years ago."

"Everyone *knows* this story," said a boy with carroty hair.

"Ah, yes, we all know the story, but today we will examine it more closely." She laid two objects on the wool rug. The first was an oblong stone, about the size of a field mouse. The second was a delicately carved ring. Both were a fluid silvery color that caught the light coming through the window and sent rainbows dancing across the boys' polished boots.

Carrottop scooped up the ring and slid it on his finger. "Fire-iron!"

"Yes," said Rosemary. "The ring is Fire-iron. But what about this?"

The question transported Eleanor back ten years, to the Brice House and her own rendition of this lesson. The stone had been lighter than a brick or a chunk of gravel, and her fingers had slid over it as if it were wet. At one end the smoothness turned to rough edges.

"I think this is Fire-iron too," the boy said, "but no one's made it fancy yet."

Rosemary nodded. "Now boys, everyone in Cartheigh knows the importance of Fire-iron. We all know its many uses. Jewelry, statues, fighting metal, even buildings—"

"It's what makes us rich! Richer than the Svelyans or the Kells or anyone in the world!" said another boy.

"Well," said Rosemary, "Fire-iron does indeed make some people rich. But before a piece of Fire-iron can become a ring or a sword it looks like this." She held up the stone. "And how do we get this stone?"

"From the Dragon Mines," said Carrottop. "The dragons make it."

"Correct. Can you explain how the Bond between the unicorns and the Desmarais kings controls the supply of Fire-iron in Cartheigh?"

Every young Carthean knew the answer to that question. The boy stood and cleared his throat, but when he caught sight of Eleanor in the doorway he dropped to the floor.

"Pass the stone amongst yourselves, children," Rosemary said, "but take care you don't lose it. And no fighting. If you leave here with singed hair and blue noses I'll hear it from Mister Oliver."

Rosemary embraced Eleanor and they sat at a small table beside one of the library's two skinny windows. "You can't resist a lesson, can you?" Eleanor asked with a smile.

"Of course not, dear. What's an old teacher to do but teach?"

"You're not old."

"Ninety-five this spring."

"The prime of life for a witch."

Rosemary laughed. "I suppose you're right. Although I do feel a century in these feet." She took Eleanor's hand. "And how are you?"

"I'm well." Suddenly Eleanor didn't know what she wanted to say to Rosemary. "Just fine. Excited."

"I'm glad to hear it. I feared something amiss."

Eleanor shook her head. "No, I just wanted to see you. I…I thought I might visit with the Oracle." In truth she'd thought no such thing since that very moment, but once it was out it seemed a fine idea.

Rosemary's mouth turned down at the corners. "You haven't seen her since just before your father's death."

"Perhaps it's time I saw her again."

"It's not that easy, Eleanor. She does not take many visitors. You only met her that once because she asked me to bring you to her."

"I've always wondered about that visit. Why did she want to see me?"

"I'm sorry, darling, but it's not possible. Not now. You're far too busy—with the wedding—"

"I'd like to see her before the wedding."

Rosemary squeezed Eleanor's hand. "The Oracle of Afar Creek Abbey is not a dealer in tarot cards, child."

Eleanor fell silent. She blinked at the bookshelves, the volumes crammed together like the condemned awaiting the scaffold on execution day.

"Shall I ask the Abbottess for leave?" asked Rosemary. "I could attend you in your preparations."

Some of the tension leaked out of Eleanor's shoulders. She found the idea of Rosemary attending anyone laughable, but she nodded. "If your students can spare you."

Rosemary smiled. "I think they can. After all, what did my red-headed scholar say? Everyone already knows this story."

The rest of the week passed in a whirlwind of fittings, tastings and, of course, parties. Try as she might, Eleanor could not regain sense of ease she had experienced for a short time at her Engagement Ball. Dorian Finley's presence at every event, no matter how large or small, did not help matters. It became clear how close he and Gregory were. While the prince's other friends rotated in and out, Dorian always stood at his side.

I'm just going to have to get used to him, she thought before bed one evening. *I'll be sitting beside him at least once a week for the rest of my life!*

She decided to think of him as Gregory did, as an older brother. She could not help but look for him when she entered a room. He seemed to know just when she had run out of things to say or would soon choke on her own foot. He would appear at her shoulder and lead her to the dance floor or to Gregory's side.

She spent an entire dinner party two days before the wedding engrossed in conversation with him. As they talked over their salads they somehow found the topic of the conditions in the slums of Meggett Fringe, which led them to the work of the witches in the city, which wound on to the state of Carthean women in general. At some point Dorian left his seat and made his way around the long table. He sat beside her, and they agreed and argued and laughed over the roles of men and women until she noticed the servants clearing the dinner dishes. She stood and looked for Gregory. She smiled when she saw him sitting on the edge of the table, a glass of wine in one hand, waiting for her. Usually she retired hours before he did.

He teased her and Dorian about their debate. "It's wonderful, you can bore each other instead of me."

She convinced herself Dorian was just a friendly face in a sea of suspect ones, and he watched out for her as Gregory's inexperienced fiancée. She ignored the fact that she caught his eye whenever she looked through a crowd or across a table.

The evening before the wedding found Eleanor in her room in her nightgown and housecoat. She took advantage of a few quiet moments to pick up a long neglected volume of poetry. Rosemary and Eliza were also engrossed in reading, Anne Iris was knitting, and Chou Chou was snoozing on the mantle. Eleanor vowed after the wedding they would spend more evenings like this.

The chambermaid entered and announced Gregory. The four women stood and waited to greet him. He came into the room, holding a small wooden box. Eleanor's casual dress obviously embarrassed him. "Good evening, ladies," he said, "I'm sorry to disturb you."

Eleanor smiled. "Not at all, you're always welcome here. Won't you join us?"

He ran his hand through his hair. It stood up from his forehead in confused question marks. "No. No, I'll come back." He started to leave and changed his mind. "Eleanor, might I see you alone for a few minutes?"

"Of course," she said, taken aback. The others gathered their things, excused themselves and made a hasty exit.

Gregory came to offer her a wedding gift, a Fire-iron necklace and a set of earrings with a simple design of small diamonds. He told her they had been his mother's favorites and he remembered her wearing them often.

"I know you've probably already picked something fancier," he said, almost shyly, "but it would mean a lot to me if you wore these tomorrow."

She told him she would be honored. He took her in his arms, whispered her name, and ran his hands over her hair. They sat by the fire until she dozed off on his shoulder. He gently lifted her and laid her on the bed. When he slipped her house shoes from her feet he ran his fingers over the damage done by the cracked slipper. He kissed the healing wound and helped her out of her robe. She asked where he was going.

"I have some last-minute preparations to make, and my father needs to see me," he said. "You just rest tonight, sweetheart. I know all of this has been a change for you. I'll tell them not to disturb you."

She smiled and closed her eyes, warmed by his love, and that last bit of understanding.

Dorian sat beside Gregory in King Casper's private receiving room. Gregory fidgeted as they waited for the king's acknowledgement. He leaned forward on his elbows, and then slid back. He crossed and uncrossed his legs. He fiddled with his hair, a gesture Dorian could read like a follicular weathervane. As various ministers and advisers came in and out, searching for instructions or signatures, Gregory settled into a stance Dorian assumed his father would dislike. He slouched, and crossed his arms over his chest. He splayed his legs and tapped one black boot impatiently.

Finally Casper looked up. "Son, don't sit like that. You look like a school boy waiting for a thrashing, not the heir to the throne." He waved away one of his generals and told Oliver, who crouched over a smaller desk by the door, to hold the visitors. The king rubbed his eyes and put down his quill. "Gregory, this wedding…I just don't know."

"What? The wedding is tomorrow, for the love of the Bond. We've already discussed it a thousand times."

"Yes, but son—"

"Have you found some problem with her family?"

"No, this isn't about her family. It seems both her parents spent time at court, and nothing can be found against them. In fact some remember her mother as quite amiable. Surprisingly, the same has been said of the stepmother."

"So what is it?" Gregory asked.

"It's her…manner…something…it's just not right," Casper threw up his hands. "Oliver, can you help me here? Or perhaps you, Finley? Talk some sense into him!"

"Certainly, sire," said the magician, before Dorian could open his mouth. "You father believes she does not have the right…" He tilted his head and pursed his thin lips. "…temperament…to be a Desmarais princess."

Gregory's face reddened, and Dorian put a cautionary hand on his arm.

Oliver held up his hands. "It is true that she knows nothing of womanly pursuits. From what she says she has spent the last eight years in the company of a parrot."

"She wouldn't know the first thing about entertaining a visiting ambassador, or planning one of the hunts you love so much," said the king. "She told me she hasn't even ridden since she was a girl. How would she carry off her duties as the hostess of the whole court?"

"Pardon me, sire," said Dorian. "If I may, Mistress Brice seems quite capable. I'm sure she could learn."

"She's far too opinionated," the king said. "She goes on about her education. How this witch friend of hers schooled her extensively in history, literature, and science. How she's anxious to use her learning to support you and help the kingdom. I've had the same speech from apprentice magicians trying for a place in Oliver's office."

Oliver rubbed his chin. "In my view—"

"Dragonshit. It's hardly your decision to make, Oliver," Gregory said. He tugged at his hair.

"Son," Casper said, "you need someone more prepared, and more… subdued…for a bride. Desmarais women are always beautiful and admired, but they know their place. It's your wife's duty to amuse and delight your courtiers, and bear your children, not provide counsel. This girl will prove too willful."

"I admit she will need some training, Father. We can have someone teach her what is expected, and of course I'll put her in her place." Each word escalated Gregory's anger. "Do you think I won't be in command of my own wife?"

"No, Gregory, but it might not be as easy to change her stripes as you think. You've spent enough time around horses to know the older they get, the harder it is to break bad habits. There are so many beautiful young women. Why must it be this one?"

"Enough. The wedding goes forward tomorrow. Dorian, come. I need a drink."

Gregory stood and left the room before his father could respond. Dorian followed him into the hallway. He had to jog to catch up with the striding, muttering prince.

"A man-to-man discussion…not a truncated council meeting…"

"Greg, I—"

Gregory spun around. His jaw jutted. "I didn't ask for Oliver's judgment, and I don't need yours, either."

Dorian held up his hands. "Peace, friend. It's your choice, of course…but…why *do* you want to marry Eleanor?"

Gregory paused, as if in search of an explanation himself. "She didn't even know who I was, Dorian, but when she looked at me… she…approved."

Rebuttals danced on the edge of Dorian's tongue, some wise, some practical, all a bit self-serving. He opened his mouth, and then closed it. "Well, if that's reason enough for you, it's reason enough for me."

Eleanor awoke hours later in disorienting darkness, unsure if her eyes were open or if she was caught in a dream of blindness. She strained for a spot of light to focus on. She finally fixed on the faint glowing stripe at the bottom of the door. Once she got her bearings, she reached across the bed. She searched the small nightstand for a candle and match. The candlelight cleared her fuzzy head. From the inky quality of the darkness, she knew she'd slept well past dinner and into the night. She swept the light over the room, pausing at Chou Chou's empty perch. Perhaps he had stayed with Rosemary.

The fire had gone out. She shivered as she carefully rebuilt the flames, grateful that she was not as helpless as other ladies. As she watched the fire grow, popping and snapping and reaching it arms up the chimney, she went over Gregory's visit in her mind. She tucked her face into her knees.

There would be no sleeping anytime soon. With a pleasantly jittery stomach she cast about for something to do to tire herself out. She picked up a book, a biography of the first Desmarais queen, but she couldn't concentrate. She kept thinking of Gregory's soft mouth, and how carefully he had laid her on the bed. She imagined him standing at the far end of Humility Chapel waiting for her. After she read the same page three times without remembering any of it, she gave up and set the book aside.

Suddenly a wicked idea leapt into her mind. She could visit him. His rooms were directly below hers. She passed his door several times a day, but she had never been inside. It could not be so improper. Tomorrow they would be man and wife.

She took up her candle and tiptoed out the door. She caught the sleepy sentry off-guard, but she quieted him with a quick lie about going to see Rosemary and ran down the stairs before he could argue with her. She rubbed her bare arms and chided herself for leaving without house shoes or a robe.

She poked her head around the corner. Another sentry stood guard under a flickering torch outside Gregory's door. He was thickset, with a mustache, and looked much more intimidating than her own young soldier.

She stepped into the hallway and his head snapped in her direction. She smiled and walked toward him, as if it was not the middle of the night and she was not half-clothed. His eyes widened.

"Please, sir," she said. "I need to speak with the prince for a moment. Would you grant me entry?"

He stared straight ahead again, as if hoping she might disappear. "I can't do that, Mistress," he said.

She frowned. "Why not? I'll only be a few minutes, and it will be our secret, I promise."

"I can't."

"Sergeant, I promise you won't be in any trouble."

He tugged at his earlobe. "I can't, Mistress, and I would, just to get you out of this hallway, but Prince Gregory is not here."

"Not here? What do you mean? It has to be—"

"Two in the morning."

"Two in the morning," she said. Something icy formed in her chest, and it wasn't from the cold tiles beneath her feet. "I see. Well, I'll be going." She turned slowly.

"I'm sorry, Mistress." The gruff voice followed her, but she didn't want to turn around and see the sympathy on his face. She started up the steps but stopped midway.

There must be an explanation. She could not face tomorrow not knowing. She would wait and see, and it would all be revealed. Probably just some late-night meeting with his advisers, a problem that must solved before the wedding. She would wait until he returned, and then go back to bed happy.

Exhaustion caught up with her and she sat on the bottom step out of view of the guard. She wrapped her arms around her knees, and in spite of the cold she nodded off. After some time, maybe ten minutes or maybe an hour, she heard voices. She sat up.

They were male voices, and some of them sounded familiar. She rocked forward on her numb toes and peered around the corner again.

She recognized Dorian first, and then Brian, Raoul, and several of Gregory's other friends. Dorian struggled to hold someone up. Her heart sank as she recognized Gregory's auburn hair.

He could barely stand. His legs kept buckling underneath him. Each time they crumpled he reached up with both arms. He grabbed

Dorian's neck and nearly dragged them both to the floor. The other men kept up a constant stream of harassment. She lost track of who said what, but their words rang painfully clear.

"What's that Gregory? Those two Talessee girls where too much for you?"

"We should have quit after the redhead. She took care of him quite nicely."

"Did you see the tits on that one?"

"Old Greg was probably seeing four of them. He was so smashed he was already falling over."

"But his flagpole was standing up!" They all roared with laughter.

"A fine tribute to Cartheigh!"

"Tell me, Gregory, how will your sweet little maid compare with those last two?"

Gregory's head swung up. "See, what you boys don't realize…is I can have the sweet little maid and still bang as many whores as I see fit. Benefits of the crown."

Eleanor could barely breathe. She heard Dorian's voice for the first time. "All right, all right, let's get you to bed or you're liable to pass out on the altar."

Gregory spoke again. "And you know, boys, little Eleanor is not quite as sweet as you may think— I've already had my hands on her—"

"Enough, Gregory," Dorian said. He thrust the stuttering prince off on Brian and Raoul. He took the keys from the guard, who gazed resolutely at the wall.

"Tonight was just practice for tomorrow—"

"Enough!" Dorian exclaimed.

Eleanor couldn't take any more. Without any further thought she stepped out into the hallway.

They all froze, a bunch of possums blinded by a woodsmen's torch. Eleanor couldn't speak. She simply stood there, staring at Gregory strung between Brian and Raoul like a pair of wet stockings left out to dry. Her hands clenched at her sides in tight fists. Blood roared in her ears, but her eyes were dry.

Dorian finally broke the silence. "Eleanor."

Gregory cocked his head. "Sweetheart, how good to see you."

His body jerked and he vomited. It covered his boots, and the sentry's. The guard never moved. The acidic scent hit Eleanor's nose and broke her paralysis. She fled up the steps. She heard Dorian calling after her but she didn't stop. She brushed past her own sentry, threw the door open with both hands, closed it and drew the latch. She leaned against it. She had left her candle in the hallway, but she'd built the fire well and it still burned. She jumped at a gentle tap on the door behind her.

Dorian's voice through the thick wood loosened the tears that had not come downstairs. "Eleanor," he said, "please open the door. Let me explain."

"No, go away."

"He's just drunk. It's just talk among men. He didn't mean any of it."

"So where were you all? You weren't out pitching lawn bolls!"

"I don't deny it, or defend it. But Gregory loves you. He never meant to hurt you."

She leaned her head against the door. There was no way she could open it. "I don't know what to believe," she said. And then, louder, "Please go away, Dorian. Please."

"As you wish."

She sensed him standing on the other side, and then his footsteps moved down the hallway.

Eleanor lay in bed for the rest of the night but she did not sleep. The servants were just creeping into the room when the door banged open. She heard the maids cry out. She sat up, her heart racing, as the bed curtains were ripped aside.

There was Gregory, unshaven, with dark circles under his eyes. He wore the same clothes she seen him in last night, and the sour smell of old booze and vomit clung to him. He looked more like an escapee from one of the witches' asylums than her handsome prince.

"Eleanor," he said. "I'm so sorry."

Her nostrils flared and she jumped out of bed. "Get out."

"No, listen to me." He followed her to the window. The two maids were frozen, trying to blend in with the furnishings.

"What are you playing at? Leave!" he yelled. He did not need to repeat himself.

"How could you?" Eleanor sputtered. "How could you, and then to speak of me like that..." She couldn't even finish.

"I'm so sorry, I don't know what I was thinking. I don't even remember it, Dorian woke me just now and told me." He grabbed both her forearms but she pulled away. "You must believe me. I barely remember anything past leaving the palace. I had so much to drink, and I think I smoked something...the boys were having a laugh...if I did those things I never meant them."

She turned away and hid her face in her hands.

"Please," he said. She opened her eyes and he was on his knees, gripping her nightgown. "You have to forgive me. I love you. I would never hurt you intentionally. I know I've been neglecting you. I can change. I promise."

Why now? Why is he telling me this now?

She was supposed to marry him in less than eight hours. The whole kingdom waited. So she slapped him. "I have no choice but to forgive you."

The surprise on his face would have been comical under other circumstances. He leapt to his feet. "I'll make it right to you, I swear it. I want to show you something."

He dragged her toward the door but she dug in her heels. Wandering in her nightclothes had gotten her nowhere last night.

"Come, who cares? Look at me!" he said.

She couldn't argue with him there. He held her hand, and they ran down the staircase, past his chambers, and through the quiet Great Hall. The servants glanced at them with raised eyebrows but said nothing. He led her down another staircase, out a side door, and into a small courtyard.

He spun her around. "There, I have something for you."

At first she didn't understand. A groom held the halter of a black horse. She took a few steps closer and studied the animal's fine head. She put a hand over her mouth.

"Ellie, Ellie, Ellie," the horse said.

It was High Noon.

"Oh," she said. "Oh."

She took the halter from the young man. The horse sniffed her palm, and lipped at her hair. "Ellie, all big now," he said.

She turned to Gregory. "How did you—"

"I remembered the name, and you said one of your father's friends had bought him. I asked around at court until I found an old business associate of Mister Brice. He told me who your father hunted with, and I tracked the gentleman down. He has been cared for. He's old now, but still a fine animal."

She stroked his nose. He seemed much smaller than she remembered.

Gregory tentatively put a hand on her shoulder. "You can start riding again. High Noon will help you. You'll be able to join me on hunts soon. We can start your unicorn training."

She looked up at him. "This is a fine gift, Gregory Desmarais. About the finest you can give me."

"You give me a gift with your pardon."

How can he be so thoughtful one moment and so callous the next?

In the end, she chose the thoughtful moments. "I give it," she said.

He lifted her up, and she wrapped her arms around his neck. They stood there in the weak LowWinter sunlight. High Noon nibbled at the pockets of her nightgown, looking for the apples a small girl had always remembered to bring him.

CHAPTER 8

CONSUMMATION

When Eleanor returned to her room the chambermaids were bustling around as if nothing had happened. Her wedding gown hung from one of the posters on her bed, draped in a linen sheet for protection. The trim consisted of hundreds of tiny jewels of every color. The Fire-iron thread woven through it, added to the rainbow of diamonds, amethysts, sapphires, emeralds and opals, made the dress sparkle like sunshine on the water. For the past six generations every bride of an heir to the throne had worn this gown. After each wearing magicians treated the dress with a preservation spell. The silk was as white as the day it was sewn. Eleanor was taller than any previous Desmarais bride so the magicians lengthened the hems and sleeves. It fit as if it had been made for her.

Gregory's mother's jewels lay on the dressing table. Eleanor thought she'd finally summoned the nerve to wear her own mother's hair comb, but in the end it stayed nestled in the jewelry box beside the cracked slipper. She'd wanted to wear the glass slippers to the wedding, but Rosemary found the cracked one too damaged to repair. Eleanor picked up a wooden box, painted pink and engraved with the legend *Telbright and Spat: Maliana's Finest Luxury Cobblers.* A pair of silver slippers with tiny purple and green bows nestled inside. She remembered the nursery rhyme,

Something purple and something green
Must be worn by the future queen
On her wedding day or she be struck
With never a son and only bad luck.

With that merry thought ringing in her head she went to the bathing room. The maid had filled a steaming bath. She stripped off her nightgown and then sunk down until only her nose and eyes were showing. She inhaled the scent of peachberries. The maids had learned she preferred to bathe on her own. She liked the quiet moments stolen in the hot, soapy water.

She spent half an hour in the tub, convincing herself she had done the right thing. She had decided to forgive, and she could not dwell on it if she meant to keep her word. She would think only on Gregory's good qualities, and believe he could change.

He wanted me. He saw me in my filthy rags, and he still wanted me. My children will never be cold or hungry. Their father will protect them.

Images of him barely able to stand, snippets of his harsh words, tried to sneak through. She shivered and shoved them aside, her toes curling under the bubbles. She reminded herself he had been out of his mind with drink. She particularly avoided the memory of Dorian's voice through her bedroom door. It was the day of her wedding, a new beginning, and a time to start over. She ignored the voice in her head saying it seemed a bit early for a new start.

Eleanor waited in the vestibule of Humility Chapel on the arm of her soon-to-be father-in-law. If not for the need to stand properly beside him she would have paced the floor. It was all she could do to keep from peeking around the purple and green brocaded tapestry the Godsmen had hung in the doorway to hide her from the congregation.

The babble of the guests and the scrapes and whistles of the orchestra tuning up crept around the tapestry. The king's brooding did nothing to assuage her nerves.

He did not speak as they waited for their cue. She winced when he caught her eye and looked away.

This just won't do, she thought.

"Your Majesty," she said. He turned. His eyes were the same chestnut brown as Gregory's. "I know you don't approve of me."

"What?" he stammered. "What do you mean? I never said—"

She put her finger to her lips. "Shhh...please. Let me speak."

He shut his mouth. She wondered if anyone had ever shushed him before, but she could not take it back now.

"I probably would not approve of myself," she said. "Some girl who comes out of nowhere. I can tell you, sire, I'm as surprised to be here as you are to have me. I don't know what I'm doing, but I will work hard, and I will learn, and I do love your son. I think he will be a fine king and I'll be proud to be his wife. I'll do my duty to him and to Cartheigh, whatever that duty entails."

King Casper's mustache quivered for a moment before he spoke. "My own dear wife wore that dress. She was a very different woman, but it suits you both."

"Thank you."

The trumpets sounded.

"We're off," the king said.

She barely recognized the simple chapel. Flowers covered every bit of white space. The magicians had brought in live trees, and struck up a cool breeze to fan the hundreds of guests packing the benches. Giant butterflies, the size of flying dinner plates, floated lazily around their heads. Six unicorns stood behind the altar. They tossed their heads and their silky manes lifted in the enchanted breeze. Eleanor smiled and nodded at the familiar faces jumping out at her from the crowd. She caught sight of Rosemary with Chou Chou on her shoulder. Ironically,

Imogene, Sylvia, and Margaret sat in the front row, in the place of honor as her only family. Dorian sat across the aisle from them. She let her gaze slide over him as she passed.

Gregory waited for her, straight and handsome, in a white tunic trimmed in purple and green. She climbed the two steps to stand beside him and he took both her hands. The ceremony flew by, the vows, the ring, the Godsman's compulsory speech. Only the kiss lasted any time at all, and it must have gone on because the audience began twittering. Cheers and whistles went up from the crowd.

Gregory's mouth slid to her ear. "You have done me the greatest honor."

They faced the congregation. The Godsman called out, "Prince Gregory Desmarais, heir to the throne of Cartheigh, and his wife, her Royal Highness, Princess Eleanor!"

The chapel erupted in applause. As he led Eleanor down the aisle Gregory drew his sword and slashed the ropes strung at intervals across it. In the old tradition each clean cut would result in a healthy babe. Gregory did not miss one. They climbed into the waiting carriage, where he promptly drew the curtain and spoiled all the hard work that had gone into pressing her gown. It was shockingly wrinkled by the time they reached Eclatant.

As they entered the Grand Ballroom Eleanor wondered how the magicians came up with new decorative enchantments. In keeping with the Waning Fest theme the entire room had been winterized. Fat snowflakes swirled above their heads as if a blizzard were brewing against the ceiling. Icicles hung from the chandeliers, and ice sculptures dotted the room and danced in time to the music. Huge pine trees, which only grew in the farthest north past the Dragon Mines, towered over the dance floor. They glistened with snow. A treat for the guests, as it never snowed in Maliana. Of course, the magicians produced a snowstorm yet maintained the temperature of a summer morning.

Gregory and Eleanor made the rounds, saying hello and accepting congratulations. Brian, Raoul, and Gregory's other friends avoided her, and as well they should. She was feeling fine, however, and so she released those fish from the hook. She walked into the middle of their little cluster, and offered hugs and kisses. She chided them for being hung-over at her wedding, and made each one promise a dance to make it up to her. They all blushed and apologized and swore to spin her around until she fainted. When she took her leave she knew her point was taken.

Brian Smithwick said it best. "You are too gracious, Your Highness."

"Oh, don't I know it, Brian," she said.

She had the perfunctory chat with her stepmother and stepsisters to give everyone a good show of family unity. Imogene made a point to introduce Eleanor to Hector Fleetwood, Duke of Harveston, who was indeed Sylvia's husband. Anne Iris had not exaggerated his age.

Eleanor had to shout so he heard her congratulations. She beamed at Sylvia. "Sylvia, you must be so thrilled. I wish you years of love and happiness, and many, many children."

Sylvia grimaced at her, but before she could reply Eleanor turned to Margaret. She asked with genuine concern after her health and happiness. Margaret curtsied and shyly offered good wishes. Eleanor made up her mind in that instant to call Margaret to the palace, if only to get her away from Sylvia. She murmured her intentions in Margaret's ear. "Our past familiarity has not left my mind. Hold fast."

Margaret curtsied. She did not need to lower her perpetually whispering voice. "I shall, Your Highness."

Eleanor squeezed her hand, then eased through the crowd toward her husband. Dorian Finley stepped in front of her before she was halfway there. His gold tunic turned his eyes amber. "Good evening, Your Highness."

"Good evening, Dorian," she said, with a wooden smile.

"Will you dance with me later?"

"I'm sorry, I'm a bit tired."

He went to the point. "Eleanor, last night—"

"I don't want to talk about it," she said.

"But—"

"I've put it out of my mind."

His silence spoke loudly.

"Don't look at me that way. What would you have me do?"

"I suppose I don't know."

"Exactly." She peered around his shoulder. "Let's not speak of it again, shall we?" She silently begged him to leave it alone.

He bowed and moved aside. She rushed to find Gregory.

The rest of the evening went smoothly. Gregory gave a heartwarming toast. He praised his bride and thanked all eight hundred guests for sharing this special occasion with them. The dancing began in earnest, with the new couple taking the first one on their own. Eleanor recognized the waltz as the first dance they had shared at the Second Sunday Ball. She kissed him for remembering. She avoided looking at Dorian as he watched solemnly from the edge of the crowd. The music picked up when the song finished and to Eleanor's joy nearly every person in the ballroom joined in. She danced with men she knew and those she didn't, and even took a reel with the king himself. Dorian disappeared, and she did not seek him out. Like he had in the beginning, Gregory filled her eyes.

At one o'clock in the morning they made a grand show of leaving the ballroom amid good-natured wolf whistles and shouts of advice. By the time they saw Gregory's door they were nearly running. Despite her happiness Eleanor was glad the guard was not the same man who witnessed her shame last night. He stepped back and gave the prince room to open the door for his new wife.

The flames in the fireplace threw shadows on the white silk curtains cascading around Gregory's bed. Eleanor watched the patterns change. She glanced enviously at Gregory lying on his stomach. She could not see his face, but the slow rise of his back and a gentle rasping snore told her he slept soundly. Eleanor, on the other hand, found sleep eluded her again.

How am I laying here, my husband sound asleep, when I was just now rushing to this room in the heat of passion?

Things had gone dodgy as soon as they entered Gregory's chambers. First, she quickly realized how drunk he was when he tripped over a sheath of hunting arrows and spilled them all over the floor. The complicated buttons on her dress presented quite a challenge. He turned her this way and that, one eye screwed shut, until she finally reached up to undo the ones she could manage herself. This disrobing would prove to be the longest part of the consummation of her marriage.

When he finished the unbuttoning ritual Gregory wasted no time. He yanked his tunic off. Her dress fell to the floor and he scooped her up. She landed on the bed with a soft *whup* and sank into the thick coverlet. She looked up at him as he yanked at his own belt. It nearly whacked her as it slipped from the loops.

She wasn't sure of the exact position, but she gamely bent one knee to give him room.

"This one, too." He grabbed her other knee and forced it up.

"Sorry," she said.

He leaned forward until her eyes met with his breastbone. Tufts of brown chest hair peeped at her from his undershirt collar. Something poked urgently at her belly, her pelvic bone, and the top of her thigh.

Curiosity and a desire to help made her reach down tentatively.

She touched something hot and hard, and her hand darted away as he moaned. She tried again, but he seemed to have found the proper path on his own.

What followed was a push, a few pulls, a few more pushes, a sharp jab of pain, and a grunt on his part. She tried to see his face, but as his shirt buttons were practically rubbing against her nose she had to be content with a glimpse of his open mouth and a few teeth. He collapsed against her, and for a moment between his weight and the blankets around her face she feared she might suffocate. She was about to shove him off when he rolled over, breathing hard.

Is he really sweating? She thought.

He kissed her cheek, and mumbled a few words of affection. She had barely responded before he turned away.

Eliza, as Eleanor's one married friend, had enlightened her to the intriguing realties of the marital bed. Upon examination Eleanor found a sticky wetness between her legs, and a dark smudge of blood, which were part and parcel according to Eliza's instruction. She had indeed been inducted into the rites of marriage. There was nothing, however, of the evening's excited anticipation, or the pleasure Eliza had hinted at in her prim description. At this juncture she had to conclude that Eliza's spectacled country gentleman was a more skilled lover than the crown prince.

Perhaps I did something wrong. After all, he has some experience with this subject, even if it is the paying kind, and I have none.

She resolved to ask her friend as soon as the opportunity arose if she had missed some trick. The whole experience left her empty, as if she had started a five-course meal and been allowed only the soup.

She decided to see if Gregory had anything to read. It hadn't worked last night, but books where always her fallback when she saw no other option. Her husband was no academic but there had to be something around. As she climbed out of bed she remembered her nakedness. Her eyes fell on a nightgown laid out on the footrest, the lacy arms akimbo, waiting for an embrace that hadn't come. She slid it over her head and made a cursory check of the bedroom. She found nothing but a copy of *A Magician's Guide to Poker*.

She knew Gregory's chambers were larger than her own and consisted of several interconnected rooms. She opened the first door and discovered a large washroom. The second was the servants' closet. On the third try she succeeded.

Gregory's study was a cozy rectangular room that oozed manliness. A fire crackled in the deep hearth across from several high-backed couches upholstered in dark cowhide. A few unfortunate foxes and deer graced the walls, along with several more exotic creatures; a furry monkeyfish, a rare spiked tortoise, two fairies who glared at her from beady glass eyes, and something like a giant rabbit with sharp front teeth the length of her arm. So many vanquished beasts gave the whole place the faint odor of old hair. A round card table and a strikestick table rounded out the furnishings. Nothing appealed to Eleanor but the hundreds of books lining the shelves.

She ran her finger over the bindings and found one of her favorite authors. She selected a likely volume, a novel she had heard of but never read.

"You appreciate Geoffrey Ellington?"

She dropped the book and spun around. Dorian sat on one of the couches in front of the fire, a half full glass of whiskey in his hand.

"What are you doing here?" She put her hand over her heart to slow the pounding.

"King Casper asked me to wait here for a while, to make sure Gregory managed to...that everything went... I assume it did."

"Yes," she said. She bent and picked up her book. "I couldn't sleep, so I came out here for something to read."

"Try this," he said. He held out a small black volume. "It's one of my favorites. Meryl Tressa. Do you know her?"

"Of course, I love her poetry, especially *The Beekeeper*," Eleanor said.

Dorian poked the fire with a long stick as he recited.

"*The beekeeper's charges his life and his bane,*

a drop of honey and a prick of pain

Never raises his hand to the tripping wing—"

"*To have the sweet he must face the sting,*" she finished. "I always loved that last stanza."

"Yes, I thought you might."

She tried to lighten the mood. "Lately you see too much of me in my nightgown."

"I have no problem with it." His mouth turned up at the corners.

"Hush," she said, and the silence fell hard. An urge to sit beside him overwhelmed her. She took two steps forward and he spoke.

"Maybe you should try harder to sleep. Your long journey starts tomorrow."

"Will you be here when I return?" she asked.

"Gregory has removed me from active duty and made me an adviser, so I will be in Maliana for the foreseeable future."

"Good," she said. He looked up at her. "I mean, it's good you will be out of the line of fire, and able to help Gregory more often. I know how he values your counsel, and your friendship."

Dorian rubbed his temples. In Eleanor's mind she saw herself kneeling in front of him, reaching her own hands up to his face. She shook her head at the image.

"Then I shall see you in a month," she said. "Thank you for the book."

"I'll bank the fire and go. I've done as I said I would."

She turned back once as she walked away, half hoping he would be watching her, but he simply prodded the fire.

CHAPTER 9

EVERY RUT IN THE ROAD

ELEANOR AND GREGORY'S HONEYMOON, if it could be so called, was really a progress through the countryside. They would leave Maliana for Harveston, travel south to Point-of-Rocks and Solsea, then head northeast toward Harper's Crossing, and finally cut across the center of the country back to the capital. It would not be the romantic trip she had imagined, but she was excited to see so much of the kingdom since she had never left Maliana in her eighteen years. Besides, after the events of her wedding night, she did not know how much enjoyment she would take from a more traditional honeymoon with her new husband.

She spent the morning following her wedding packing and hashing things over. She had been in an odd frame of mind when Dorian sprang on her last night. Best she not see him for a while, but a pang of disappointment went through her each time the chambermaid announced a visitor and it was not him.

She paused before climbing into the waiting carriage to take in the size of their retinue. Eight white horses pulled their coach, and at least fifty soldiers would march in formation around them. Four other carriages brought up the rear. The first transported three advisory magicians. Eight more magicians rode inside the next open-air carriage, but they were martials, magicians who used their powers to fight and defend. The last two carriages carried provisions and the couple's clothes and personal belongings, as well as several servants. Two mounted unicorns brought up the rear with Vigor, who walked alone.

Eleanor hugged Anne Iris and Eliza, and kissed Chou Chou on his beak. She scanned the courtyard and the drive a last time, but saw no sign of Dorian. Gregory lifted her into the coach and climbed in after her. He had been gracious all morning, but she could tell he felt the effects of two nights of hard drinking. Eleanor could have asked Rosemary for a tonic to help, but in her opinion he did have it coming.

Her teacher climbed into the carriage with the advisory magicians. The Oracle had asked Eleanor and Gregory to stop at Afar Creek on their way down the Outcountry Road. After Rosemary's recent hesitation Eleanor immediately accepted the invitation. She sensed the request irritated Gregory, but he seemed willing to placate her. She wondered if he had some idea of last night's, shall we say, shortcomings.

As soon as they closed the doors Gregory shut his curtain. "I have a bit of a headache, sweetheart. I think I'll rest if you don't mind."

She patted his knee. "Of course not. I'll wake you when we reach the Abbey."

The procession made its way slowly out of the palace gate, like a cumbersome, undulating caterpillar.

No wonder it will take a month to see all of Cartheigh. I could run faster, she thought.

As they left the palace grounds the townspeople started milling around the soldiers. They yelled and threw flowers. They were young and old, merchants, workingmen and women, and the poor. She waved through the window.

Gregory opened his eyes. He picked an apple from the basket on the floor and took a bite. "They love you. I've heard they think of you as one of them, for what it's worth."

I was, and I could easily be one of them still.

There was no need for torchlight inside the Oracle's cavern. A pool threw mottled blue light against the dank walls, and while it wasn't cheerful, it was effective. As she had on her first visit on the eve of her father's death, Eleanor found it difficult to tell the true size of the chamber. The light came from nowhere in particular, perhaps from the walls themselves, which she saw in some spots but faded into darkness in others. The air should have been stale but somehow Eleanor caught a faint smell of fresh lavender. When they reached the pool's edge Rosemary sat and tucked her long legs beneath her. Eleanor imitated her, although her full skirts turned what should have been a simple plop on the ground into a complex and haphazard maneuver.

Sitting beside the water, propped on countless homespun pillows and wrapped in piles of furry robes, was an impossibly ancient, impossibly tiny, impossibly alive woman. Eleanor saw only her small face through the layers of cushions and blankets, a head covered in wispy hair floating in a bubble of supporting warmth. She was called Hazelbeth, and she was the Oracle of Afar Creek Abbey.

Eleanor knew more of the Oracle from her studies than from their brief meeting eight years ago. She was timeless, permanent, existing without food or water, kept alive by her own magic and strange intellect. No one knew when she had arrived at Afar Creek or where she had come from. Her life stretched back so far she had forgotten her own origins.

At first it seemed the Oracle was ignoring them. The scented air, heavy with magic, moved and stood still at the same time. It rocked Eleanor toward sleep. She blinked and pinched her own arm. Just when the dirt floor started looking like a particularly fine spot for a nap, a surprisingly strong voice floated across the water.

"Eleanor Brice, now Eleanor Desmarais. You have changed since our last meeting." Hazelbeth's eyes seemed to float across the water and hover in front of Eleanor's face. She tried to think pleasant thoughts, just in case the old witch could hear them.

"Greetings, wise one," said Rosemary. "We trust you are well and comfortable."

"Comfort is irrelevant," said Hazelbeth. "I am as I am. The sun goes up and down, the pool is full, and I watch." She turned to Eleanor. "You may wonder why I asked you here. I have heard young people, recently married, prefer to spend time alone. Where is your husband?"

Eleanor colored, at both the witch's reference to marital intimacy and her embarrassment over Gregory's absence. "He's not feeling well. He sends his regrets from the carriage." She returned to a more comfortable topic. "Of course I'm honored you asked me to visit, but I did wonder why."

"I would speak to you about your position. In all honesty, even I underestimated the signs about you. These things are never written clearly, you know."

"Signs?" asked Eleanor.

"Rosemary, explain it to her."

"I—what shall I tell her?" Rosemary glanced at the pool, at the dirt floor, at her own hands, everywhere but at Eleanor's face. "Perhaps you should tell her."

"If you wish it." Hazelbeth's voice lacked any emotion. "Shortly before your father died, child, I felt you in the pool, but I could not see you from the other side. What has meaning and consequence became soft and harmless."

Eleanor's brow furrowed. "What—"

Hazelbeth continued plowing through each word, without changing tone or cadence. "I asked Rosemary to bring you to me. I found nothing particularly special about you, no magic, just a strong mind and a strong will. Rosemary had fear for your safety even then, with your father still alive. She made a promise to you mother—"

"What promise?" Eleanor asked.

Rosemary shut her eyes. "Do you remember what I told you about your mother? About when she was my student?"

"You said she was smart. A quick learner. Always questioning."

"She was more than that. She was exceptional. When she turned thirteen your grandfather said it was time she finished her schooling. She cried at our last lesson. I begged your grandfather to allow her to continue her studies, but it was no use. He was just like every other Carthean man. He didn't care if she was brilliant. He only wanted Leticia to make a good marriage, and he made sure she spent the next few years finding one. She was fortunate in that regard, because she loved your father so."

Eleanor's lip trembled, as if she'd not grown up. As if Rosemary were delivering a particularly sad history lesson.

Rosemary continued. "Before she died she—she asked me to look after you if she could not. She made me swear it."

"Rosemary wanted to bring you here to the Abbey to live," said Hazelbeth, "but I cannot allow those with no magic asylum in our walls. Besides, I felt you were living the lot you were meant to live, and after your father died I knew I was right."

"The lot I was meant to live?" Eleanor annoyed herself with her flummoxed repetition.

"Yes. Rosemary came to me again after your father's death, but I convinced her to leave you where you were. You needed to be there."

Eleanor turned to Rosemary. "I thought you had to leave me there."

"I could not bring you here—"

"But you could have sent me somewhere else. Maybe to a farm, in the country." As child Eleanor had dreamed some long lost relation would appear and take her away from her stepmother's house. It is the great fantasy of all orphans and street waifs and poorly parented children. "You left me with Imogene on purpose!"

"Eleanor, I have never known the Oracle to be wrong, nor has any other witch at Afar Creek. She knew the right path, and now here you are."

"Yes, here I am, after eight years of misery and loneliness and—"

Hazelbeth broke in. "And the best education any noblewoman in Cartheigh has ever received. You have known hardship and overcome it, and you would not be the person you are today without those eight years. It is all clear to me now. Finally, we have a Desmarais woman with the brains and the strength to do some good in this land."

Eleanor heard the Oracle, but she focused on Rosemary. "You swore to look after me, and this is how you kept your promise?"

"I understand you pain, more than you know. I was a child alone myself."

"You grew up here, at the Abbey," said Eleanor. "You weren't alone."

Rosemary gave an adamant shake of her head. "But I was. I was five years old when the Abbey claimed me. A witch appeared at my family's farm outside Maliana and took me away. I never saw my parents or my three older brothers again."

Rosemary had never spoken of her childhood, and Eleanor realized she'd never asked. The idea of Rosemary as a child, or a young woman, was bizarre.

"Young witches and magicians must embrace a new life," said Hazelbeth. "Holding onto the past is not helpful. Most girls accept our creed in a few days, but Rosemary was one of the unusual ones. For a month we worried for her health, until she found solace in magic and learning."

"This life has never come easily to me, Eleanor. All these years, teaching girls only to have them ripped from me just as they begin to flower. I begged HighGod to give you magic, so I could bring you to the Abbey. So I could have something I should not want. One child of my own, whose brilliance I could lead in so many directions. I never imagined He would make me cage your body so I could set your mind free." Rosemary took her hands. "Please know I agonized over this decision. To put you through the fear and loneliness I remember to this day, and for years instead of weeks." Tears streamed down Rosemary's cheeks. "I did what I hoped was right, and I pray I kept my promise. Please, do not hate me."

"That's why you seemed nervous that night, before I left for the ball. You defied Hazelbeth to help me."

Rosemary nodded. "Disobedience. For the first time in one hundred years."

"Were you punished?" Despite her anger Eleanor's eyes stung at the thought.

"We have our own castigations," said Hazelbeth. "Now I thank HighGod for Rosemary's waywardness."

Eleanor's own words to Dorian Finley during her Engagement Ball flashed through her mind. *I'd be a better dancer, but I'd rather have other talents.*

She wiped away her tears, and then embraced her teacher. "I could never hate you, never. For better or worse, you made me, Rosemary."

Rosemary whispered in her ear. "For better, dearest, better every day."

Eleanor did not discuss the visit with Gregory. She simply kissed his cheek and gazed out the window.

Do some good in this land.

The mob thickened as the carriage rolled beneath the Abbey gate. The carriage stopped and started as the soldiers forced people back. She watched the faces go by, not one of them powdered or bejeweled. They were calling her name and singing songs. She saw more than one woman crying. Eleanor pressed her face to the glass.

The carriage stopped again. Eleanor slid the handle up, opened the door and stepped into the dusty street. The soldiers were not prepared when the people surged forward. They pressed in on her and shoved gifts into her arms. Snippets of shouted sentiments rang in her ears.

She was nearly knocked off her feet but she kept reaching out, clasping hands and collecting piles of flowers. Someone yanked hard on the gray tulle lining of her dress, perhaps in search of a souvenir. She kept smiling and turned to the carriage, but the surging throng of admirers blocked the way. Just as alarm set in the crowd melted away as if blown by a strong wind.

Gregory stood behind her with his sword drawn. "Get back," he shouted. "Get back, all of you, I command it."

Everyone fell silent and those closest dropped to their knees.

"The next person that touches my wife, I'll cut off his hand." He brandished his sword at a heavy-set woman holding a bunch of wilted daisies. "Or her hand."

He took Eleanor by the arm.

"Wait," she whispered. She cleared her throat. "Good people. Thank you for seeing us safely out of Maliana. I will think of home and your fond farewell on the dusty roads. Pray for our safe passage."

He squeezed her arm again, this time more forcefully.

"Bless you!" came the cries from the crowd. "An angel come to Eclatant!"

Gregory slammed the door behind her. "Are you out of your fucking *mind*?" he shouted.

"I'm sorry, I don't know what came over me—"

"You could have been killed!"

"Gregory, they want to wish us well, not harm us. You needn't be so cruel."

"HighGod in tears, Eleanor! They're peasants! They will smother you with their love; trample you to death in their stupidity! My cruelty saved your life!"

"I was one of those peasants until a month ago," she shot back.

"You were never a peasant."

"Maybe my name was in Mister Oliver's book, but I had far more in common with those people out there than with you. Perhaps I still do."

"Don't you say that a second time." His voice was dangerously hard. "You are my wife. You are a Desmarais princess. You are nothing like those people. You'll do as I say, when I say it, and you won't ever try something like that again. It's for your own safety, *my love*."

He threw his apple and it split against the carriage wall. Seeds and juice sprayed into his lap. She seethed, her head against the window. They lumbered down the Outcountry Road.

"Another thing," he said mildly. "It's not a good idea to second guess me in front of my subjects. It doesn't look good. I'll let it pass this time because you're still learning, but I won't expect it to happen again. Do you understand?"

She did. Anger and confusion rolled over her with every rut in the road. After a while Gregory slid across to her side of the coach and rested his hand on hers. The sudden warmth raised gooseflesh on her arms.

Eleanor and Gregory were finally alone.

PART II

CHAPTER 10

A True Bond

WINTER ARRIVED AS HARD as it ever does in Maliana, bringing with it chilly days and cold nights. Cartheans are a sun-loving people. Most of the thin-blooded courtiers left Eclatant Palace and hibernated in their own homes, confident they would not miss much. Eleanor had arrived during one of the busiest times of year, the long social season that started just before the Harvest Fest and culminated in the Waning. By the end of MidWinter the wealthy took a much needed break from ale, wine, and company to hunker down and regain the strength to do it all again in the spring.

Eleanor welcomed the relative quiet when she returned from her honeymoon. Most of the guest bedrooms were empty and only those closest to the family or necessary to the country remained at court. She missed her friend Eliza, who had retired to the country with her husband, but Anne Iris stayed and kept her company. Even in the dark months Anne Iris had an uncanny ability to keep up with gossip. Eleanor was half convinced she snuck off to Afar Creek Abbey and spied on her friends and relations in the watching pool.

As promised, Eleanor saved Margaret from a long winter in Harveston with her mother and Sylvia by calling her to the palace. Anne Iris heartily disagreed with this turn of events.

"I don't understand," she said to Eleanor over a game of Dragon-eyed Jack on a lazy, rainy afternoon. "She's quite possibly the most milquetoast creature I've ever encountered."

Eleanor laid a pair of cards on the table. "You just need time to know her. We'll have lunch together when she arrives tomorrow."

"I shall need an ear trumpet to pick out one word."

"She can be quite funny."

"It's true," said Chou. "I once witnessed her attempting to speak with a handsome woodcutter. Hilarious."

"Now, Chou," said Eleanor. "That's unkind."

Chou hung upside down from the chandelier. He swung to and fro. His waving cheek feathers gave the impression he'd sprouted a red mustache. He rather resembled Eleanor's father-in-law. "I'm only jesting. Margaret Easton does indeed have admirable qualities."

"Even if she proves to be the most charming lady at Eclatant," said Anne Iris, "I don't fancy her reporting our every conversation back to her mother and sister."

"You could hardly refer to Sylvia as an insufferable bitch," said Chou, "or Imogene as a pitiful social climber."

"She wouldn't," said Eleanor.

"How do you know?" asked Anne Iris.

"Tell her," said Chou. He dropped onto the table, scattering queens and a pair of sevens. "Tell her how you came to befriend Margaret."

"It's rather embarrassing," said Eleanor.

Anne Iris scooted closer. "All the better."

"Well..." Eleanor collected her thoughts. "Imogene married my father a month before his death. I was excited at the thought of having sisters, but once I met Margaret and Sylvia I lost my enthusiasm. Sylvia...I'm sure you can see why. Margaret had nothing to recommend her. A plain, frizzy girl with no apparent opinions. After my father died she wasn't kind or cruel, helpful or uncooperative. The opposite of Sylvia, who went out of her way to be as mean, messy and lazy as possible. All with my stepmother's encouragement."

Chou's whistle became a chortling growl, and Eleanor stroked his head.

"In my thirteenth year I started having pains in my back and stomach. They'd come and go—"

Anne Iris nodded. "Ah, I remember those first pains. They kept me awake for hours."

"I thought them the result of hunger...or hours bent over a washtub. And one morning I woke...and the blood...I thought I'd hemorrhaged."

"You didn't." Anne Iris's mouth hung open.

"How was she to know any different?" asked Chou.

"I'd never been so frightened. Chou was off on a tour around town..." Eleanor smiled at him. "And honestly, darling, as dear as you are I don't know that I could have discussed my mysterious condition with you. Not then."

"You humans. Everything is dirty and embarrassing to you. Birds are hardly humiliated by laid eggs."

Eleanor went on. "I hid in my room, under a sheet. When I didn't turn up Imogene sent Margaret and Sylvia after me. Sylvia tried to yank me out of bed. She tugged at the sheet...and you could see..." She could still feel the mortification. Sylvia's look of disgust. Her words to her sister.

Look, Margaret, Skinnybones is finally growing up. It had made no sense to Eleanor, but it had obviously made sense to Margaret.

"Margaret sent Sylvia back to the house. She told me I wasn't bleeding to death. I remember thinking she'd been waiting weeks to find someone willing to do address the topic. She and Sylvia were only several months into the whole business themselves. Sylvia refused to acknowledge it, no matter how Margaret tried to confide in her. Imogene's first concern was for their dresses and the bed linens. She insisted they attend to themselves and rinse away any stains, She even made them see to their own chamber pots."

"You can imagine how that went over with Sylvia," said Chou. "Like a dragon with a broken wing."

"It was all about shame, not useful information," said Eleanor. "They hid soiled rags in sealed burlap sacks until the knackerman came to collect the garbage we couldn't compost each week. I never knew."

"HighGod above," said Anne Iris. "I thought my own mother was a prig."

"So Margaret brought me tea, and then..." Eleanor's eyes stung. "She went to her mother and asked for extra rags. I'd not have thought her capable, but she pushed until Imogene gave in. After that, she changed. She handed down old dresses. They were too short, of course, but better than what I had. She cleaned up after herself, and after Imogene and Sylvia. And the smiles...passed jokes..." Eleanor remembered Margaret sticking her tongue out at her mother's back, her stubby nose wrinkling like a baby piglet's. "We were not the best of friends, but I had one less enemy in the house."

"I commend her generosity," said Anne Iris, "but in the end her loyalty must remain with her blood."

"If Imogene hadn't had Eleanor she might have very well set Margaret to be the maid," said Chou. "She has two horses, but she's always bet on the flashy one. Margaret disgusts her."

Eleanor's jaw clenched. "All the more reason to bring her to Eclatant."

"As you wish, Your Highness," said Anne Iris. "I hope she thinks of you with as much affection as you do her. For your own sake."

During Margaret's first days in Eleanor's service they tiptoed around each other, but within a week Eleanor felt the cautious affection between them had won out. Anne Iris grudgingly accepted Margaret's presence, and the three young women spent the remaining winter evenings huddled around the fire. Chou Chou sent them into peals of laughter with ribald tales from his flights around the castle and the marketplace. Eleanor found herself a font of knowledge for her unmarried friends. Anne Iris was predictably frank in her curiosity about Eleanor's love life with Prince Gregory, and after the first few nights of feigned mortification Margaret joined in the questioning. If anything after several drinks Margaret's prodding became an interrogation.

"I do wonder," said Margaret late one night, "is it preferable to lie there or move about?"

Anne Iris's eyes widened, and then she looked to Eleanor for an answer.

"I suppose some form of enthusiasm is needed," said Eleanor.

Margaret swirled her wine around her goblet. "In the stories the women are always very keen, but I do wander if that would give one's husband the impression of wantonness."

Margaret had an abiding fondness for romance novels. She'd been allowed to borrow her mother's books, and Imogene's tastes did not run toward the highly intellectual. Not being highly intellectual herself, this had suited Margaret just fine. She'd sometimes handed off a particularly torrid volume to Eleanor, and even Eleanor had found herself drawn into the longing and passion that came along with brave knights and damsels in distress.

"One must indeed reach a middle ground," Eleanor said.

Margaret stood. "How depressing. I should hope I can reach the precipice of the mountain when my love reveals himself." She excused herself to use the chamber pot.

"Perhaps I was incorrect in my assessment of her docility," said Anne Iris.

"Now that she's out from her mother's skirts I'm sure she'll surprise you."

Anne Iris seemed unconvinced, precipice of love or not. "We'll see," she said.

Margaret returned with more questions, and Eleanor answered her with cautious optimism. While Gregory had not yet transported her to the heights of passion, he had not repeated the disaster of their wedding night. He drinking, while still a daily occurrence, was more subdued. He spent most of his days hunting *j'rauzelles*, the four-horned antelope that roamed the low hills outside of the city, with Dorian, Brian and the other young men who remained at the castle. They hunted on horseback because the unicorns could not be risked on such diversions, and anyway they were so fleet it would have been unfair to the quarry. The hunting parties left at dawn, and after a full day in the saddle Gregory came to her door, tired and in need of comfort. She would dismiss her ladies, rub his back, and listen as he told another variation on the same old hunting story. After he ate and relaxed he almost always took advantage of his rights as her husband. While she usually found her mind wandering, he was gentle enough and it wasn't unpleasant. She enjoyed his company, and appreciated the peace.

Dorian Finley remained the itchy button in her bodice. She found if she casually let slip she would be in the library he would find an excuse to drop in. He was always passing by on his way here or there, or returning a book he'd had in his room for weeks. He would fall into the next chair, and two hours disappeared. They poured over history and religious documents. They discussed great works of literature. They argued over current affairs, from the crown's tithing of the Coveys (Dorian supported it and Eleanor did not) to the allegiances of the surrounding nations (both agreed the loyalties of Kelland would always lie with Svelya).

He enthralled her. She had never found anyone other than Rosemary who shared her passion for learning and discourse. And Rosemary, while smart and insightful, did not share Dorian's low drawl, nor did her mouth curve up so sensually before making a point. After one poetry discussion left her with sweaty palms she avoided any vaguely romantic topics. She usually brought Chou Chou, and asked him to bring along his grouchy raven, Frog. The two birds snoozed through their meetings like bored chaperones. She told herself she was married, and would not act on her infatuation, so it was all right.

The fact that Gregory seemed thrilled his best friend and his wife got on so well made her squirm. Throughout the winter Eleanor rode High Noon in the indoor ring every morning, and Gregory was highly impressed. He called her a natural rider, and said she was ready to begin unicorn handling. He wanted Dorian to help him teach her.

The Paladine, the sprawling complex of buildings that housed the Desmarais unicorn herd, was a mile outside the palace. It consisted of several long stone stables, a brood mare barn, two training rings, acres of pastureland, several warehouses and granaries, and the Paladin House. There were no guards or fortifications. The horned residents were their own protection. The Paladins, or unicorn-keepers, were all fit men in the prime of life. They had great status among the common people, and the position usually ran in families. Every few years a new man would come to the stable, show a connection with the creatures, and be allowed to stay on as an apprentice, but it was rare. Eleanor had heard the Paladins were an arrogant, uncooperative bunch.

A balding man called Welker Tubbetts stood in front of her. Eleanor smiled at him and held out her hand, but he merely bowed and adjusted his chewing wad. "Pardon, Your Highness," he said, "but I heard the princess just started riding a horse this winter. And you think she's ready for this?" He scuffed his battered work boots.

To Eleanor's surprise Gregory took no offense. "I do, Welkie, and you know I wouldn't waste your time."

"I don't know," Welkie muttered.

"You'll find her an apt student, like Mister Finley." Gregory waved up at Dorian, who was seated on his black stallion, Senné.

"I doubt it," said Welkie. "Will give you credit, sir, I weren't sure that black devil would ever submit. We don't get many black 'uns but they're always flighty. You had him wrapped up in no time."

Dorian tipped his head at the compliment.

"Ach, sire," Welkie continued. "Seems soon to train your wifey here, and a waste of a good brood mare if she don't take to it."

Eleanor prickled. "Excuse me, Mister Tubbetts, but I recall my husband telling me you managed five live births last year. I believe you have over one hundred breeding mares in the Paladine? If only five deliver foals, I think you can spare one for my training."

Gregory cleared his throat, Dorian coughed, and Welkie looked at Eleanor as if she had just sprouted a horn herself. "If you put it that way, Highness," he said, and spat. "Come, there are a couple ladies over here you can meet."

She hitched up her skirts and followed him to a nearby paddock. Three unicorn mares grazed in the weak sunshine, their silver horns nearly brushing the ground. Each raised her head as they approached. The mares were shorter than the stallions, and more delicate of bone, but no less powerful.

Gregory and Dorian stood on either side of her. She reached out and squeezed each man's hand in her excitement, before remembering herself and dropping Dorian's. Welkie opened the paddock door. The mares tossed their heads and moved to the back of the enclosure. He waved the three visitors in and spoke under his voice to Eleanor.

"Now you know, m'lady, you can't just talk to a unicorn. We Paladins spend our whole lives with them. We understand them. Fine men like your husband and Mr. Finley, those that keep their own stud, are near as fluent as we. The mounted soldiers can get by, enough to work together, but they don't have a true bond. The magicians and witches have a bit of a way with them. Most other people couldn't make out a word."

"A stallion on guard spoke to me once," Eleanor said. "It was only a few words, but I understood him."

"Really?" said Welkie. "Then maybe your husband's right. Anyway, as I was saying, unicorns ain't chatterboxes. They speak in words, but also in breaths, and gestures, and with their eyes. Humans can't replicate their language, but fortunately they understand everything we say. The trying part of the understanding is on our side. If you can learn to read every sign your unicorn offers you can have a conversation with her just as we're speaking right now. They're just as clever as people, maybe cleverer."

Gregory spoke up. "It's a different kind of intelligence, Eleanor. It's more..."

"Sensate," said Dorian. Gregory nodded.

"Now it will be a while before you can think about riding one of these ladies. Some unicorns are trained to accept different riders, like the war mounts and sentries. When we hand a unicorn into the keeping of one person, like Vigor to the prince or Senné to Mister Finley, we like to give a young, green animal. One likely to accept only one rider, so there is no chance of an abuse of the privilege."

Welkie motioned for them to wait, and walked further into the ring. He spoke in a breathy voice too low for Eleanor to understand. He held both hands out, and the mares came to him. He turned to Eleanor.

"Let's see if one of these three takes a shine to you."

A month later Eleanor sat astride Teardrop, the mare she had chosen from the three in the paddock. She was a skittish thing, named for the birthmark on her right cheek. Eleanor had been drawn to her appraising look, but the pink splotch on her face sealed the choice. The other mares seemed too perfect, and Teardrop's birthmark reminded her of the flaw in her own eyes.

Few women ever rode unicorns, but the ones who did were permitted to wear leggings while mounted. For Eleanor, who had spent her whole life in heavy skirts, it was liberation. The soft calfskin riding pants made her silk stockings feel like sausage casings, and she rejoiced in the ease of loosening a belt and a few buttons to use the chamber pot without fear of wetting a petticoat. Riding astride was comfortable and easy after sitting sidesaddle on horseback.

Welkie had been astonished at how quickly she began an earnest communication with Teardrop. Eleanor appreciated his praise, but did not fully understand it. She found the mare's subtle cues and nuances, along with her airy speech, obvious and easily interpreted. She simply took in the whole picture, from the set of her ears to the swish of her tail, and Teardrop's meaning could not have been clearer had she picked up a quill and written it out. Within a week Eleanor had been ready to ride.

"Not meaning any insult, young masters," Welkie had said to Gregory and Dorian, "but you two were plain slow compared with Princess Eleanor here, and I would have said you was some of my best students."

As Welkie gained confidence in Eleanor's abilities he let her ride in the ring alone. This afternoon she looked up from checking Teardrop's lead and saw the Paladin and Dorian leaning over the paddock gate.

"Visitors," Teardrop said. "What do they want?"

"Let's go find out." Eleanor dismounted and Teardrop followed her to the gate.

"Got some good news," Welkie said. "You two are getting along right well. You ready for some new scenery?"

"Do you mean it?" Eleanor clapped. She and Teardrop were both bored with circling the ring.

"I do," he said. "Why don't you head out into the south pasture? There's a nice trail back there. It passes the brook and heads out toward the Abbey. Mister Finley and Senné will join you. Make sure everything goes smooth-like."

"Gregory stayed up a bit too late playing sharpstick with Brian, so I offered," Dorian said. "I hope you don't mind."

"No, of course not." In truth, she was genuinely disappointed

Gregory wouldn't be coming along. She hoped their shared love of the unicorns would give them something they could enjoy together. She fumbled as she checked Teardrop's girth. The thought of spending several hours virtually alone in a field with Dorian unnerved her. The mare nibbled at Eleanor's hair as Eleanor examined her hooves. She whispered in her mistress's ear. "All fine." Eleanor straightened so she could read the whole message. "We will watch over each other."

"I know we will."

She kissed Teardrop's muzzle and grabbed the braided rope woven into her mane. She couldn't reach the stirrups and swinging herself into the saddle took all her strength, but it got easier each day. She guided Teardrop through the open gate.

As Dorian watched them approach his respect for Eleanor increased by the moment. Teardrop required constant reassurance, but he could tell she would become a fine mount and friend under Eleanor's patient guidance. He saw her body responding to the mare's movement, her long legs strong in her hunting leggings. He hoped his admiration was not too apparent.

As they left the Paladine grounds the dirt path widened and they rode side by side. Heat radiated up from Senné's thick mane, and Dorian took off his riding gloves. He told Eleanor how impressed he was by her natural way with Teardrop, and her obvious pleasure at his compliment warmed him.

She asked about Senné. "What does the name mean?"

"It means darkness in Svelyan," he said. "It was his sire's name, and his grandsire."

Senné tossed his head and snorted. "Great-grandsire," he said.

"Yes, and his great-grandsire. Senné comes from a long line of black unicorns." Dorian patted Senné's neck.

"He's quite handsome," Eleanor said, and blushed.

"Thank you."

They rode on, splashing across the creek Welkie had mentioned. There were no buildings and few trees, mostly wide-open fields of low grass in varying winter shades of brown and gray. They had crossed onto the grounds of the Abbey. Dorian reined Senné in. A light breeze lifted the feathering on the stallion's hooves. He snorted and tossed his head, eager to stretch his legs. "Go," he said.

"Hold on, Sen." Dorian turned to Eleanor with a grin. "We should test your progress."

"What do you mean?"

"That tree over there." He pointed at a live oak at the far end of the meadow, half a mile away. "Let's race."

She shaded her eyes and gathered her reins in the other hand. "You mean that one? It is far. And we're already ten paces in front of you!"

She leaned forward and Teardrop took off. Senné jerked the reins from Dorian's hand and went after them.

Senné was larger than Teardrop, and longer of leg, but he did not catch up until they were nearly halfway across the field. The two unicorns raced along beside each other, kicking up clods of mud and dead grass. Dorian stole glances at Eleanor through Senné's black mane. She ignored the reins she had looped over the pommel and clung to Teardrop's mane. He might have thought her afraid if not for her whooping yells.

They reached the tree together. Eleanor slid from Teardrop's back and landed nimbly on both feet. She shook out her tangled hair and wiped at the tears the wind had sent streaming down her face. She beamed at Dorian.

He remembered his first gallop with Senné. He had spent his life on horseback, as a child and then in the army, but when Gregory offered Senné to him three years ago he realized he had never known real speed or power. The thundering hooves, the rushing breath, the flexing muscle and bone, were all tenfold from the back of a unicorn. He understood Eleanor's joy.

"Fantastic," she said. She hugged Teardrop around the neck and flopped down on the grass. He sat next to her on the damp ground. She laughed and lifted her seat. "These leggings don't provide as much protection as three layers of petticoats and a skirt. I must look frightful."

He reached out and took a twig from her hair. "No, it suits you."

He studied her dark and light eyes. He had heard talk of bad spirits, and spiteful women thanking HighGod their daughters were not so scarred and abnormal. He disagreed with them all. Without the birthmark Eleanor's face was lovely. With the birthmark it was interesting.

His hand slid down her cheek and she didn't move. She didn't close her eyes the way a girl might in a poem. When his thumb brushed her lips her jaw clenched.

"Welkie might worry," she said. She placed his hand in his lap. "We don't want to cause any trouble."

"No, we can't have that." He wondered why he was angry. It wasn't her fault. It wasn't anyone's fault, but the joy had gone out of the afternoon. He offered her a leg up on Teardrop's back. The mare snorted and sidestepped and Eleanor scrambled more than usual to find her seat.

"I'm sorry," he said to Teardrop. She squinted at him, and then blew a long blast of air into his hair.

Apparently Teardrop wasn't sure what to make of him, and Dorian couldn't really blame him for her suspicion. They cantered back across the field. Eleanor tried to engage him as they slowed to a walk, but he answered her in monosyllables. He had to. Everything he said gave him away.

CHAPTER 11

SOMETHIN' BREWIN'

ELEANOR SURVIVED HER FIRST Breaking of the New Year at Eclatant. The somber week of fasting and chapel services at the start of LowSpring made Gregory moody and irritable, and even cheerful Anne Iris began to show the effects of too little food and drink and too much preaching. "I'm supposed to be repenting for my sins, but all I can think about is wine and men," she complained on their fifth day of water and flat bread.

Eleanor sighed. "I know. What time is it?"

Chou Chou answered for her. "Four o'clock."

"Ugh," Anne Iris said. They were not allowed to eat until six. "Why don't birds have to fast?"

"It's common knowledge that we can't understand the moral complexities of fasting," Chou said, through a mouthful of walnuts.

Eleanor scowled at him. "I hope you choke!"

He lit on the bedpost. "It's only a week ladies. Soon we will be overrun with indulgences and friends and relatives we didn't know we had."

He was right. Once the fast ended the nobility trickled back to Eclatant in preparation for the Awakening Fest. Dressmakers and pastry chefs consumed Eleanor's attention through most of LowSpring. As the highest-ranking female member of the royal family, Eleanor needed to both look the part and participate in the planning. Once again she thanked HighGod for Anne Iris, and for Eliza, who had returned from the country. Both of her friends enjoyed the preparations, from the menus to the magicians, and Eleanor gladly let them take charge of much of it. She stored away their arguments over table linens and guest lists, so she would be better prepared in the future.

As the castle grew more crowded the days and nights were again busy. Eleanor could hardly find the time to visit Teardrop or High Noon. Although she no longer needed the old horse for riding practice, and her unicorn's training had progressed rapidly, she hated to neglect either animal. When she could, she rose early and rode High Noon down the private road to the Paladine for her training sessions with Teardrop. She needed an escort, but as the nights got later she rarely managed to drag Gregory out of bed. Most mornings she settled for a few mounted sentries. One evening she asked Dorian to come with her, but he demurred.

He had been distant since their ride over the Abbey grounds. She told herself it was better this way, but she still looked for him whenever she entered a room. The evenings fell into a predictable pattern of harmless pleasantries and stolen glances. He kept up his maddening habit of meeting her eyes whenever she turned in his direction.

She tried to focus on Gregory, who was in a better mood with his barrel tapped and the contests in full swing, but she could never gain his full attention. The comfortable intimacy that began during the winter over quiet evenings and long rides stopped mid-blossom. His visits, both during the day and late at night, were hasty affairs. They spoke of nothing but the next event, and once again spent most of their time in the company of dozens of jostling courtiers. She danced with him, cheered him on, and laughed at his antics, but whenever he turned his back on her in a crowd she looked for Dorian. Whenever he rolled away from her in her darkened bedroom she thought of Dorian's hand on her cheek. She often wished Gregory would spring one of his endearing romantic gestures on her, in the hope it would drive Dorian and his coldness from her mind.

Then, abruptly, Dorian began to thaw. It began when Anne Clara Finley Tavish and her husband Ransom arrived to celebrate the Awakening. It was their first visit to Eclatant since the birth of their twin daughters the previous year.

"I've heard nothing but praise for your sister," Eleanor said, when Dorian mentioned the visit at a picnic. "I would love to meet her in my chambers, away from all this."

"I'm sure she would like that. She looks forward to meeting you as well. I've often written of you." He gave her a real smile for the first time in weeks.

"You're too kind, as usual," she said. "Please ask her to let me know as soon as she's settled."

The next day, in her room, Eleanor and her teakettle were introduced to a shorter, dark-eyed, female version of Dorian. Eleanor and Anne Clara passed an easy hour getting to know each other, chatting about palace life, and Anne Clara's three children and her home in Harper's Crossing.

"The Lake District is beautiful, and the people were so gracious," Eleanor said.

"We are known for our hospitality," Anne Clara said. "Ransom and I would be honored if you would come and stay with us."

"What a wonderful idea. It would be nice to get away from here for a few days. Not that it isn't wonderful…being here, I mean." Eleanor sipped her tea.

"Eleanor, dear, don't think I need an explanation." Anne Clara reached over and tapped her knee. "I hear enough from my brother about this place. It can make anyone want to escape for a while, even the princess."

"Dorian makes it all look easy," Eleanor said with a smile.

"Easy? No, he's just had more practice. I know everyone here thinks he's all confidence and arrogance, but it wears him out. He comes home a few times a year and it's like watching the wind let go of a banner. He's a sensitive one, my big brother. More than he lets on, even to himself. He esteems you greatly."

"And I him. There is no finer gentleman at court."

"Except your husband."

"Of course." Eleanor set down her teacup.

"I am fortunate," Anne Clara continued. "Ransom might not be the most handsome man in the world, but I understand him. We've known each other since we were children. He's always been my friend, and he's become my great love. I know others are not so lucky."

Eleanor did not speak. She gazed out the window at the gardeners pulling weeds.

Anne Clara went on. "My brother is in a strange position, in our family and at court. I fear for his happiness. I think he knows I will always support him. I will stand by those he cares about, and those who care about him."

"He's fortunate he has you," Eleanor said. "I hope you will call me your friend."

The conversation returned to more mundane topics, and soon both Eleanor and Anne Clara had to prepare for dinner. They said their goodbyes, but when Anne Clara stood Eleanor embraced her before she could curtsy.

Perhaps his sister's presence relaxed him, or something in her report back eased Dorian's mind. Eleanor only knew over the next few weeks Dorian slowly returned to her, and somehow Gregory's carelessness hurt her a little less.

Dorian and Gregory sat by the banks of Afar Creek passing a flask of pomegranate whiskey between them. The Awakening was over, and Dorian relished the peace. The morning was all light greens and soft blues, broken up by flashes of red and purple in the form of new tulips. Dorian loved how HighGod could make any colors blend together.

Senné and Vigor fanned out away from them, grazing and cooling down after the hard run across the Abbey grounds. The two stallions had grown up together, but they rarely spoke. In the wild a dominant stallion might not see any males other than his own sons for years, and he would eventually drive even his offspring away from his mares. The stallions of the Desmarais herd tolerated each other and worked well together, but they avoided close contact when they could.

"Too bad Eleanor couldn't join us," Dorian said.

"She was needed at a ladies' sewing circle or some ridiculous thing," said Gregory. "Knowing Eleanor, she'd rather be out here in pants with Teardrop than knitting."

Dorian laughed. He lay back in the grass and it tickled his ears. "Another reason I'm thankful I'm a man. More opportunities for escape."

"Speaking of escape," Gregory said as he took a long swig from the flask. "I'm thinking it's time we head into Maliana and visit the Hussy."

Dorian blinked at the fat clouds above him. The Red-headed Hussy was a bordello named for and run by Pandra Tate, the most famous prostitute in Maliana. She was known for her beautiful girls, heavy security, and dedication to the privacy of her wealthy patrons.

"Why the Hussy?" he asked. "We haven't been there in months, not since the night before the wedding."

Gregory leaned on his elbows. "And I bet Pandra has some new girls!"

"What's wrong with the girl you have?"

"Oh, please, Dor, this has nothing to do with Eleanor."

"Really? I think she might disagree. Aren't you…" Dorian's discomfort increased with each word. "Aren't you pleased with her?"

"Of course I'm pleased with her. I love her. She's kind and pretty of course, but more than that she's actually funny and rather adventurous."

He seemed to think Dorian needed convincing. "She's really quite fascinating. And I do love the way she keeps father and Oliver on their toes. If I must be married to anyone I'm glad it's her."

"That's good to hear." Dorian ground his teeth. Lately his temper sat in the back of his throat. He swallowed it.

Gregory threw a clod of dirt at him. "Oh, come now, I just want a change of scenery. Don't you go all moral on me. You've been with half the women at court. Come to think of it, you've been rather chaste this spring. Run out of conquests?"

Dorian had waited for this line of questioning. Gregory never tired of discussing his legion of admirers. He sat up. "Nothing new sparking my interest. I have other things on my mind."

"Well, you can use a run down to the Hussy to clear your head. Remember Trudie, with the giant—"

"Frankly, Greg, I think we're too old for all that. What if it got out you're still running around Pasture's End? You should be more discreet."

Gregory frowned at this new idea. "Maybe you're right. What if I had them brought to me?"

"That's not the point—"

Gregory stood. "What is the point? That I should be loyal to my wife? You show me one man at court that is and I'll eat this flask! Besides, you can fuck anyone you want. Talk to me after you're married."

Dorian could not suppress the anger this time. "If I was I wouldn't be sleeping with hookers and bringing home the weeping pox!"

Gregory's ears were redder than his hair. It took the brunt of his temper as usual. Dorian knew he had pushed too far. "Peace, Your Highness. I beg your pardon. I'm not myself and I spoke out of turn."

"Damn right you spoke out of turn. I should have you flogged." Gregory squatted in front of Dorian with his forearms on his knees. Myriad birds screamed their springtime love songs from the trees behind them. "What is it, friend? Is it Abram? Is it money?" Gregory understood how Dorian's brother held money over his head. "Haven't I been generous in the past?"

"Yes, you've always been generous, probably more so than I deserve," Dorian said. "You're a true friend, Gregory, and I am sorry."

Gregory clapped him on the shoulder. "You know you just need ask. Think, soon we leave for Solsea, and the ladies will be at their summer best. You'll find plenty of distractions, I'm sure."

Dorian stood and whistled for Senné, who came at a gallop, followed by Vigor. The two stallions eyed each other, flexing their necks, while their riders tightened their girths.

"Thanks for the advice, by the way," Gregory said from behind Vigor's wide belly. "I'll keep it in mind."

Gregory seemed to have put their disagreement aside as they returned to the palace and the barn that housed the royal family's unicorns. He dropped Vigor with the groom and excused himself, Dorian noted ironically, to visit Eleanor. Dorian stayed behind and rubbed down Senné himself.

Senné was tired and didn't say much, which suited Dorian. He couldn't begin to sort out his emotions. Gregory's callous treatment of Eleanor infuriated him. His own feelings for her haunted him, no matter how he tried to stifle them, through his waking hours and in his guilt-ridden dreams. To say Gregory had been a friend was an understatement. Dorian owed him everything, from the unicorn in front of him to his position at court. Gregory insisted Dorian be included in the High Council, when Dorian knew he was too young and inexperienced, and in all honesty lacked the social standing, to be there. Gregory's steadfast confidence in his abilities humbled him, to say nothing of the true affection Dorian felt for him, even when Gregory was at his most exasperating.

Dorian had spent the last six years on a slow climb up a steep hill. He'd reached the top, and should be pausing for breath. Taking in the view. Instead, as he picked burs from Senne's mane he wondered how he had become so beholden to one man.

Eleanor followed Ezra Oliver's trail from his office to the library to King Casper's receiving room. She stood outside the sealed Fire-iron door with a book and a ledger tucked under her arm. Her stomach grumbled. She'd left her room before breakfast, but she dared not step away for a bite, lest Oliver emerge and she lose him again. She opened the book, took a quill from her pocket and clenched it between her teeth. She'd been awake until the wee hours reading. Her eyes stung as she flipped the pages. "That quote…page four hundred twenty-seven…"

"Don't mumble, Your Highness. It's not becoming."

Eleanor looked up at her stepmother. She spit the quill into her hand. "Good morning."

Imogene bit the inside of her both cheeks, whether from disgust or an attempt to hide a snigger Eleanor could not be sure. With her full lips pursed so she had the look of a coquettish trout.

"Pray," said Imogene. "Can you tell me if Mister Oliver is inside?"

Eleanor nodded. "I'm waiting for an audience with him myself." It was quite possibly the most pleasant exchange she'd ever had with her stepmother. No harm in encouraging congeniality. She cleared her throat. "Do you seek his advice?"

"We wish to expand the Duke of Harveston's presence at Eclatant. We require more rooms, and Mister Oliver handles such delegations."

"Does His Grace not already occupy the entire second floor of the East Wing?" Eleanor asked. She'd meant no offense, but Imogene's lips went fishy again.

"What about you? What could the princess possibly need from Mister Oliver?"

"I've come to share a book with him."

Imogene touched the book's spine. "*Women, Magic and the History of Afar Creek Abbey*," she read. "You're bringing *that* to Mister Oliver?"

"Ah...yes," said Eleanor. "Why do you speak so?"

"Oh, no reason. Do carry on." Imogene sat in an upholstered chair across the alcove from the door. She took a doily from her pocket. The pouty smirk on her face made Eleanor want to jab her with one of her own embroidery needles. *So much for congeniality*, she thought, as an apprentice magician opened the receiving room door. Imogene leapt to her feet. She and Eleanor curtsied as the king swept past.

Eleanor straightened and poked her head around the doorway. Oliver was pressing a seal into purple wax on a folded document.

"Mister Oliver?"

He jumped at her voice. "Horns and fire," he said, shaking his thumb.

"Pardon," said Eleanor. "I didn't mean to startle you. Did you burn yourself?"

"It's nothing, Your Highness." He inserted a few more documents into a velvet bag. "Do you have need of me?"

"I just wanted to share something with you." She smiled her enthusiasm. "Do you remember, last fall...we spoke of the witches' dedication to desperate cases? I thought you'd enjoy this book. The Oracle gave it to me years ago. It gives insight into Afar Creek's philosophy on the impoverished—"

"Please forgive me, Your Highness, but I'm terribly busy."

"But there's a quote—it reminded me of how Rosemary helped me—"

"Did you get the silk I sent you?" he asked. "From Point-of-Rocks."

She nodded in confusion at Oliver's apparent preference for talk of fashion over philosophy. "Yes, thank you."

"Good. I'm sure you'll make good use of it." He smiled his crooked smile. "Such fine craftsmanship. As soon as I laid eyes upon it, I knew no other lady could do it justice. Now, please, excuse me." He bowed, and left Eleanor to her ledger and her seemingly uninspired reading habits.

Summers in Maliana were miserable. The rains were sparse, and the Clarity River dwindled to a warm brown puddle, exposing smelly clay and sending hordes of mosquitoes into the city's streets. As LowSummer wore on and the buzzing became intolerable the entire court packed up and left for the resort town of Solsea, eighty miles south of Maliana on the coast of the Shallow Sea. Even the king would join them for a while, leaving Eclatant in the care of several armed legions and the Unicorn Guard. Eleanor had visited Solsea for a few days during her honeymoon the previous winter, and she wanted to see the town in its summer glory.

As Eleanor oversaw her packing in the week before they were to leave she tired easily. Three evenings in a row she retched into her chamber pot. Her new lady's maid, Pansy Ricketts, suggested she needed a witch's attention.

"I think there might be somethin' brewin' in there, highness," said Pansy. She was a short, square woman with limp blondish hair. Eleanor had chosen her for her take-charge attitude and bluntness. Better a smart, honest servant than a pretty one.

"It's just a flu," Eleanor said, but she sent for Rosemary anyway.

Rosemary arrived with another witch, a healer and babycatcher called Mercy Leigh. Mercy Leigh's red hair made Gregory's look brown in comparison. She did not appear much older than Eleanor, but with witches it was difficult to tell such things.

Mercy Leigh examined Eleanor and declared her pregnant. "I can read it in your energy, but your body is not yet showing signs. It's very early. I would keep it to yourself, Your Highness."

"Of course," Eleanor said. The more she thought about it, the more thrilled she became. She beamed at Rosemary, Pansy and Mercy Leigh.

"It will be our secret. Though I will tell Gregory, of course. I can't wait to see his face!"

"Maybe you should wait a few weeks before telling him," said Rosemary.

"Why?" Eleanor asked. A dash of fear pushed her already buoyant stomach further into her throat. "Is something wrong?"

"Everything seems fine," said Mercy Leigh, "but this is your first pregnancy. We don't know how it will progress. Sometimes...Sometimes these things aren't meant to be."

"What they means, Highness," Pansy broke in, "is you don't want Prince Gregory all puffed up for nothin'."

"He's my husband, and I will tell him."

Rosemary kissed her. "As you wish, my dear. Besides, I'm sure everything will be just fine. You're young and healthy. And stubborn as a mule."

Eleanor laughed, her worry forgotten, and sent Pansy to find Gregory. Mercy Leigh left some tonics for the nausea and the health of the baby, and Eleanor promised to write Rosemary daily with updates on her health. After they left she sat back and waited for her husband.

As she expected, he was ecstatic. He lifted her up and covered her face with kisses, then set her down just as quickly. He was afraid he had shaken her too much. She laughed and begged him not to leave her unkissed for the next eight months. He sat beside her on the couch and rested his head on her lap, as if already waiting for a kick. She ran her hands over his thick hair.

"Let's have dinner here tonight," he said.

"Really? I'd like that."

"What is our child in the mood for?"

"I'd say anything but broccoli," she said. "A berry tart would be nice."

He turned his face up to hers. "No broccoli and a berry tart. You shall have it."

He called for Pansy and gave her the instructions. Over a quiet meal they discussed baby names and laughed over when the child had been conceived. She tired early, but for once it didn't bother him. He helped her out of her dress and into a simple satin nightgown. He took off his own tunic and slid under the covers next to her. For the first time since they had been married he slept beside her without any expectations. She curled comfortably in the crook of his arm and snuggled close to him. She laughed to herself when he fell asleep first, as he always did, even though there had been no eruption to tire him out. As she lay under the light covers with Gregory's arm around her, she realized she had not thought about Dorian all evening. As soon as she let him in he didn't want to leave. She finally drove him from her mind and fell asleep. It was one night she should share only with her husband.

CHAPTER 12

THE PRIZE FOR EXTRAVAGANT LIVING

SOLSEA MEANDERED ALONG THE cliffs overlooking the Shallow Sea. The town itself consisted of a few winding streets of shops and a chapel squeezed into the rock. The villagers, who lived in small hamlets behind the cliffs, made their living as domestics during warm months. They survived the winter by fishing and caretaking the great houses dotting the cliffside. Magnificent estates could be found throughout Cartheigh, but Solsea took the prize for extravagant living. To Eleanor each home was larger and had more pillars than the next.

Several steep wooden staircases provided access to the white beach below the village. They needed replacing at the beginning of each summer season because the high winter tides washed them away. The mansions had private staircases made of Fire-iron and anchored deep into the cliff walls. The tides did not affect them, and they hung over the sides of the cliffs like frozen silver waterfalls. Eleanor's first descent down to the beach left her clenching the railings and muttering prayers. On the way back up she abandoned counting the stairs at four hundred. Once she got used to the height she tried to walk the stairs at least once a day. The climb would add strength to her saddle seat.

The royal residence, Trill Castle, was really a compound of six houses and a stone barn. It dated to the days of Caleb the Second, and while luxurious, was not as opulent as some of the newer estates. She would stay with Gregory and his father in the largest of the six, Willowswatch, and their closest friends would spread out in the other buildings. Each cottage, as they were called, was unique. Some were stone, some brick, and the smallest, Speck Cottage, was made of ancient interconnected logs. Stone paths woven through riotous gardens connected them. Flocks of bitterbits swarming the flowers gave Trill its name. The tiny birds made up for their size with their piercing voices, and they woke Eleanor before the sun some mornings.

Willowswatch (Eleanor could not help but laugh at its designation as a cottage) was the only building at Trill with any Fire-iron construction. The alternating granite and iron gave it the look of a giant, cube-shaped chessboard. Six crooked willow trees shaded the front walk, and Eleanor had to duck dangling fronds to reach the door. There were three round turrets, one on each end and a larger one at the front and center. Eleanor sometimes caught King Casper peeking out the windows of his bedroom in the center tower.

Gregory offered Eleanor the south tower, with its stunning views of the Shallow Sea from the rounded wall of windows. She demurred, because she knew he always stayed there, but he insisted.

"The north tower has fewer stairs, sweetheart," he said. "I'll be less likely to crash to my drunken death after some party. Besides, I want you to have the best of Solsea this summer."

She was touched by his thoughtfulness, and even more touched at his attempts to make her feel at home. Before they arrived he had the whole south tower redecorated. It was hilariously feminine, all lace and pink bedding and furniture so dainty she feared it would collapse if anyone actually sat on it. She would hardly have chosen any of it, but no matter. She thanked him sincerely, and kissed him when he pointed out the pieces he had selected himself.

To Eleanor's delight, there was little formal entertaining at Trill Castle. The grounds were lush and rolling, perfect for games and picnics. The interiors, however, were full of small, cozy rooms cramped with furniture. Willowswatch had one dining room, but it got little use beyond Eleanor, Gregory and the king at breakfast. The royal family would be the guests of honor at the more spacious mansions of their subjects, and invitations were waiting as their carriages pulled into the drive.

People were still airing out their houses, but they didn't waste any time. A traveling tennis competition sprung up among the young men. It moved from home to home over the first week, long warm days of shouting fans and spiked punch. Gregory performed well and with high spirits in all his matches. Eleanor noticed he never played against Dorian, and after she watched Dorian play a few rounds she knew why. He crushed each opponent handily, never raising his voice, while the unfortunate fellow on the other side cursed and fumed. She knew of the widespread admiration for his skill at all male pursuits, but he had been subdued during the Awakening Fest and avoided sport. With an improved mood he dominated not only at tennis, but jousting, archery, fencing, and even lawn bolls. His graciousness in victory only irked his opponents. Eleanor thanked HighGod he and Gregory avoided each other. She didn't think her husband's pride could take it.

Gregory had never been so attentive. He brought her drinks and sat on a blanket with her during lunches. He even held a parasol over her head as she walked between the cottages. Why, then, did Dorian still invade her thoughts? Why did she find herself shading her eyes with her hand so she could watch him without being obvious?

Early one Tuesday morning she positioned herself on the edge of the fountain between Willowswatch and the unicorn barn. Gregory had not yet recovered from the previous nights' bought with a particularly potent cask of northern rock gin, but she'd noticed Dorian never suffered such ill effects. He joined her after he saw to Senne's morning feed.

"What are you reading?" he asked. He wove a piece of straw through his long fingers. She held up her book. "*The Fallen Woman*, by Sara-Susan of Afar Creek Abbey," he read. "How incredibly inappropriate."

She laughed. "I had Rosemary send it from the Abbey. You don't find such material lying around the Willowswatch library."

"Why prostitutes, princess?"

The endearment warmed her. She watched his moving hands until the corners of her mouth stopped twitching. "I suppose all woman have some morbid curiosity about those...ladies."

"Morbid, yes. Rich or poor, women like to feel there is someone else worse off. I suppose men do, too, but we prefer to beat each other into subjugation." He threw the straw into the fountain. "You're not one for idle curiosity."

"I suppose..." She shook her head. "No, you'll think me morally deficient."

"How fascinating. Now you must tell me."

"I understand how they come to it. The whores, I mean. There are so few opportunities between marriage and Pasture's End for non-magical women in Cartheigh. Look at me. I have an education to make any witch or magician or nobleman proud, and I could think of nothing to do with it."

"So you stayed in your father's house."

"I always knew I couldn't hide away forever but..." She hugged the book to her chest. "In the first months after my father died I did the work my stepmother set for me, because I didn't eat if I refused, but I fought back. I sassed her and stormed around the house. Sometimes I broke her trinkets or purposely let her underthings go sour after washing."

"Am I to be surprised?"

"The scale finally tipped when I stomped on her foot and refused to polish my father's pocket clockworks collection before she sold it. She beat me...and then locked me in the closet. I could hear Chou screaming curses at her through the door for hours...and then she stuffed me into a hired carriage. We ended up in some seedy square.... watching the street children begging for alms from the Godsmen..."

Eleanor trailed off at the memory. Bits of the scene jumped out, like pieces of a wooden puzzle dangled before her. Round, staring eyes. Heads either shaved or topped with mats of never-brushed hair. Gaunt faces, raw with running sores. Knees and elbows and collarbones so sharp they might have caused the holes in the children's ratty clothes. Their voices had streamed into the carriage, begging, pleading, each trying to outdo the other's tales of woe. They screamed threats and insults at one another, and Eleanor had not believed such foul language could come from such small people. The Godsman dolled out lumps of bread and cheese, reaching for the tiniest hands, but the older children slapped the little ones away. They grabbed what they could and beat a quick retreat into the crevices between the shops and stalls.

"She told me I would join them if not for her generosity. And then she pointed down an alleyway off the square. At the older girls, not much older than me but painted and cinched and gussied up in a way that made me blush."

"Even then, you knew."

She nodded. "Imogene asked me if Rosemary had taught me about Pasture's End. She said it's a bad place, full of bad girls and bad men who make them do horrible, dirty things. They get sick and they die and no one cares. No one loves them. No one will ever love any of them."

Dorian rested his hand on the marble ledge. His fingers just brushed the edge of her skirt.

"I had nightmares for weeks. Dreams she'd left me there with those girls. I don't remember the details of my father's face, Dorian, but I can't forget the eyes of a few anonymous whores."

"What of your mother?" Dorian asked. "Do you remember her? You never speak of her."

She considered telling him, but in the end the old discomfort got the better of her. She set the book on the ledge. "She died so long ago… not like your father."

"It *has* been almost nine years. My mother died two years before my father, of a sudden apoplexy. You know, there are other similarities in our situations. Not just our parents' early deaths. My choices were also limited. After Abram pushed me out of the house—"

"Why would he do so? To his own brother?"

Dorian took a moment. "Mother once told me she thought HighGod had played a trick on her by sending Abram first in out family. He's not terribly bright, and he's a poor marksman. He's not a strong rider…and he's…rather…how can I say it? He's homely."

"So he's just the opposite of you."

"Here's where I once again prove my conceit."

"It's not conceit if it's the truth."

"Debatable. Anyway, Abram has all the responsibility and no means to cope with it. It's not really his fault. I try to help him…when he lets me." He absently rubbed the bit of silk under his fingers. "I wanted to stay on for an advanced course at Academy, but he threatened to disown me. It was the army or nothing."

"You became a soldier to avoid your brother's wrath. I remained a maid to avoid becoming a whore."

"Don't say that," he said, and the intensity in his voice frightened her. "I can't stand the thought of you in one of those places."

She looked down at his hand on her skirt. "I'm here now," she said. "And so are you. All for the best."

He chuckled and handed the book back to her. She touched the spot on her skirt where his hand had been. "I'll let you return to your reading," he said. "I've a bow to string."

They said their goodbyes. As she watched him disappear into the unicorn barn she wondered how she'd managed these past months when he withdrew his friendship. She wished she could tell him about the baby, if he was indeed her friend, but she couldn't do it. Her pregnancy brought her joy regardless of her confusion. She could not bear the thought it would cause him pain.

She stopped lying to herself. She could not blame Gregory's neglect anymore. Her feelings for Dorian were not under her control.

Near the end of their second week in Solsea, the royal family and their guests were invited to the home of Sir Maxmilon Faust, whose family had made a fortune in shipping several centuries ago. Faust was a contemporary of Sylvia's husband, the Duke of Harveston. Eleanor's toes curled when Margaret read a note from her mother expressing Imogene's happiness at their reunion at Faust's dinner party.

"Mother and Sylvia have just arrived. They are staying at the Fleetwood place, of course," Margaret said.

"Charmed," said Eleanor. Eliza pinched her arm.

"Perhaps we should invite them to Trill," said Anne Iris. "Dorian can stay with me and they can have his room. Supposedly he has a large…bed."

"I doubt they would enjoy sharing a cottage with Brian and Raoul," said Eleanor. "I hear your brother snores something terrible when he's drunk."

"I bet Margaret would love to find out," said Eliza.

"Eliza! How saucy!" Margaret laughed. "Besides, I mean no offense, Anne Iris, but your brother is a bit wild for me. Raoul, on the other hand…"

Eleanor shook her head and adjusted her necklace. She had started feeling better over the last few days. Her nausea had disappeared and she had more energy. She looked forward to having a glass of wine at Faust's party, but the thought of an evening with Imogene and Sylvia put a damper on her good mood.

Oh, to the dogs with them, she thought. *If I can finally stomach a glass of wine I will have it.*

Eleanor's belly acquiesced, but her bladder did not. She squirmed throughout the bumpy carriage ride to the Faust estate, her legs crossed at the thigh and again at the ankle. HighGod forbid she should arrive at the party with wet petticoats. As soon as the carriage stopped she dashed for the nearest water closet, which happened to be on the opposite side of the house from the ballroom.

Horns and fire, she thought, *where do they expect the dinner wine to go?*

A servant tried to accompany her, but she couldn't bear the idea of some stranger listening outside the door, so she took directions instead. She went left, then right at a tall mirror, but she missed the next left and came to a dead end. She wheeled in frustration, certain she'd have to relieve herself in one of Lady Faust's famous antique vases. She took the first available turn in the hope of meeting someone who could redirect her, but at the sound of sniffling she slowed. She paused before a cracked door. The smell of leather and old pipe smoke told her it was a study of some sort.

"I can't do it anymore," said a watery voice from beyond the doorway. "I just can't."

"Sylvia, darling, you must." Imogene's voice held a rare hint of compassion. "I know it's not ideal—"

Sylvia laughed.

"—but he takes care of you. You'll never want for a thing."

"Nor will you."

"It could be worse. He's not unkind, is he?"

"No—"

"Does he hit you? Pinch?"

"No! He's just ancient and hideous and he never let's up!" Eleanor peeked through the crack as Sylvia stood. "And she…she has him…" Sylvia dissolved into noisy sobbing.

Imogene rose and tried to embrace her daughter, but Sylvia pushed her off. "It's your fault! She should have ended up in a whorehouse in Pasture's End, not sitting on a throne. Her eyes...all the bad signs...she killed her own mother!"

Eleanor sucked in her breath, waiting for Imogene to shudder in disgust and agree with her daughter.

"Ridiculous," Imogene said. "Half the city would be murderers. Women die in childbirth every day. Your own grandmother among them. She no more killed her mother than I killed mine."

Air left Eleanor's lungs in tiny puffs, as Imogene unintentionally gave her the reassurance she'd never been able to ask of her father, or Rosemary.

"Everyone knows such children are cursed," said Sylvia. "The Godsmen say it!"

Imogene crept close to her daughter's face. "The Godsmen are superstitious fools. Leticia Brice died of childbed fever when Eleanor was five days old. Sickness and bad luck kill new mothers, not babies."

"I wish you'd thrown her out on the streets."

"You think I don't know it? I see what my pity has wrought. I dwell on it day and night." Imogene took Sylvia by the shoulders. "But I won't take the blame for your being married to an old man over a prince. Besides, you're young. You think love matters, but it doesn't. In the end, you have only your family."

Sylvia laughed again. "That's rich...coming from someone who has dwelled on that unimportant emotion for years."

Eleanor pressed her face to the door and it gave a disloyal squeak. She jumped back, afraid of both revealing and wetting herself, and escaped down the hallway.

Eleanor finally found the water closet. She entered Maxmilon Faust's ballroom feeling much lighter, in more ways that one. Her mind wandered as she found her seat. Who would have thought Imogene would be the source of some relief from eighteen years of guilt over her mother's death? But what could Sylvia have meant? Eleanor couldn't think of one person less concerned with love, her own or anyone else's, than Imogene Easton Brice.

The party was an intimate affair by court standards, with only about twenty-five guests. A musician serenaded the long table with soft flute music. There was no magical entertainment. Several magicians were in attendance, including Ezra Oliver, but they were a more serious, powerful lot.

King Casper sat at the head of the table, with Faust on his left and Gregory on his right. Eleanor sat beside Gregory and across from Dorian. Ezra Oliver sat on Eleanor's right. She made a few attempts at conversation, but he answered her in mutters around his roast duck. His eyes flitted between the king and Faust like two well-played tennis balls. While Sylvia's outburst lingered in a faint redness around her eyes, a seat beside Dorian reinvigorated her. She flirted with him shamelessly. Eleanor's mood was dour until it became apparent Dorian was paying her no attention. Sylvia turned on the hapless Raoul. Eleanor glanced down the table at Margaret, who seemed to lose her own appetite as she watched her sister. Imogene was at the far end, surrounded by Faust's daft wife, Hector Fleetwood, Brian, Eliza, Anne Iris, and several other prominent citizens Eleanor couldn't place. Eleanor could not decide which end of the table was heavier with poor company.

At least the discussion provided some intellectual stimulation on this end. Once she knew Dorian was not ensnared in Sylvia's net, she relaxed, finished her wine, and focused on the conversation. Common knowledge said a glass of wine strengthened the baby, but until now she had felt too queasy for alcohol. The drink went to her head.

"I think you're right, Oliver," Faust said. He was a fat, pompous old man. Eleanor struggled to like him. "The witches take up far too many resources for what they give back."

Eleanor's head whipped in Oliver's direction. Gregory took her hand and squeezed it.

King Casper broke in. "I spoke with the new Svelyan ambassador just yesterday. He told me witches are much less influential in his country. Interesting."

"It's true," said Oliver. "In Svelya witches only practice healing, which is after all more womanly. They leave the learning to those more capable, and the sorcery to those more powerful. The magicians."

Eleanor leaned in Oliver's direction, until her head hovered over her water glass, but he peered around her. She felt her face redden and Gregory squeezed harder. Dorian tried to catch her eye from across the table but for once she ignored him.

"What do you think, young sire?" Faust asked Gregory.

"I haven't thought about it much, honestly," Gregory said. "I do see the redundancy in both witches and magicians pursuing scholarly…I mean, the Abbeys and the Coveys don't both require huge libraries and dedicated scholars. Maybe the witches should concentrate on healing the sick and catching babies."

Eleanor dropped his hand. "Mister Oliver," she said, "I must interject. The witches have always focused on literature and natural philosophy, while the magicians deal in history and mathematics. It is a good division, and has given all who have the opportunity to take advantage of it the finest wealth of knowledge in the world."

Oliver sipped his wine. "Yes, but here is the point. Magicians could easily do all that and more—"

"I say there is room in the world for all learning. I would think you, of all people would agree with me."

"—if given the proper resources."

"The crown supports you. The witches must rely on the common people."

"This isn't about money. It's about our national security," Oliver said.

Eleanor laughed. "National security? Please, you don't like the competition for the people's coin."

Oliver's nostrils flared. His voice held none of the vague camaraderie or absent kindness she'd sensed in her earlier interactions with him. "You have no idea what you're talking about. Cartheigh needs magicians for protection, and we can't reach our full potential with witches dabbling about looking for a magical cure for the common cold or a spell to pull out a peasant baby stuck in its mother's belly."

"Oliver," Dorian said. "There are ladies present."

The table went quiet, and even Sylvia set down her glass to listen. Oliver's distaste for *Women, Magic, and the History of Afar Creek Abbey* suddenly made sense to Eleanor. "No, Dorian, it's fine," she said. "You act like there is a finite amount of magic in the world, sir."

Oliver spoke slowly, as if addressing a distracted schoolgirl. "Any student of sorcery knows the atmosphere can only support so much magic at a given time. The more enchantments spinning around, the weaker they all become. There are forces out there that would destroy our kingdom. Magicians must be given free rein in defense of our country!"

Several men at the other end of the table applauded. The king started speaking but Eleanor cut him off. The gasps of the other guests rolled down the table like falling dominoes.

"Let me tell you something, you—you self-righteous—" She somehow stopped herself before the words *horse's ass* could slip between her teeth. "If you went out on the streets of Maliana and asked the people who does them more good every day you know what their answer would be. I believe they put a lot more stock in the witches' dabbling than your greedy need to defend Cartheigh from imaginary enemies!"

Gregory grabbed her arm, and now there was no support behind his grip. "That's enough, Eleanor."

Oliver's round eyes bulged from his face and wisps of gray smoke leaked from his ears. "I won't be insulted by some peasant in—"

"Enough!" King Casper roared. "Oliver, you overstep your boundaries. You're speaking to my son's wife, your future queen."

Oliver's mouth snapped shut.

"Thank you, Your Majesty," Eleanor said. "I just can't believe—"

"Silence, madam," the king said. "Oliver has forgotten himself, and so have you." He spoke slowly to his son. "Control your wife. Take her home."

Gregory's face went crimson. He stood with Eleanor's arm still in his grip and she had to follow him. Dorian rose as well. "I can take her home, Your Highness, so you can continue your evening," he said.

Gregory glared at him. Eleanor wished her husband would yell, or pound his fist on the table as he usually did. His silence terrified her. He dragged her from the dining table, into the hall, and out the front door to the waiting carriage. She did not even have time to collect Chou Chou. Gregory never loosened his hold on her.

Gregory's stony silence continued until they reached Eleanor's bedroom at Trill Castle. She hoped they would part ways at his own door, and spend the night cooling off, but he made a straight line for her room. As he flung open the door a drowsing Pansy leapt to her feet and stumbled a curtsy. Gregory dismissed the servant, kicked the door closed, and unloaded on Eleanor.

She had never seen him so angry. She knew she had crossed a line at dinner, but all of her explanations floated away under the pelting rain of his rage. Over the next few days she winced when bits of the long and horrible argument popped into her head.

"What did you expect of me? Should I sit there while Oliver spews bigotry and suspicion?" she had screamed at him.

"Yes! Yes! That's exactly what I expect of you! Unless I give you permission to do otherwise! That's what my mother would have done!"

"I am not your mother!"

"That is painfully obvious," he sneered. "Oliver is right for once. What you are is a result of the influence of that woman who filled your head with the useless idea that your opinion matters!"

He paced the room, and his boots left dark smudges of dirt on the prissy pink rugs he had bought for her. "I admit, I've found it funny when you've sassed Father. I've given you too much freedom, but you're fucking crazy if you think I will allow you to throw a hissy fit, and insult the king on top of it!"

She narrowed her eyes. "This isn't about what Oliver said, or about me, it's about the fact that you can't stand up to your father! You think I should be a proper lady. I will be when you can be a real man."

"If you weren't pregnant I would beat you for that." He crept in close to her face. "Remember who fucking brought you here. Maybe I could send you back down again."

Eleanor's breath came so hard she could feel her nostrils flaring. "I have nothing more to say."

"Good. Let's keep it that way for a long while, shall we?" He swept his hand across her dressing table, sending bottles of perfume and creams flying across the floor. They shattered and sent a nauseating mix of scents into the air.

"Why don't you clean that up," he said. "I've heard you used to be good at that sort of thing."

He slammed the door on his way out, and it ended at that. They were stiffly polite when they had to be together. Eleanor refused to talk about the argument with her friends or her bird. The walls at Trill were thin and she was sure everyone already knew the sad details.

Chapter 13

Little Assasins

Any uneasiness Eleanor had felt in her position up to this point paled in comparison to the strain of the next few weeks. Chou's report the morning after Faust's party left her with a deep sense of foreboding. He had watched Imogene approach a brooding Ezra Oliver on the balcony after the infamous altercation. Chou had been alarmed by their sudden and untimely intimacy. He did his best to spy, but he could not find an advantageous perch. The crashing waves below the estate drowned out their whispering, even to his sharp ears.

"They were tight as kernels on a cob," he said. "I can't imagine the conversation revolved around your finer attributes."

Oliver's further betrayal hit Eleanor hard. She asked Chou to watch for additional fraternization between the magician and Imogene, but Oliver appeared to be burying his humiliation in his office. She envied his seclusion. News of her chastening at Faust's dinner party traveled along the cliffside, bouncing from manor to manor like a carriage wheel rolling down a bumpy road. Of course no one said a word, but she read the tide of opinion in the forced gaiety. She stuck close to Anne Iris, Eliza and Margaret when she could. Brian and Raoul maintained a polite distance, but she could hardly blame them. Only Dorian, as usual, seemed beyond the prince's reproach. He stood casually at her side, smiling and laughing his low laugh. He almost dared anyone to insult her in front of him.

Sylvia took it upon herself to reinvigorate the summer party circuit while Eleanor stood humiliated on the outskirts. The Fleetwood estate, called The Falls, was one of the most beautiful on the cliffs. Sylvia took advantage of the setting to host an impossible number of dinners, dances, picnics, hunts and tournaments. Eleanor wondered how the Fleetwood servants managed to keep up.

For his part, Gregory drank more and laughed less, but he attended every event and Eleanor had to go with him. Sylvia fluttered around them, radiant in a pastel rainbow of gowns, chattering gaily and gushing over everything Gregory said. She concocted the perfect way to make sure no one forgot Eleanor's disgrace, and repeated her compassionate message to anyone who would listen. How the witches had corrupted her poor, dear stepsister, and how it really wasn't her fault she was so rude and tactless. She truly pitied the unfortunate girl, but really, it was hopeless and Prince Gregory deserved better. What could be expected from someone whose own eyes did not even match? A bad sign, tut tut.

Eleanor wanted a distraction, and she found it in the famous Rockwall Chapel Gardens. The royal family refurbished the gardens at the beginning of each summer season. Eleanor oversaw the planning and the dedication ceremony, and she spent several days selecting plants with the Godsmen and a master gardener. As she worked the villagers came and went from their prayers and an idea took shape. She knew the seasonal life of the town strained the locals, so she asked the Godsmen to invite the parishioners with children to attend the dedication. She thought the children would enjoy a romp through the flowers and a treat of cake and sweet lemon juice. The Godsmen were surprised at her offer, but warmed to it quickly.

So, about a week after Faust's dinner party, Eleanor waited in green silk to ceremoniously plant a purple orchid. The summering noblewomen clustered behind her, like too many pale flowers crammed into a small vase. The Godsmen were surrounded by a dozen nervous-looking women in plain gingham dresses whose children milled around their legs in a happy pack.

Eleanor gave a perfunctory speech about the beauty of the gardens and the honor of helping preserve them. She had just knelt to place the bulb into the freshly turned dirt when a whirring sound overpowered the gentle crash of the waves on the beach below. She looked over her shoulder for the source.

Something shiny flashed past her on silvery wings. Another clipped the back of her head. She reached up to rub the spot and found herself face to face with what seemed at first to be a giant, hovering damselfly.

She had seen stuffed fairies, and paintings of fairies, but they were much nastier when animated. This creature was just smaller than Chou Chou, with four arms, a round potbelly, spindly legs and a long, sharp tail. Mischievous intelligence twinkled in its bright green eyes. Its wings were a vibrating blur. Like a cunning flying monkey, it grinned and scratched her cheek.

She spun around. There were hundreds of them. Some swarmed her head, pelting her with dirt. The others went to work on the garden. They flew in and out of the rows. They picked flowers and yanked plants out by the roots, and overturned birdbaths and benches. They buzzed around the refreshment table, scattering food and dumping out the punch bowls. The other women screamed and the children clutched at their mothers while the Godsmen tried to drive them off, but Eleanor could tell through the haze of battering wings that they focused their attack on her. They didn't touch anyone else.

It only took a few minutes to destroy the master gardener's work. As suddenly as the fairies appeared they were gone. Anne Iris and Eliza pushed through the crowd of gasping, pointing noblewomen, followed by Margaret. Eleanor saw Imogene grab her daughter's arm, but Margaret shrugged her off.

"Oh, HighGod above, you're bleeding," Eliza said.

One of the villagers came forward and knelt before Eleanor. She held out several clean handkerchiefs. Eliza put one to Eleanor's swelling mouth. The sound of children crying cut through her fog.

She shook the dirt from her skirt as she wandered to the dining tables. The punch was gone, and the grapes smashed, but one of the cakes had survived the mêlée. She turned when she heard the women squeal again. She raised her arms to cover her face.

Teardrop trotted through the garden. "I knew something was wrong," the mare said. "I am sorry I arrived too late."

"No, you arrived just in time," Eleanor said. She spoke to her friends. "Make sure the children have some cake."

They nodded. She reached for her unicorn's mane and swung up onto her bare back. The villagers dropped to the ground in front of Teardrop. Eleanor knew she should say something to the crowd, apologize or laugh it off, but she couldn't. She had to escape.

Later, back at Willowswatch, she sat with Dorian in one of the parlors. He handed her a cloth soaked in herbs to bring down the puffiness of her lip. "Fairies," he said. "Little assassins."

"What do you mean?" she asked.

"Someone paid them. Fairies care nothing for right or wrong. They'll do anything for a good price. Someone hired them to sabotage you."

Eleanor had bathed and donned a clean dress, but her arms were covered with scratches and she had a pounding headache, as if the fairies had returned in high-heeled boots and were dancing in her hair. "Imogene and Sylvia," she said.

"You can't prove it. We'll never see those creatures again. It takes magic to call them."

"Magic?" Eleanor wondered if Ezra Oliver would possibly stoop so low.

"I've seen many a family feud at Eclatant, Eleanor, but yours is one for the magicians."

Eleanor couldn't help but chuckle at the thought of magical scholars, bent over historical tomes, charting the course of her stepmother's hatred for all posterity. "She's cruel to everyone. Me, Margaret...even Sylvia at times. My father..." She scowled, trying to find a story that would best illustrate her stepmother's temperament. A candle lit an old memory, and she leaned toward Dorian. "You should have seen how she mistreated the little amount of hired help we could afford. Even her own groom. She brought the poor man to the Brice House, but she abused him so soundly he left within a month."

"How so?"

"You should have heard her. She'd scream at him, call him names. Idiot, Shit-Shoveler, Fringe Filth—his Meggett Fringe accent was so thick I couldn't understand him. She'd make him repeat himself over and over and mock him the entire time. He slept in the hayloft—"

"With you?"

Eleanor blushed. "No...this was before my father died. But she'd always go out there, before the sun even rose, and drag him from his bed...Robert...that was his name. Margaret and Sylvia called him Robin. He'd been in the Easton family's hire for some time."

Eleanor closed her eyes, and the groom swan out of her memory. Darkish skin, dark eyes. Thick, curling black hair. A prominent nose, but it fit him. Surprisingly white teeth that lit up his face on the rare occasion he had reason to smile. A soft voice around his slum accent.

"He must have hated her so. One afternoon I found him in her bedroom. He had a knife...some kind of long carving knife. He was slashing away at one of her lace nightgowns. Just ripping it to shreds with that huge knife. He looked so angry...his face was bright red and he was sweating, even though it was sometime in winter...a freezing cold day, I remember, because the fire had gone out and I could see his breath. He looked rather like a dragon. Terrified me. He saw me in the doorway. I ran away and told my father."

"Did your father dismiss him?"

"No. He just told me to stay away from him. I think father was afraid, too."

"Of Robin?"

"No, of Imogene. For who would she have screamed at without Robin? But Robin left anyway, not long after. Just disappeared one night. I suppose he decided the wages weren't worth the abuse.

Gregory came in without knocking. "I heard," he said. "Are you all right?"

Eleanor twisted in her chair. "I'm fine."

"What a horrible thing." He came closer, and stood between Eleanor and Dorian.

"Yes, it was," she said. She saw Dorian's jaw working. She knew the ceasefire she had wanted would come, but when Dorian stood tears stung her eyes.

"Excuse me," he said, and left the room.

Gregory sat on the low table in front of her. He took her hands, as he always did when he couldn't say what needed to be said. "Don't cry. Is there anything you need?"

She shook her head. Whatever she needed, she doubted Gregory would ever be able to give it to her.

Sylvia and Imogene would not allow the fairy incident die the slow death of normal gossip. Admittedly, it was more interesting than your everyday so-and-so got drunk and pissed in the bushes story. The topic was discussed ad nauseam over the next few days. Everyone had a different theory on the identity of the saboteur. Imogene and Sylvia fed the fire, whispering names left and right. Eleanor had no proof her stepmother and stepsister were behind the attack, but in her eyes Imogene gave herself away with her zealous concern.

At least she and Gregory were on speaking terms again. Eleanor had not forgiven his cruelty or his threats, and she didn't think she could ever forget them, but she stood at his side day and night and she welcomed the civility. The awkwardness lingered, but they were both trying. He started small, by standing up for her at Sylvia's next party.

It was a dance on a Saturday evening, attended by over one hundred guests. Sylvia made an announcement during the musicians' intermission. "My lords and ladies, please welcome Maliana's favorite puppeteers, Tellis and Twig!"

Two thin men, dressed all in black, wheeled an elaborate puppet stage to the front of the room. They both turned cartwheels before it as the guests formed a semicircle. Tellis and Twig and their bawdy shows were a fixture at Eclatant. The crowd cheered as they threw in a few pelvic thrusts and ass wiggles before disappearing behind the stage.

The show was clearly a roasting. The puppets were fashioned after various characters at court, and Tellis and Twig poked fun at everyone's idiosyncrasies. Many courtiers hoped to be lampooned. It showed one was important or interesting. Nearly everyone was fair game, even Dorian had been parodied this summer. His puppet leapt around with a giant penis for a tennis racket.

The royal family, however, was granted honorary clemency, so it took the guests by surprise when a blond puppet wearing a crown appeared on stage. She carried handfuls of flowers and sang old drinking songs. It went downhill from there. The fairies attacked, the flowers flew, the Godsmen fainted and the children cried. At the end a new, dirty, crownless princess appeared onstage only to be dragged off again by a unicorn.

Eleanor watched in silence, her face burning. Dorian sidled up beside her and took her hand. Reckless, but she didn't care. She gripped his as if she were dangling from the side of a boat and couldn't swim. This silly reenactment was worse than the original humiliation.

When the show ended the guests shifted uncomfortably. The ladies fanned their necks and the gentlemen cleared their throats and excused themselves to smoke. No one knew the correct response.

Dorian let go of Eleanor's hand, and she rubbed her palms together at the loss of warmth. She turned to him, and the look on his face was one she had never seen before. He was even paler than usual, and she could almost hear his teeth grinding over the noise of the party. His eyes shimmered in their sockets, the pupils reduced to tiny specks. He resembled a rabid wolf, minus the foam.

"Excuse me," he said. "I must speak with our hostess."

Gregory stood on her other side, and for once he was the calmer of the two men. "Wait, Dor," he said. "I'll speak with her."

"No, I'm sure more important matters need your attention."

Gregory grabbed Dorian's arm. "I appreciate your defense of my honor, and that of my wife, but I'll handle it."

"As you wish."

Eleanor divided her attention between placating Dorian and watching Gregory approach Sylvia and Imogene. They were laughing and sipping wine as if they had not just broken the universal convention of respect. Gregory got his point across quickly, and although Eleanor could not hear his words she saw those around him watching as well. It seemed Imogene tried to explain herself, but Gregory silenced her and returned to Eleanor. "She claims she thought you would appreciate the unfortunate incident being treated with humor."

"She was wrong," Eleanor said.

"She's a nasty bitch, and so is her daughter," spat Dorian.

"Dorian, stop. I wish we could just forget the whole thing."

Gregory put his arm around Dorian's shoulder. "He's a man of the crown, Eleanor. He'll always defend what's mine."

Imogene and Sylvia backed off the fairy attack but continued undermining Eleanor in a hundred other ways, the most obvious being Sylvia's undisputed reign as the social butterfly of the summer. She was beautiful. She was fun. She flirted and danced and complimented everyone. In short, she was the effortless, perfect hostess Eleanor needed to be.

Why can't I be that way? Eleanor asked herself. *Why does it drain me?*

She posed the question to Chou Chou one cloudless, breezeless morning as she sat in a rocker on the porch of Willowswatch.

"Why compare yourself with her?" he asked. "People like her because she tells them what they want to hear."

"I've never been very good at that," Eleanor said.

"No, you haven't, and those who know you love you the way you are."

Except my husband, she thought.

Chou went on. "Just because you don't excel at party planning does not mean there is anything wrong with you."

"Oh, I know, Chou, but life would be smoother if these things came easily to me. I never know where I stand with anyone."

Eleanor had been thinking. She saw no reason Sylvia should have all the devious fun. As she told Chou Chou her plan she ignored the voice in her head that railed against being as shallow and vindictive as Imogene. Childish or not, she was sick of taking whatever dish they served.

The Fleetwoods were to host a hunt on their property. It would start in the early hours, so the royal family and their friends arrived the night before. As soon as they unpacked Eleanor sent Chou Chou to the kennels on a mission of canine bribery.

"Remember, promise the dogs that meat," she instructed. Eleanor had smuggled ten hams into her dressing trunk under her riding habit and dresses. If the servants wondered about the smell of salt pork among her belongings, they kept it to themselves.

The morning of the hunt dawned clear, and a breeze rolled off the water. Eleanor waited with Anne Iris for the grooms to bring High Noon from the guest stables. Margaret was not a strong rider and

Eliza was uncomfortably pregnant so they would stay behind. Eleanor still kept her own pregnancy a secret. She felt perfectly fine and there were no outward changes in her body, but she planned on avoiding the fences. High Noon's age provided a good excuse.

Teardrop asked if she could follow along. Eleanor knew the mare wanted to keep a close eye on her. "It's a beautiful morning," Teardrop said.

"Of course you can come, but please be careful. If you bruise a hoof Welkie will lock us in the Paladine when we return to Eclatant. You know you shouldn't run hunts."

Teardrop snorted. "Run? I doubt I'll break a trot. Poor horses. Such plodding creatures."

"Here they come," Eleanor said, at the sound of clopping hooves. She stretched up to tug Teardrop's forelock. "Don't rub it in."

She greeted High Noon. As she mounted the old horse chewed his bit in excitement. "The fox, the fox, where is the fox?" he asked.

Dorian was already up and mounted. He trotted over, followed by Christopher Roffi, the new Svelyan ambassador. They exchanged good mornings all around. Roffi, a strapping man with the closely cropped, shockingly white blond hair common among his countrymen, asked after Gregory's whereabouts.

"I'm not sure," Eleanor said lightly. Although they were beginning a tentative understanding, Gregory had not visited her chamber at night, and she had not encouraged him.

"There," said Dorian. Gregory, Raoul, and Brian came out of the mansion. Eleanor could tell they'd had a hard night. Gregory hunched and squinted, and none of the three had shaved.

"Well, at least they made it," she said. She changed the subject to the weather, all the while looking for Sylvia. The barking that had been background noise all morning grew louder as the hound master led the pack into the courtyard. The dogs rushed around, yelping, sniffing, and snapping at each other.

Just when Eleanor had decided Sylvia would miss her own hunt their hostess appeared, dressed in a low-cut white riding habit and matching feathered hat.

Perfect, thought Eleanor.

One by one the dogs lifted their heads and sniffed the air, as if they already had a line on the fox. They turned, a hairy brown stream, and rushed Sylvia, whose back was to the pack. Imogene screamed a warning. "Sylvia! The dogs!"

Sylvia spun around, her eyes widening. The first dog reached her. He planted his muddy paws on her shoulders. The others were right behind him, and it was clear to all watching the duchess would soon be on her ass covered in slurping, yapping hound dogs.

Sylvia didn't dally. She scrambled onto the picnic table behind her. In an act no one saw coming she leapt into the arms of the unsuspecting and hung-over Brian Smithwick, already mounted on his tall gray hunter. The dogs milled around the horse's legs. It reared, sending Brian's arms around Sylvia's waist as he prevented both of them from tumbling backwards. The effect was heroic.

The hound master ran after his charges, yelling and beating them off with a stick. They retreated and sat thumping their tails in shame. "Sorry, sorry, so sorry, verrry verrry, sorry," they chanted.

Brian slid to the ground with Sylvia in his arms. "Are you hurt, Your Grace?" he asked.

Sylvia held her hand to her heart and steadied herself on his arm. Imogene burst through the crowd and embraced her. "Darling," she said, "Are you sure you can lead us?" She put a palm to Sylvia's forehead.

"I think so," Sylvia said. "I just thank HighGod you were here to rescue me, Mister Smithwick."

Brian swelled. "It was nothing. Quite clever of you to climb onto the table, and quite nimble." He led her to her mount and gave her a leg up.

She adjusted herself prettily in the saddle. "A thrilling beginning to our morning, my friends. Let's hope the dogs are as excited on the field, and the fox not so quick!"

The other riders laughed, the dogs yipped, and Eleanor scowled. Instead of making Sylvia the fool of the day, Eleanor had made her the star.

CHAPTER 14

REAL PROBLEMS

ELEANOR WOKE THE NEXT day with a throbbing ache in her lower back. It didn't subside when she got up, or as she got dressed. She was not in the mood to face Gregory and his father so she called Anne Iris, Eliza, and Margaret to her room for breakfast. She picked at her grapefruit and toast. "Eliza, I wonder how many babies you have in there? You're eating more than Anne Iris," she said.

"I HAVE TOO KEEP these bosoms inflated, you know," Anne Iris said with a shimmy. The girls always teased Anne Iris about her healthy appetite, but fortunately she was her own favorite joke.

Margaret changed the subject. "I *do* think someone set those dogs on my sister."

Eleanor excused herself to use the chamber pot. She was still annoyed by the unexpected turn of her plan to embarrass Sylvia. A sharp pain jabbed through her belly when she stood. She caught her breath, and worry set in. She would send for a local witch as soon as possible. She wished Rosemary were near.

As she headed to the bathing room Chou Chou flew in the window and landed on her shoulder. "I must speak with you," he whispered. "Go to the window. We can admire the view."

She shrugged and humored him. She sat on the windowsill and adjusted her weight around the pain in her back.

"I don't know how else to put this." His black tongue darted back and forth. "So I will just out with it."

She nodded.

"I was in the kitchen this morning. The cooks always save yesterday's rolls for any birds willing to rise early and claim them. Lemonseed today."

"Go on." She knew he was stalling.

"As I left, I passed Melfin."

"Gregory's manservant," Eleanor said. Melfin was an old man, a lifelong servant of the Desmarais family, who ruled Gregory's personal staff with an iron first.

"He was with a woman, a…flashy woman…in red silk."

Eleanor nodded, her heart sinking. "Red silk, in the early morning."

"Yes," Chou went on. "I flew past, but then I changed my mind and followed them. He led her out the side door, the one that leads to the barns. I hid in the branches of that old oak. Before she got in the carriage, he asked her if the prince was satisfied. He told her if she was lucky she would be called again, and she should be ready and keep her tongue in her head. He said if it got back to the princess she would regret it."

"She would regret it," repeated Eleanor.

"I'm so sorry," Chou Chou said, "but I had to tell you. Maybe it's not what we think."

"Chou, you're a wise bird, and I'll give myself credit for not being a fool. We both know exactly what it was." She covered her eyes. "Excuse me. I need a moment."

She opened the bathing room door. The need to relieve herself overwhelmed her. She squatted over the pot, cursing her cumbersome skirts. When she finished she stood and tried to collect herself.

Gregory was taking the favors of another woman, and a hired one at that. She didn't know if that fact made her feel better or worse.

Why? Because I'm pregnant? Because he's still angry with me? Another thought struck her. This might not be new. Perhaps he'd never stopped straying.

What about Dorian? Am I a hypocrite? She no longer denied her feelings for Dorian, but she had never acted on them, nor did she ever plan on it. She had sworn herself to Gregory.

How can he do this to me? How? How? The refrain ran through her head like one of the Godsmen's hypnotic chants.

She must confront him, and she needed to do it before she drove herself into a lunatic asylum. She wiped her eyes and turned to cover the chamber pot as she always did. Her stomach clenched when she saw bright red, harsh against the white porcelain. The pot was full of blood.

Eleanor lay in her bed. Her friends crept around her, removing soiled linen and cold cups of tea. If they had suspected her secret they had not pressed her, and they didn't question her now. Chou Chou curled on the pillow beside her head.

"How far along were you?" An old witch attended her. She was kind enough, but Eleanor ached for Rosemary's voice.

"Eight weeks," she said.

"Early," the witch said. "Some would just consider it a very late flow."

"The witches in Maliana found the baby, and I was sick until two weeks ago."

"It can be a bad sign when the symptoms end suddenly. I agree the child began, but it's gone now. You must rest and wait for your body to be done with it."

Eleanor swallowed her grief. "Can you tell me why it happened?"

"No one knows," said the witch. She gathered her tools. "Did you have a bad fall? Have you been upset?"

"No, nothing," Eleanor lied.

"Then HighGod did not mean for this child to be." She put her hand on Eleanor's cheek. "Don't fret, Your Highness. There's no reason you should not catch again soon. It's just sad luck." She left instructions with Eliza.

Anne Iris and Margaret sat on Eleanor's bed. Margaret took her hand. "You must rest, darling," she said.

Eleanor shook her head. "Have Pansy call Gregory."

"Today? Give it a while," Anne Iris said.

"We'll tell him you're ill, and don't want to see anyone," added Margaret.

"No, I want to see him now."

"Eleanor—"

"Now, Margaret. Call him now."

Pansy announced Gregory and the room cleared. Eleanor sat up and pulled the pink coverlet toward her chin. She couldn't stand his eyes on her body.

"Husband," she said. She pointed to a chair beside the bed and he sat down. He wore his hunting clothes, all browns and greens, a walking hedgerow.

"You're unwell?" he asked. Eleanor heard something creeping in his voice, as if his camouflage would hide him from an unwanted answer.

"I lost the baby."

He took her hand, but she didn't return his squeeze. She drew her knees closer to her chest and eased through another cramp. He asked what had happened, and she told him about the witch's visit.

"Did you do something to bring it on?" His words struck her like a fist.

"The witch said it's not unusual. She asked if I had been upset."

Gregory didn't respond.

"I told her no, but indeed I was upset this morning."

"Why?" he asked.

"I was upset by a story I heard. A story about a woman in red silk." It was a strong counterblow, and Eleanor knew the baby had probably gone with her nausea before Faust's party. But she said it anyway.

"I don't know what you mean," Gregory replied.

She turned her own face to the wall. Pink again. Too much pink, too much red. Pink walls and red dresses. Pink and red streaks in the chamber pot. "Red silk. How trashy."

"You're talking nonsense. I'll leave you."

"Yes."

He stood to go, and for a moment she thought he might take her in his arms and apologize, or promise it would all be all right and they could try again. Instead he took a more objective route. "Did she say there is something wrong with you? Something that will prevent you from carrying a child?"

"There is nothing."

"Then rest, we have work to do."

Eleanor refused to see anyone but Pansy and Chou Chou. After a few days the bleeding stopped, but she could not get out of bed. A terrible melancholy gripped her.

Her friends came and were dismissed. Dorian knocked on the door several times a day, but she could not face him. On the fifth day Gregory returned. Perhaps he would have set things right, but she never gave him the chance. Although she permitted Chou to perch on the headboard behind her, she didn't respond to his gentle prodding. She couldn't talk about the lost baby. In her mind the miscarriage became *the thing, the thing-that-had-happened.* She didn't want to give anyone the opportunity to make her say the words, as she had to Gregory, in all their terrible finality. She couldn't stand the thought of the questions, or anyone's accusations, or worst of all, their pity.

Perhaps Sylvia is right. Maybe I am cursed.

Sleep was the only respite from the questions running through her head. On the seventh day she sought that relief by lunchtime, although she'd only been awake for a few hours. Regardless of the humidity, she closed the curtains to block the sunlight that bored into her forehead. She threw back the covers and curled on her side, and within minutes she drifted off.

A cool breeze wafted over her body. She stirred, annoyed with Chou Chou for opening the curtains. She opened her eyes and sat up in surprise. Rosemary sat in the chair beside her bed. "How did you get here?" she asked.

Rosemary smiled. "I'm not here, darling. Look around you, you're dreaming."

Eleanor peered over the edge of the bed at the grass beneath the bed frame. The sky was bright blue, the air sweet with lavender and a recent rain. She recognized the meadow at the entrance to the Oracle's cavern, back at Afar Creek. "It feels so real," Eleanor said.

"It is more than a normal dream," Rosemary said. "Your letters of late have born a trace of false happiness, and I have heard nothing these past few days. I had a sorceress teach me this spell so we could speak. I've been worried about you."

Eleanor needed no further encouragement. Choking back sobs, she told Rosemary everything. Her fight with Gregory, his infidelity, her misjudgment of Ezra Oliver, her humiliation and insecurity at court, the loss of the baby, even her feelings for Dorian. Rosemary listened without speaking, letting Eleanor go on until she ran out of words.

"You have been holding all this inside?" Rosemary asked. "It's no wonder you stay in bed." Rosemary spoke in the calm voice Eleanor remembered from her childhood. "First, let me say I love you dearly." She touched Eleanor's cheek. "But this mooning about will get you nowhere. You must come out of it. It may sound harsh, but you have real problems, and hiding away in your room will not solve them."

There it was, as always, the truth from Rosemary. Eleanor sighed, and the wind seemed to sigh with her. "You're right. I've been remiss."

"We all need a sympathetic ear, darling, but we don't have much time. We must focus on solutions and I will start with this: I'm disappointed you have let Imogene and Sylvia run away with your confidence. What happened to the girl at the ball? The one who proved she was worthy?"

"I don't know, Rosemary. I feel like I've lost her."

"Well, you must find her, and quickly. You say everyone loves Sylvia. Being a coquettish entertainer works for her. Now, what works for you?"

"I'm a scholar."

"Beyond that. How did you win Gregory over at the beginning?"

"By answering the questions he asked me. By being honest."

"So what does that say about you?"

"I tell things as they are."

"Yes," Rosemary said. "You have used that bent, and a rare one it is, in the past. React to people in the way that comes naturally to you. It will always be most effective."

"I try, but it always comes back to haunt me."

"I admit, you are not very diplomatic, but you can learn. You'll never please everyone, but you'll please yourself, and they will respect you for it." Rosemary sat beside Eleanor on the bed. Her dark eyes held Eleanor's, not with magic, but with the intensity of her concern. "Now I must give you some advice you may not want to hear. You must forget about Dorian Finley."

Eleanor bit her lip, but she could not look away.

"Eleanor, as a witch I'm no expert on these matters, but this cannot end well. Gregory is your husband, and he is the future king. I fear for your safety if this continues. You know there is only one end to marriage."

Eleanor nodded. In Cartheigh nothing but death could divide a couple joined in a chapel before HighGod. History was dotted with wives who mysteriously disappeared when their husbands found no other option to be rid of them.

"Gregory is no angel, but I don't think he's capable of that," she said.

"You have no idea what he's capable of. This is a man who has had everything delivered to him with the ring of a bell his entire life. We're speaking of someone who is more a brother to him than a friend."

"It's not fair."

"I agree, but there have always been different standards for men and women. We must be realistic."

Eleanor could not hide her bitterness. "Better to be a witch, and not have these troubles."

"It may appear so, but we have our own trials. This goes beyond threats, beyond arguments. Gregory could kill you. And Dorian."

Rosemary's words struck home. "I will try harder to get along with him," Eleanor said.

"I will never advise you to be straw under his feet. I know you couldn't live that way, and I wouldn't want you to. You are married. No amount of wishing will change it. But you have the tools to manage not only Gregory, but everyone at court."

"I understand."

Rosemary tugged gently at a lock of Eleanor's hair. "Remember Hazelbeth's faith in you. How did she put it? Oh yes...do some good in this land. If you focus on that perhaps it will take your mind off Mister Finley."

"I will, Rosemary," Eleanor said, abashed. "I haven't forgotten." She squirmed, and something poked her thigh. She looked down at her mother's Fire-iron hair comb.

"Wear it," said Rosemary.

"Would she want me to?"

"Think of how you've felt the past few weeks and ask that question again."

Eleanor ran her fingers over the raised design of flowers and butterflies. Solid, even in the dream.

Rosemary put her arms around Eleanor and whispered in her ear. "Summer will be over soon and you will come home. In the meantime, if you need me, this spell will linger for a while. Call me in your dreams and I will hear you. Now someone is coming. You must wake up. Wake up, Eleanor! Wake up!"

Chou Chou's scaly feet scratched her bare shoulder. He nibbled at her ear, and then on the end of her nose. His breath smelled of almonds.

"Wake up!" he said.

"I hear you, Chou."

"Good! It's a lovely afternoon and the girls are picnicking by the big magnolia. I said I would try and entice you."

"All right."

"Do you mean it?"

"I do, you old feather duster. Call Pansy to help me dress before I change my mind."

He fluttered off, calling for the maid. Eleanor swung her weak legs over the side of the bed and steadied herself. It was nothing a little exercise wouldn't cure. The strength of Rosemary's confidence ran through her veins, and she was determined to turn things around. She wasn't so sure, however, about keeping her promise to forget Dorian. She already hoped he would be at the picnic.

Two days later Eleanor gave Pansy the afternoon off and waited in her room for Chou. She'd claimed that mysterious ailment, *female troubles*, and lay across her bed on her stomach enjoying a few snippets of solitude. She flipped through one of her favorite books, *A Botanical Encyclopedia of Cartheigh*, and compared leaves and flowers she had collected from Trill's gardens to the drawings.

Chou finally soared through the window and landed on the poofy skirts covering her rear end.

"Hello, Chou." Eleanor closed the book. She rolled onto her back. He fluttered for a few seconds to keep from being squashed and landed again on her belly. "You asked to see me in private. What news?"

He arched his neck. "News? Perhaps I just long for the old days of our chummy twosome."

"Perhaps. Or perhaps you've seen something interesting."

"All right," he said. "You've plucked it out of me. Imogene was here at Trill morning, and she visited Oliver's office in Looksee Cottage."

Eleanor sat up and Chou hopped onto the bed. "Indeed. Do you know why?"

"She left with a basket of tonics, but she stayed for nearly two hours. Longer than one needs to gather a few medicines."

"Did you hear anything?"

Chou's eyes rolled his frustration. "Oliver closed the windows. You would think they were engaged in a passionate liaison, but Oliver cares nothing for such dalliances with men or women or a flock of sheep. Anyway, I lit on the chimney—"

"Clever," said Eleanor.

His chest feathers puffed at the compliment. "Wasn't it? Unfortunately, only a few words drifted up. *Visit Margaret. Fool. Enlighten. You may have fabulous powers but you may be an idiot.* I only caught the last because Imogene got a bit testy."

Eleanor scowled. "Hmmm. Anything else?"

"*Three hundred years. Follow.* Soot in my feathers for an unheard conversation."

"Why are they conversing at all? Our argument proved that Oliver has no fondness for the fair sex, witch or not. He obviously detests forceful women, and I'll give Imogene her due. She's no damp daisy. Why waste two hours holed up with her?"

Chou took a moment. Eleanor could almost see threads of logic twisting around his birdie brain. "Everyone knows Oliver doesn't see eye to eye with Gregory. Gregory doesn't hide his feelings, for sure."

For some reason Gregory's accurate assessment of Oliver irked Eleanor. Her husband might have more years in the chief magician's acquaintance, but she still considered herself a more astute judge of character. "Oliver serves the king, not Gregory."

"True, but some day the king and the prince will be one in the same. Oliver will want allies when that day arrives, and Imogene wields some influence over the Fleetwoods."

Unfortunately, Eleanor found Oliver and Imogene's shared dislike of herself to be a more compelling reason for their sudden camaraderie. "Maybe," said Eleanor, "but I still wonder…an odd twosome." Her voice trailed off and she bit her lip. "A little more poking around won't hurt, will it?"

"I live to poke," said Chou.

"Then please, carry on."

CHAPTER 15

DANCE WITH ME

ELEANOR'S FIRST FORAY BACK into society was a party held at an estate owned by one of the many Smithwick uncles in honor of Brian Smithwick's birthday. It could hardly be called a dinner, since there were nearly two hundred guests, but the hosts made an attempt at intimacy by seating the guests at long tables at the head of the ballroom. People shouted across and down the tables to their friends and relations, and Eleanor avoided taking a seat as long as she could. She feared she would lose her voice before the soup arrived.

She stood sipping a goblet of wine beside Margaret. Her free hand repeatedly wandered to her mother's hair comb pushed snugly behind her ear. The Fire-iron teeth digging into her scalp felt reassuring, not painful. People stopped to pay their respects and ask after her health, since word had gone out she had suffered a bad cold. Eleanor was grateful to her friends and Gregory for concealing the truth. True to her new resolution, she was firm and friendly with everyone, even the women whose eyes raked her in an obvious attempt to find a more significant ailment. The well-wishers finally dispersed.

"Anyway," said Margaret, "when Mother told me I just couldn't believe it…the ambassador? He's so…worldly." Margaret raised her voice to be heard over the shouting, the music, and the magicians' popping and fizzing light displays.

"He is handsome and charming, but you give Christopher Roffi too much praise and spare none for yourself," said Eleanor. She waved away the smoke drifting down from the dissipating spellwork. "He would be a lucky man if a lady such as yourself showed him favor."

Margaret slipped her arm through Eleanor's and gave her a little squeeze. "You're the sweetest of friends, but I've never attracted men like Roffi. Still, he has been very attentive, so maybe Mother is right. Maybe he does fancy me!" She giggled and blushed as if Roffi were standing right in front of them. "Roffi asked Mother if he could call on me. Would you mind? We would see a lot of him."

"Of course I don't mind, if it makes you happy, but what about Raoul? You've been eyeing him all summer. I think he likes you. Poor thing, he's more than you are!"

Margaret sighed. "Yes, Raoul is a sweet boy. But the ambassador, that is a man."

Eleanor could not help but laugh at the changes a few months had wrought in Margaret. When they could put it off no longer they made their way to the dining tables and found their place cards. Eleanor would sit between Gregory and Christopher Roffi, with Margaret on Roffi's far side. She thought Margaret might faint when she read her name, but her teasing was cut short by a fluttering at her shoulder.

"Chou!" she said, waving at him. "Watch my hair."

"Very funny," he said. He landed on her outstretched arm. "I'm so pleased by your good spirits I hate delivering this message."

"Then don't. Lately you bring me too much disturbing news."

"I only tell what needs telling."

"I know," she said with a sigh. "Out with it. I would rather it was not about my husband."

He crept up her arm and spoke in her ear. "No, it's about Sylvia."

"Not much better."

"She'll make an announcement tonight. She's pregnant. Four months along."

Eleanor pressed her lips together. "Well, she should be congratulated. As should her husband, for the strength to hold her down long enough to mount her."

"There are rumors about," said Chou.

Eleanor nodded. Sylvia was universally praised as a hostess this summer, but she was not above reproach. When the women were not deriding the princess's unladylike outbursts of political opinion, they were hinting that the Duchess of Harveston's eye, and perhaps the rest of her, often wandered from her elderly husband.

Gregory appeared beside Eleanor and pulled out her chair. "Chou Chou," he said. "Good evening."

"Your Highness," said Chou, bowing.

"We're about to begin. The bowls are stocked with berries, if you would care to join the other birds at the roost."

"Certainly." Chou nipped Eleanor's ear before taking his leave.

"Your parrot is always very gracious," said Gregory.

"Thank you," said Eleanor. "I'm sure he would be pleased to hear you say so." Eleanor hated these conversations. How ridiculous, talking about the manners of a bird with the man who had shared her bed until three weeks ago. She wished something hilarious would happen, perhaps a pie falling out of the sky and landing on Oliver's head, so they could have a good laugh together. She didn't know what else might break the tension.

She sat down. Christopher Roffi joined them, and he whispered to Margaret, who colored yet again. Roffi turned to Eleanor. His face was all strong angles, as if carved out of the rocky faces of the Scaled Mountains that divided his country from Cartheigh. Even on this muggy summer night he wore a red tunic trimmed in black fur, but not one bead of sweat dampened his forehead. The goatee covering his chin was the one distraction from his pleasing appearance. The only

Carthean men who wore facial hair were contemporaries of the king and older, and it seemed out of place.

"Your Highness," he said. His accent was thick, the consonants harsh, as if he were swallowing them. "What have I done to deserve a seating between two such ladies?"

Eleanor smiled. "You flatter me, Mister Roffi, but I do agree Margaret is glowing tonight."

He was witty and interesting and the conversation flowed with the wine. As the servants passed the bread he lowered his voice. Margaret and Eleanor leaned in.

"You know I am only recently arriving," he said, " and sometimes I am…how are you saying it? At a losing for who is who."

Eleanor laughed. "Oh, Mister Roffi, I share your pain."

"Please, call me Christopher. I would be greatly appreciating it if you two ladies would be my…my…"

"Confidants?" offered Margaret. The color had not left her face in half an hour, so another blush left her near purple.

"I am not knowing the word…but if I could look to either of you for help in these matters I would be grateful."

"Of course," said Eleanor. "You just come to Margaret or myself. If we can, we will enlighten you."

Their host, Sir Robert Smithwick, rose and gave a toast to the health of his nephew. Other speeches followed, each more suggestive than the next. She laughed out loud when Dorian subtly mocked Brian's inability to hold his liquor. Gregory spoke last, and gave a surprisingly thoughtful salute to his cousin. She patted his arm when he sat, and he gave her a tentative smile.

As everyone returned to their venison and cliff shrimp Imogene tapped her goblet. She rose and lifted the cup. "I must ask you to pause for one more moment," she said. "I have another announcement."

"My darling," she said to Sylvia. "We've all so enjoyed your hospitality this summer. But now my daughter must remember herself, and rest, for with the winter will arrive a future duke! Our dear Sylvia is expecting!"

The guests applauded, congratulating Imogene and Sylvia. Sylvia gazed demurely in her lap, as if embarrassed by the association with procreation. As for the expectant father, he was nowhere to be seen. His wife's entertaining had proved too much for him, and the duke returned to Harveston for some peace.

Eleanor glanced down the table. Anne Iris retched into her cup, but it was Dorian's calm face that inspired her. She stood and the room quieted. "My dear sister," she said. "Let me extend my good wishes."

Sylvia's simpering went rigid.

"I will say, Sylvia always had a flair for the dramatic when we were children. Who knew you would entertain so many with your widely varied talents? While I have recently been ill, I've heard you neglect no one, from the loftiest lord to the most common stable hand. We are so fortunate there is one among us who gives so generously of herself to others. It's no wonder His Grace, your husband, took his leave. It must be difficult to share you with so many."

Imogene's eyes bulged and her nostrils flared, while Sylvia gave an uncertain twitter. Eleanor looked at Dorian again. He winked.

"So I salute you, Your Grace," she said. "May your child look just like you. Just as lovely."

The guests applauded, all the while hiding their smirks and chuckles in their goblets and napkins. Eleanor sat down. This time Gregory touched her arm. "Well played," he said.

Sylvia and Imogene were subdued for the rest of the night. Gregory and Eleanor spoke more than they had in weeks, and danced several waltzes and a reel. She could feel him making amends in his creeping way, like a cat twisting around its master's legs. She sighed as she watched him teasing Brian, who was already pissing drunk before the meal was through.

He is as he is, she thought.

For the first time she acknowledged she might not be able to change him. There was something freeing in the acceptance. Now she must figure out how she would live with him.

Dorian took her arm, interrupting her musings. They'd had no chance to talk since she emerged from her bedroom.

"You are a fine speaker. Would you deliver the eulogy at my funeral?" he asked.

She punched him. "How dare you bring up such a depressing thought when I am only just delivered from my sickbed."

"How are you feeling?" The humor left his voice.

She did not know if he understood the true nature of her illness, but she didn't want to speak of it here. "I'm well, thank you. I've missed everyone."

"We missed you. It's not the same without you."

She did not know how to respond, so she pointed out the commotion at the head of the ballroom, where the dining tables had stood. "We're in for a show. What are they doing?"

"Arranging their drums."

"Drums?" Flutes and fiddles drove the music of Cartheigh and the surrounding nations. Court music did not call for many percussion instruments.

"Yes. The performers are a traveling troop from Mendae. I saw them last time they came to Eclatant. They're fascinating."

Five men, with the dark skin and hair of the far southern kingdoms across the Shallow Sea, arranged themselves in front of the drummers. They wore baggy white trousers and had bare chests and feet. One of the magicians lowered the candlelight and the guests hushed. The drums started, slowly at first. Each drum had a different size and shape, yet the drummers worked in precise time together. The men came to life, leaping and spinning as the rhythm built. Every tiny movement synchronized with the throbbing drums in unison with the other performers. Unlike dancers in Eleanor's experience, they stayed low. The muscles in their thighs strained, like predators about to spring. It was perfectly controlled and perfectly wild. Her head bobbed, almost of its own accord.

"You like it," Dorian said into her ear. She grinned her answer.

The beat built to a frenzy before crashing to a halt. The dancers froze, and Eleanor could see the sheen of sweat on their bodies. The guests applauded and pushed forward, eager to meet their exotic entertainment.

Eleanor was surprised at how readily everyone accepted the colorful foreigners and their outlandish performance. Even Lady Chesterwaite, who was so proper she had refused to show her gout-ridden ankles to a witch and now walked with a cane. The old crone shook hands with one of the performers and gushed as if he were the king's long lost brother.

"Dorian, how long will the Mendaens be with us?"

"They usually stay on for a few days," he said. "They'll do some private shows and rest their horses."

"Wonderful. That's all the time I need."

"Why? What are you up to?"

She laughed. The orchestra started up again. "Dance with me."

The next day Gregory suggested an overnight hunting trip to the Egg Camp, one of the royal hunting lodges outside Solsea, and Dorian agreed it was a fine idea. He hoped for a hard ride and a peaceful evening, but he should have known better. Gregory included not only their usual retinue but also the sons of several important courtiers and Christopher Roffi.

The Egg, which could hardly be called a camp, was a three story, oblong stone house that made Dorian feel as if he were sleeping in a giant jam jar. During the summer, a full-time groundskeeper kept the Egg well stocked with wine, spirits, and clean linens. Ancient beams crisscrossed the ceiling. There were no paintings or decorations on the dark wood walls, only a huge stuffed bear in the corner of the sitting room. Dorian and Gregory had christened the bear Fluffernuts one drunken evening years ago, and the name stuck. They drank several toasts to his health during each stay, although, since he was dead it was not much help to him.

The hunting party had a successful day in the fields. Gregory took down a ringbuck, and promptly sent the beast back to Solsea to be stuffed, mounted, and added to the furnishings at Trill. The cooks they brought along produced a fine meal from their other killings. Dorian reclined in a squashy armchair in front of the fire with a pint of ale. A belly full of pheasant made him sleepy.

Gregory, on the other hand, was not sleepy at all. Dorian had not seen him so buoyant in weeks. He banged his fist on the table. "Gentlemen! I'm so pleased you all joined me today." They men raised their glasses, toasting his generosity. "Now, it was a long afternoon, and we're all well fed, but I think we've worked up other appetites."

Gregory nodded at the butler, who opened the kitchen door to a flood of gingham and lace. Dorian counted a dozen young women, all of them attractive, before he gave up.

"My friends, enjoy yourselves," said Gregory.

The women dispersed among the ever more enthusiastic men. Dorian drained his glass, and settled back to watch his friends make fools of themselves in ways never tolerated in polite society.

"Dorian!" Gregory called. Two ladies had joined him at the table. A dark-haired girl stood behind him, rubbing his neck, while her blonde companion slithered into his lap.

Dorian took the seat beside him. When she realized her friend was making more headway with Gregory, the dark-haired girl transferred her attention.

"She's nice, huh?" said Gregory, leaning close.

"Nice, yes."

"Oh, come on. I don't understand you lately. We've been here over a month, and I've not yet heard any scandalous stories about you."

"I'm sorry to disappoint you. It's just getting tiresome, I suppose."

"Afraid you'll end up with another Lady Lynwood?"

"HighGod forbid."

Dorian had become involved with Lady Jane Lynwood, the wife of an elderly wine magnate from the town of Sage, last summer during the Solsea holidays. She was ten years his senior, and beautiful, and she wore him out for half the summer. Gregory had teased him mercilessly that he would walk with a permanent limp if he didn't get rid of her. Lady Lynwood, however, had other ideas. Even after the summer's end, when Dorian thought himself well finished with her, she continued writing, professing love and demanding to see him. When he didn't respond, she came to court and heartily embarrassed herself by getting drunk and crying in the corner at the Harvest Ball. He stuck to simpler dalliances after that, but even those had lost their appeal in the last few months.

"I learned my lesson with that one." Dorian shook his head.

"True. It's much better for men like us to stick to more anonymous encounters."

Dorian let the comment lie. He removed the dark-haired girl's hands from his shoulders.

"Anyway," Gregory said. "I can't let you wallow, or get out of practice. What kind of friend would I be?" He pointed at the narrow stone staircase.

"What do you mean?" Dorian asked.

"Go upstairs, my friend, and find out. I've left something there for you."

"I don't know, Greg, I'm tired."

Gregory whispered in the blonde girl's ear. She smiled sweetly, slid off his lap and disappeared under the table. Gregory leaned his head back and closed his eyes. "Go upstairs, Dorian. Third floor, second door."

Dorian walked across the room. The staircase, and whatever the third floor held, both beckoned to him and repulsed him. He found the second door and opened it to a bedroom full of heavy furniture upholstered in blue and green plaids, the kind one would imagine in the home of a well-to-do farmer. A patchwork quilt covered the bed. The only light came from two ornate candelabras, one on the mantle and one beside the bare hearth. A young woman in a plain gray dress, the kind the servants wore to chapel, turned when she heard him enter. She had light brown hair, and was pretty in a fresh, country way. Dorian could almost smell the sea air rolling off her. "Hello," he said.

She curtsied, and held the pose. He came closer to her, and he saw her tremble. He set his drink on a chest of drawers. "What's your name?" he asked.

"Molly, sir."

"And do you live close by?"

"Aye, sir. My father is a fisherman in the village."

She wouldn't meet his eye. "How did you end up here, Molly?"

She swallowed. "I'm a good girl, sir. I am. The prince's men came, and they offered us…my father don't make much…a lot of people to feed…"

"Shhh, I understand." He lifted her chin. "You can go if you want. I'll not say anything."

She finally looked at him. Her eyes flickered over his face. She bit her lip. "No," she whispered. "I'll stay."

"Face the hearth," he said. In the candlelight her hair seemed paler. He pushed it aside and kissed the side of her neck. Her dress was a simple affair compared with the ornate gowns of the court ladies, and he loosened it with the tug of a ribbon. It slid off her shoulders and formed a heap of cheap cotton at their feet. He ran his hands over her body, feeling her chest rising as he cupped her breasts. He wandered down between her thighs. She gasped, but he didn't stop. She might not have wanted to come here, but it shouldn't be unpleasant for her.

A few minutes later her knees buckled and she cried out. He held her up. "Now, this part may be a little more uncomfortable, but I promise I'll be as gentle as I can."

She nodded and tried to face him, but he didn't want to look at her. He didn't want to see her simple gray eyes, with no hint of dark imperfection. He eased her to the ground and loosened his own belt. She lay on her side on the thick bearskin rug with her back to him. He watched the flickering candles over her shoulder as he made love to her.

Dessick, the leader of the Mendaen dance troop, had thought Eleanor crazy, and told her so. Now, as she was about to enter a packed ballroom, in pants no less, she began to think he was right.

Eleanor had invited the Mendaens to stay at Trill for a few days, in the guest quarters of Speck Cottage, under the pretext of learning about the culture of the southern kingdoms. She assumed Gregory had granted her request out of guilt, but no matter, because she had been telling the truth about her curiosity. She just left out the particulars of how she would expand her knowledge.

At first Dessick refused her request. She persisted. "Master Dessick, don't women dance in your country?"

The fat drummer licked his mustache. "Of course, Your Highness, but we always assumed you Cartheans would not appreciate our ladies. They are a bit...raw for your tastes."

"Perhaps our tastes are changing."

"There is another problem," he said, with brutal honesty. "I don't think one with your training could ever master the technique. All those years of stiffness suck the life out of you."

"Well, we are in luck, sir," she said. "I may be the only lady in Cartheigh with absolutely no training."

He finally agreed to teach her. They pushed the furniture against the walls and brought out two drums because the whole set would be too loud, even on the far side of the grounds. Only Margaret, Eliza, Anne Iris, and Chou Chou were allowed to enter the cottage yard, and Gregory and his friends were thankfully off on a hunting trip. Eleanor talked Dessick's wife Tressanel and his daughter Mendi into performing with her. She saw they were grudgingly impressed with her attempts. Their respect lifted her confidence.

She examined Mendi's costumes and declared Cartheigh was not ready for their skimpiness. She called in a peddling magician from the village to magically alter her riding leggings. He ballooned the legs and cinched them under her knees for freedom of movement. Next he detached the bodice from one of her dresses. He removed the stiff capped sleeves and replaced them with gauzy silk. Her leggings sat low on her hips, and her navel peeking over the waist sash made her self-conscious.

Tressanel would not let the magician raise the waistline. "How can your hips move," she said, "if they are bound in fabric?"

So after two days of practicing, Eleanor and her unhindered hips waited for their cue at the home of Eliza's in-laws, Sir Edward and Lady Alice Harper. The Harpers were well liked, and their parties legendary. Eleanor knew no one would miss this ball. It celebrated the height of summer, the beginning of the weeklong Waxing Fest.

The guests had seen the Mendaens set up their drums and eagerly awaited another performance. The drummers struck their gong and Eleanor walked to the center of the room. The conversation hummed in her ears as people recognized her. She knelt on the floor in front of Tressanel, her heart pounding. Mendi had rubbed a *jezza'min* cream on her shoulders for good luck, and the spicy sweet smell clung to her nostrils. She hoped the sweat already beading on her forehead would not send her heavy Mendaen makeup running down her face.

The drums were beginning, slowly as they always did. She unfurled her body, and with no need to watch for her partner's clumsy feet her limbs relaxed. The rhythm led her as it built. She focused on the front of the room and did not see any specific person. Three women and a driving beat, and she lost herself.

The drums crashed to a stop and she dropped to the floor with Mendi and Tressanel. Her knee slammed the marble, adding insult to the deep bruises of her practice sessions, but she hardly felt it. She lay prostrate on the cold stone. As her breathing slowed she heard something. She lifted her head.

The guests were cheering and yelling. Mendi and Tressanel were already on their feet, and they blew her kisses and applauded. Mendi reached down and helped Eleanor stand. She curtsied to the crowd. Her cheeks burned with pleasure.

Gregory strode across the floor, lifted her into his arms, and kissed her mouth before setting her down. He held both her hands and bowed before her. She laughed and he pulled her close again. He whispered in her ear.

"You always surprise me," he said.

She smiled at Gregory and linked her arm through his. Her eyes scanned the crowd for the one person whose opinion mattered most. She couldn't find him.

She couldn't find him because he had excused himself as soon as Gregory swept her off her feet. He moodily walked the garden paths for half an hour, exorcising the sway of her hips, the flash of her belly, the joy crying out in every twist of her body. Dorian sat on a bench, trying to suppress the ache that followed him everywhere these days, but he couldn't beat it down because he wasn't sure where it originated. It traveled from his head to his chest to his stomach to his groin. He managed it on a sober afternoon but tonight it was a living, breathing monster. He knew he should go inside. She was probably looking for him.

He grabbed another whiskey from one of the serving trays as he entered the ballroom. Eleanor was still in the middle of the floor, accepting compliments in her makeshift Mendaen costume. He wished she would change. He knew every man in the room appreciated the view. Gregory didn't seem to mind. He stood proudly at her side.

As if he deserves to be there. Dorian pushed the thought away. *She's his wife, his wife, his wife.*

Eleanor excused herself, rubbing her shoulders, and made for one of the doorways. Her face lit up when he stepped in her path. "Dorian! Where have you been?"

"I just took some air," he said. "You were marvelous." He couldn't help it. His eyes raked her body. He took a tiny step closer and she held her ground.

"Thank you," she said. "I'm so glad you think so."

"How could I, or anyone else, think otherwise?"

Something hard set in her eyes. "I wanted to slap them in the face. To wake some people up."

"You slapped them, and they liked it." He drained his whiskey. "And Gregory looks wide awake."

As soon as he said the words he regretted them. She started to walk away, but he took her arm. Perhaps the night air brought on the gooseflesh he felt as his fingers trailed down to her elbow. "As he should be," he said.

She gently removed his hand. "I do as I must."

"I begrudge you none of it."

"Thank you." She glanced over her shoulder. "I have to change."

"I can come with you, if you need help," he said, hoping for a smile.

He got his wish. "Now that would not be helpful at all."

He watched her go, graceful in her bare feet. People called out, and she took their hands and their good wishes. Dorian was proud of her, even if it was not his place.

Once she disappeared he turned his attention to the myriad women circling the dance floor. That release brought him no relief after the Egg Camp, but he tried again. It did not take long to find someone amenable to helping him.

CHAPTER 16

HER TRUE FACE

ELEANOR ASSUMED SYLVIA MUST be the owner of an enchanted wardrobe. She had managed to attend at least two social events a day for weeks and Eleanor swore she never saw her in the same gown twice. On this fine afternoon she drifted around The Falls in pink and green organza like a cherry blossom caught on a light breeze. She was supervising the Annual Fleetwood Fencing Tournament. It seemed odd to call it the annual tournament, as it was the first one, but Sylvia was already creating her own summer traditions. Eleanor had to give Sylvia her due. Her pregnancy had not slowed her down, or so far even expanded her waistline.

Eleanor sipped her punch beside Margaret. Some vaguely remembered baroness had cornered them. Eleanor looked for Anne Iris or Eliza as the woman droned on, in the hopes of providing both Margaret and herself with an escape.

"...and you just would not believe how expensive it is to have anything sent to Solsea. I've had my eye on a dining table in Pettibone Lane for months, but the cost to ship it by carriage would be more than the table itself! Not that money is an obstacle of course..."

Sylvia waved and started toward them. For the first time in their long acquaintance Eleanor greeted her appearance with relief. She beckoned Eleanor and Margaret toward the narrow creek that gave the estate its name. The water ran across the property before pausing in a wide pool in the garden. It left the pool in a series of terraces and made its way to the cliffside, where it plunged into the sea.

Sylvia addressed the martial magician standing at the pool's edge. "My sister and the princess are here to offer us advice. Your Highness, Margaret, the falls are boring me. I thought we could dress them up a bit for the royal family. What do you think, purple or green?"

The magician waved his hands and the pool flashed between the two colors.

"I prefer green," said Eleanor, and Margaret nodded.

"Really? Purple is so much more dramatic. Purple it is." Sylvia dismissed the magician. "So, Margaret, Mother tells me you have an admirer in our new Svelyan friend."

Color flooded Margaret's face, and Eleanor doubted it had anything to do with the summer sun. "So she tells me as well," Margaret said.

"Well, aren't you lucky. He is something."

"He's been very gracious."

Sylvia snorted. "Gracious? Please, you can't play the innocent with a man like Christopher Roffi. Although he does have unusual taste."

Margaret started in with a stumbling rebuttal, but Eleanor knew in Sylvia's presence Margaret's mind always went blank.

Sylvia shrugged and flashed her most charming smile. "Well, I've heard Svelyan women are a tough lot. Anyone with a Carthean accent must seem attractive!"

Eleanor had hoped to give Margaret a chance to defend herself, but she could not let that last comment lie. "Some hide malice behind a sweet voice and pleasing countenance, Your Grace. Excuse us."

"Oh, ladies, your corsets must be too tight. I'm just teasing. Don't run off yet." Sylvia pointed across the lawn. "Look, there's the Svelyan in question!"

Roffi joined the crowd of men practicing outside the fencing court.

"Aren't you going to speak with him?" Sylvia asked Margaret. "Too shy? Dear sister, you must let me show you how to handle him. I can help you!"

Before Margaret could reply Sylvia made a straight line for Roffi and slipped her arm through his. Margaret frowned as Roffi's handsome face lit up. Sylvia laughed and ran her hand over the hilt of his sword.

Eleanor tried to drag Margaret away. "Come, don't give her the pleasure. We'll speak with him after the match."

"No, wait," Margaret said, and tipped her head in the direction of the court.

Christopher Roffi was looking over Sylvia's head in their direction. He said a quick goodbye and strode across the lawn. Eleanor did not miss the surprise on Sylvia's face. When he stopped in front of Margaret he cut quite the dashing figure. His hair had grown over the summer. It danced around his head in soft white curls. He had shaved the goatee, and it softened the angles of his face.

"Mistress Margaret," he said in his exotic voice. "My match is next. It would be honoring me if you would stand on my side, for I am sure you will bring me luck."

Apparently Margaret was at a loss for witty words. She just nodded. She took Roffi's arm, and when she looked back at Eleanor over her shoulder her face somehow conveyed both panic and exaltation. Roffi led her to the edge of the court and kissed her hand before trotting out to meet his opponent. He reached Gregory and put a hand on the prince's shoulder. He said something Eleanor could not hear, but it must have been amusing. As Gregory laughed Margaret waved to Eleanor. Eleanor smiled and returned the gesture.

Roffi had abandoned Sylvia for Margaret, something Eleanor imagined both sisters would have believed impossible. She counted anyone who would make such a choice a fine gentleman indeed.

Eleanor enjoyed the Waxing Fest more than the other revelries of the past year. No longer so consumed with her own worries, she appreciated the little intrigues around her. Margaret grew more enamored with Christopher Roffi, and Eleanor watched with pity as Raoul followed her around every party. She couldn't blame Margaret, but Raoul was a gentle soul. Eleanor wished Margaret had not forgotten him so quickly. Anne Iris flirted with anyone who paid her mind, and transferred her affections nightly. Eliza, who would soon return to Maliana and wait out her pregnancy under the eye of the witches of Afar Creek, chastised Anne Iris regularly for her lack of decorum.

"You only care," Anne Iris sniffed, "because you finally have cleavage but your belly takes all the attention."

As for Gregory, after threatening to disown her, he proved again to have a short memory. Eleanor found she admired his ability to move on. Eleanor, on the other hand, could never completely set aside the last few weeks. They never spoke of the woman in the red dress or the lost baby, but the night of her performance with the Mendaens he returned to her bed. The first time she fought the urge to turn away from him, but she got used to his affections again. She did give up, however, on his attempts to pleasure her. Through quiet exploration of her own body, often long after Gregory had fallen into a satisfied sleep, she learned to relieve that pressure herself. Neglect could be a good teacher.

She saw no other choices, and she preferred the happy, life-of-the party Gregory to the silent, sulking one. She grieved as she came to this conclusion, for it meant her love for him was wearing away, like the face of a statue long battered by changing weather. She might envy his uncomplicated happiness, but she couldn't replicate it.

She did keep her promise and show her true face. Whether people's opinions of her changed, or if she just stopped paying attention to them, she didn't care. Rosemary's soft admonishment that she do some good with her position stayed with her. Even after Hazelbeth and Rosemary's expression of faith in her abilities, she had been so focused on trivialities she neglected the real problems of everyday people. She sought the Godsmen for better understanding of the challenges faced by the villagers, and what she learned alarmed her.

She called on the most desperate cases, the mud and thatching shacks hunched like cowering rabbits in the rocky fields beyond the cliffs. She doled out her allowance, which had always seemed silly since her staff met her every desire with the snap of a finger. She listened to the people's woes and complaints and promised to deliver their messages to the king. After a few visits she dragged Gregory along with her. At first he balked, but she pushed until he gave in.

She took him to three tiny cabins on the first day, and they heard the same story at each. At their last stop a man called John Blade offered Gregory a cup of weak tea and sat across from him on an overturned stump. His ragged children danced around them in excitement over their elegant visitors. Eleanor sat with his wife and held their new baby.

"I have six children, Your Highness," John Blade said. He couldn't have been much older than thirty, but his hair was thin and his teeth were dark and cracking. "In the summer we scrimp by serving in the big houses, but in the winter it's a hard row around here. We can't grow nothin' in this soil, and the seas get so rough we lose men each year at the fishin'. The rich folk need us to keep up the empty places, but they know we're desperate so the pay is, pardon me, chicken shittings. Even in the summer they know we're too afraid to ask for a decent wage. You get tossed out and your children ain't eating."

"No pardon needed, sir," said Gregory.

"All I want is just pay for the work I do, sire. I ain't got no sights on being rich, but I'd like not to starve."

That evening the king called Eleanor to his receiving room on the third floor of Willowswatch. Casper finished reading a document, signed it, and handed it to Ezra Oliver. The king dismissed him. Neither Eleanor nor Oliver acknowledged the other's presence. She and the king exchanged greetings.

Casper tapped his fingers on the arm of his throne. "Gregory tells me you have been visiting the local people. He said you took him with you today. Why?"

"I'm called to it as a human being who has been elevated to a position of great fortune. I'm also called by my love of the crown to spread good will."

"And you bring Gregory as a chaperone."

She spoke frankly. "Yes, as a chaperone, but also because I think it will serve him well if he understands the needs of his people."

"He demanded I set a fair wage for the people of Solsea," Casper said.

"I believe in the justice of his request, Your Majesty, but I would not suppose to know your mind."

He walked to the window. "I think you have good instincts with the commoners. Do you have a desire to continue this work?"

"I do."

"Then you have my blessing, but you must keep Gregory informed of your endeavors. If we reject one of your plans, you will stand down without a word. Understood?"

"Of course."

"I'll have Oliver draw up the decree on the standard wage. You may go." She curtsied and made to leave but the king called her back. "Oh, and Eleanor, do take Gregory with you when you can. I admit in this matter you may teach him something."

After Chou observed Ezra Oliver accepting a message from the Duke of Harveston's private courier, Eleanor redoubled her efforts to understand the unfathomable friendship between her stepmother and the Chief Magician. She sent Chou on a fact-finding mission, as while she had first-hand knowledge of Imogene's unsavory personage, she knew little about Ezra Oliver beyond what he had revealed in their notorious argument. Suspicion now tainted her previous congenial interactions with him.

Chou delivered his report in her bathing room as Eleanor soaked away the grime of a long ride with Teardrop.

"So," Chou said as he paced the edge of the bathtub like a strategizing general. "Here is the first thing one must know about Mister Oliver. He is indisputably the most powerful magician to emerge in Cartheigh since the Desmarais came to power. He's served the past three kings. Longer than any other Chief Magician in history."

"Yes, the history books are clear on those facts. How did he come into their service?" Eleanor asked. She blew a clump of lavender-scented suds off her nose.

"An interesting question," Chou said. He whirled around to march back down the tub, but he lost his balance and nearly tumbled into the bubbly water. When he regained his footing and his dignity he continued. "Oliver was born in Meggett Fringe. On the seediest street in the slum, so they say. His mother was only fourteen at his birth, and she vanished into Pasture's End. She left him in the care of his grandmother. I hear tell she hated both the boy and his powers from the first day. It must have been a relief to both of them when the Covey claimed him. I think he was about five years old."

"Ezra Oliver is from the Fringe," Eleanor said. "I never would have expected it."

"It's true. An old martial magician told me Oliver's better-born peers at the Covey hated him just as much as his teachers loved him. He showed tremendous power early, you see. Somewhere in his childhood he must have learned the art of solicitude. He's been crafting relationships as well as he crafts sorcery ever since."

Eleanor thought of Oliver's initial friendly overtures. "I must count myself formerly under his spell."

"I assume he thought you'd make a malleable ally, but Faust's party showed him the other side of the coin. He's always calm—"

"Except in the midst of a screaming match with me."

"An unusual display of emotion on his part. In all honesty I could not find one person who would say a word against him. Maybe fear drives some of the respect shown him, but the consensus seems to be thus: powerful, hardworking, patriotic, and loyal to the death. Everything a king would want in a Chief Magician, I suppose."

Eleanor swirled the water around her hands. "Gregory doesn't like him. Why, I wonder?"

"Because the king put Oliver in a strange spot with his son. King Casper has always tolerated Gregory's...temper tantrums..." Chou paused for Eleanor's reaction.

"I'll not disagree with you."

"Casper has trouble saying no, so he's always made Oliver do it for him. Someday Oliver will be slaving away for a king who hates him."

Eleanor sunk deeper into the water and into silence. She ran a scrub brush over her dirty fingernails. For a moment she almost pitied Oliver, until she remembered his obnoxious comments at Faust's party. Her sympathy washed away with the dirt.

"Well done, Chou," she said, as Pansy knocked on the bathing room door.

"Your Highness?" she called. "Come, please. You'll be late for dinner."

"I'm coming, Pansy."

"Don't forget to wash behind your ears," Chou said.

She splashed him, and he landed in the tub with a squawk.

As the hot days wore on Eleanor missed more of the daytime social functions. She couldn't justify attending another luncheon or fencing match when there were so many more worthwhile pursuits. Her new work energized her, and gave each morning a sense of purpose. She continued visiting the poor in their homes, but she also read to the children in Rockwall Chapel and organized donations from the summer visitors. She made appeals for charity at every party, and used carefully worded peer pressure to ensure near universal participation. She sent soldiers mounted on unicorns back to Maliana and Harveston to collect old coats and cloaks from the nobility's winter residences. She spent a joyful afternoon organizing piles of warm clothes with Dorian, Anne Iris, and Margaret. They draped the bundles over the backs of Teardrop and Senné and delivered them to the chapel. The villagers eagerly sorted through the garments and marveled at their thickness and fine stitching.

While Gregory cheerfully supported her and sometimes came along, Dorian was a far more willing participant. She was glad of it, because it was a harmless way to spend time with him. One afternoon Margaret caught her watching him teach two village boys to fence with willow branches.

"Dorian will make a fine father one day," Margaret said.

"He will." Eleanor returned to sorting books she had collected for the chapel library. Dorian sat down in the grass and the boys joined him. "Now, boys, you know how Fire-iron was discovered in Cartheigh eight hundred years ago, don't you?"

They boys shook their blondish heads.

"HighGod, how can you be proper soldiers for Cartheigh if not? We must rectify this injustice. Listen well." His voice floated over the chapel yard toward Eleanor and her friends. She knew the story well, and fell into the rhythm of his low drawl.

"...when a rogue dragon attacked the Village of Pearl on the Tala River. The dragon was barely even grown up, probably only about eighty years old, but the village lost thirteen men in the battle. The villagers finally chased the creature into a cave. They trapped it by sealing the entrance with a boulder. Then they all said they heard it raging and growling away inside for two weeks before it finally ran out of air."

Dorian grasped his throat, his eyes bugging from his head, and the boys scooted away from him. He waved them back. "Or maybe it starved."

"After several days of quiet the villagers rolled away the boulder," he continued. "All were amazed at the beautiful glowing stones surrounding the dragon's big, dead body. They tried lots of ways to get the Fire-iron out of the rocks. They finally extracted some while it was still pliable."

"What's pliable, sir?" asked the older of the two.

"It means bendy, son. Now, water does not cool Fire-iron but the villagers of Pearl realized animal skins did the job quite well. The fur absorbs the heat and chills the stone enough that pieces can be chipped from the larger blocks. Fire-iron can be molded into almost anything when it is still warm, and pieces hold warmth for about a month after they are knocked out of the main rocks."

"It did not take long for news of the discovery to travel. The Malian kings of Cartheigh found a colony of dragons in the mountains of the far North Country, but before they could make a plan to begin mining the Fire-iron, the Svelyans invaded with a terrible and *ferocious* army."

The boys scrambled back again. Dorian laughed and continued. "For five hundred years the two countries fought over control of the Dragon Mines, even though they are on our Carthean side of the border, and of course the Svelyans should have just gone home. The Cartheans watched as Svelya got all the benefits of the Fire-iron trade—"

"Sir, like what?" asked older boy.

Dorian ruffled his hair. "You're a curious lad. Mostly a lot of money. You see, Cartheigh did not have the armies to drive away the invaders or control the herd of dragons who lived in the mine caves and created the Fire-iron with their breath. Everything changed when Caleb Desmarais found an orphaned unicorn foal—"

At that moment a Godsman emerged from Rockwall Chapel and called to the boys. Dorian scooped the younger one up under his arm and carried him to the priest.

"I wonder who Dorian will marry," mused Anne Iris.

"I have no idea," said Eleanor. Anne Iris could hint all she wanted, but Eleanor would never discuss Dorian, not even with her closest friends.

She could not ignore the fact that Dorian would marry someday. Gregory continued to rely on him, and gave him more responsibility all the time. People speculated Gregory would give him a title once he was king. In the meantime, even with his limited means, women swarmed him like cats to cream. Unlike other courtiers, he never needed to draw attention to himself. Attention came with his quiet confidence and understated wit. Even when surrounded by wealthier, more seasoned men, he took up the room.

Eleanor watched him each night as he flirted and danced. Even though she knew his conquests were legendary, she struggled for evidence he favored any one of his admirers over the others. She took heart she could always find his pale eyes in any crowd, no matter how large. When she was being honest with herself, she knew it would be better if he just chose one of them and married her. Eleanor had no claim on him, and she never would.

CHAPTER 17

COMPASSION

ONE MUGGY FRIDAY MORNING Dorian asked Eleanor if she would ride with him down to Porcupine Bay. Gregory was holed up in misery with the king and Oliver reviewing tax revenues. She found Anne Iris and Margaret on the veranda searching for a breeze with Brian, Raoul, and Christopher Roffi. They were playing swords and arrows, a local dice game.

"Stay with us," pleaded Roffi. "With Eliza gone back to Maliana we are an odd number."

"You know I'm not one for dice," Eleanor said.

"Eleanor would rather be out enjoying nature," Anne Iris said.

"Nature is too bloody hot," Brian countered irritably.

"Be careful," said Raoul in his soft voice. "The path to Porcupine Bay is difficult."

Roffi scowled. "It is hard for me to be believing Mister Finley would put the princess in . . . how do you say it? Jeopardy."

"She's couldn't be safer with a dragon as her guide. Dorian and Senné can navigate a mudslide and come out clean," said Brian, tossing his cards on the table.

Eleanor said goodbye and ran down the path to the unicorn barn.

She greeted Vigor and Fortune, the king's stallion, and then opened the door to Teardrop's stall.

"Thank HighGod," said Teardrop. "I need some wind in my mane."

"Let's leave the saddle. It's just too hot." Eleanor climbed onto Teardrop's back. "I tell you, friend, if ever I am glad for these britches, it's today. I think we'll be out all afternoon so I can stay out of a petticoat."

"Humans should forego all of your trappings in the summer. Your modesty makes no sense."

"I agree, but I would suffer a wool coat today over dining with Sir Faust and his fat wife just as HighGod made them."

Teardrop whinnied her shrill laugh. There was an answering neigh, and Senné and Dorian rounded the corner. Senné's ears pricked. "Share the humor," he said.

"We were just talking about naked humans," said Teardrop, with a unicorn's forthrightness.

"Really?" asked Dorian.

Eleanor hushed him. "Which way are we headed?"

"Past Neckbreak Cottage and the main staircase."

They crossed the grounds of Trill Castle. When they reached the top of the path Eleanor leaned up Teardrop's neck and looked down the steep incline. "Are you sure we can make it?" she asked.

"A horse couldn't do it," Dorian said. "Don't try and steer. Just let Teardrop lead and you'll be fine."

Eleanor patted her unicorn's neck. "Do you hear that?"

Teardrop shook her head. "It's not so bad. I see where the rocks are holding and where they will soon slip free."

Eleanor gripped the mare's sides with her legs. "I'm glad you see it."

Teardrop followed Senné down the cliff. She placed one wide hoof carefully in front of the other. Once Eleanor got used to the rocking motion, and realized Teardrop was perfectly confident, she relaxed and enjoyed the ride. Scrappy trees clung to the rocky hillside, and insects sang and hissed in a million clattering languages. She caught flashes of bright blue in the scrub around them.

"What's making that noise?" A call, a loud *Waa-eee, Waa-eee,* sounded through the branches.

"Cliff lemurs," said Dorian. "They're smart and curious. Don't be afraid if one jumps in your lap." He had no sooner said it than a blue creature dropped from the rocks to her right. The lemur swung onto Teardrop's horn.

"Hello, little one," Teardrop said.

The lemur whispered in Teardrop's ear in a scratchy voice and eyed Eleanor over his pointed snout. His brown eyes were ringed in white circles, as if he were wearing a seeing glass.

"We are just passing through," said Teardrop. "I'm sure my mistress can offer you a gift."

Eleanor pulled a few dried figs from her pocket. The lemur reached across with tiny, almost human hands and took the fruit. He sniffed it, and licked one with his pointed pink tongue. The figs must have passed his test, because he climbed into Eleanor's lap. He reached up and tickled her chin, then crept up her shoulder and onto her head before leaping onto the rock wall beside her. She turned around. He watched her, flicking his bushy tail and nibbling the figs, before lifting his hand and waving.

The way leveled out as they splashed through the blood-colored waters of Redwine Falls. They cantered down the sandy path to the wide beach at Porcupine Bay, so named because of the thousands of bright sea anemones that washed up from the tidal pools. Dorian and Eleanor slid off their unicorns. Teardrop and Senné chased each other and splashed in the cool shallows. Dorian spread a blanket on a rock. Eleanor pulled off her boots and soaked her feet in the salty water.

"This is far better than dice," she said.

Dorian chuckled. "I agree. It's well worth the effort in getting here." He passed her a piece of cheese and a water jug. "It's fine fare, I know."

"If only you had bread I'd feel like I was back in my father's house in Maliana."

He fished in his canvas bag and brought out a round loaf.

"Perfect!" she cried. "All I need is a broom and an apron."

They sat in comfortable silence for a while, listening to the screaming gulls and the hiss of the waves lapping in and out. She studied his chiseled profile.

"You know," she said. "Your eyes don't really have a color. Right now they're blue, because you're framed against the sky. Blue, green, gold. Always changing."

He looked down. "Even when I was a small boy it made me uncomfortable."

"I'm sorry, I didn't mean—"

"No, I like the way you put it."

"I understand how you feel. Here we are, two oddities together."

He faced her. "Do you want to tell me something?"

She brushed a piece of hair behind her ear. "I lost a baby," she said.

"I'm sorry. I wish I had known."

"There was nothing you could have done."

"I could have comforted you."

She shook her head. "It was not your duty."

"But I could have taken it up when others did not."

"I know you would have," she said. "That's enough."

They stayed a while longer, talking about their friends and the upcoming parties, but there was no excuse to linger much longer than it took the unicorns to cool down. She slipped on her boots and called to Teardrop. She and Senné stood in the surf, nose to tail, resting on one another.

"Senné likes her," Dorian said. "She's a fine mare. Perhaps the Paladins will put them in the breeding program."

"Now wait," Eleanor scolded. "Don't think about retiring my mare for a year or more yet. She's too young for that kind of thing."

A wicked grin crossed his face. "So are you."

Eleanor kicked water in his face, and then sprinted toward Teardrop. The mare tossed her head and met Eleanor halfway. Dorian followed her, soaked and laughing, and they made their sweaty way back to Trill Castle.

Dorian hardly made it back to his room before Gregory summoned him to the financial review. Apparently Gregory did not wish to suffer alone. By dusk Dorian assumed they had reviewed to the penny the tax money collected from every city, town, village, hamlet, and farm in Cartheigh, not to mention the crown's varied business interests and the fluctuating price of Fire-iron. As the royal comptroller droned on Dorian stripped to his shirtsleeves, but after a long ride in the sun and a half-day of financial minutiae he was near comatose. Not a hint of breeze blew through the propped open windows of Looksee Cottage.

"Well, that was very thorough. I think we could all use a drink after such a productive day. Oliver, is there anything else?" asked Casper.

Oliver shuffled his papers. "There is one other matter, Your Majesty, I would ask you to address."

Dorian's plan to retire in a cool bathtub and scrub the sand from his hair went up in puffs of steamy air.

"Get on with it," said the king. Dark sweat stains leached down the sleeves of his tunic.

"I'm sure Master Comptroller's wife is waiting with his dinner," said Oliver. The comptroller gathered his ledgers and heeded the message. Oliver continued. "It's about Thomas Harper Rowe, sire."

Thomas Harper Rowe was a promising apprentice magician, one of Oliver's personal charges. Several weeks ago Dorian had overheard Oliver informing the king he suspected Rowe of thievery.

"Yes, that." Casper said. "Have you reached a conclusion?"

Oliver nodded. "I have, and it's not a pleasant one. Rowe has confessed to stealing from you. He admits he replaced the jewels in the necklace with false stones."

"What necklace?" asked Gregory.

"I asked him to transport a valuable piece from Maliana to Solsea. A gift for the Talessee queen. It took several days, and much convincing, but we have a confession. He also confesses to skimming from the treasury."

Gregory mopped his face with a handkerchief. "What do you mean, much convincing?"

Oliver could not have been blander if he were discussing the humidity. "He's been locked in the sheep shed at the top of the Ramlock Face. We tried starving him, and then whipping him, with no success. He was probably near caving when we removed his fingernails, but it was a night hanging by his wrists from the wall that finally called forth the truth."

Gregory scowled in distaste. "Aren't you a magician? Couldn't you hypnotize him?"

"There are some instances in which mundane interventions are more effective than magical ones," said Oliver. He turned his attention back to the king. "Your Majesty, what would you have me do? There is the question of his family connections."

"Yes," said King Casper. "Since his mother was a Harper and he uses her name it would be embarrassing to the family despite the fact he's been claimed by the Covey all these years. A trial would still cast the Harpers in a bad light."

"I'm sure they would appreciate the attention to their honor," said Oliver.

"How can we get rid of him without a trial?" asked Gregory. "It's not like he's some peasant and we can just lock him away and lose the key."

"You're right, my son. The line is a fine one. How to placate our dear friends yet show such behavior will not be tolerated? Oliver, take

Gregory with you. He should see how we handle these delicate matters. Finley, you go too."

"Now?" said Gregory. "It's late, Father. I'm starving. Can't it wait?"

Casper clamped a hand on Gregory's shoulder. "I'll have the cooks send something to your room. You boys fetch Vigor and Senné. I'll send Oliver along in a few minutes."

"Yes, Your Majesty," said Dorian. He hustled Gregory out the door.

Dorian and Gregory collected their unicorns from the barn. Dorian hated disturbing Senné. The hike down the cliffside had tired the stallion, but he didn't complain. Dorian took a soft rag and rubbed his legs. By the time Oliver appeared in the courtyard it was dark. Three martial magicians, somber, bearded men in simple black tunics and leggings, accompanied him.

No one spoke on the way up the Ramlock Face, the highest point above Solsea village. The path was a daunting mix of sliding rocks and a dizzying drop edged by scrubby bushes. Senné shuffled along, adjusting his pace to the magicians' horses. Each magician conjured a ball of light to guide his mount, and the spells cast a gray, red, and blue glow over the horses' feet. It was hard going, and Dorian appreciated Senné's easy confidence.

When they crested the top of the path the wind whipped over a day's worth of dry sweat and raised gooseflesh on Dorian's forearms. The full moon cast light on great houses of Solsea dotting the cliffs below them. He could see the cottages of Trill Castle, and the steeple of the Rockwall Chapel.

"A fine view, is it not, gentlemen?" asked Oliver. Gregory grunted in agreement, and Dorian nodded. Fine view or not, he wanted to get back.

Everyone dismounted. Dorian and Gregory followed the magicians across a rough field to a stone sheep shack, long abandoned by some village farmer. Thick ivy vines covered the shack, as if it has sprouted arms and dug into the rocky ground to keep the wind from blowing it into the sea.

The three martials opened the warped wooden door. Dorian heard them cursing inside, and rays of enchanted light snuck through cracks in the shed walls. Someone cried out and was silenced with a meaty thump.

Dorian barely recognized the prisoner as a man when they dragged him from the shed. He wore nothing but a pair of ragged leggings, and his buckling knees lent a bowlegged roll to his stumbling stride. His arms hung uselessly at his sides. He looked like an oversized skinned monkey.

"What's this?" Gregory asked.

"This, Your Highness, is the thief Thomas Harper Rowe," said Oliver.

Rowe raised his battered face, and a hopeful flame of recognition lit in his eyes. Gregory took a few steps back. "Your Highness!" Rowe called. "Your Highness, I swear, I swear to you I am innocent!"

"Ignore him, sire," said Oliver. "He knows the end is nigh. He'll say anything."

One of the martials punched Rowe in the stomach, and he doubled over. Oliver tugged a burlap bag over Rowe's head and cinched it under his chin.

"What are you doing?" Gregory held his own hands in front of his mid-section, as if waiting for a blow himself.

"I'm doing as your father commanded."

Oliver spoke in a low voice and raised his hands. Two sets of heavy shackles formed out of the mist swirling around his head. Rowe screamed as the chains attached themselves to his fractured wrists and tightened. The others wound around his legs and he fell to the ground.

"Thomas Harper Rowe, you are condemned here on this cliff for the crime of theft of crown possessions."

Rowe's weeping voice escaped his burlap mask. "Please, Your

Highness. I'm sorry. I didn't mean it. I swear to HighGod." Dorian wondered if Rowe even remembered whether he was guilty or innocent.

"It is His Majesty King Casper's wish that you atone for your sins with the highest price."

Rowe struggled. Sparks flew around his head and danced off the chains.

"Wasted effort, Rowe," said Oliver. "My chains are much more powerful than anything you can conjure."

"Even I can see that," Gregory said to Dorian.

Senné's breath grazed Dorian's neck. He wound his fingers through the stallion's black mane.

Oliver's chant carried over the Face. Rowe's bound body rose into the air in a cradle of gray mist. He thrashed and moaned.

"Can't they shut him up?" Gregory muttered. He tugged at the back of his neck.

Rowe floated out over the edge of the cliff, hovered, and spun slowly. Oliver raised his arms and his chant came to an abrupt end. The gray mist winked out, and Rowe plunged out of sight. Gregory ran to the edge of the cliff. Dorian followed him, but Rowe had already disappeared into the dark water below. All Dorian could make out were the tossing whitecaps.

Eleanor often delivered extra food to the chapel for the Godsmen to distribute among the poor. Gregory's request to tag along on her next trip into the village surprised her.

"I've been so busy with Father and Oliver I've been no help," he said.

"I would welcome your assistance, and your company." She stood behind him at the breakfast table, rubbing his shoulders. "If you feel up to it. You seem tired."

He looked up at her with the brown eyes of a tired puppy. "Maybe I am, but I'm afraid if I stay around here Father will call me into another assembly. Besides, there's something else I want to see to in Solsea."

In the courtyard Eleanor directed the stable boys and kitchen maids in sorting bushels of food that would spoil if not eaten soon.

"Why do the provisioners bring us so much?" she asked. "We can never eat it all."

Gregory shrugged. "I assume they want us prepared if we are struck with the urge to hold a ball."

"Ha," she said. "It's a help to the Godsmen at any rate." She bustled about, enjoying the task. She hoped the afternoon would lift Gregory's spirits. He'd been unusually distracted the past few days.

Eleanor and Gregory mounted their unicorns and followed the horse carts into the village. The Godsmen welcomed them, and they passed the time while the goods were unloaded with a glass of pear juice. Once the carts were empty, Gregory sent the drivers back up the road to Trill, took the Godsmen's blessings, and swung onto Vigor's back.

"Where are we going?" Eleanor asked.

"Just follow me."

Teardrop fell in line behind Vigor and they trotted down Solsea's quaint high street. On the west end the shops gave way to small, well-kept fishermen's cottages. Gregory reined in at the last one on the block. It had its own wooden staircase down to the beach. Eleanor and Gregory dismounted and climbed the whitewashed steps. He knocked on the door and a voice called from within.

"Hold on, I hear ya." The door opened a crack, revealing a young woman with black hair and buckteeth. Her eyes widened. "Oh, Your Highness, please forgive me." She opened the door wider and dropped to a curtsy.

"Don't worry, Millie," said Gregory. "I know you weren't expecting me." He brushed past her and called for Eleanor to follow. Millie stayed at the door with her eyes on the ground.

"Princess Eleanor, it is just an honor, an honor to have you in our house."

"Thank you," said Eleanor. She still no idea what they were doing here.

Gregory had disappeared. Eleanor peered around the corner into a tiny, but meticulously neat, sitting room. A large window let in the sun and a beautiful view of the Shallow Sea.

"There she is," Gregory said. "My girl." He knelt by a battered couch. A tiny old woman was propped up on it, wrapped in a patchwork quilt. Her white hair, still streaked with black, was piled on top of her head in several squashy layers. One side of her face stayed frozen when she smiled at them.

"Eleanor, let me present my dear friend, Nanny Flossa," Gregory said.

"I'm pleased to make your acquaintance," said Eleanor.

The old woman covered her mouth with two wrinkled fingers. She spoke around them in a slurred voice. "Oh, Gregory, she's just lovely, she is. To think I would meet her."

Eleanor silently asked Gregory for an explanation.

"Nanny Flossa took care of my mother as a child, and then she looked after my sister Matilda and me."

"I did, Your Highness. Two generations. And the late queen and princess just as angelic as your husband was a rascal."

Gregory and the old lady laughed, and she beckoned Eleanor into a chair next to her. She rambled on, stories of Gregory and Matilda and the troubles and joys of their childhood. Eleanor listened with interest, and glanced now and then at her husband. He opened a box of chocolate truffles from one of Maliana's finest confectioners.

"Oh! Look how he spoils me," said Nanny Flossa. "You know, love, Gregory bought me this house when I retired. He knew I had grown up here in Solsea, and he sent me home for some rest in my old age."

"Did he?" Eleanor asked.

Nanny Flossa wagged a finger at Gregory. "Now then, don't you be keeping your generosity from your own wife. Ain't like kindness will stop the hair growing on your chest." She turned to Eleanor. "Millie looks after me and Gregory pays both our keep. We are right comfortable."

Eleanor took Gregory's hand. "I'm glad."

Gregory colored, but Eleanor could tell her words pleased him. "I do as my mother and sister would have wanted. Besides, I gave Nanny most of those gray hairs. It was the least I could do. I'm sorry I haven't visited sooner."

Nanny Flossa shrugged. "You're here now, son, and I know the life of a prince is a busy one. I thank you for bringing your rose here to me. Everyone in the village speaks so highly of you, Princess Eleanor. I'm blessed to meet you. Hmmm…blessed."

Millie tucked the blankets around her chin. "I think it's time for a nap, Nanny."

Nanny Flossa nodded. She squinted at Gregory, and Eleanor saw confusion in her eyes for the first time. "Where's Matilda?" she asked. "She should come in for dinner."

"We'll find her. You rest. I'll stay until you fall asleep," said Gregory.

The old woman put a papery hand on his cheek and closed her eyes. Within moments she drifted off.

Eleanor and Gregory rode up the Cliffside Road to Trill Castle. As they entered the courtyard Eleanor tried to praise his kindness to his old servant. "Nanny Flossa was right," she said. "Why hide your compassion? It's a fine quality."

She meant it as a compliment, so his irritation surprised her. "I'm tired of this topic," he said as he dismounted. "She wanted to meet you, so we went. Let's be finished with it."

"As you wish," she said. She joined him on the ground.

Dorian walked purposefully out of the barn as she handed her gloves to a groom. "You're back," he said. "Good."

"What is it?" asked Gregory.

"Is something wrong?" Eleanor added.

Dorian hesitated. His eyes flicked between them. Eleanor felt a twinge of annoyance when she understood Dorian did not want to speak in front of her.

"You know I'll hear of it anyway," she said.

Gregory shrugged, and Dorian waved both of them out of earshot of the grooms. "Some fishermen found the body of Thomas Harper Rowe."

Eleanor had heard of Rowe, and how he had been accused of thievery and then disappeared. "Did he drown?" she asked.

"In a way, yes," said Dorian. "He was tortured, bound, and thrown off a cliff."

She gasped. Gregory, however, did not appear surprised in the least. "What are people saying?" he asked.

"People say it is frightening, but not unexpected if he was guilty of these crimes."

"What of the Harpers?"

"They haven't addressed it."

Eleanor turned on Gregory. "Someone needs to address it. It sounds like he was murdered without a trial."

"Eleanor—" Dorian began.

"He confessed," said Gregory.

"So you knew about this? Dorian said he was tortured. You or I might confess to giving birth to a dragon under such duress."

Gregory's hands roamed from his eyes to his hair. "I'm tired. It's been a long week."

"I'm not finished!"

"Well I am," Gregory said. His volume rose with each word. "An example needed to be made and it was made. Honor needed to be retained and it was retained. Why am I justifying myself to you? It's not your place, and it's beyond you anyway."

Eleanor's mouth fell open. "Beyond me?"

"I said I don't want to bloody talk about it anymore!"

He stormed toward the groom leading Vigor into the barn. The boy saw him coming and tripped. He did not drop the reins, and the nose strap scraped across Vigor's muzzle. It pulled Vigor's head down and he stumbled along with his guide.

Gregory talked softly to Vigor until he calmed. The groom knelt on the ground, his head lowered. "I'm sorry, Your Highness, I'm sorry—"

Gregory jerked him to his feet before he could finish.

"Stupid ass!" he screamed into his face, and threw him to the ground again. He kicked the boy in the stomach. Vigor tossed his head and backed away.

"Gregory!" Eleanor cried.

"Stop," said Dorian. "Don't judge him this time, Eleanor."

"He should judge himself!"

Dorian shook his head. "I would not be him in these matters. You don't know what choices he has to make. Let me take care of it."

Dorian trotted across the yard. Gregory was yanking the scrambling groom back to his feet and cocking his arm when Dorian took his shoulder. Gregory turned, his fist still raised.

"That's enough, Greg, don't you think?" said Dorian. He put his other hand on Gregory's upraised arm, and eased it down.

The groom fell again, his forehead against the ground and his arms over his head, in a position of subjugation and defense. Eleanor saw the redness drain out of her husband's face as he looked at Dorian.

"Let's have a drink," Dorian said.

Gregory nodded. He said something Eleanor couldn't make out, and another groom took up Vigor's line and lead him into the barn. Gregory started up the stone path to Willowswatch, but then turned back to her and bowed his goodbye. She returned it with a curtsy, and the two men disappeared, Dorian a step behind Gregory.

At a bit of a loss, Eleanor approached the offending groom, who still crouched in the dirt.

"Rise," she said. He leapt up. "Are you badly injured?"

"No, Your Highness," he said.

"You should take the rest of the day."

He shook his head. "I was at fault. I'll not ignore my duties."

She exhaled. "You're a brave boy." She pointed at Teardrop, who still waited patiently by the fountain. "Will you look after my lady mare? I trust you will take care. She is a gentle creature and easily frightened."

The eagerness on his face tugged at her heart. He couldn't have been more than twelve. "Yes, I will take care, I promise. Thank you, Your Highness."

She kissed Teardrop goodnight and went to prepare for dinner.

CHAPTER 18

THE BROOM CLOSET

THE SEASON WOUND DOWN, and one by one the summer families prepared to return to their year-round homes. The carriages were packed, the furniture covered, and the windows nailed shut against the driving wind that battered the cliffs all winter. The king had returned to Eclatant, but Gregory and Eleanor and their friends lingered to enjoy a few more days. Eleanor had been content in Solsea these last weeks, and she although she wanted to see Rosemary and start her charity work in Maliana, she would miss the quaint beauty of Trill Castle.

Two days before they were to leave they met on the south lawn for a game of lawn bolls. The servants piled fruit, sweets, and bottles of wine and liquor on a long table.

"No need to drag it all back with us," said Gregory. He poured a flask of whiskey into the bowl of tangerine punch.

"Hear, hear," said Raoul.

Chou Chou flew around their heads as the game started, shouting advice on proper pitching form. Eleanor's first two throws went wide, and her third came up short.

"Your Highness," said Roffi, "with your husband's permission I will show you the way we are playing in Svelya. We are internationally known for our skill at lawn bolls."

Anne Iris and Margaret laughed.

"Don't forget, Eleanor," said Brian. "Svelyans are also internationally known for their skill at bullshitting."

Gregory nodded at the ambassador. "By all means, Roffi, help the girl. She stands to lose all her money, and then where will the poor children of Solsea be?"

Eleanor stuck her tongue out at him. Roffi came up behind her. He reached around her waist and put his hands over hers on the ball. His mouth brushed her ear when he whispered directions.

Eleanor was concentrating on easing away from Roffi's awkward embrace and barely registered what he said, but when he swung her arm for her the ball arced up. It plopped gently in the grass and rolled to a stop beside the target. She couldn't help but beam at him. "You are indeed a master, sir," she said. "I've always been rubbish at this game."

"I am at your service, as always," he said.

Gregory applauded, and then spoke to Brian. "Smithy, where's Dorian?" Irritation crept into his voice.

Raoul answered for Brian. "He was writing to his sister. You know she's expecting again."

"Yes, I know," said Gregory, "but it can wait. I told him I wanted him here."

Brian snorted. "Your dog not jumping fast enough?"

Eleanor bristled. She knew Brian liked Dorian, but sometimes resented his elevated status. As Gregory's cousin Brian should by any measure outrank a former soldier.

"I doubt you would say that to his face," said Gregory. "Play on."

The game became wilder as the players sipped Gregory's spiked punch. A tipsy Anne Iris argued with Chou Chou, who kept landing on her shoulder and giving her pointers. Eleanor chuckled as Anne Iris turned this way and that, trying to swat him. Chou clung to the back of her dress between her shoulder blades, giving the impression she had sprouted wings. On her last attempt to dislodge him, the ball slipped from her grip. It flew through the air and landed with a splash in the glass punch bowl. The bowl shattered and sent shards and punch flying. As Eleanor stood beside the unlucky bowl her bodice was drenched.

Gregory examined her face for cuts. "Are you hurt, sweetheart?" he asked.

"Eleanor, I'm so sorry," Anne Iris said.

"I'm fine, everyone, don't worry. It was an accident." She wiped at her neck with a napkin as the servants scurried about cleaning up the mess. "I'll just run into the boys' cottage and wash before the bees smell me."

She lifted her skirts and walked up the low hill to Walnut Cottage, the summer home of Dorian, Brian, Raoul, and for the last month or so, Christopher Roffi. She went around to the back door, hoping to find some linens and a washbowl on the porch. When she didn't see any, she opened the door. Dorian was just clipping down the staircase in front of her.

It happened quickly, and with little fanfare. Later she would wonder what had sparked it, when there had been so many other opportunities.

Dorian paused on the third step when he saw her. She smiled, and was about to say hello, when he stepped down to the landing. He crossed the front hall in three strides. He took her firmly by the waist and pushed her backwards through a flimsy door into the broom closet. He kicked the door shut behind them, and his mouth met hers.

He was everywhere, his hands, his mouth, and she was kissing him back. He pressed her against the wall, knocking over a bucket of mops. She thrust her fingers into his hair, and heard a moan escape her lips. Months of restraint flew out the window like so many bursting soap bubbles. His hands locked on her shoulders, and their foreheads touched. She tilted her head and bit his lip. He clamped down, his fingers digging in, but it wasn't painful. As he leaned against her she could feel his strength and his pent-up emotion.

She looked to the ceiling as his mouth moved to her chest, and down to the hem of her bodice. He ran his tongue over her bare skin, licking away the traces of sticky sweet punch. She cried out and slid down the wall. As she threw her head sideways she saw a window over her left shoulder. If anyone walked by there was no doubt they would be seen.

"Dorian," she said. "Dorian, stop."

He didn't slow down. He kissed her again. She turned her head.

"We have to stop." She tried to grab his hands, but he caught hers instead. She tugged them away and pushed at his chest, hard. "Dorian, stop!"

He pulled away from her, his chest heaving, his dark hair tousled. His eyes were vacant; the pupils dilated to pinpricks as they did when he was angry. His lips were raw and red.

"I'm sorry," he said. "I have offended you."

"No. No, you could never offend me." She was near tears, her frustration about to boil over. "We can't, we just can't. Gregory is right there…if he saw us…"

Dorian's heel struck a watering can as he stepped back. She jumped at the noise. "I have to go," she said, and fled into the hall.

She ran up the stairs to one of the bathing rooms and examined herself in the mirror. She was flushed, but it could have been the drink. She sprinkled water on her messy hair and rubbed her face and bosom, trying to create the illusion the color was the result of a hard scrub. She peered out the window at Dorian crossing the yard. She gripped the sides of the basin.

I won't cry, I can't cry, not now.

When she knew she could control herself she returned to the game. Once again she assured everyone she was uninjured. She declined her turn and sat on a bench, stroking Chou Chou. After a while Gregory commented on Dorian's silence.

"HighGod, man, you're a gloomy one today. Why be glum? It's a beautiful day and we're surrounded by such lovely company." Gregory squeezed Eleanor's shoulder. She managed a stiff smile.

"I'm sorry, Greg," Dorian said. "I'm not feeling well. A headache."

"I'm sure you're just worried about Anne Clara. You know she'll be fine."

"Yes, perhaps that's it."

Gregory crossed the playing field and stood by Dorian. "You're planning on visiting her, correct? You should go straight there from Solsea. There's no need to return to Maliana and then backtrack all the way to Harper's Crossing."

"That would be wonderful, as long as you can spare me."

"We'll manage without you for a few days, will we not?" They nodded and agreed like a congregation at chapel. "I give you permission to go. You may take your leave at your leisure."

"You're too kind," Dorian said. "I will go now, and prepare, if it pleases you."

Gregory nodded, and Dorian bowed and walked back to Walnut Cottage.

"Eleanor," Gregory asked. "Are you sure you're all right? You look pale."

She made her reply as light as possible. "Yes, I'm fine, thank you."

He knelt down in front of her. "I'll be visiting you tonight. I want to make our last nights here at Trill as memorable as we can."

"I'll be waiting," she said brightly. She wiped her eyes. "Oh, the sun is harsh today."

Eleanor could not sleep after Gregory's attentions, and the next morning she was exhausted. She wanted to see Dorian alone before he left, but with few people to provide a distraction she struggled for an excuse. Last night, before falling asleep himself, Gregory had told her he would not be returning to Maliana either. He had been called to the Dragon Mines, and he would head north straightaway.

"Brian and Raoul will see you back to Eclatant."

She spent her sleepless night thinking it over, and could come to only one conclusion. The next morning at breakfast she begged Gregory to take her with him. He raised his eyebrows, his spoonful of oatmeal pausing before his mouth.

"To the Dragon Mines? Why would you want to go there?"

She smiled. "You know me. I'm curious. How can I be a true Desmarais princess if I've never seen a dragon or visited the most important place in the whole kingdom?"

"I don't think my mother or any other Desmarais woman ever saw a dragon."

"Then I'll be the first." Eleanor was purposely pert and positive. He liked her that way. "Please, Gregory."

"Woman, you are hard to resist. You may come." He put down his napkin, then stood. He wagged a finger at her and she resisted the urge to push it back in his face. "Now I don't want any complaining, mind you. The Dragon Mines are not Eclatant."

"I promise. I'll be a good soldier."

"Start packing. We leave first thing tomorrow." He patted her hair and left the room.

She sank into her chair. While she had always been interested in the Mines, the real reason she wanted to accompany Gregory had nothing to do with dragons. He would be gone for over a month. The thought of returning to Eclatant and stewing over Dorian, only to have him arrive at the palace in advance of her husband, spelled disaster. She had to make an effort to forget Dorian and resurrect her affection for Gregory. She needed a long spell with her husband if she had any hope of success.

She handed her plate to the servant, then went to her room to give a few packing directions to Pansy.

"Chou," she said. The parrot lifted his head from his watering bowl. He shook and his feathers stood out in stiff spikes.

"A morning wash always awakens the senses," he said.

"Will you come to the Dragon Mines with me?"

"Dragon Mines! Cold, wet, and full of…dragons?"

She nodded.

"I can't wait," he said. "I'll pack a cloak."

She stroked his back. "Help Pansy with the packing, will you? I'm going to tell Teardrop." She knew the mare would be excited by the prospect of a long journey. She also knew Dorian would probably be at the barn with Senné.

She found him running his hands down the black stallion's legs, checking for soundness. She could smell the harsh protective ointment he had rubbed onto Senné's hooves. It made her eyes water, or at least she told herself so. His back was to her, and she hesitated to disturb him. Senné did not speak. He just waved his ears.

"Dorian?"

He didn't jump, and she wondered if he had indeed known she was watching him. He straightened and turned. His boots rustled the thick hay around Senné's feet. There were pieces of it stuck to his dark blue tunic. She wanted to go to him, to pick them off, to be close enough to touch the pricks of dark scruff on his face. He hadn't shaved since the broom closet. She held her breath until the urge passed.

"Are you packed?" she asked.

"Yes."

"You're going alone?"

He nodded. "I can use the time to think."

Best just to tell him. "I'm going to the Dragon Mines with Gregory."

He opened his mouth, and then shut it.

"I have to go," she said, soundlessly begging him to understand. *I'm doing this for you, too.*

"You'll be gone for—"

"Six weeks."

"Then I wish you a safe journey."

She wanted to say more, but the conversation was ending without her permission. "And you. I will see you at Eclatant, before the Harvest Fest."

He leaned on his unicorn. She kissed Senné's silky muzzle. "Take care of him, Sen," she whispered, knowing Dorian heard her. Then she fled.

Eleanor sat on Teardrop's back in the front courtyard of Willowswatch with Chou Chou on her shoulder. The grooms and servants ran from the cottages to the carriages, their arms laden with boxes, as Trill Castle prepared for its long winter sleep. Anne Iris and Margaret had forsaken their own packing this morning. They followed Eleanor around the grounds and begged her to return to Eclatant.

"It's far too treacherous!" Margaret gave one final appeal. She wrung her hands. "What if you're attacked on the way? What if a dragon breathes on you and you're burnt to a crisp?"

Christopher Roffi agreed with her. "It is not wise for a lady to be visiting such a place."

Eleanor gave them a weary smile. "I could just as easily be burnt up leaving a candle lit in my bedroom at night."

Anne Iris took another route. "The food will be horrible, and the company worse."

Gregory glared at her.

"Except for you, dear cousin," she said, "but you must admit, everyone says the miners are a frightful lot."

Raoul added to their cautions. "It's true you must take care, Your Highness."

"I will, Raoul, I promise. I'll stay away from the dragons."

"I worry more about the miners. They don't often see beautiful women," Raoul said.

Gregory's face darkened. "Enough, all of you. Don't you think I will protect my wife?"

Their friends were full of apologies and reassurance.

"We should leave," Gregory said. "The sun will only get hotter."

Eleanor and Gregory, mounted on Teardrop and Vigor, led their unusually small procession. An apprentice magician by the name of Orvid Jones would ride seated behind one of five Unicorn Guards. They would stop at several estates on the journey to eat and sleep, but if they were caught in the elements Orvid could provide temporary magical shelter. They would travel light and fast, and carry few belongings. Anything else they needed would arrive later by horse-drawn carriage. Eleanor looked forward to the freedom.

She blew final goodbye kisses. Christopher Roffi strained on his tiptoes to kiss her hand. He startled Teardrop, who jigged sideways until Brian grabbed her bridle. Before they left the courtyard Gregory asked the question Eleanor wanted to ask herself.

"Smithy, has Dorian left?"

"Yes, before breakfast this morning. He left a note sending his good wishes. He must be anxious to see his sister."

Gregory nodded. Vigor tossed his head, ready to be off.

"HighGod grant him a safe travel," Gregory said, "and safe travel to you all!"

He grinned at Eleanor. His brown eyes were clear and sober, and his enthusiasm heartened her. He had let his hair grow this summer, and a lock slipped from behind his ear. He tucked it back. "Well, sweetheart, you asked for this journey. Let's see what you make of it."

"I'm waiting for you, husband," she said, determined to return his smile.

Gregory tightened his grip on the reins with one hand and slapped

Vigor's shoulder with the other. The stallion reared, but as always Gregory had a strong seat. "That's the spirit. Off, then!"

Chou Chou slipped into the deep pocket of Eleanor's cloak. "Tell me when we get there," he said.

Eleanor kicked Teardrop and they raced after her husband, out the gate and down the Cliffside Road. Vigor's hooves sent gusts of wind and dust into Eleanor's eyes. The Unicorn Guard pounded behind them, and within minutes Trill Castle disappeared.

PART III

CHAPTER 19

WHERE THE CLARITY FLOWS

DORIAN PUSHED SENNÉ HARD and the one hundred miles between Solsea and Harper's Crossing flew past under the unicorn's hooves. The rocky, barren terrain of the southern cliffs gave way to rolling hills and thick forests. Most people of the Lake District made a living logging and raising sheep, but a community of Fire-iron artisans also thrived in the Crossing. The town was famous for its finely crafted jewelry, sculpture, and military equipment. The comfortable village bustled with specialty shops and small inns.

Dorian rode down Main Street. It took him nearly two hours to get through town because he had to stop and speak with old friends who recognized him and called out. He followed the road along Lake Brandling, but he didn't stop at Floodgate Manor, his childhood home. It was late afternoon by the time he reached his sister's house, Tavish's Fifth, so named because there were four other mansions owned by the Tavish family on the lakeshore.

Senné could easily cover twenty miles in an hour, but a whole day of such exertion with only a few rest stops had exhausted him. Dorian offered to rub him down, but the stallion insisted Dorian leave him with the groom and go up to the house. Dorian agreed and promised to return after dinner. He said hello to Anne Clara's old pet goat, who munched thistles in the stable yard.

"Whadja bring me?" the goat asked. It devoured the dried apples Dorian threw over the fence.

Two butlers opened the heavy silver doors as he climbed the stairs. Dorian removed his traveling cloak and gloves and handed them to the servant. His brother-in-law, Ransom, waited for him. They embraced.

"We heard you arrived in the village," said Ransom. "Your bath is filled. When did you leave Solsea?"

"Early this morning."

"HighGod, you must have been flying. I'll send some extra grain down for Senné. The poor lad must be worn out."

"Thank you," Dorian said. "He deserves a good meal and a long rest. If he were a man I would say offer him a stiff drink."

"Ah, but if he were a man he would have fallen by the wayside," said Ransom.

"Where is Anne Clara?"

"She's resting in her bedroom. The witches have advised her to stay off her feet if she can. She said she's sorry she can't meet you, but she wants to join us for dinner."

"Really." This bit of information, so calmly given, worried Dorian. "Just give me a few minutes to change and I'll be down."

He hurried through his bath, and met Ransom and Anne Clara in the dining room with damp hair. With her bright eyes and good color she looked better than he had expected, but she could barely reach the table in front of her. Her yellow dress made her seem like a ball of sunshine come to dinner.

She teased him. "Brother, don't look at me so, as if you're afraid I might explode."

"I'm sorry, darling, but I can't help it. It must be painful." He kissed her cheek.

"It is uncomfortable at this stage, but what do the witches say? The bigger your belly, the more pain you're willing to suffer to get the baby out."

Dorian did not appreciate the humor. He hated the thought of his sister in agony, pushing and heaving. He loved his nieces and nephew, but he wished she would take a break.

"The children are excited to see you," she said, as if reading his mind. "We had a time getting them in bed. They will abuse you soundly tomorrow."

"Then I, too, should be in bed early." Over fresh lake flounder and summer squash he listened half-heartedly to Anne Clara and Ransom's updates on the goings on in Harper's Crossing. He was about to excuse himself after dessert but Ransom beat him to it.

"Well, that was a lovely meal, but I think I'll turn in. The children will be up early, and I know you two want to catch up."

"We'll sit and talk a while, won't we, Dor?"

Dorian leaned back, eyeing his sister. She knew him too well, and got to the point as soon as Ransom left the room.

"What's the matter? I don't think I've ever seen you so tired. And don't blame it on the ride."

Dorian buried his hands in his hair, and then scraped them down his face. "You know what it is."

"Eleanor."

"I don't know what to do, Anne Clara."

"Tell me."

"I feel like I'm going mad. It gets worse every day."

"How so?"

"The more I'm with her, the more I..." He had never said it aloud. "The more I love her."

Once it was out he couldn't stop. "She's everything I didn't know I needed. I wake up each morning and promise to keep my distance, and then I see her and do just the opposite. I'm terrified I'm putting her at risk, but I can't stay away from her."

"I thought you felt better about it after my visit to court last spring," Anne Clara said.

"I did. After you met with her I was elated. I suppose I felt I wasn't an idiot, imagining she cared for me. I don't know what good I thought it would do."

"Do you think she feels as strongly?"

He paused, his heart heavy in his chest. "I know she does. I almost wish she didn't."

"How far have you taken it?"

"She stopped me, thank HighGod, when I couldn't stop myself."

Anne Clara took a few thoughtful moments. "What of Gregory? Does he suspect?"

Dorian threw down his napkin. "That's the most damnable part of it all. I don't think he does. Gregory is so used to everyone agreeing with him and doing his bidding I think it's beyond his imagining. I hope he's not so naïve when he's king."

He wanted his sister to believe him. "How can I look him in the face, knowing I'm in love with his wife? I hate myself for it. I go back and forth, wanting to strangle him for how he treats her and wanting to encourage him so she hates him. It's disgusting."

"Can you retreat from him?

Dorian snorted. "You know I can't. You don't just retreat from the Crown Prince of Cartheigh. Besides, you know what he's done for me. I'd still be a soldier. I might be dead. He made me into something."

She took his hand. "He didn't make you into anything. He just saw what was already there."

"And this is how I thank him for it. Gregory has his flaws. Believe me, I know the worst of them. But he has goodness in him as well. I have hope he will be a fine ruler someday. I can't hate him. We've been through too much together. And even if I did I'm too entrenched."

His throat constricted. He could not remember the last time he cried. He had not shed a tear at his parents' funerals, or through the violence of his military career. He rubbed a rough fist across his eyes and hoped Anne Clara hadn't noticed.

"I'm not my own man, sister," he said. "It weighs on me."

She shook her head. "Don't say that. I wish you had been at the Second Sunday Ball and not here with me. It could've all been different."

"No, you needed me. I would not change it."

Anne Clara wrapped her arms around her swollen belly. "I would offer you a solution, Dorian, but for all my heart I can think of none," she said.

He stared into his whiskey as if it might provide the answer that eluded them both. He took a drink, but familiar taste and smell brought him no comfort. "I know it. I know it too well."

"What will you do?"

"I'll enjoy my time with you and Ransom and the children. I'll stomach a visit with our dear brother Abram. Then I'll return to Eclatant and serve them both. I couldn't stay away if I tried."

It took Eleanor and Gregory and their party three days to reach the North Country. They followed the Clarity River, skirting Maliana on the way. For a few hours Eleanor could see the silver turrets of Eclatant shining on the hillside. They met a light mist on the second morning as they left the home of a wealthy cattle farmer. It became a drizzle as they traveled north, and it didn't let up. Chou Chou complained in her pocket. Eleanor finally snapped at him to shut his beak, at least it was dry in there. The damp crept inside her clothes and she shivered, even though the mountains trapped the fiercest weather on the Svelyan side of the border. She imagined it must be miserable in winter, and understood why the farms and towns were few and far between.

They stopped for lunch and Gregory pointed at a low hill. "On the other side are the Great Marshes," he said. He took a bite of dried beef and pointed east. "It's said that Caleb Desmarais's farm was somewhere in that valley, but it's long since disappeared. Wild unicorns still live in the Marsh. If we're lucky we might see them."

They ate quickly and mounted again. The Marshes were passable by only one road, the Path of Nine Bridges, so named for the crossing points where the land became too boggy to support travelers. Eleanor strained for a sight of the wild unicorns. Gregory asked Thunderhead, his falcon, to fly high and see what he could see. The bird took off and disappeared against the cloudy sky. Chou Chou poked his head out of Eleanor's cloak.

"Such speed," he said with admiration.

"Yes, he's fast, but he eats rats," said Eleanor.

"Point taken."

When Thunderhead returned he reported to Gregory like any sharp lieutenant. He had seen a group of mares and a foal two miles east.

"Thank you, Thunderhead. Good work."

Teardrop pricked her ears. "We should call them. They will hear us."

"Maybe," said Gregory. "What do you think, Vigor?"

Vigor tossed his head up and down. "If they are mares and I call, they will come."

"You should cover your ears, Eleanor," Gregory said.

"My ears? Why?" She got her answer as Vigor let out a piercing cry, almost a screech. She clapped her hands on the sides of her head. Chou Chou twisted in her pocket and scratched her through the thick wool.

Gregory laughed. "That's why."

They waited for a few minutes, watching the horizon.

"They are coming," Teardrop said.

Vigor and Thunderhead nodded. Eleanor didn't see anything at first, until she caught flashes of white. Four mares and a foal leapt over the pools of water and landed easily on solid ground. They stopped about twenty paces away. The mares nudged the little one behind them, but it kept peeking at the visitors from behind their tails.

Vigor called out. "We send you greetings."

The wild mares danced on their hind legs.

"I am called Vigor, and this is Teardrop." He did not bother introducing any of the humans. "We are passing through on our way to the place where the dragons sleep. We won't disturb you, but we wanted to pay our respects."

One of the mares stepped in front of the others. Eleanor supposed if you could say a unicorn spoke with an accent, she did. "Our stallion is Terin."

"I have heard of him, even in the cities of men where we live. Please send him my regards."

The wild mare nodded. "We will. It is good to see a friend of man remember to show respect. You will have easy passage here."

Vigor thanked her. The first mare nipped at the others and got them moving. The foal bucked and capered. She snorted and pushed it in line with the others. Soon they were white dots on the horizon again.

Gregory reached over and squeezed Eleanor's thigh. "You don't see that everyday." He called to the soldiers. "Move out!"

As Eleanor took up her rein, she noticed Teardrop looking after the wild mares. Eleanor wondered if she could still see them. "Teardrop? Are you ready?"

Teardrop fell in behind Vigor. "Does it make you sad when you see the wild unicorns?" Eleanor asked her.

"No," said Teardrop. "Not sad. They have their allegiances. I have mine. It's a different life. But no thinking being can help imagining herself in someone else's footsteps. At some point we all ask, what if my path had been different?"

Eleanor knew just what she meant.

The terrain itself could not be called beautiful, but it demanded respect. There were no trees, just damp hills and sparse grass bunching up on each other as they rolled toward the mountains. They passed two shipments of newly mined Fire-iron being sent south. Gregory stopped and spoke with the transport guards, a rough mix of soldiers and martial magicians.

The Clarity River wound down from the Scaled Mountains and through the North Country on its way toward Maliana. Once it reached the port town of Navigation Ford it widened out, but up here it was rocky and wild. Raw Fire-iron traveled south in clunky horse drawn carts until it could be loaded onto barges in the Ford. Transport guards ensured the precious cargo got there.

"Dorian served on transport when he first came north," said Gregory.

Eleanor kept her reply casual. "Oh?"

"He was promoted within a month. Unheard of, really, but General Clayborne had never been so impressed with a lieutenant." Gregory's chest swelled with pride, as if her were talking about his own offspring instead of his friend. "You've seen his skill with a blade...but his men loved him, too...and he singlehandedly dispatched a Kellish magician bent on stealing a shipment of raw iron. Clayborne brought him south a few weeks later. He still had a gash on his chin when I met him." Gregory smiled at the memory before trotting ahead.

By the evening of the third day the journey lost its romance. Eleanor was wet through and her rear-end was sore. She longed for a cup of hot tea and a crackling fire.

"We'll soon reach Peaksend Village," said Gregory.

"Good," Eleanor said. It had been several hours since they passed any settlements.

"Don't get your hopes up. It's nothing but miners' cabins and a dry goods merchant."

He did not exaggerate. She saw only a few women in the village, who seemed to be peddling themselves over any dry goods, and no children. Eleanor was on the far side of town before the last of their party passed the first cabins. They came to a fork in the road.

"Where does it go?" she asked.

"To Peaksend Castle." Gregory pointed east. "And the soldier's encampment."

Several hundred squat cabins cowered in Peaksend's gloomy shadow. Granite turrets loomed over the camp like a stern father wagging disciplinary fingers at his errant children. Peaksend had none of Eclatant's graceful angles. There were no grounds, just a steep path up the craggy mountainside. Castle or not, the whole scene depressed her. She could not believe Dorian had spent years up here.

They pressed on. Eleanor was about to break her resolve against complaining when Gregory stopped Vigor.

"Here we are," he said. She eased Teardrop beside Vigor and looked down over a narrow valley. It was as if they had stumbled upon an oversized anthill. Men hauled carts loaded with digging tools and huge hunks of meat. Chunks of raw Fire-iron, wrapped in the thick hides of various animals, were loaded onto rough horse-drawn carts and dragged out of the valley. Merchants gathered in noisy clusters around piles of used hides; an earthy rainbow of browns, tans, reds and blacks. The hides, known as dragon robes, absorbed the Fire-iron's heat and held it forever. Magicians believed the robes held warmth because they had once held life, a fact Eleanor had always found fascinating. Her own great-grandfather had made his fortune in dragon robes. An unlucky herd of sheep grazed in rickety paddocks outside the Gate, blissfully unaware they would all end up as a combination of dragon feed and cooling skins.

There were at least fifty unicorns at work, some mounted, some wandering free. A few stood watch at the Gate but more came and went from the twelve cavernous openings in the mountainside leading into the mines themselves.

"We move the dragons from cave to cave." Gregory pointed at the six caves that glowed orange and spewed thick black smoke at regular intervals. "Those caves are active; there are dragons living in them. Those over there—" He turned to two caves that had lost their hot glow but still leaked smoke. "—are inactive, but the Fire-iron is still too hot for extraction. And those four quiet ones are being mined right now."

Only the unicorns entered the active caves. Most had bushels of raw meat strung over their backs. *It must be too hot for humans,* Eleanor thought.

The men did come and go from the smoking inactive mines. They carried animal skins down into the caverns to cool the iron.

"The smoke must be horrible for them," she said.

Gregory nodded. "It is, but there's no other way and the pay is good. Men come up here from all over Cartheigh to do this work. It doesn't kill them, if they don't stay too long, and we have magicians who cast spells to clear the air. The cooling is the worst. The extracting is dark but not very dangerous."

Eleanor's brow furrowed.

"And yes, I have been down there myself," Gregory said. "Don't give me that look."

"What look?"

"The one you always give me when you think I'm being a pampered dandy."

"I never—I don't know what you're talking about—"

He laughed. "Peace, sweetheart, here are our quarters."

With two rooms down and a large bedroom upstairs, their cabin was larger than the others, but still rustic. Simple wood furniture sat on a floor with no rugs. Dragon robes made of different animal skins covered the bed; fox, bear, wolf, rabbit. A line of rusty hooks on the bedroom wall served as a wardrobe. They would take their meals with the miners in the eating hall.

"So this is the Desmarais version of the great outdoors," Eleanor said. She opened the shutters to let out the musty air. She took her mother's music box from her saddle bad and set it on the rough table beside the bed.

"Do you plan on playing a tune for the miners? Dancing a jig in that broken slipper?"

Eleanor didn't know what possessed her to drag the music box and the cracked slipper from Maliana to Solsea to the Dragon Mines. "I couldn't wear it even if the miners planned a ball at Peaksend. It's too fragile. I've had dreams of it falling to pieces on my foot."

In truth the dream had become an ever more frequent nightmare. The slipper always shattered as soon as it touched the floor. Glass sprayed across marble in glittering needles. Eleanor fell on her knees, desperately sweeping crystals into her bleeding hands, but she could never catch all the shards.

She unwittingly rubbed her palms on her tunic, but Gregory had already moved on. "I told you it wouldn't be much."

She flopped down on the warm robes. "I love it. I'm so tired I wouldn't care if we slept on a pile of new Fire-iron."

"Wife, you're soaking my bed. As your prince and your husband I command you to remove those wet clothes immediately."

She threw a pillow at him. "You first."

"You know you won't have to ask twice." He was not nearly as tired as she was.

When their other belongings arrived two days later Eleanor unpacked her extra riding leggings. Her dresses were too valuable for the rough terrain. While it never poured rain, some form of precipitation fell every day, be it mist or drizzle or lazy plunking drops. She imagined the curses of the laundresses at Eclatant should she return with a trunk full of mud-stained hemlines. Eleanor doubted she would see a petticoat for the next six weeks, not such a bad thought. She relished the idea of free movement from dawn until dusk.

Chou Chou, on the other hand, relished nothing. After a few half-hearted attempts at keeping up with Thunderhead on his exploratory flights Chou gave up and rarely left the cabin.

"I stick out like a tulip among ragweed out there," he complained. "Everything is gray and brown. A Giant Buzzard will likely eat me. I've heard they live around here."

"They only eat carrion," said Gregory.

"Regardless, I should never have come. I need sun."

"Oh, Chou, hush," Eleanor said. "Speaking of eating, why don't you try one of those tasty moles Thunderhead brought home for you?"

He retreated in a pique and sat muttering by the fire. "Parrot abuse, I tell you."

King Casper had sent Gregory to the mines to ensure the smooth leadership transitions of a new general and a new mine boss. Casper had not planned on the latter, but the former boss met an early end when a horse bolted and overturned its heavily laden cart. A cascade of warm Fire-iron crushed him. The king thought Gregory's presence would keep things in order while everyone adjusted to the new regime.

Gregory's understanding of the mines and his rapport with the men who worked them impressed Eleanor. Each morning he kissed her and disappeared into the morning haze as she huddled under the dragon robes. He visited the soldiers in their camp. He helped fix broken equipment. He consulted with the magicians over air quality. After several hours of searching she finally found him one afternoon as he emerged from the shaft of one of the inactive mines. Shiny gray dust covered him from head to toe.

He spent hours with the working unicorns, listening to their reports from the active caves and asking after the well being of the dragons.

Were they eating well? Were any breeding? Had there been any illness? The unicorns themselves also needed constant tending. They came to the mines in six-month stints before returning to the Paladine for rest and a change of scenery. Gregory kept a lookout for those who might need to return early.

One morning he called a young stallion from the entrance to one of the active mines. "What's your name?" he asked.

"Chalice, sire," the stallion said.

"You look weary. Is this your first posting here?"

"Yes." Like most unicorns, he did not elaborate unless asked specifics.

"Go have a rest. I'll see you cycle south when the relief arrives." Gregory ran a hand over Chalice's smooth foreleg. Chalice nodded and walked to the barn.

"What's wrong with him?" Eleanor asked.

"I'm not sure," said Gregory, "but he didn't seem right. Being up here takes a lot out of the young ones. I think the dragons drain something from them. I'll keep him on gate patrol for the next few days."

"Will he get better?"

A gruff voice answered her. "Aye, Your Highness, he'll be better in no time. He'll be go south and be happy to return in the spring." The new mine boss, Matt Thromba, was a fierce-looking bald fellow, with a stringy gray beard he braided into three long twists.

"Why?" she asked.

"They don't mind it up here in the badlands," he said. "It would be their natural habitat, anyway. They just need to learn to control their energy, like."

"What do you mean?" said Eleanor.

"For my life, sire, I never knew a woman to ask so many questions." Thromba winked at Eleanor. "Don't know if I could stand it, even from such a pretty thing."

Gregory clapped him on the shoulder. "Aah, Thromba, you haven't had a conversation with a woman you weren't paying to be there in years."

Thromba laughed in a series of snorts. "Ain't it the truth, Highness, ain't it the truth."

Thromba might feign annoyance at Eleanor's curiosity, but she could tell he and the other miners respected her for it. They watched with admiration as Eleanor and Teardrop followed Gregory and Vigor on long scouting rides and gave her thoughtful answers to her never-ending stream of questions. They even offered her shots of their preciously horded rock gin. To pass the time she joined them at cards and strikestick, and even though she lost every game they didn't mind. Their colorful language became as polite as any Godsman's when they saw her coming. The euphemisms she overheard when they weren't aware she was listening were enlightening, to say the least.

One cold night Thromba invited Eleanor and Gregory to join the miners for an outdoor roast. One of the men had killed a passing buck, and the smell of fresh meat permeated the air. She sat in front of Gregory, between his bent knees. He draped a dragon robe over the two of them and wrapped his arms around her. She leaned into him. He kissed her temple and the fuzz on his cheek was pleasantly scratchy. Thromba's old terrier inched so close to the cooking meat Eleanor feared the dog would singe his hair.

"What about the dragons?" she asked. "Won't they smell the meat and…come out?"

"They rarely come out. We feed 'em so well there's no need for it," said Thromba.

Eleanor enjoyed the excellent meal, and the men's stories of mishaps and adventures, rookie miners and grouchy dragons. The drink flowed and a few of the men sang tavern songs. Gregory joined them for the choruses. As the evening wound down a young man Eleanor knew only as Jeb spoke to Thromba.

"Come, Mattie, give us a song," he said.

"No, boy," said Matt.

"Yes, please, sir, one of those old ones, that make us think of home."

"Why do you want to feel sad? Do you want to make the lady sad?"

"On the contrary, Mister Thromba, I would love to hear your song," said Eleanor.

Thromba shrugged. "All right, then." He didn't stand, or even sit up straight. His high, sweet voice belied his rough exterior.

I left a girl in the south
Where the Clarity flows
As soft as the silken
Gown of my rose
I come to the north
To work in this hole
To buy her a ring
So she'll salvage my soul
It's dark down below
But in the dark I can see
The light in her eyes
When she looked at me
Maybe the light
Is nothing but fire
Maybe the dragon
Will come when I tire
And carry me back
Where the Clarity flows
I fear that another
Has stolen my rose.

His voice tapered off, and the men watched the flames. Thromba broke the silence. "Ah, there you have it, boys. Another cheerful miners' tune to end the night."

"It was lovely, Matt, thank you." Eleanor wiped her eyes. She and Gregory excused themselves to retire.

"It must be lonely for the men, so far from their families," she said, as they got ready for bed.

Gregory pulled off his boots. "Oh, I don't think they dwell on it when they're sober. They like the pay just fine."

"Are they ever allowed a visit home?"

"We can't exactly stop the mining so they can go on holiday, Eleanor. Besides, we have a two-year wait list for these jobs. It can't be that bad."

"They don't have any choices closer to home."

"It's late. I don't want to discuss this right now."

And the conversation ended. Eleanor puttered around the room, waiting for him to fall asleep as he usually did when he'd been drinking. At the sound of his even breathing she slid under the robes. She wasn't angry. They had been getting along fine, but she couldn't help but wish Dorian could have heard Thromba's song. It would have made sense to him.

CHAPTER 20

The Most Stubborn, Disobediant, Brave, Exasperating Woman

"Eleanor, come, wake up. You'll want to see this."

She squinted into Gregory's face. "What is it?" she grumbled.

"Don't you want to see a dragon?"

"Are they transferring them?" She sat up.

He grinned and yanked back the covers. "Hurry, fair lady. Dragons wait for no one, not even a Desmarais princess."

She jumped out of bed and pulled a long tunic over her head. She bounced around on one foot as she tried to hop into her leggings. "Where are my boots?"

He threw them to her and she yanked them on. She didn't bother brushing her hair, just twisted it in a thick knot around itself. She wrapped a robe around her shoulders, grabbed an apple from the fruit bowl, and followed Gregory out the door and into the mine yard.

It looked like all the mine personnel, magic or not, plus half of the soldiers, had assembled in the yard. They held blazing torches in the dim early morning light. The unicorns formed a white wall between the seventh cave and the first. Eleanor waved at Teardrop, who joined the end of the line.

Gregory elbowed through the crowd and Eleanor ran to keep up. He stopped beside Matt Thromba. Thromba had never led a transfer, and the pressure showed in his nervous hand ringing.

"You'll be fine, you have my utmost faith," said Gregory.

Thromba exhaled. "Thank you. I'm glad to hear you say it."

Gregory took Eleanor's hand, and they moved behind the line of men and unicorns. Thromba called out, and the men hushed.

"All right, boys, you know the plan. We have thirty-six dragons to transfer."

Thirty-six! thought Eleanor as Thromba went on.

"...and sixteen males. From cave seven, which will go inactive, to cave one, which has been mined of all Fire-iron and is ready to go active again. Tremor!" he called.

One of the unicorns broke from the crowd. "We are ready, Thromba."

Tremor walked to the entrance of the seventh cave, and called out in the same shrill whinny Vigor had used to summon the wild mares in the marsh. As answering cry came from the bowels of the cave. The orange glow brightened, and Eleanor could feel the temperature rising, as if she were approaching the hot ovens in the kitchen at Eclatant. Two unicorns trotted from the mouth of the cave and whinnied again.

A different cry answered them. It was a sound like none Eleanor had ever heard. She could not call it a roar, or a snort, or a scream, but it had elements of all of them. Others joined the first, until the very air vibrated. Streams of pebbles slid down the steep valley walls. She grabbed Gregory's arm as the first dragon emerged.

It was at least as tall as her father's house in Maliana, with a dark green hide that sparkled in the glow of the men's torches. It shrieked and threw back its head, spraying fire into the air. Tremor reared on his hind legs. He whinnied and shook his head. The dragon collapsed on its front legs with a rumbling growl, and crept close to the stallion's face.

Eleanor found she saw a resemblance between the two creatures. Both had long, thin faces, although the dragon had three horns and teeth hung over its black lips like giant arrowheads. Long, folded scales sprouted down its neck, in a sort of mane, and tapered off at neatly folded brownish green wings. Its tail, capped with more long scales, swept the ground. Powerful rear legs clenched with its shifting weight, and it clicked the talons on its shorter arms. It stared at Tremor with half-closed orange eyes. She could not hear what, if anything, Tremor said to the dragon, but its growl subsided to a low rumble. It sounded absurdly like a cat's purr heard through the court caller's megaphones.

The dragon stood and lumbered toward the first cave. It passed the other unicorns, slowing every few steps, and they responded with reassuring whinnies. The next dragon appeared, followed by two more of Tremor's unicorn guides. The first dragon called to the second, who screamed once in return. Both creatures seemed eager to get underground.

The transfer continued for nearly an hour without much fanfare. Eleanor thought she must have miscounted when there was a break in the procession.

"This will be the last one," said Gregory. "I wonder what's taking so long."

Tremor paced at the mouth of the cave. Dark smoke rolled from under the ground. Tremor sent two of his fellows down below, and when after a few minutes they did not return, Thromba called to him to send two more.

Without warning, and with an earsplitting scream, and a new dragon burst from the cave. Stubby horns revealed her as a doe.

"Ho!" Gregory yelled. "Nestlings!"

Three baby dragons, about the size of saddle horses, squealed and circled their mother's feet. She screamed and shot fire at the wall of men and unicorns. The men fell back. The unicorns just shut their eyes. As

Gregory steered Eleanor toward the cabin she caught a flash of white behind the dragon's legs.

Teardrop had somehow been pushed from the line. She was pinned between the raging dragon and the canyon walls. As the dragon backed and reared, her massive tail, all wrathful muscle, swung in a deadly pendulum.

"Teardrop!" Eleanor screamed.

Teardrop zigged, looking for a way around the mother dragon. The dragon's tail came down hard and clipped the mare across the shoulder. Teardrop slammed into the rock wall. She cowered, stunned and heaving.

"Teardrop!" Eleanor yanked free of Gregory's grip.

"Eleanor, stop!"

She ran past the startled guards and into the chaos.

"Get back!" Tremor snorted.

"I won't!" She yelled to be heard over the dragon. "I'm going to help her."

"You can't, and we must control this situation."

"I will, damnit!" She tried to get around the stallion but he stepped in front of her again. "Get out of my way!" she stormed.

He lowered his head. "If you insist on this foolery at least let me help you."

Gregory was shoving past the guards, but she climbed onto Tremor's back before he could reach her.

"Eleanor!" Gregory screamed.

She clung to Tremor's mane as he raced at the dragon. Her eyelashes stuck together in the blinding heat. Tremor dodged and wheeled as the dragon spit fire. Two other unicorns flanked them.

Tremor skidded to a stop. Eleanor leapt off and ran to Teardrop.

"Hurry!" Tremor called.

Foam dripped from Teardrop's muzzle as she pressed against the wall. She wasn't bleeding—her thick hide was nearly impenetrable—but a raised welt marred her shoulder. Her eyes rolled.

"Teardrop," Eleanor tried to keep her voice calm over the screams of the dragon as it went after Tremor. "Help me. Take me back to Gregory."

Teardrop swung her head at Eleanor's voice. Her dark eyes came into focus. "Why are you here?" she whispered. "You will be killed."

"So you must take me out."

Teardrop nodded, and Eleanor grabbed her mane and pulled herself onto the mare's back. "Go, now," she called. "I need you to get me past this dragon."

Teardrop scraped at the ground with one hoof and pricked her ears. She watched Tremor and his helpers and the mother dragon. She spotted an opening and dove for it. The dragon spun and swung her tail again. Eleanor held on as Teardrop leapt. They barely cleared the spinning spikes.

They came to a stop past the line of unicorns, and Eleanor's legs gave out when she slid to the ground. Gregory caught her, cursing and kissing her.

"Dammit, Eleanor," he said. "You're the most stubborn, disobedient, brave, exasperating woman."

She sat on the ground with her head between her knees. The magicians bustled around Teardrop. They tried to examine her injury, but she snorted them away. She stood over Eleanor, breathing down the back of her neck.

Eleanor raised her head as Tremor called a dozen of his fellows into the skirmish. The doe blew fire, but more unicorns pressed in and she backed down. Her children squeaked and smoked around her. Tremor stepped from the line and knelt on one knee. To Eleanor's amazement one of the nestlings crept out from under its mother's belly and slunk toward him. The doe hissed a warning. Tremor stood, and gently touched the baby dragon with his horn.

The doe exhaled a long blast of fire, but this time there was no fight in it. The other baby dragons came forward, and Tremor touched them all before nudging them toward the new cave with his muzzle. Their mother let our several low whistles and followed them.

Once the doe disappeared under the ground, Thromba ran to Eleanor and Gregory. "Dear HighGod, sire," he said. "It was a botch-up, and the princess nearly roasted."

"No, Thromba," Gregory said. "We both know you can never tell how the does with nestlings will react. Last year we lost three men to a new mother. Not so bad, really." He knelt beside Eleanor.

"Are you angry with me?" she asked.

"No," he said. "How can I be angry? But you must be more careful."

He helped her stand on her shaky legs. She ran a hand over Teardrop's withers and the white hide twitched under her fingers. "Does it hurt?" she asked.

"Some, but we heal quickly."

"Princess," said an airy voice behind her. It was Tremor.

"Thank you," she said. "I'm sorry if I made things more complicated."

Tremor lowered his head. "I thank you," he said. "For reminding me of what is important."

Six weeks in the North Country is a long time. Eleanor had seen enough to fill several Fests worth of dinner conversation, and she had enjoyed her husband's company. He was as tender and sober as she had known him, and he continued to impress her with his diligent attention to the mine operations. Their disagreements were mostly around his habit of destroying any semblance of order in their tiny cabin. Eleanor and Gregory had never occupied the same space for more than a night, and never without the assistance of a troop of servants dedicated to preserving order around the chaotic prince.

Eleanor could hardly blame him. He had never needed to take

care of himself. On the other hand, years of meticulously fighting off dust in the hayloft had left her fastidious to a fault. Gregory's mining tools, leftover dishes, and muddy boots all over the cabin drove her to distraction. She asked the miners to bring her a washboard, and took to scrubbing his clothes as well as her own. She might respect the miners, but she did not want to smell like them, nor bed someone who did. In light of past arguments, however, their spats were quickly forgotten.

Unfortunately, her goal of falling desperately in love with him again did not happen. Up here she had only a bunch of dirty men and scaly beasts for competition, and she had no doubt Gregory would return to their old routine when they returned to the palace. Maybe the past month would have made up for what she faced at home if she hadn't known any different, but she did. By now Dorian had returned to Eclatant, and she was no closer to keeping her promise to Rosemary and forgetting him than she had been the morning of their tumble in the broom closet.

She missed him, simply, every day and in every new experience. She stored up anecdotes to tell him, hoping she could do justice to the people and land and creatures around her. She wanted to hear him retell his stories of his first year here, now that she could appreciate what it must have been like for a boy of seventeen fresh from the lush forests of the Lake District. Twice she sat down to write to him, but nothing she wanted to say was safe to put to paper. She tucked the half-finished notes into a feed sack and asked Teardrop to take them into one of the active caves. She fed her words to the dragons' breath.

She took long rides across the foothills when Gregory was otherwise occupied, as he would not approve of her wandering on her own. She wondered what he thought could bother her with Teardrop's protection, but decided the solitude was worth it. It would be in short supply when they returned to Maliana.

A week before they were to leave she called her mare to a halt at the top of a steep ridge. She recognized the gray dot that was Thunderhead by the white patch on his breast. He floated lazily on the currents. Even a mile from the Mines the smell of Fire-iron dust hung in the air. She took off her gloves and buried her hands under Teardrop's warm mane. The wind blew into her eyes and she wiped them.

"We will be going home soon," said Teardrop. "It won't be long until you see him."

"How do you do that?" asked Eleanor.

"What?"

"Tell me what is on my mind before I say it."

"I can see him, inside you, looking out."

Eleanor nodded. In her way, Teardrop always made perfect sense.

CHAPTER 21

MY HIGHEST REGARD

ELEANOR STOOD AT THE foot of her bed, unpacking her personal valise. Jewelry, perfumes, books and stationery were spread over the light silk bedcover. She had opened all the windows, and was enjoying the warm MidAutumn morning after so many long damp days in the North Country.

Chou Chou fluttered through the window and lit on her head. He flapped his wings as she leaned over and untangled a pearl necklace.

"Ouch, Chou." His talons dug into her scalp. He dropped a folded sheet of plain white paper into the valise. She crossed her eyes and looked into his upside-down face. "Get down, you're making me dizzy," she said.

He dropped onto the bed. "From Frog," he whispered. "He asked that you burn it."

Eleanor glanced at Pansy hanging clothes in the wardrobe. "What else did he say?"

"You know Frog," said Chou.

She nodded. Dorian had named Frog for his croaking voice, but the raven rarely used it with anyone but his master.

Eleanor excused herself loudly and went to the bathing room. She closed the door behind her. She leaned on the tub, afraid to read the note. Eleanor and Gregory had arrived at Eclatant late the previous night and gone straight to bed. She and Dorian had not spoken since he left Solsea.

Her hands shook as she unfolded the paper.

> *Dear Lady,*
>
> *Let me apologize again for my conduct when last we were together. It was wholly my fault. Please do not worry. Nothing need be different or strange between us. You can trust I will never put you in such a position again. I am, as always, at your disposal.*

Her disappointment grew as she reread the note. If she hoped for a declaration of some sort she would not get it. She tried to be sensible. He was right. There was no hope in all this.

She left the bathing room and gathered some stationery on the way to her desk. She sat down and picked up her quill and ink, and on second thought put the thick vellum aside and took out a piece of scrap paper.

> *Dear Sir,*
>
> *As I said on that day, your actions caused no offense. It was a mutual transgression, and you are right, it should not happen again. I bid you know you remain in my highest regard.*

She folded the note and held it to her lips.

"Here, Chou. Please take this to Frog."

When the parrot had gone she lit a candle and did as Frog had asked. Dorian's note curled up and disappeared into a pile of ash on the table. She pressed her fingers against her temples, trying to relieve the pressure behind her eyes.

Eleanor was determined there would be no discomfort between them. She went straight to Dorian at the first opportunity and asked if he would join her in the library to review some books on the relationship between unicorns and dragons.

"I would love to hear your opinions. The theories on the Bond are so varied," she said.

He put on a cheerful face, even through his halting voice. "As I have said, I am at your disposal."

"This afternoon, then. Chou and I will meet you there." And so they continued their friendship that was not a friendship. Barely tolerable, but better than nothing.

Eleanor's interest in the Bond did not wane. Whenever a topic caught her attention she immersed herself in it. Last spring, she collected books on unicorn handling. After the dreaded attack in the garden, fairies became her subject of choice, then Mendaen culture. Two weeks after her return from the Dragon Mines she had barely skimmed the surface of the ocean of literature on unicorns, dragons, and the royal family. She sat by a wide window in one of the studies adjoining the library waiting for Dorian to return from the Paladine and join her. Chou dozed on the arm of the chair. She propped her feet on a painted wooden stool and turned the pages of a battered book in her lap. *Scale, Steed, and Scepter: Theories on the Triple Alliance of Cartheigh.* She sipped a cup of tea as she read.

Caleb's Horn is a neither legend nor a reality. It is true the object itself exists, and is kept under the heaviest of Unicorn Guard at Eclatant Palace. What no one knows, however, is whether it has the powers ascribed to it. Most scholars believe the Horn holds the key to the allegiance of the unicorns to the Desmarais family.

It is not written, in any book, exactly how Caleb Desmarais secured the loyalty of the herds. It is commonly thought he must have had the help of magic. Some say he was a magician himself, while others believe he had outside assistance. Believers agree, however, on the role of the Horn in his success.

Unicorn foals shed their horns several times as they mature. According to the Horn legend, Caleb took the first horn of the great stallion Eclatant, the one he shed as a foal under Caleb's care, and sealed it in a piece of warm Fire-iron. Through some unknown sorcery the mystic residue in the chunk of Fire-iron bound Eclatant and his descendents in service to the Desmarais family. The Fire-iron hardened, became impenetrable, and is now known as Caleb's Horn. Believers say as long as the Horn remains in the hands of the Desmarais family, the unicorns will be loyal.

The royal family neither confirms nor denies its powers. It is possible even they are not sure whether the Horn is the key to their power. The unicorns themselves, when asked, offer no explanation for their dedication to the royal family. The Desmarais, however, are taking no chances.

Eleanor knew of the Horn, as it was one of the famous magical objects in Cartheigh, but her current obsession lent it a new fascination. *The key to the Bond! Right here at Eclatant*, she thought. But where? She'd never seen any sign of it.

As she mulled over possible locations the study door swung open. She looked up with a smile on her face, and caught herself before it could falter. The visitor was not Dorian, but Gregory. He informed her that her presence was required at lunch, as some visiting Kellish duke had unexpectedly arrived with his wife in tow.

"I need you to converse with her. About womanly things," Gregory said. He looked over her relatively simple afternoon gown. "You'll have to smarten up."

She closed her book. "Of course," she said, trying to hide her disappointment. She stood, and it occurred to her that the answer to her question was in the room with her. "Gregory, where does the family keep Caleb's Horn?"

"The Horn?" Gregory repeated. "It's in a secret chamber, here in the palace. Why?"

"Oh, I'm just interested. I've been reading up on it." Chou landed on Eleanor's head and yawned. "Would you take me to see it?" she asked.

Gregory shook his head. "No. Few people ever see it. Only my father and I may touch it. I doubt a woman has ever crossed the chamber's threshold."

"I'm a Desmarais now. Doesn't that count?"

"Unfortunately not. I can't think of anyone besides the Unicorn Guard who has...oh, except Ezra Oliver."

She scowled her opinion, and Gregory laughed. "Come now, he's been the Chief Magician for a century, and it's a magical national treasure."

She gathered her belongings, and Chou flapped around her head like a living hat. "Please," he said. "Must you bob so?"

She ignored him. "Reading about it is one thing. Seeing it is another. Can't you ask your father?"

Gregory's nostrils flared, and she could tell she would get no further. "You have a unicorn. You've been to the Dragon Mines. Isn't that enough?"

"I suppose it will have to be," she said.

"Try reading about something else. Sewing perhaps. Or maybe childbirth. Both useful topics."

"Darling, I think your green silk gown would be just perfect for today's lunch," said Chou. "The one with the lace bodice? Don't you agree?"

Eleanor took Chou's hint. She excused herself before she said something she would regret.

Dorian knew it was a bad idea to accept Gregory's request for a fencing match. Gregory hated losing, but he also hated when someone else lost for him, and Dorian never let him run away with any contest. Gregory had years of training with a sword, and few men at court other than Dorian presented a challenge. Gregory's practice in the ring couldn't compete with Dorian's combat experience, or his long arm span.

They had both stripped to their undershirts in the lingering LowAutumn heat. Dorian squinted against the glare of the washed-out sky and wiped at the bead of sweat trickling down his nose. Gregory took a cloth from Melfin, mopped his own face and threw the cloth across the deep grass of the topiary garden. It snagged on one of the tall hedges and waved at both of them like a white flag of surrender. Dorian wished Gregory would just accept the inevitable, but the prince ran a hand through his wet auburn hair and tightened his grip on his sword.

Dorian lifted his own sword and the ching of Fire-iron on Fire-iron rang through the garden again. Advance, retreat, feint, parry, counter parry, thrust, thrust, thrust. Gregory's nose was a few finger widths away from Dorian's own. Blasts of air shot into Dorian's face through their crossed swords. They strained against each other for a few moments, until Dorian turned the edge of his blade and bore down hard. Gregory's sword spun out of his hands and landed on the gravel path several paces away. The thud was embarrassing, even to Dorian. The sword could have done Gregory the favor of a dramatic, upright landing.

"Fuck an ogre!"

Dorian raised his eyebrows. "That was colorful, even for you."

Gregory retrieved his sword, took another cloth from the servant, and wiped the dust off the thin blade. He called for wine and whiskey. Melfin retrieved the drinks from the wicker basket left under a decorative cherry tree. Gregory handed the whiskey to Dorian and they both sat in the grass. It was not so lush this time of year, and scratched at Dorian's rear-end through his calfskin leggings. The gardeners couldn't drag enough buckets of water out here to keep it green this late in the season. Flecks of brown shot through the dark green.

"Out with it," Dorian said. "You never stew over anything. You might strain something." Dorian hoped to insult Gregory out of his foul mood, but to no avail.

"That business with Thomas Harper Rowe last summer. I can't put it from my mind. It didn't seem right. Why would Rowe steal those jewels? His family is one of the richest in Cartheigh. He'd been trying for a position in Oliver's office for years, and he was so close to it."

"Have you discussed it with your father?"

"He says what's done is done. Won't hear a word. All he cares about is a new Desmarais heir. Humiliating, having your bloody father question your vigor. As if it's my fault she hasn't caught ag—er...yet."

Somehow Dorian managed to keep his tone light. "The fate of the nation lies in your lap, man. You must start procreating."

"No." Gregory shook his head. "Even if Eleanor pushes out ten children in as many years it won't matter."

Dorian blocked that image from his mind and focused on his best friend in front of him. "Your father would do better to use the talents you have than try to make you into something else."

Gregory's mouth twitched. "Don't get all sweet and sugary on me."

"I'm being about as sugary as this whiskey," Dorian said. "You'll be a great king someday. I've been with you on warships, in the Dragon Mines—"

"In the whorehouses."

Dorian choked on his whiskey. He spit a mouthful on the grass. "Not quite the picture I was painting."

Gregory called for a hunk of cheese and some bread. He chewed thoughtfully for a while. "You know," he said once the bread disappeared, "I don't want you to exert yourself flattering me. You might run out of things to say."

"Oh, no, Your Highness, I could write a sonnet."

Gregory laughed. "Cheeky bastard. Your poetry is fairy shit. Even I know that."

"Forgive me if I disregard your opinion," said Dorian. "I think the last book you picked up voluntarily had no words. Maybe just some sweet little drawings of fairies? A wolf chasing after a few pigs, perhaps?"

Gregory finished his wine in one long swig. "Who needs books when I have you? When I'm king we'll rely on my charisma and good looks and your brains and we'll be unstoppable. Cartheigh will rule the world."

Dorian chuckled.

Gregory stood and offered Dorian a hand up. "Thank you, friend," he said. "I am fortunate among princes to have found the likes of you." He punched Dorian's arm, hard. "As long as we're being sweet and sugary. Melfin! Clean this shit up. I want to visit my wife." He winked at Dorian. "No time like the present to fulfill father's great wish, eh?"

Dorian trailed behind the whistling prince on the short walk back to Eclatant. His arm throbbed, but it was pithy compared to the ache in his chest.

CHAPTER 22

SHENANIGANS

ON ANOTHER FINE MORNING a few days later Eleanor and Gregory and their friends lounged on blankets on the south lawn sharing a picnic breakfast of scones and fruit. Eleanor lay back and watched the fat clouds disappearing behind the great silver bulk of Eclatant. She ran her fingers through the grass.

"What a day," she said. "I think everyone should visit the North for a month so we can all appreciate Maliana. It may be crowded, but at least it's dry."

"Your description will have to be enough for me," said Eliza.

"You never know, Liza dear, you may feel adventurous one day."

"I doubt it. I don't want adventure. I just want a full night's sleep."

Eliza's son, Patrick-Michael, was two months old. She and Patrick-Clark had brought him to Eclatant for a visit and the king's blessing. He was a sweet, fat little thing, but he drove his mother hard with his night feedings.

"When will Patrick-Clark reclaim your bosoms?" teased Anne Iris.

"Just wait," said Eliza. "Someday you'll be sitting in my chair and I won't have any sympathy for you."

"I have plenty of sympathy for you. I just have more sympathy for

Patrick-Clark. Besides, when I have a husband and a baby there will still be enough of me to go around."

Brian choked on his sweet bun. "Please, Anne Iris, I'm trying to eat."

"Speaking of eating," said Margaret, "Have you seen the deliveries to the kitchens? The cooks are preparing for the Harvest Fest invasion."

"Oh, already?" sighed Eleanor.

Gregory tickled her and she sat up. "Sweetheart, you sound positively unfestive." He draped an arm around her and she glanced at Dorian, who was suddenly fascinated by his teacup.

"The Waxing seems like just yesterday," Eleanor said. "I guess we missed the peace and quiet."

Christopher Roffi joined the conversation. "You Cartheans are so formal. You are needing a good Svelyan Fest."

"What makes a Svelyan Fest?" asked Raoul.

"Many, many beers."

Eleanor smiled at Dorian's laughter. It was a sound like no other. "The townsfolk have those Fests every night," he said.

"Perhaps that's what we need. Let's start the Fest right, and put our princess in the mood," said Gregory.

Dorian grinned. "You know, Greg, that's the best idea you've had in a long time."

The next night they met in the royal stables at nine o'clock. Eleanor, Margaret, Anne Iris, and Eliza all wore leggings and tunics. Eleanor had been surprised when Eliza decided to join them.

"Should you leave Patrick-Michael?" Margaret had asked.

"I think the wet-nurse and Patrick-Clark can keep him for one night. Besides, I once heard beer thickens your milk."

The women were nervous, for they knew the king would not approve of their plan. Margaret jumped when the barn door swung open.

Orvid Jones, the apprentice magician who had accompanied Eleanor and Gregory to the Dragon Mines, crept inside and shut the door behind him. He was a timid man, quite unlike most of the blustery magicians Eleanor had met. She liked him.

"Orvid, thank you for coming," she said.

"Yes, Your Highness," he whispered. "I must return to the Covey before Oliver notices I've gone." Orvid shed his shyness once the conjuring began. He gazed at all four women like a theater director sizing up his actors. "This won't do. You're all far too obvious."

He set to work disguising them. First he magically shortened their hair, and Eleanor's blond became bright ginger. Both Anne Iris and Eliza were wrapped in baggy tunics that hid their ample cleavage. Margaret squealed when the stiff whiskers of a small goatee sprouted on her chin.

"Don't worry," said Orvid. "These disguises never last long. You'll be yourselves by morning."

Eleanor thought of Rosemary's spellwork at the Second Sunday Ball as she ran her fingers through her short hair. "I feel naked without it."

"Sweetheart, don't tease me."

Eleanor turned around and burst out laughing. The men had already been subjected to Orvid's handiwork.

Gregory had sandy blond hair and a long handlebar mustache, and wore a seeing glass. Orvid had curled both Roffi and Brian's hair so tightly they appeared to have sheep attached to their heads. Brian had shrunk while Raoul had grown, so they were roughly the same height. Dorian, however, had the worst of it. His dark hair hung down his back and over his shoulders, and a thick beard obscured most of his face.

"Mister Finley is well-known in Maliana, so I disguised his more recognizable features," Orvid explained.

"Orvid would hide the tiger eyes behind a lion's mane," said Gregory.

Dorian scowled. "I won't be able to find my mouth to drink."

Hilarious tears streamed down Eleanor's cheeks. "Don't worry," she choked out. "We'll all assist you."

A groom brought their horses, and each lady climbed up behind one of the men. Margaret sat nervously behind Christopher Roffi. She didn't grab his waist until the last possible second. Eleanor stifled another laugh when his horse lurched sideways and Margaret threw her arms around him. She'd waited for months for the opportunity.

They trotted behind the barn to one of the smaller exits in the back wall of the palace. Gregory had spoken with the guard and he waved them through. They cantered down the Hundred Heralds Street in high spirits.

"How did I end up with no fair lady's arms around me this evening?" lamented Brian.

"We aren't so fair tonight, brother," called Anne Iris as she brushed Dorian's overgrown hair out of her face.

"I'm sure you'll find someone willing before long," said Raoul.

They crossed Smithwick Square and headed for the more decent taverns marking the first blocks of Pasture's End. Gregory and Dorian reined in at a substantial brick establishment where scantily clad women lounged in hammocks on the wide front stoop. The sign hanging from the eaves read The Ogre Bar.

Eleanor dropped to the ground. "Charming. Does that describe the décor or the clientele?"

Dorian's white teeth flashed through his beard. "A bit of both."

The reclining ladies called to them as Roffi opened the door. Eleanor waved away the smell of burnt stew and peered through the thick pipe smoke.

The Ogre Bar was a great square room, full of long wooden tables and benches filled with men of all shapes, sizes and ages. Most were drinking thick ale out of heavy tankards. Behind the bar were several voluptuous young women and a huge bald man in a dirty white shirt. The scar cutting across his lip showed his two jagged front teeth.

"That's the proprietor." Dorian yelled in Eleanor's ear over the shouting and cursing. "He runs a tight ship around here. He won't put up with any shenanigans from these boys."

"I feel very safe," said Eleanor. "Are you sure he didn't name this place after himself?"

Dorian pointed at the walls. They were covered in mural-sized paintings of the Ogre Wars of five hundred years ago. Eleanor shivered at the violent, lifelike portrayals.

"A businessman and an artist," Dorian said, and winked.

Brian and Raoul claimed a table and the women sat while Dorian, Gregory, and Roffi pushed their way through the crowd to the bar. They returned, arms laden with beer tankards, and passed out the drinks. Gregory squeezed in beside Eleanor.

"Remember, I'm a boy," she said.

Roffi raised his glass. "Orvid Jones may be having much genius, but you ladies are still the loveliest here."

"Facial hair and all," said Raoul. Margaret giggled.

Fine Carthean ladies did not drink beer, but the new taste went down easily. The women in the bar, both those that worked there and the other patrons, smelled money and flocked to their table. They slid into the men's laps and whispered HighGod-knows-what in their ears. Eleanor nearly spit her beer back in her tankard when cool hands touched on her own bare neck.

"You look sweet, boy," said a buxom girl younger than herself. Her teeth were yellow. "Can I do for you tonight?"

"I'm fine, thanks," said Eleanor, trying to deepen her voice. Dorian sniggered into his glass across from her.

"Furrball," she said.

The beer flowed and the conversation coarsened. Gregory was already slurring by the time Dorian suggested they order something to eat, and he waved off the suggestion. A dark-haired girl, one from the porch, stationed herself firmly in his lap and he seemed perfectly comfortable. She ran her hands though his hair and dragged her cleavage across his nose each time she reached down the table for a drink. Eleanor caught Dorian's eye, and shrugged. She was having too much fun to be angry with Gregory. She rolled her eyes when he wagged his eyebrows at her over his new friend's shoulder.

Do I even care? The thought swam through her fuzzy mind and she drowned it in a swig of beer. She noticed Margaret was quiet. Eleanor followed her line of sight. Roffi had bellied up to the bar with a pretty barmaid. He wound one of her blond curls around his finger. Margaret smiled weakly and lifted her shoulders. Eleanor squeezed her hand. She tried to distract her by pointing at Brian, who had, as Raoul predicted, found company. Two girls in matching black gowns were dragging him away. He did not reappear for nearly an hour.

"If only Father knew how you spend his money," Anne Iris chided in disgust when he returned to the table.

Brian he leaned back in his chair, all smugness. "Father was a young man once himself."

"You're not so young," his sister grumbled.

A quartet of musicians squeezed into the corner across from their table and struck up a jaunty tune.

"Let's get closer," Eleanor said to Margaret and Eliza.

Dorian grabbed her arm. "Be careful," he said.

The drink made her bold. "Why should I fear when I know you'll be watching me?"

So he did. Eleanor and her friends elbowed their way to the band and stood tapping their feet and clapping. Dorian wondered how anyone could believe they were men. He focused on Eleanor's new red hair, and waited for an excuse to go to them if anyone got too close.

Someone cleared a table beside the performers and a young man wearing the tall boots of a stable hand leapt onto it. He danced a lively jig, the metal on the soles of his boots firing off a sharp rhythm on the tabletop. The audience cheered and lifted him down. Another young man followed, and then a fat woman who swished her skirts and kicked up her thick ankles, much to the men's drunken appreciation. Eleanor yelled with the rest of them. She said something into Eliza's ear, and Eliza shook her head. She yanked at Eleanor's arm as Eleanor pushed toward the table.

"Here we go," said Dorian as Roffi handed him a drink.

"Should we stop her?" Roffi asked. "Eleanor!"

"Shut up, man!" Dorian stood and Roffi followed him to the musicians. By the time they reached the table Eleanor was already in full swing. The crowd screamed for more as she spun down the table. Dorian swore he saw her hair getting longer. He glanced at Roffi, who watched her as aptly as anyone. Roffi caught Dorian's lifted brow and chuckled.

"Now that," Roffi said, "that is entertainment."

Dorian clapped him on the back. "Have another beer, friend."

The crowd thinned as late night bled to early morning. Most of the patrons had either passed out or were tossed out. Only a few sturdy souls managed to stumble home under the power of their own two legs. Eleanor stopped drinking, and as her head cleared an ominous throbbing began behind her eyes. She yawned.

"If we can't drag these three out of here soon Raoul and I will take you ladies home," said Dorian. Raoul nodded. Margaret had dozed off, her head on his shoulder.

"They don't show signs of slowing yet," Eleanor said.

Gregory, Brian, and Christopher Roffi were leaning on the bar. Roffi was teaching them Svelyan drinking songs. Since neither of them spoke the language, it was a useless exercise. Their voices carried in the emptying tavern.

"Ah, boys, look there." Roffi pointed at a group of five men gathered around a card table. "I think they are playing De'menna. How do you say it, Tailspin?"

Gregory squinted. "Yes, yes, Tailspin."

Roffi's eyes lit up. "My favorite game! A pastime at court in Nestra." He slid off the bar stool and lurched across the room. Gregory and Brian followed him.

"This won't be good," Dorian said. He gave Anne Iris a bag of coins. "Take these to the barkeep. It's time we paid our bill."

Eleanor turned her attention to the men and their cards. Roffi placed his beer on the table. "Gentlemen," he said. "Are you having room for one more at your table?"

One of the gamblers, a rangy man with his black hair tied back in a ponytail, rubbed out his cigarette. "No," he said.

Roffi laughed. "Ah, you have only five players. In my home we know more players are better for Tailspin. Better odds."

The man glared up at him. "Better odds, right. Don't matter, we ain't got room for you."

Roffi threw up his hands and started to walk away. "Well, then you will keep your money."

"Where you from, anyway?" asked one of the others, younger, and heavyset, with bad skin. "You from down the way of Sage Town or somethin'?"

The first gambler spit. "No, you daft bastard. Can't you tell he ain't from Cartheigh at all? I'm thinkin' he might be from far north."

Roffi turned around. "Is there a problem?"

"Are you a Svelyan?"

"Yes."

"Then yeah, there's a fuckin' problem."

Brian put his hands on Roffi's shoulders. "Come on, Chris, no need."

The ponytailed gambler kept at it. "You know, boys, I heard all

Svelyans look like this bloke here. Big, blonde. You know why they all look the same?"

"Why, Pat?" asked the pimply one.

"Because they're all related. They all fuck their mothers."

Roffi lunged at them. Gregory and Brian held him back.

"Yeah, Svelty," sneered Pat. "You got your rich Maliana boys behind you. Maybe Svelyans don't just fuck their mothers. You must give them some reason to protect your ass."

That was enough for Gregory. He let go of Roffi and went in swinging himself. Unfortunately, he was the drunkest of the lot.

Eleanor leapt to her feet, but Dorian was faster. He climbed over the table between himself and the prince. He yanked Gregory back by his collar. His fist plowed into Pat's nose and it exploded. Blood sprayed across the table. The pimply instigator and one of the other players tried to make an exit. Dorian took both of them by their ears and soundly whacked their heads together.

One of the other gamblers tried to scramble past Eleanor. She reached down, picked up her abandoned tankard, and smashed him in the face with it. He hit the floor like a bag of rotten tomatoes. Gregory got back on his feet, and he grunted and ran through the fat doorman who tried to break things up. At least a dozen men joined in the scuffle, and the few women who were still sober enough to realize what was happening jumped onto the tables to avoid being trampled. Eleanor's friends gathered behind her, as if she might offer them some protection.

"Let's get to the door," she yelled over the ever-growing pack of swearing men. There were more people left in the Ogre Bar than she had thought. Maybe the noise of the fight had rousted the ones sleeping under the tables.

She scanned the room as they worked their way to the exit, and caught glimpses of their male counterparts in the mêlée. They were holding their own. She noted with perverse pride that Dorian had cleared a wide swath around himself, and even her drunken husband was making a solid go of it. The best moment of the night, however, came when the four women bumped up against a woozy old codger, who wrapped his arms around Eliza. Her dark blonde hair hung down her back again.

"Hey, pretty, where did you come from?"

Eleanor tried to drag Eliza away, but Margaret came to the real rescue. She grabbed a heavy candle made from an old bottle of wine and covered in dried wax. She blew out the wick, and hit the old man squarely on the back of the neck.

"Margaret!" shouted Eleanor as the old man sank out of sight. "How clever!"

They huddled by the door, uncertain as to their next move. Eleanor started to suggest they retrieve their horses and wait outside when Dorian appeared above the crowd. It took her a moment to realize he had climbed onto one of the tables. His enchanted hair was retreating, but he still had to push it back from his face. He pulled out a Fire-iron dagger. He swung it over his head and sliced one of the chandeliers clean off the ceiling. It slammed onto the table, overturning cups of beer, which fortunately doused the few remaining candles. Everyone froze as if in a children's game of ice tag.

"Ho!" he called. "We've had enough. If anyone else needs to prove himself, he can do so against me. Right now."

No one stirred.

"All right then." Dorian sheathed his knife. "Enjoy the rest of your evening."

Gregory, Brian, Roffi, and Raoul fell in behind him. The bald proprietor stepped from behind the bar.

"You lot don't need to come back here anytime soon," he growled.

"Very good," said Gregory. He took a small gold ring from his finger and handed it over. "Sorry about that chandelier."

The sentry at Eclatant waved them through the back gate. Their disguises had mostly worn off, and they rushed to their chambers. Eleanor shushed Gregory and Roffi, who hung on each other professing their true friendship and love like any drunken sailors on weekend leave. They dumped Roffi with his valet, who mumbled under this breath in Svelyan. The others broke for their own rooms and Eleanor and Dorian were left to shove Gregory into his bed and tug the boots from his feet. He showered them both with praise, and promised Eleanor he would make it up to her tomorrow night. She laughed and kissed his forehead.

"You're a silly man, Gregory Desmarais," she said. He was already asleep.

His two hounds leapt onto the bed. They circled and scraped at the sheets. "Move over, move over," they growled at each other.

She turned to Dorian. Nothing remained of the spell but a touch of five o'clock scruff. She pulled her own hair over her shoulder. It was long and blond again.

"You should let me look after that cut," she said. She reached toward the gash under his ear.

He put his own hand over it. "Don't worry, it's nothing."

Eleanor gently closed the door behind them. They walked up the stairs, but she stopped before they reached the landing. She stood two steps above Dorian, so they were eye-to-eye.

"The witches will be busy repairing broken noses in Pasture's End this morning," Eleanor said.

"Don't forget concussions. That man you hit with the beer mug got more than he was gambling for, should you pardon the pun."

"What a night."

"Yes, it was."

She lingered, trying to think of something else to say. She reached for the wound under his ear again. Her fingers grazed it, then traveled down his neck and caught in the dark hair curling around his collar.

He took her hand and held it to his lips. He took the other hand

and balled both her fists together, and eased them toward her chest. When he let go his own hand brushed the loose cotton covering her breast. Her skin tingled.

"I will sleep better knowing you're protecting the castle," he said.

"And I you."

"Sweet dreams, princess."

"Good night, Dorian."

He disappeared up the staircase. She sat down on the hard stone, and wrapped her arms around her knees.

CHAPTER 23

SUSPICION AND OUTRIGHT HOSTILITY

AS ECLATANT FILLED WITH guests in preparation for the Harvest Fest, Eleanor threw herself into her charity work. She wanted to eke as much support out of the gathered aristocracy as possible. Since Afar Creek Abbey provided so much aid to the poor people of Maliana she started her planning there. Rosemary arranged a full afternoon of tours and meetings, and Eleanor arrived ready to work.

Eleanor's carriage passed under the stone gate and into the bustling outer courtyard, where witches mingled with visiting townsfolk. They doled out medications, sold creams and tonics from rickety wheelbarrows, and bartered the fruits and vegetables grown at the Abbey for cloth and other sundries. Obviously ill patients were directed toward the sick rooms. Some were carried on stretchers, and their mournful cries rang out over the squawk of chickens and the friendly arguments between the merchants and the witches as everyone tried to drive a bargain.

Eleanor climbed five uneven steps into the stone edifice of the Abbey itself. Rosemary met her at the entrance. Countless wooden doors lined narrow corridors lit with sputtering torches. There were few decorations, a portrait of some long-gone Abbottess here, an ancient, faded tapestry there. Women walked with quiet purpose on the gray flagstone floors, talking softly amongst themselves. Eleanor flattened herself against the wall to make way for an old woman who seemed to be consulting a fat pony on the best treatment for colic in babies and horses. Weird smoke in a prism of colors drifted from the cracks under the doors. The scents matched the colors: blue-green smoke hinted at salty ocean air, yellow held a bit of lemon, dark brown the warm odor of a barn full of cows. Eleanor tried to peek around the few open doors but Rosemary urged her on.

First Rosemary led Eleanor past the sick rooms that took up much of the first floor, where witches cared for the poorest citizens of Maliana, those who could not afford to have their illnesses treated in their homes. There were two chambers, one for those with contagious diseases and one for injuries and chronic conditions. Eleanor stopped in the baby-catching room, where a woman could seek care before, during, and after the birth of her child. She chatted with the new mothers and left coins for the tiny bundles nestled in their arms.

"How do the witches avoid falling ill in the sick rooms?" Eleanor asked.

"In general we have a higher tolerance for these kinds of things," said Rosemary, "but not always. Some do sicken, and some do die."

They climbed a steep stairway to the library, two full floors of books and manuscripts. They perused the stacks for several hours. Eleanor enjoyed their conversations with the scholars. No one curtsied or paid her false compliments. The witches were open and honest but not overly deferential. It was a refreshing change.

They left the library, and climbed yet another flight of stairs to the dormitories. Eleanor had begun to wonder how the witches did not go blind in such perpetual dimness, but there were more windows on these three floors. They wandered through the simple but comfortable adults' quarters and into the children's wing. Eleanor gazed in wonder at the mish-mash of childish magic in the gathering room. The girls had brought in giant flowering plants and live trees, and monkeys and squirrels capered in the branches. The bone-dry floor appeared as running water below her feet, and great bands of color swirled around the ceiling like captive rainbows. Eleanor felt as though she had stepped into a little girl's storybook about the Talessee jungles.

She pulled up a mushroom shaped stool and talked to the girls, who ranged in age from about five to fourteen. Their hard questions belied the whimsy of their decorations. They grilled Eleanor about the conditions in the slums of Meggett Fringe and what the prince planned to do for the poor people. She whispered in Rosemary's ear. "This is worse than a High Council meeting."

"We tell them the truth," said Rosemary. She stood, and asked one of the girls to join her. "Eloise would like to read you the story of the Great Bond, in her own words."

The witch, who looked to be in the realm of ten years old, cleared her throat. Aside from her pitch, she sounded as strident any Godsman at the pulpit.

"In honor of your visit, Your Highness," she said with a quick curtsy. "It all started three hundred years ago. A young farmer by the name of Caleb Desmarais, a poor and lowly born man who owned a plot of land outside the marshes south of the Dragon Mines, found an orphaned unicorn foal. He raised the colt to adulthood when no one had ever been able to keep one alive. To this day no one knows exactly how he did it. Some say he was a magician, but all agree it was the most important thing ever in the whole history of Cartheigh. He released that first unicorn, a stallion called Eclatant, back into the marshes. Amazingly, Eclatant brought together a herd of mares and returned without anyone even asking him to Caleb's small farm."

"Unicorns are mystical creatures. Through fear or respect, the dragons became quiet as kittens among the unicorns and their chosen people. Well, almost like kittens. They are still big and fiery. But even so, the Svelyans had always used force to control the beasts. With the unicorns at their sides, the Cartheans mined larger piles of Fire-iron for both for trade to other countries and their own use. They did not have to work anywhere near as hard as the Svelyans had and not too many men even died doing it. Caleb was hailed as king of Cartheigh. The Great Bond has continued these three hundred years, and all Cartheigh has flourished."

The child swept her hand through the air. Rosemary nodded encouragingly, and the girl continued.

"Although Cartheigh is a small country with not so many people, and surrounded by larger countries with lots and lots of them, Cartheigh has kept control of the Dragon Mines for three whole centuries, which is a very long time. There are few dragons left in the world, and no other mines in any of the kingdoms surrounding Cartheigh. We, the Witches of Afar Creek Abbey, send our thanks to King Casper and your husband Prince Gregory for ensuring the continued prosperity of our beloved kingdom."

Eleanor clapped, then stood and hugged the girl. She laughed when embarrassed orange steam floated out of the child's ears.

They visited the sorceresses last, on the top floor. Witches hunched around glowing fires and kettles of bubbling liquid, or sat mumbling while smoke or light swirled around their heads. So many smells filled the air, Eleanor could not pick out any one. Their enthusiastic guide, called Alesson, explained the work of her colleagues.

"Over there," said the young sorceress, "she's trying to remove contaminants from water. It will help in the Fringe, where sickness runs rampant when the Clarity is low. Those two over there are channeling their minds to put words to paper without writing them. Imagine how much faster the scholars could work!" She nodded at one of the witches enveloped in pearly light. "We're so close to finishing this spell. It will be a magical breakthrough. She's trying to slow her heartbeat enough that she feels no pain. We hope to transmit the spell to our patients, and eliminate the need for opiates."

"How fascinating. What about her?" Eleanor asked.

Alesson colored. "Not so noble. She's trying to brew a magical sweetener. Some of us are quite addicted to the Abbottess's chocolate truffles and marzipan balls, and it's starting to show."

Late in the afternoon Eleanor shared a cup of tea with Rosemary in a comfortable parlor. "I'm impressed," she said. "I never grasped the depth of the work you do here. I don't know if the rest of the city knows either."

"I think the common folk understand," Rosemary said.

"Well, the king certainly doesn't." Eleanor remembered his comments at Faust's disastrous dinner party last summer.

"We've always done our work with little fanfare. It's in our nature."

"Fine," said Eleanor, "you don't need bugle calls, but you could use money."

Rosemary laughed. "Our wealthier patrons pay for our services, but the cost of supporting the poor of this city drains the fees the teachers and public healers bring in. We have to compete with the Godsmen for patronage, and while we help each other where we can, there is never enough to accomplish everyone's goals."

"And the magicians are flush with money from the state treasury," Eleanor said with a scowl.

Rosemary shook her head. "We have no quarrel with the magicians. There are many fine men in the Coveys doing important work. Their magic is just as vital as ours. Still, we wouldn't turn down some new beds for the sick rooms, or ink pots. Do you have any idea how much ink we use?"

Eleanor jotted notes in a ledger. None of Rosemary's requests were exorbitant or out of the ordinary, just practical items to ease the witches' burden. She didn't think she would have too much trouble convincing the visiting courtiers to open their change purses, and she couldn't help but feel gratified their donations would irk Ezra Oliver to no end.

Dorian could name most of the bearded men glaring down at him from the white walls of the Council Hall. Kings, dukes, magicians, royal relations, scholars; all captured for eternity in life-sized oil paintings. Apparently nothing about the Council Hall had changed in several hundred years, as the décor in the portraits mirrored the furnishings in front of him. The same long rectangular table, the same high-backed chairs, the same tapestries from the mills in the Harveston with their traditional geometric patterns. Huge windows let in floor-to-ceiling light. Unlike most of the rooms in the palace, there were no draperies. According to Gregory, the lack of shade was intentional. One could not fall asleep during a lengthy review of cattle inventories or trade policy with sunlight streaming into the room and glaring off the polished table. While Dorian found the Council meetings fascinating, even his analytical mind wondered at times. A pack of wolves couldn't make him admit it, but he sometimes imagined where his own solitary likeness might fit into the portrait collection.

Only the men at the table were different, save one. As Ezra Oliver had been at Eclatant for ninety years, his face appeared in several paintings of the full High Council. With every depiction his somberness increased. In the most recent painting he stood beside Dorian with a positively grim expression. Dorian assumed a direct correlation between mood and position. He knew his habit of voicing his opinion drove Oliver mad.

They were three hours into session when Oliver stood and delivered his final report on upcoming criminal trials. He read the names and supposed crimes of the accused. The Council asked a few clarifying questions but they appeared anxious to return to their meat and wine.

"Lastly," said Oliver, "the proprietor of Clarity Fine Jewelers has been accused of selling false jewels to the crown. He has admitted wrongdoing and will seek a plea bargain."

Gregory had not said much throughout the meeting, but he was suddenly interested. "Selling false jewels?"

Oliver nodded. "Yes, he has offered to repay any losses—"

"As in false jewels in a necklace bought for the Talessee queen last summer? As in jewels Thomas Harper Rowe admitted to stealing before his untimely tossing off Ramlock Face?"

Oliver's mouth hung open for a moment, but Gregory had no such difficulty finding words. When he stood, his chair caught in the thick rug and tick-tocked precariously on its legs. It tipped over and hit the black and white marble floor with a resounding whack.

"Nothing to say, Oliver? Nothing to say about throwing an innocent—"

"I'd say we're finished, gentlemen," interjected the king. "You're all dismissed. Except you, Oliver."

The other members of the council gathered their papers and cloaks and said hurried good-byes. Dorian made to go with them but Gregory stopped him. "Stay here, Dorian."

"As you wish." Dorian turned around, draped his cloak over his chair again, and stood beside Gregory.

When the room cleared the king spoke. "Sit down." Gregory didn't move. "Gregory! Sit down."

Gregory left his own chair on the floor and sat in the one next to it. Dorian sat beside him. The king asked Oliver to explain himself. "Did Clarity Fine Jewelers have anything to do with that necklace for the Talessee queen? The one you said had false jewels, false jewels put there by Thomas Harper Rowe?"

Oliver nodded, and shuffled his papers with his eyes on the desk. "I'm sorry to say, sire, yes. The proprietor included the necklace in the list of tampered items."

Gregory's fist hit the table. "You dragged me up on that cliff, you made me watch that disgusting display…like a pack of animals…and you were not even sure Rowe was guilty?"

"Sire, I truly thought—"

"HighGod in tears, Oliver! That's what your tactics get us! An innocent man tortured and murdered…I haven't been able to sleep for—" He stopped abruptly. Oliver's eyes darted between Gregory and his father, as if hoping for salvation from his sovereign.

He did not get it. "Shoddy work, Oliver," the king said. "By the Bond, there will be some conciliations to be made if the Harpers find out we gave one of their kinsmen the ax under false confession. My son is right. We expect more from you. It will be on your head to sort this out if it comes to light." He wagged a finger in front of Oliver's nose.

Oliver's face now resembled like an overripe tomato. His usual eloquence disappeared. "Sire…when we suspected a thief in the government ranks I indeed suspected Rowe…uh, we never had proof but the necklace…set an example…followed your plan to the last letter."

Dorian caught a few wisps of hostile gray light seeping from under the table before Oliver sucked them back into his hands. Gregory continued his diatribe. "If you think you will be allowed to run amuck like this when I am king you are sorely mistaken, Oliver. Sorely fucking mistaken."

It seemed a good time to intervene. Dorian spoke up. "You've said your piece, Greg. Why don't we let your father sort this out?"

Gregory stood and Dorian followed him. He caught a last glimpse of Oliver's bulging eyes as the two of them left the Council Hall. Gregory kept fuming down the passageway, through the Great Hall, and up the staircase to his chambers. He yelled at Melfin to shut the study door behind Dorian and poured himself a hefty goblet of wine. All the while he muttered under his breath. "Time for a change…a hundred years is long enough."

"Peace, Greg," said Dorian. "Your face is the same shade as your hair."

Gregory whirled around. "Spare me your impudence, for once. You have no idea…" He gulped his wine.

"In fact, I do," said Dorian. "I was on the cliff, remember?"

Gregory poured Dorian a glass of whiskey, perhaps to make up for going off like an ogre with a toothache. "I'm the future king."

"You are that."

"I won't tolerate sloppiness, or hold onto servants who have outlived their usefulness." Gregory started to put a hand to his hair, but stopped himself and twisted the Fire-iron ring on his right index finger instead. He'd let Dorian try it on in their younger days. It had belonged to Caleb Desmarais's grandson, Gregory the First. He would be the Second.

Dorian could almost hear the king's words ringing through Gregory's head.

My son is right…we expect more…

Gregory's chest swelled, even as his right hand closed in a tight fist. "My opinions will be heard."

Eleanor sat on a throne, under a pavilion, observing her first magicians' joust. It was nothing like an ordinary joust, as it involved no horses but did include a plethora of whizzing fireballs. Two martial magicians, each dressed in the color his magic assumed (in this case bright yellow and purple), hid behind Fire-iron shields and flung enchanted projectiles at one another. Yellow and purple fireballs spun around the arena like out-of-control, overgrown hummingbirds. The crowd pressed in as close as safety allowed, and Eleanor was one of the few with a clear view. Ironic, as she found the whole scene distasteful.

The gathered courtiers screamed and cheered any time one of the fireballs found its mark. Eleanor winced as blood and sweat flew from the combatants' faces and swinging arms. Gregory had left his throne. He paced the bit of open space in front their seats, shouting profane encouragement at the yellow magician.

The sight of men with such rare abilities reduced to sparring partners saddened Eleanor. She turned to Rosemary in the wooden lawn chair beside her. "Why do the magicians participate in this ridiculous display? It's like a magical cockfight. There's no dignity in it."

"I agree," said Rosemary, "but martials are a strange breed. Magic is not beauty to them. They see it as a means to a living, nothing more."

"Sometimes I wonder why magicians and witches don't rule us all."

Rosemary never coated any answer with sugar. "I think HighGod had a plan in creating magical beings. Perhaps ten magical children are born in Cartheigh in a given year. We are simply to few to hold power, even with our talents."

After another interminable thirty minutes the match came to an abrupt end. The purple magician flung two desperate fireballs at his opponent's knees, but yellow dropped to a crouch. Both purple balls ricocheted off yellow's Fire-iron shield and catapulted back into their creator's face. He was blasted into the air and landed on his back ten paces away.

As the crowd went wild Eleanor leaned closer to Rosemary. "What in the name of HighGod was that?"

"Fire-iron repels magic." Rosemary almost shouted to be heard over the yellow magician's supporters. "And no magic is as dangerous to the conjurer as his own turned against him."

As Eleanor stood and applauded politely Margaret appeared at her shoulder. "Walk with me?" her stepsister asked.

"Gladly," said Eleanor, and they curtsied their way past the mob and into the autumn sunlight. Anne Iris joined them on the edge of the crowd.

"Margaret, I noticed you've been walking with Raoul in the garden," said Eleanor, after they passed a few words about the weather and the joust. "How is he?"

Margaret blushed, and smiled. "He's well. He...he took my hand yesterday, and asked me to visit with his parents at their townhouse in Maliana."

"How sweet!" said Eleanor.

"No more Mister Roffi?" asked Anne Iris.

"I've grown bored of the idea of him," Margaret said with a shrug. "He's never spoken of his supposed affections, or acted on them."

Eleanor wondered if Margaret was thinking about their night in the Ogre Bar. In truth she was relieved. The idea of Margaret and Roffi had always seemed as natural as a witch and a magician setting up house and raising triplets. "Raoul is a good man," Eleanor said.

"If only Mother thought so." Margaret sighed. "She never tires of discussing Roffi. She always wants to know if he comes to your chambers to visit me. How often does he visit? Does he stay long? What does he talk about? I've told her he's about nearly every day but she won't let it be. She even asks about his friendship with Gregory. Of course anyone close to the crown fascinates her."

"Imogene isn't known for her tolerance, but perhaps his full purse makes up for his unbecoming accent," said Eleanor with a laugh. "You should explain how Roffi comes to teach us all about Svelya. I'm sure her interest would wane at the mention of anything academic."

"Eleanor," Margaret said, with sudden seriousness. "I would discuss my mother with you. Our last conversations have not only revolved around Roffi, but around you."

"Indeed," said Eleanor. For some reason this brought her no surprise.

"Yes, she often asks after you and Gregory. How well you get on, if you're happy. She asked me if you'd shown signs of pregnancy."

Anne Iris scowled. "The nerve. How did you respond?"

"I called her a nosy, spiteful gossipmonger," said Margaret.

"Margaret, you didn't!" said Eleanor. "By the Bond, sister, you aren't yourself these days."

"In all sincerity, Eleanor, you must take care. Remember, my mother was not so different from me, or Sylvia, or even you. She had an old name and no funds to shore it up. The fifth of five daughters. She didn't even have a dowry, just her face and her charm. She never loved my father. He was a drunk, and a mean one at that, but she married him with the hope of bearing a son and securing some of the Easton money. When he died after gambling away the little we had she survived alone for five years. She bundled us from house to house, distant relation to more distant relation, before she married your father. She got another roof over her head, but no boy to go out and secure a fortune."

"Just another leftover girl," said Eleanor.

Margaret nodded. "Sylvia was always her great hope. Her one chance for safety. It's why she always hated you so, I'm certain. It must have driven her mad, having Sylvia's greatest competition under the same roof. I think she saw it from the first moment she laid eyes on you. For all those years she kept you close and strangled your spirit to make room for Sylvia's. I couldn't be what she needed."

Eleanor took her hand. "Thankfully."

Margaret smiled and went on. "So now she's climbed higher than we had any right to expect, on Sylvia's coattails. But it will never be enough for her."

Margaret stopped, and Eleanor and Anne Iris had to stop with her. "Somewhere in her heart I believe she wants the best for me and my sister, but if that means the best for herself all the better. Look how she forced Sylvia to marry that old man. I tell you this because I fear she'll never put aside her anger. She'll never forgive you for stealing the crown she hoped to put on Sylvia's head."

It was a long speech for Margaret. Perhaps she had written it down to ensure she remembered all that needed to be said. "Thank you," Eleanor said. "Your words have fallen on alert ears, and a grateful heart."

Margaret excused herself to find Raoul, and Anne Iris took Eleanor's hand. "You were right, dearest," she said. "Margaret Easton has many admirable qualities."

Eleanor enjoyed Roffi's lessons about his country. Relations between Svelya and Cartheigh had always varied between suspicion and outright hostility, and Eleanor felt her previous education on the subject therefore tainted with Carthean bias. Roffi brought her Svelyan literature and history books, and even had the cooks make Gregory and Eleanor a bragga, the traditional Svelyan rabbit stew.

"Ugh," said Gregory as he spit out a small bone.

"Shhh," whispered Eleanor. "You'll hurt his feelings."

"I'd rather hurt his feelings than choke to death." Gregory pushed his plate aside.

As always, Eleanor wanted to share her new interest with Dorian, so she asked Roffi to join the two of them in Eclatant's cavernous library. His presence had the added effect of preventing Eleanor and Dorian from being alone. Roffi began turning up every day, and soon all three were equally engaged in the discussion. They rattled on for hours under the flickering chandeliers, sipping pear juice and coughing when flipping pages threw old dust into their faces.

"You can see how it's difficult for us to trust your nation's intentions, Chris, and it's not just your hideous accent and tendency to wear more jewelry than my grandmother at chapel," said Dorian one afternoon as they leafed through a study called *One Hundred Years Behind the Mountains: Memories of a Carthean Magician in Svelya.* The three of them always sat at the same Fire-iron table, strategically located between the literature and history sections. Their only company was an old magician whose sole purpose seemed to be wandering the stacks and reorganizing books that looked as if they had not been moved in a hundred years.

"Having spent time here, yes, I am understanding it. You protect what you see as yours," said Roffi. After five months in Cartheigh he had shed not only the fur on his face but also the fur on his tunic. Apart from his white Svelyan hair he looked like any Carthean nobleman.

"What *is* ours," Dorian said. Frog spat at Roffi from his perch on Dorian's shoulder.

Roffi ignored the raven and nodded. "Accepted. But you must understand our position as well. We held the mines for five hundred years before the Desmarais came to power."

"By all accounts you made a shoddy mess of it," said Dorian.

"I will not be arguing. Once the unicorns joined your kings, we lost any chance at controlling the mines. But Svelya is a hard land. We don't have your endless fields and forests, your gentle climate, nor even your rivers and access to the Shallow Sea. We have mountains, cold plains, and the jagged coast of the Quartic Ocean. Other than raising sheep and mountain cattle there is little way for the people to thrive."

Eleanor admired Roffi's restraint as Dorian pushed his position. His diplomatic training served him well. She spoke for the first time. "What of the banking industry in Nestra? Didn't your own family make a fortune in the money trade?"

Roffi nodded. "Yes, we did, but it is concentrated in the hands of a lucky few like myself. It is great wealth for a small minority and poverty for the masses in Svelya. So we cannot help but…" He waved his hands nonchalantly. "…feel nostalgic for the days when we were having access to other resources, no matter what a poor job we did at handling them."

Dorian laughed. "Always the charmer."

"How did you become Ambassador, Christopher?" Eleanor asked. "Aren't you young for the job?"

"I am, Your Highness. The youngest ambassador Svelya has ever sent out. My family has always represented our country at Eclatant. My grandfather was wanting to retire, and my father is in poor health. So here I am, just earlier than expected. My valet, my magicians, and me. The only Svelyans in a sea of Carthean…what is the word? Refinement."

"And we are all the more fortunate for it," she said. "Do you miss home?"

"Of course, Nestra is a wonderful city. You would both love it."

"I'd like to visit someday."

"I don't think your husband would allow it," said Roffi. "He would be fearing some evil Svelyan lord would steal you and hold you for ransom. While our women are known for their beauty, we have none such as you."

"Oh, stop," said Eleanor. "You would flatter my maidservant if she walked in this door."

"You are right, but I would not mean it."

Eleanor threw a crumpled piece of paper at him. It bounced off his head and disappeared under the table.

"Men always desire most what they cannot have," said Roffi. "Is it not true, Dorian?"

For once Dorian seemed caught off guard, but he recovered quickly. "Yes," he said, "but I believe it true of women as well as men."

Eleanor looked at Roffi, who met her eye with none of his usual lightheartedness. "If you are right," he said, "then we are all doomed to unhappiness."

He laughed and the tension passed, and they broke up a few minutes later for dinner. Eleanor mulled over Roffi's comments during her bath that evening. Something there unsettled her.

CHAPTER 24

A Sign Around Her Neck

ELEANOR HAD OTHER REASONS to be unsettled during the Harvest Fest. She feared her feelings for Dorian were becoming obvious. She gave up trying to forget him. The futility of that exercise had become undeniable. Instead, she tried to be as close to him as possible, as often as possible, without attracting any suspicion. Her stomach churned with longing, paranoia, and guilt.

She had become used to Gregory's drinking and carousing, and learned to ignore the little cruelties that lashed out with his temper. He had strayed from their bed, HighGod knew how many times. There had been clues; scratches on his back, a delay in opening his bedroom door, a long dark hair screaming at her from the whiteness of his tunic. His infidelity sat in between them, like an embarrassing cousin that was never discussed. But he was still her husband, and her prince, and Dorian was his best friend. She told herself he had pushed her toward Dorian, but in her heart she knew that even if Gregory had been the most dutiful husband the world had ever seen, she could not have known Dorian Finley and not been in love with him.

She felt as if she wore a sign around her neck. They continued studying and riding, and she still sought some form of chaperone, be it unicorn, parrot, or person. It was worse at the Fest parties, after a glass or two of wine. She stood close to him, close enough that their elbows just brushed. She touched his long fingers when he handed her a drink; she touched his chest when she spoke to him. She cut into conversations he had with women who were too pretty or flirtatious. Chou Chou landed on her shoulder during the Harvest Ball after she monopolized three of his waltzes.

"Careful," said the parrot.

"What do you mean?"

Chou's yellow eyes rolled. "I mean Mister Finley should spread his wings a bit, yes?"

"I'm tired. I think I'll go to bed." She set down her drink.

"Fabulous idea."

She resolved the next morning to pull back, and she succeeded in avoiding him for one entire afternoon, until they met at a chapel service. She knelt beside him, trying to pray, and before she knew it she edged so close her skirt covered his calf. Through it all he was stubbornly unflappable. He didn't egg her on, but he didn't discourage her, either.

Eleanor had always been slight, but she progressed to painfully thin. Food had no taste, and she lost much of the sparse cleavage she had with her appetite. She was snappish and moody with her friends. While Eliza was too proper to let on, Margaret's gentle prodding and Anne Iris's lack thereof gave away their concerns. Thankfully none of them pressed her. Although she trusted them all it was too dangerous to talk about it. She didn't know what she wanted to happen, but this certainly could not go on. Just when she decided she must confront Dorian for her own sanity, a chain of events changed her mind.

She was unusually tired. At first she blamed the hectic Fest schedule and her strained emotions, but when her stomach began rolling in the evenings she took out her calendar. She was late. There was no doubt about it.

Gregory visited her chambers with the same regularity as always. She had never discouraged him. Regardless of her feelings for Dorian,

Gregory was her husband and in Cartheigh, husbands had their rights. Besides, no matter how much of an ass Gregory could be she never stayed angry with him. Even if she doubted she would ever love him the way she once had, she was fond of him. She felt like a bit of an ass herself. She had been so consumed by her romantic notions she overlooked the inevitable consequences of her marital relations.

About a week after the Harvest Fest ended she sat sewing by the fire. She rarely dabbled in embroidery, but tonight couldn't focus on anything of substance. She had claimed a headache for the privacy it brought her, and sipped a cup of green tea. She hoped it would ease her spinning stomach and kill the sour taste in her mouth. She draped High Noon's old red blanket over her legs. It clashed horribly with the rest of the décor, but she didn't care. Pansy sometimes tried to move the blanket to a less conspicuous spot in the room, but Eleanor always returned it to its rightful place in the center of the couch.

"Your Highness," said Pansy. "Prince Gregory is here."

"Thank you, Pansy. Send him in," Eleanor said.

She welcomed Gregory and shifted over on the couch, but he chose the chair across from her. He hadn't shaved.

"Husband, are you feeling well?" she asked.

"Honestly, no," he said.

She put a hand to his forehead. "You aren't feverish. Should we send for a witch?"

"It's not that kind of feeling. There's nothing wrong with my body. It's my heart that's ill."

This time Eleanor's flipping stomach had nothing to do with her tender condition. It was a hollow pit, and the rest of her slid inside. "Has something happened?"

"I don't know. That's what I'm here to find out."

Sweat beaded on her upper lip.

Gregory went on. "Can I be frank?"

She smiled, but it felt like puppeteers pulling strings attached to her cheeks. "Of course. I hope I can help you."

He stood and leaned on the mantle. It seemed even the furniture waited on his words. When he spoke she saw nothing but his broad back. "You know my sons will be kings of this country. I cannot tolerate any...suspicions about them."

"Suspicions?" She hoped the panic rising in her chest would not make her voice shake.

"If anyone were to...cause such suspicions...they would face heavy consequences. Mortal consequences." He turned to her.

"Gregory, I don't know what you mean."

"You've been meeting with Dorian in the library."

"Yes, as we always have. We both enjoy scholarly pursuits. You know that."

"Why did you ask Roffi to join you?"

Eleanor shook her head as Roffi entered into the conversation like a sheep tossed into a chicken coop. "Roffi?"

"Yes, Roffi." Gregory grabbed a pillow and threw it on the bed. "Why did you invite him? And why does he visit your chambers?"

Eleanor's mouth fell open. "You think I'm having an affair with Christopher Roffi?"

Gregory glared at her. "There are people who are saying as much. Your stepmother and Sylvia Fleetwood are first among them. They say Roffi toys with Margaret's affection to hide your...dalliances."

"And you believe them? You know our family history. Besides, I've never heard one word of it. Nor has Chou."

"HighGod's eyebrows, Eleanor. These are treasonous accusations, not petty rumors. No one will say them to your face, feathery or otherwise. Perhaps you would be more aware if you conversed with anyone other than Margaret, Anne Iris, or Eliza."

"I'd choose three true friends over a hundred acquaintances." She laid the half-finished pillowcase on the couch. "While we're speaking of friends, I thought you enjoyed Christopher."

"I do, but why does he come here? Every day, it seems."

"He drops off books, and he stays and chats with me and my ladies. I always assumed it was because of his feelings for Margaret."

Gregory flopped into his chair. His legs splayed out in front of him. "Do you really believe he wants Margaret?"

She shrugged, relieved she could tell him the truth. "I don't know, but I know I don't want him. Gregory, I promise you, I have no interest in Christopher. He comes to the library to study with Dorian and me. I've never even been alone with him."

His desperation tugged at her. "Do you swear it?"

"I swear."

She thought of the mysterious woman in the red silk dress. Of the countless others that had definitely proceeded and probably followed her.

He left the chair and sat beside her on the couch. "I just had to ask you."

"I'm glad you did." She made up her mind about what she needed to do. "Now I have something to tell you." She put his hand on her stomach.

"Again?" he asked. His hand slid over the blue silk of her nightdress.

"Yes. It's early, so I can only pray it goes better this time, but I wanted to tell you."

"This makes me happy, Eleanor. I know all will be well."

She kissed the end of his nose. "Yes, if we believe it, all will be well."

With that, she made preparations for her baby, and coddled her husband. As for Dorian, she loved him quietly.

The Waning came and went and the palace moved into the slow days of winter. Eleanor's pregnancy progressed with no complications, and to her amusement a protective circle closed around her. Margaret, Anne Iris, and Eliza followed her everywhere. Between Gregory, Dorian, and Christopher Roffi she could barely carry her own water cup or climb a flight of stairs without one of them appearing at her side. King Casper rarely made personal visits to anyone, but he began stopping by her chambers. He even asked Ezra Oliver to brew a tonic for the unborn child. Much to her annoyance, her father-in-law insisted on referring to the baby as *he* or *my boy*. Eleanor in turn referred to the child as *she*. Pointless, since HighGod had long since made that decision for both of them.

One lazy HighWinter afternoon Eleanor and her popping belly had nothing in particular on their agenda, other than a half a box of chocolate covered almonds and a long nap, so she took a turn around the palace. Chou sat on her shoulder, and she stopped to chat with servants who curtsied or bowed and offered respectful blessings to her and the child. Between compliments Chou whispered in her ear. "I believe I know where we're headed."

"Do you? Clever bird." The oak-paneled doors of the Chief Magician's office appeared around the next corner. "My child is in need of a tonic," Eleanor said. "I might as well have a look around."

"You have my eyes, as always," said Chou.

The guard announced them, and soon Eleanor greeted Ezra Oliver across his wide Fire-iron desk. "Your Highness," he said, staid as ever in his dark gray robes and silly cow patty hat. "How might I help you?"

She forced a smile onto her face. "I so enjoyed the tonic you brewed for me. I wondered if you might stir up another."

"Of course," Oliver said. He smiled back, but he looked as if his face might crack from the strain.

Could I have been so desperate for camaraderie? Eleanor wondered.

She took a seat in an embroidered armchair as Oliver busily gathered the ingredients from the apothecary cabinet beside his towering bookshelves. As he chopped and stirred and whispered enchantments Eleanor's eyes darted around the room.

Broken quills and blotters and bottles of ink huddled in the shadow of the mountain of paper and parchment on Oliver's desk. A half-eaten plate of bread and butter sat beside a cup of dingy tea. More baskets of documents lined the floor around the desk's Fire-iron legs. An apprentice collected a pile of completed correspondence and dropped a stack of new letters twice as high.

He's more glorified secretary than sorcerer.

She let Chou pace the bookshelves as she was too far away to read the titles, and anyway there were so many volumes it would have taken both of them a week to peruse them all. She searched for anything else that seemed out of place, but the chaos overwhelmed her. Even the smell of the place was jumbled. A scent of mint and lemon mingled with the familiar odors of ink and dusty paper. She was drawn to the one bit of serenity in the room.

A small potted plant sat on the window ledge. Its glossy blue leaves drooped as if it had not been watered in a week. She stood and walked toward it. "What an interesting plant," she said.

Oliver looked up. "A Blue Weathervane," he said.

Eleanor touched one of the plant's leaves and she swore it shuddered. She sniffed at the trace of blue powder it left on her fingers, and realized the lemony-minty smell came from the Weathervane. She wiped her finger on her handkerchief. "Pardon, sir, but it appears thirsty."

"It's not," said Oliver with a haughty sniff. "It always looks that way. Weathervanes are highly sensitive to different stimuli. The common yellow variety reacts to changes in temperature or precipitation." He sounded much like a talking textbook. "The blue variety reacts to magic. It's relatively healthy in Solsea, where I'm one of the only practicing magicians and the witches live in the countryside. Here in Maliana the magical weight is so heavy I sometimes fear it will kill the Weathervane altogether. Such a shame. It's very rare."

Eleanor sensed a reference to last summer's argument over the superfluity of magic in Cartheigh. She swept back to her chair, and the grin plastered on her face felt almost Sylvia-like. "Ah, Mister Oliver, one plant in exchange for a world of magical innovation and good deeds. A just compromise."

Oliver's nostrils flared. He shoved a stopper in the glass tonic jar. "To your health, as always, *Your Highness*," he said as he handed it over. "And to the health of your child."

Chou landed on her shoulder once more. He'd been unusually quiet throughout the visit. She commented on his diligence as they walked back to her room.

"I don't blather about when there's work to be done," he said.

"I didn't see anything alarming," Eleanor said, "but then again I don't know what I expected."

"You're right. Oliver isn't going to write a book entitled *My Deep and Abiding Friendship with Imogene Brice* and leave it on his desk."

"Did you see anything on the book shelf?" she asked. "No, but I did see something under the desk."

"Ah, Chou! Tell me."

"Two books. One on rare enchantments and one called *Legacies of Caleb Desmarais*."

"Well done," she said. "I believe I must have copies of both. Winter is a splendid time for reading."

Eleanor watched the crowd of dancers swirling about the Grand Ballroom and sneezed into her hand. The magicians had overdone it with the giant Awakening flowers, but at least they hadn't brought in any matching bees. She sat at a dining table at the head of the room beside Gregory. Dorian stood quietly in front of them like a dark sentry. He swallowed whiskey by the glassful.

Margaret sat on Eleanor's other side. A combination of wine and her newfound romance with Raoul made her giddy. She leaned over and whispered in Eleanor's ear. "You know, darling, I've always found Dorian a bit intimidating, but he does look lonely. Do you suppose he's ever been in love?"

Eleanor gave her a wide-eyed shrug as Gregory stood and called to Anne Iris. He met his cousin on the other side of the table and led her onto the dance floor. Eleanor's pride and a swelling belly kept her from joining them, but she wouldn't deny Gregory a good time. She sneezed again and dabbed at her watery eyes with the napkin.

The Duchess of Harveston and her mother had arrived to celebrate the Awakening Fest, and Sylvia would not let a little hay fever ruin the party. Eleanor watched her stepsister maneuver her way through the line of dancers. She was none the worse for wear after the birth of her son last winter. Her waist was just as tiny, her spirits just as lively. She sidled up to Gregory. She laughed and tossed her dark hair and clung to him whenever she got close enough. She touched his face. Through three reels she kept it up, and she was conveniently beside him when the orchestra struck up a waltz. She stumbled and fell against him, and he had to grab her to keep her upright. Eleanor's eyes narrowed. Sylvia had never missed a dance step in her life.

Eleanor glanced around the ballroom, and found her stepmother shared her interest in Sylvia's performance. Imogene stood on the edge of the dance floor, beside Ezra Oliver, with a goblet in her hand. They conversed from behind their cups as they watched the dancers. Eleanor observed them for ten minutes, burning with curiosity all the while.

Chou Chou was laid up in her room with a strained wing, so Eleanor had to be her own spy. She got up from the table and made her wobbly way across the ballroom. Much to her annoyance people bowed and curtsied and moved out of her path. Their respect only drew attention to her progress. By the time she reached Imogene, Oliver had disappeared.

I didn't cross this room with aching feet for nothing. Without any further thought she sidled up to her stepmother.

"Good evening, Missus Brice," she said with a smile.

Imogene turned, and made a poor attempt to hide her distaste. Her smile seemed made of jelly. "Good evening, Your...Highness," Imogene said. "I trust you're well?"

"Healthy as a herd of horses, thank you. How do you find our hospitality?"

"Incomparable, of course. A lovely evening."

"Isn't it? Such fine conversation tonight! Mister Oliver is quite entertaining, don't you agree?"

The wiggly smile left Imogene's face. She adjusted the huge sapphire necklace resting in her cleavage and tugged at the neckline of her gaudy blue gown. While most ladies always seemed to be adjusting theirs up, Imogene's usually trended down. "He's very interesting."

"You two have struck up quite a friendship, I hear. I'll admit I was surprised, as I remember you referring to magical folk as *conjuring oddballs* on my last visit to my father's house."

"Would you care to come to the point, Your Highness?" Imogene's sharp white teeth flashed as she took a sip of wine. She resembled a small, fluffy dog, the kind that look pretty and harmless but will bite an ankle if stepped on.

"Come, now. I'm just musing. Court life does make for unusual alliances."

Imogene did not reply.

"A shame Mister Oliver had to retire, but I'm sure you'll find others to willing to trade rumors with you. There are some simply fascinating ones circulating about Mister Roffi." Eleanor curtsied with as much grace as she could manage. "Well, I do hope you enjoy the rest of the party. Goodnight."

She returned to the table, sat, and took a few bites of cake before letting her eyes sweep the ballroom again. Imogene was gone. Maybe the party had lost its appeal.

Gregory stumbled when he handed his mount off to the groom. Dorian caught his arm. "All right, Greg?" he asked.

"I'd be better if we had caught something," Gregory said. "All damn day in the saddle and not one bloody *j'rauzelle*."

Dorian, Gregory, Brian, and Roffi had left Eclatant as the sun rose. They rode due east, toward Rabbit's Rest Lodge, one of the crown's hunting estates. Their party had included several mounted servants, two members of the Unicorn Guard, and a large picnic basket. They covered many miles and many flasks of whiskey, but had seen no quarry. Dorian suggested they stay at Rabbit's Rest for the night, but Gregory was in a foul mood and wanted to get back. By the time they passed through the palace gate the dinner hour loomed, and both Gregory and Brian were decidedly drunk.

Brian was still rolling. "Let's have a game of strikestick."

"I can't," said Gregory. "I have to visit Missus Desmarais. I've been gone all day and she'll have plenty to say about it. I tell you, pregnant women lose much of their charm."

Roffi slid down from his bay hunter. "Your Highness, for such a lady you can be tolerating anything."

Gregory glowered at him. "Spoken like a true bachelor, Chris," he said, and took his leave.

Brian turned to Dorian and Roffi. "How about it, boys?"

Dorian shook his head. He had a fascinating book waiting for him, an account of Caleb Desmarais's first High Council during the Great Svelyan Wars. He wanted to return to it. "I'm worn out, Smithy. I think I'll have an early night."

"Myself as well," said Roffi.

Brian tossed his calfskin gloves and his crop to the groom. The boy dropped a glove, and scrambled to pick it up before Brian could reprimand him.

"You two are shockingly boring these days," Brian said. "I expect it from Dorian, but I thought you had a bit more life in you, Chris. Gregory's the only one who remembers how to have a good time around here, and he's tied up by his balls."

"A woman like the princess would not have to tie me up by my balls," Roffi said. "I would go willingly."

Dorian was surprised, and the comment somehow cut through Brian's drunken fog. "I would watch that kind of talk, Roffi," Brian said.

Roffi blinked, as if someone had just pinched his arm to see if he was dreaming. He smiled. "Oh, come now, I am only jesting. What man is not envious of His Highness, in everything from his seat in the saddle to the beauty of his wife?"

Brian snorted and the tension drained out of his shoulders. "Well, as long as we're being honest...I don't know about that. Eleanor is a beauty for sure, but beauty can't make up for the mouth on her."

Dorian bristled. "This conversation needs to end, now."

Brian pulled a flask from his belt. He went for a drink but it was empty. He yelled at the groom and tossed the flask his way as well. "Listen to you," he said. "Always perfectly loyal, aren't you?"

Brian crept closer, until Dorian saw the red lines radiating from the hazel irises of his eyes. His breath was a shot of whiskey. Dorian heard his own pulse getting louder in his ears with each word Brian threw at him.

"Mister Finley, perfect friend...perfect soldier...perfect rug under my cousin's feet. Anything for a seat at the Council Table."

Roffi stepped between them and put his hands on Brian's chest. Dorian's hands curled into fists. "Say what you need to say, Brian," he said.

Brian looked down at Dorian's clenched fists. He spit, and then wiped his mouth. He laughed the false giggle of a young girl flirting with a rich old man. "No worries, boys," he said. "I'm just poking fun."

He spun around and his ankle rolled, nearly sending him into a wheelbarrow full of old straw and horse manure. Dorian could still hear him cursing after he disappeared behind the tack house.

Roffi was full of apologies and excuses for Brian. Dorian shrugged him off. He said a quick goodbye and returned to his room. He went the long way, so he wouldn't have to pass Eleanor's door.

He tried to read that night, but none of it made sense. He put the book aside and poured a glass of whiskey. Brian's words stayed with him. Whether he liked it or not, some of them were true. And nearly as bad, some of them were not.

Eleanor watched Mercy Leigh over her ballooning stomach. The witch had increased the frequency of her baby monitoring to once a week. Eleanor both anticipated and dreaded her visits. Mercy Leigh never said much as she ran her hands over Eleanor's belly and down her spine. Eleanor waited for the smile that signified all was progressing well.

This morning Mercy Leigh did not grant Eleanor her usual reassuring conclusion. She turned away without any comment. Her delicate brows drew together as she wiped her hands on a towel. Eleanor waited, her heart pounding in her chest, while the witch gathered her tools. Finally she could stand it no more.

"What is it, Mercy? What's wrong?"

The witch rubbed her eyes. "Goodness, Your Highness, forgive me. All is well. I'm distracted."

Eleanor exhaled and rolled onto her side. She rested a hand on her belly. It lay beside her on the bed like an extra pillow. "Praises," she said, and then with her usual curiosity, "what is bothering you?"

Mercy Leigh shook a bottle of herbs. "Nothing to concern you, Your Highness."

"Maybe I can help you. I've little else to do these days but wait. Pray, tell me?"

"I don't want to upset you, but if you insist…" Mercy Leigh sat on the bed. "I've a patient. Very young. Poor. She delivered late last night. I…the bleeding is too heavy."

"Will she die?"

"Yes, if I cannot find a solution…I've tried thinning her blood, and nectar of cottonflower…" She ran a hand over Eleanor's forehead. "You're pale. I shouldn't have said anything."

Eleanor shook her head. "Better to know what I'm facing."

"You should be fine," said Mercy Leigh, but she turned away. Eleanor grabbed her hand. The witch rubbed her tired eyes again as she spoke. "The baby is strong. You are strong. You have narrow hips, but it shouldn't be a problem. I just—I cannot in good conscience guarantee anyone's safety. Especially the first time."

"Thank you for your candor," Eleanor said.

Mercy Leigh kissed her cheeks. Once she'd left Eleanor stood and waited for her creaking hips to settle into an ambulatory position. She crossed the room and opened her mother's music box.

Did anyone give you such an honest assessment? She wondered. She slid Leticia Brice's comb into her own hair, so thick and lustrous from the baby's energy. *Did you have an inkling of the end? Or did you careen toward it with visions of old age and a passel of your own grandchildren at your feet?* She stroked Leticia's grandchild through her own skin. "Be safe, little one," she whispered. "Little man. Little lady." She hummed a nervous tune, and her hands searched for something else to occupy them. She fiddled with a necklace, and a few earbobs, before removing the largest item from the box.

She slid the cracked slipper from its dusty green and purple bag. She held the shoe in her hand, and it felt no less substantial than it had at the Second Sunday Ball. She turned it over and over as she walked to the window. Light congregated inside it at the spots her fingers touched, the shifting grays and blues of clouds blown out over the Shallow Sea after a hard rain. The intricate web of cracks wound through the swirling colors like static lightning. Sunlight shot through the shoe when she held it up to the window.

Pansy must have announced Dorian, but Eleanor never heard her. Still, his voice over her shoulder didn't startle her. It was the most natural sound in HighGod's creation. "It is amazing how it holds together," he said.

She nodded. "Damaged, yet lovely."

He put a hand on her shoulder. "And much stronger than anyone thinks."

She turned to him and lowered the shoe. "Shall I be thus?"

"As you have been," he said. "As you shall be."

CHAPTER 25

DORIAN'S BIRTHDAY

DESPITE HER WORRY, ELEANOR enjoyed being pregnant up until the last month or so. During HighSpring things got uncomfortable. Her belly swelled to the point she could not imagine making it until her assumed delivery at the beginning of LowSummer. When dressed for dinner she resembled a giant chapel bell with a blonde head. She spent the warm afternoons walking in the garden for as long as her aching back would allow. Gregory wanted her to stay in bed, but Mercy Leigh assured him the fresh air would benefit both Eleanor and the baby.

Teardrop had been staying at the Paladine ever since Eleanor stopped riding. Eleanor had missed her, so she asked Gregory to bring the mare to the palace for the afternoon. She grazed on the lawn as Eleanor sat on a picnic blanket eating candied cherries. Gregory sat beside her, reading a proclamation of some sort. She'd brought along copies of the two books Chou had seen under Ezra Oliver's desk, but after several careful examinations she could find no glaring connection between the two. Each perusal disappointed her more, so she set them aside and flipped through her botany encyclopedia. She couldn't place a seedpod she'd found during one of her walks in the garden.

"Ah!" she exclaimed. "A weathervane seed. A red one, I think." She tilted the book to get a better look at the painting and read the few lines of information below it. "Interesting. Weathervane pollen is highly flammable, and the smoke takes on the color of the plant."

"Hmmm," Gregory said. "What? Oh, yes, interesting." He sounded anything but interested.

A scowl crossed her face as she read on. "It says here the red variety is common. Not like the blue ones. *The only known Blue Weathervane in existence has been in the possession of Ezra Oliver, Chief Magician at Eclatant Palace, for over fifty years.* Blah!"

"What's the matter?"

"It amazes me how often I come across Ezra Oliver in my studies. By the Bond, I cannot escape him."

"He's over one hundred years old, Eleanor, and he's been one of the most important men in Cartheigh for most of them. Why not just ignore him? You don't have to dance with him, or invite him to tea."

She sighed. "I know. Something about him bothers me. Gregory, I—"

"Don't worry yourself about him," said Gregory, without looking up. "He won't be an annoyance forever."

She let the conversation end with that happy thought. A few silent minutes ticked by.

"These are so good." Eleanor picked out another sweet. "Have one."

"Hmmm," he said again. "Pardon? Ah…No thank you."

"The bakers have been outdoing themselves lately. I'll be the size of a milk cow by the time this baby comes."

Gregory put down the parchment. "The bakers, that reminds me. Dorian's birthday is coming up in ten days. I think we should have a party for him. Something grand. He never puts on airs. We should put them on for him."

"An interesting idea." She knew Dorian would hate it. She ate another cherry. "Or, do you know what he might really enjoy? Why don't we invite Anne Clara and her a family for a visit? Dorian hasn't seen them since last fall. Not glamorous, but just as enjoyable."

"Maybe you're right. Sometimes I think Dorian prefers intimate affairs," he said.

"Do you think so?"

"It's done. Can you handle the planning? I don't want you to exert yourself."

"Of course I can. It will make the time pass. Right now each day seems an eternity."

"I know," he said. "It's tiring me out."

She patted his hand in sympathy.

Eleanor sent a message off to Anne Clara by private courier. She received a reply two days later.

Dearest Princess Eleanor,

What a wonderful idea to celebrate Dorian's birthday as Eclatant! We would be honored to come, and thank you in advance for your generosity.

I must ask you for a small service. Please inform Dorian that our brother Abram and his family will also be joining us. I have tried to discourage him, because Abram is sadly lacking in courtly graces, but he has not visited the palace in several years and feels it is time to pay his respects. I pray you will prepare Dorian for his visit and beseech him to remain cordial for the sake of family unity.

We look forward to seeing you in a few days.

Your devoted servant,
Anne Clara F. Tavish

When Eleanor brought Dorian news of his sister's visit he was thrilled, but elation became gloom as he realized Abram would accompany her. Eleanor hoped Abram's presence would not ruin the celebration.

The Finleys and the Tavishes arrived two days before Dorian's birthday. Eleanor planned several pre-birthday celebrations. Anne Clara's adorable children filled each picnic and tea party with good-natured energy.

"Is this what I'm getting myself into?" Eleanor laughed as Anne Clara's son chased Dorian and Gregory with a wooden sword and her twin daughters toddled across the picnic blanket with muddy bare feet. The girls babbled nonsense to each other in their own language.

Anne Clara bounced her youngest, a chubby boy, on her knee. "It is, every messy moment."

Eleanor rubbed her belly and eased her own squirming baby out from under her ribcage. She grabbed a little foot, or maybe it was an elbow, and eased the child into a more comfortable position. "This one hears them and wants to join in!"

Anne Clara took her hand. "You look lovely, Your Highness. Are you happy?"

Eleanor rested her hands on her swollen middle. The stubborn baby slid right back where he or she had been and jabbed Eleanor's ribs again.

"I am," she said. "It's a wonderful thing, no matter..."

Anne Clara shushed her. "Don't speak, I understand."

The day of Dorian's birthday Eleanor sought him out so he could approve the final dinner menu. She asked Anne Clara, who said she thought he was down in the topiary garden, shooting with Abram. Eleanor heard them before she saw them. She shuffled down the gravel paths, puffing like a hot teakettle, searching for them amidst the maze of hedges.

Eleanor did not know what to make of Dorian's brother. He was polite enough, but obviously uncomfortable with strangers. She saw why he resented Dorian. There was a family resemblance, but the puzzle pieces just did not meet well in Abram. Both men were tall, but where Dorian was lean and strong, Abram was skinny and almost frail. Dorian's fair skin became pallor on Abram, whose dark eyes were protruding rather than arresting. He was only a few years older than Dorian but his hair was thinning. Eleanor couldn't help but feel sorry for him as he stood beside his brother's robust glory.

She paused behind a hedge and rested one hand on the prickly branches. She didn't mean to eavesdrop, but she hesitated to interrupt. They were clearly arguing.

"I don't need your approval for anything, Dorian," Abram said. "It's my estate, and my money."

"You forget my income comes from the estate as well. I should at least be consulted."

"It's been a hard year. I have to sell off some property."

"I think that's rash. You can't get it back. What about your hounds? Can't you sell some of them? The kennel must cost a fortune," said Dorian.

Abram swelled. "I raise the finest hunting dogs in the east. I see no reason to sell them."

"You have over a hundred. Can you even tell which is which?"

"You know, I have come up with a way to cut costs. I'm reducing your stipend." Abram notched his arrow.

"You can't be serious. It's barely enough to get me by as it is."

Abram laughed. "Get you by? You live here, in the palace. You're the prince's lapdog. What could you possibly need?"

Dorian lowered his bow. "Is that what you think of me?"

Abram didn't answer, he just let fly with his shot. It went wide and he cursed.

"I'm trying to put aside something of my own," said Dorian. "I don't want to live here at court forever. I'd like to have my own home, perhaps in the Crossing. A place where I can escape all this for a while."

"Don't worry, I'm sure Gregory will take care of that for you when he's king."

Dorian stepped toward him. "As my brother I'd hoped you'd understand. I want to do this myself."

"Why don't you get married? Why don't you wag your pretty dick at some rich widow and have her take care of you? Or are you still too busy chasing whores and deflowering virgins?"

Dorian grabbed Abram by the shoulders and pulled him close. The look on his face frightened Eleanor.

"You know nothing about me." Dorian pushed Abram, hard, and Abram landed on his ass.

Eleanor stepped out from behind the hedge. She moved too quickly and stumbled on the sliding gravel. Her hand went protectively to her belly. "Hello, Dorian, Abram," she said in a high voice. "I hope I'm not disturbing you."

Abram stood. He wiped his leggings and gathered his bow and quiver. "No, Your Highness. We're finished. I'll leave you." He marched off.

She waddled over to Dorian, who stooped to pick up his own equipment. His arrows clacked as he shoved them into the quiver. She put a hand to his back, but he shrugged her off.

"How much did you hear?" he asked over his shoulder.

"Enough to know your brother is spiteful and jealous," she said.

He snorted. "Yes, I guess you're right."

She wanted to make him feel better. "Don't listen to him."

"Do you think I'm Gregory's lapdog?"

"Of course not." She tried to stand in front of him but he paced around her. His hair fell across his forehead, but he didn't brush it back. For once he would not meet her eyes.

"Gregory loves you," she said. "He counts on you in everything.

You've never asked him for more than he offers you, and you give him your service in return."

Dorian laughed, and it was bitter. "My service. Yes, I give him that. And he gives me a unicorn, and a roof over my head, and the admiration of the whole court. But there's only one thing I really want. And he can't give it to me, because he can't share it."

He walked to the shooting target, ripped it out of the ground, and returned to her with his eyes still on his muddy boots. "That's what a loyal servant I am."

"Dorian, tell me what you want from me," she said. "Please, tell me, and I will do it."

He finally looked at her. "You asked me that question a long time ago," he said. "You asked me what I would have you do. I don't know. I just know I can't live like this."

"Please." She wasn't sure what she meant by it.

"Maybe I should have been man enough to tell you what I wanted at the beginning. Maybe there would have been some slight chance, but there was no time to understand it." He placed his warm hand on her tight stomach. "Whatever chance there was, it's gone now."

Tears slipped down her cheeks. "You're right."

He stepped away. "I'll walk you home."

"I'm fine. I know the way."

"I can't be responsible if you deliver the future king alone among the hedgerows," he said.

She couldn't muster a smile. He followed her to the palace.

Eleanor was glad for the excuse of her heavy belly. She stayed at the dinner table and picked at her food. The fiddles and flutes ground on her nerves like a chorus of bullfrogs competing with a herd of cows. She responded to the party guests who directed questions her way, but later she remembered none of the conversations. Chou perched on the back of chair, and picked at her hair. He landed by her soup bowl.

"What's wrong?" he asked.

"I'm weary, that's all." She glanced at Dorian, who in turn focused his attention on his two fidgety nephews. He entertained them hiding a nut beneath one of two cups and asking them to find it. When she entered the dining room she had wished him a happy birthday and they had not spoken since.

"I share Chou Chou's concerns," said Gregory. "Are you feeling well?"

Her held her napkin to her eyes for a moment. "This food is just not sitting well with me. You know, pregnant women and their delicate constitutions."

"Maybe you should retire early," said Gregory. "Dorian will understand."

"I think I will. Will you tell him goodnight for me?"

Gregory helped her pull out her chair. When she stood her stomach knocked into her water glass, and it tipped over. She grabbed for it but it rolled over the edge of the table and shattered on the floor. The guests looked up from their plates.

"Damn," she said.

"Peace, Eleanor." Gregory waved over one of the servants. "Go lie down."

Eleanor turned on a heavyset woman in a bright orange dress with her fork halfway to her mouth. "Mind your eyeballs, Lady Pendleton," she said, "before they fall into your pie." As Gregory took her arm she heard drumming hooves and loud voices in the hall. She turned toward the entrance.

Two unicorns burst through the dining room door. Some of the guests screamed as a sentry slid down from the first unicorn's back. He ran to the head of the table and fell on his knees in front of King Casper.

"HighGod, what is the meaning of this?" asked the king.

The sentry raised his head. His face was ashen. "I hardly know how to tell you, Your Majesty. I can't believe it myself."

"Tell me what?"

The young man stuttered a few unintelligible words. The king gripped his butter knife. "Tell me, boy!"

"Caleb's Horn, sire. It's gone."

"That's impossible." Casper dropped the knife and it clanged off his plate.

"I wish it was, sire," he said. "I wish it with all my heart."

"How? Did someone break in? No one's ever been able to break in! Thieves have been trying for three hundred years!"

"No, sire…no one broke in…it's just gone. A magical crime. It disappeared, right in front of our eyes." He hung his head, as if expecting to lose it right there.

Gregory stood. "Father—"

The king didn't let him finish. "Gregory, come with me." He pointed at several other members of the Council. "And all of you. And you, Finley."

Dorian waited behind Gregory as the king spoke to the sentry. "Go and find Ezra Oliver in his study. We need his expertise."

Eleanor was understandably forgotten as they left. Christopher Roffi spoke from behind her. "Please, Your Highness," he said. She turned. Roffi held out his hand. "Would you let me see you safely back to your room?"

She nodded absently and called to Anne Iris and Margaret before taking his arm. They made their ponderous way back to Eleanor's chambers. She found herself annoyed at Roffi's clinging assistance. *He's just trying to be helpful*, she thought, *but I'm pregnant, not crippled.*

When they reached her door the guard opened it and Anne Iris and Margaret disappeared inside. She turned to say goodnight to Roffi, but he did not release her.

"You looked lovely tonight, Your Highness," he said.

She gave him a quick smile and tried to extract her arm. "Thank you, Christopher. Now I must really—"

"A vision, you were—"

"Yes, thank you," she said, and yanked her arm loose. It was hardly the time for courtly flattery. "Thank you for escorting me. Goodnight." She glanced at the guard. His eyes flicked to the floor.

Roffi's jaw clenched, and to Eleanor's surprise he flushed. She started to apologize for her rudeness, but he bowed and took his leave.

CHAPTER 26

DIRER BY THE MOMENT

THE NEXT MORNING ELEANOR, Anne Iris, and Margaret were no better informed. They dressed quickly so they'd be prepared to receive guests if anyone came to enlighten them. Throughout breakfast they picked at their food and speculated on the theft. As the chambermaids cleared the dishes there was a knock at the door. Pansy announced Raoul and Christopher Roffi.

Roffi and Raoul joined the three women in Eleanor's sitting area. She smiled at Roffi, and to her relief he smiled back and kissed her hand as he always did. He pushed High Noon's blanket aside and sat on the couch beside Margaret. Raoul squeezed between them.

Eleanor didn't bother with small talk. "What news, gentlemen?" she asked.

"Nothing new, unfortunately," said Raoul. He took Margaret's hand. "Gregory and Dorian haven't left the Council Hall."

"They must not be having anything to tell," Roffi said.

They sat in morose silence for the better part of an hour. Anne Iris made a few attempts at humor, but they fell sadly flat. Eleanor excused herself, and Anne Iris followed her to the bathing room. To Eleanor's embarrassment she needed help managing her skirts over the pot. By the time they returned they were minus one visitor.

"Where's Christopher?" Eleanor asked.

"He asked that we apologize for him. He's preparing a report for his king," said Margaret.

Eleanor envied Roffi's sense of purpose. Raoul left half an hour later, and Eleanor and her friends searched for a way to pass the time.

"Bunco?" asked Anne Iris. "We're only three with Eliza in the country, but we can have a ghost toss."

Eleanor shrugged and joined Margaret and Anne Iris at the card table. They started rolling, but she could not concentrate on keeping score.

"We're on fours, not threes," said Margaret.

Eleanor threw down the dice. "You know I can't stand these games."

"Pardon," said Anne Iris. "I'd be open to other suggestions."

"No, I'm sorry," said Eleanor. "We're all worried. If only someone would tell us something!"

Chou Chou landed on the table. "I could take a turn around the palace and see if I hear anything."

Eleanor was about to respond when she heard Pansy behind the door. She sounded uncharacteristically harried. "Sir, you can't go in there. You can't…stop… you must be announced!"

"Who—"

Margaret didn't need to finish the question to have it answered. Ezra Oliver flung open the door. Two armed guards followed him.

Eleanor stood as quickly as her belly would allow. "Mister Oliver, may I help you?"

Pansy rushed in behind him. "I tried to stop him, Your Highness."

Eleanor waved at her. "It's fine, Pansy." She tried again. "Mister Oliver, what do you want?"

He didn't answer. He walked across the room to her desk. He opened the drawers and pushed ribbons and packets of powder out of the way. He picked up her mother's music box. He opened it and took out the cracked slipper, wrapped in its green and purple bag, and set it on the desk. He turned the box over and shook it.

"Put that down, sir," Eleanor said.

Oliver ignored her. His eyes fell on the red blanket on the couch, and he picked it up. He reached his hands into the small pockets lining the edge of the blanket, where Cyril Brice had long ago stored hoof picks and curry combs. He removed a red and black silk bag, about the size of an apple.

"What is this, Your Highness?" he asked, holding it toward her.

"I have no idea," said Eleanor. "I've never seen it before."

"Really," he said. "Then how did it get here?"

Eleanor felt a prick of anger. "Since I've never seen it before, I wouldn't know."

He loosened the ribbon and a round object dropped into his hand. Eleanor's face went clammy as she recognized a lump of crude Fire-iron.

"You've never seen this either, I suppose?" asked Oliver.

"Never."

"I find that difficult to believe, since I found a tracking spell that could trace it, and here it is."

"That's impossible," said Eleanor, shaking her head. "How could I have stolen it? I can't perform magic. How could I make it disappear from underneath the noses of a Unicorn Guard?"

"Someone put it there," said Anne Iris.

Oliver slipped Caleb's Horn back in the black and red bag. "You may not be able to perform magic yourself, but your dear friends at the Abbey are capable."

"Rosemary? She's a teacher, not a conjurer. If I recall, *you* are the most powerful magician in Cartheigh. The person capable of the most elaborate magic could very well be behind the most elaborate magical crime in history." Eleanor started for the door. "I'm going to speak with the king."

"I think not," said Oliver. "He commanded the Horn be brought straight to him if it was found."

"I'm coming with you."

"No. The king's orders said the thief was to be contained."

"Thief?"

"That's what we must assume, is it not?" He spoke with the two guards. "Keep her here. Don't let her leave this room, nor these two, not even the bird. I'll speak with the king. He'll decide what's to be done."

Eleanor tried to pass the soldiers but they crossed their lances in front of her.

"Don't make it worse for yourself, lady. Especially not in your condition," said Oliver. He slipped the bag in his pocket, turned without bowing, and left.

Eleanor's legs started to give way. Margaret and Anne Iris helped her to the bed. Margaret knelt in front of her. "This is a mistake," she said. "There will be an explanation."

Eleanor's fist went to her eyes. "Of course. An explanation." In her opinion the explanation had just walked out the door.

Dorian and Gregory paced across the king's receiving room. Every few circles they passed each other, like dancers in a reel. Casper sat on his throne, watching them. "Stand still, both of you!" he barked. "You're making me ill."

Dorian leaned against the window. He jaw ached from grinding his teeth for hours. The situation grew direr by the moment. The unfathomable magical theft, the accusations against Eleanor, and now Oliver's latest disturbing revelation.

"Roffi," the king said for the twentieth time. "Christopher Roffi."

"Tell us again what happened," Gregory said to Oliver.

Oliver sat in a chair beside the king. His face looked like a dirt road after a hailstorm. His mouth was lacerated and he'd lost several teeth. He held a wet cloth to his blackened eye.

He sighed, but did as Gregory asked. "After I discovered the Horn in the princess's room I hid it in my pocket and came directly here. I took the kitchen passageway, the one that leads to the Covey, to avoid the Great Hall. Halfway through the passage Roffi and his men came at me from behind. You can see the result of our meeting." Oliver dipped the cloth into the bowl of medicinal water at his feet. "All three of his magicians hitting me with firepower at once...a lesser sorcerer would have been killed out right. Thank HighGod for my own strength."

"You Majesty," Dorian said. "Something is not right. Princess Eleanor could not possibly have taken the Horn."

"Then give me another solution, Finley," Oliver said thickly, through his swollen lips.

"Obviously someone stole it by magical means and planted it in her room."

"Or," said Oliver, "she was obviously involved with Roffi. Haven't there been rumors for months? Look at my face. He followed me and ambushed me! She must have been about to give it over to him."

Gregory's hands had rarely left his hair since last night, and it stood up in wild spikes all over his head. "Has there been any news of Roffi?" he asked. "That bastard."

"By the time I woke he was gone, and the Horn gone with him. He's long out of the city by now," said Oliver.

"She asked me to take her to see it. The Horn. Last fall. I should have—"

"Does that surprise you?" Dorian couldn't believe how little Gregory understood about his own wife. "You took her to the Mines. She was studying the Bond. Of course she wanted to see the Horn...it was a very..." He shook his head in frustration. "Very...Eleanor-ish...request!"

Gregory did not seem to hear him. He rattled on. "Why? Why would she do it?"

"She must be in love with him!" said Oliver to Gregory. "Let's be honest, Your Highness, you and the princess have not always had a felicitous marriage. The Svelyan king wanted the Horn, and Roffi got it by playing on the princess's female vanities. Maybe she planned to go with him."

"In her condition?" asked Dorian. "Perhaps Roffi planted it there himself."

"Perhaps," said Oliver. He took a few thoughtful moments. "But…it hardly makes sense for Roffi to steal the Horn and plant it in her room, only to have to steal it back again. Why take the risk? And to what end?"

"Oliver has a point," said the king.

Oliver nodded. "Princess Eleanor knew about the prince's indiscretions—"

"How did you know about that?" interrupted Gregory.

"—and we warned you about this girl from the beginning. She's not the type to turn the other cheek."

"She's not in love with Roffi," said Dorian.

Oliver turned on him. "How can you be sure?"

Dorian couldn't speak truthfully, so he changed the direction of the conversation. "How could she have done it? She can't perform magic!"

"I have a theory," said Oliver. "A Blood Path."

"A what?" said the king.

"A Blood Path. It's a very complicated enchantment that connects two objects that are related to each other. Related by blood. It's only been accomplished a handful of times. If done correctly, it can draw them together from great distances."

"Explain it," said Gregory.

"I can't explain it," said Oliver, "because I don't know exactly how it works, but if there were something that could be traced to the actual unicorn horn inside the Fire-iron, something related by blood to Eclatant himself, perhaps a path could be drawn. It's the only way the

Horn could have disappeared from its chamber in plain view of the guards."

Casper's eyes widened. "Every unicorn in the Paladine is somehow related to Eclatant. My stallion, Fortune, is a direct descendent."

"As is Vigor," said Gregory. "The Paladine is covered in traces of Eclatant's bloodline. Shed horns, hoof clippings, thousands of hairs. Millions of hairs."

"Even if someone did use a Blood Path," said Dorian. "It couldn't have been Eleanor!"

"Of course not," said Oliver. "I already confronted her about the witches from Afar Creek. She denied it, of course."

"I don't think that woman, her teacher, would know that kind of magic," said Gregory.

"No," said Oliver. "But I will admit there are some sorceresses in that harem with talent. There's no reason someone couldn't have performed the spell for her. The witches have every reason to detest the royal family, since the crown is so generous to the Coveys. They would love to see power fall into the hands of the Svelyan king."

"You hate the witches," Dorian sneered. "Their treachery would be convenient for you."

"You are overly emotional, Finley. You forget the Horn is out there, heading straight into the hands of the Svelyan king. Who knows what magical deviance he has planned? A breaking of the Bond? Or worse yet, a usurping of the unicorn's loyalty?" Oliver was all puffed-up rationality. Dorian wanted to knock his other eye shut.

"Oliver is right," said Casper. "Securing the Horn must be our top priority. Princess Eleanor will be held under arrest until we can organize a trial. Send her to Rabbit's Rest Lodge, under Unicorn Guard. She may take her maidservant with her."

"Sire, I don't think that's a good idea so close to—"

"Quiet, Dorian," said Gregory. "The king didn't ask if you thought it was a good idea."

Casper stood and put a hand on his son's shoulder. "Thank you, Gregory. I'm glad you're keeping your head. Now, we must organize the scouting parties."

Dorian barely heard the rest of the conversation. He was thinking about routes to Rabbit's Rest Lodge.

CHAPTER 26

NO TIME

RABBIT'S REST WAS FIFTEEN miles outside of Maliana. A short ride by unicorn, but via carriage it took all day. It was unusually hot for HighSpring, and Eleanor removed two layers of petticoats as they rolled down the OutCountry Road. Pansy passed Eleanor a water flask and tried to make her eat. Eleanor sipped the water, but she couldn't stomach a morsel of food. The rocking of the carriage together with her tattered nerves made her feel as queasy as ever she had at the beginning of her pregnancy. She closed her eyes.

Even with the baby pressing into her ribcage, preventing her from drawing a decent breath, she drifted off. The shouts of the guards as the carriage rolled to a stop woke her. She leaned out the window.

Grassy fields and rolling hills surrounded Rabbit's Rest. The lodge, a one-story stone building rambling willy-nilly around several barns and a skinning shed, had no permanent staff. Gregory brought his own servants when he visited.

"Come, Your Highness," Pansy said. She had climbed down and stood in the dirt courtyard. Eleanor steadied herself with both hands on the sides of the carriage door.

"Wait!" said a voice. One of the Unicorn Guard slid down from his mount. He reached up to her. "My family is from Solsea, Your

Highness. I know of the good you've done down south, and I'm just sorry you in this sad way. It ain't right."

She laid her hands on his shoulders and allowed him to lift her down from the carriage. "Thank you, soldier. You're a strong lad to lift such a load." She dropped her voice. "I will accept your kindness, but please don't offer it again. You put yourself in danger. If you would ease my burden, heed me."

The young man nodded.

Eleanor and Pansy entered the lodge. The ceilings were low and the furniture basic. Dented iron pots hung from hooks above a pot-bellied stove. The slanting light revealed eddies of floating dust.

"The hunting must be fabulous in these parts for the Desmarais to tolerate such lodgings," said Eleanor. The place was rustic at best.

Eleanor jumped when an old woman rose from the kitchen table. Her gray robe blended so well with the mossy stone walls Eleanor hadn't seen her.

"Who are you?" Pansy asked.

"My name is Myrtle. I'm a witch. A babycatcher."

"Are you from Afar Creek?" asked Eleanor.

"No, no place as grand as that," the old woman said. "I'm from Flat Rock Abbey. It's about five miles south of here."

"I've never heard of it," Eleanor said.

"It's a small Abbey. There aren't many towns out this way. We live quietly most of the time, and tend our crops. A rider came in royal livery and asked me to stay here with you and look out for the baby."

"We'll be glad to have you," said Eleanor. Myrtle wasn't Mercy Leigh, but she would be better than Pansy and some soldiers.

The soldiers came in behind them with their few cases and boxes of bread, cheese, and dried fruit. Eleanor found a bedroom off the sitting area. She opened the door to a simple bed with flannel sheets and a dragon robe quilt, a few wooden chairs and a low chest of drawers. An embroidered purple and green rabbit sat on the pillows. Its button eyes looked at Eleanor as if she could explain why it was here on this drab gray bed and not in some cheerful nursery. She lifted the latch on her valise. She pulled out a nightdress and shook it out. Something red and blue rolled out of the sleeve.

"Chou!" she cried.

The parrot righted himself and shook. "Never, never again," he said.

She grabbed him in both hands. "How did you get in there? Gregory said you couldn't come!"

"Margaret stuffed me inside while Anne Iris gave the guard who was supposed to be checking your bags a view down her dress," he said. "You know I wouldn't let you go without me."

"You dear old buzzard." Eleanor squeezed him, and a few feathers dropped onto the bed.

"Don't kill me after I survived in the case," he said.

She set him down.

"Did you ever speak with Gregory?" he asked.

She shook her head. "He wouldn't see me. I wrote to him. I told him I was innocent, and still he didn't come."

"What about Dorian?"

"There was no time. They came so quickly, and took me out the passageway through the Covey. I never saw anyone. To think, only yesterday afternoon I was worried about seating charts at the birthday party!" She laughed, and it had a bitter taste. "Now here we are, Chou. You and me in a leaky, drafty room. Just like old times!"

Chou landed on her shoulder. "It's been a long ride, even for you in the comfort of the carriage. Why don't you take a nap?"

"I'm sick of people telling me to rest." Eleanor rustled around in her valise for some paper and a quill. "I'm writing to Gregory again. He must believe me. Perhaps when Roffi visited…why does no one suspect Oliver? They're blinded, all of them, by his groveling…his ingratiating…his—Oh."

A spasm ripped through her stomach and stopped in a knot in her lower back. She bent over.

"Eleanor? Eleanor? What is it?" Chou swirled around her head.

"Get the witch, Chou." She crawled on the bed as he disappeared down the hallway. She lay on her side, breathing hard.

Myrtle and Pansy came into the room. Myrtle scrubbed her hands in the wash bin. "Can you sit up, Your Highness?" she asked.

Eleanor rolled onto her back, but as she sat up heat gushed between her legs. Since she had removed her petticoats the fluid soaked through her dress and onto the dragon robe.

"Her water has been pierced," said Myrtle.

"No," said Eleanor. "It's not supposed to come yet! Not for over three weeks!"

"Water's gone, my lady. The baby don't know about three weeks. It's coming sooner than later."

Not here, not here.

The next few hours passed in a haze of stabbing pain and weakness. "There's nothing to be done but endure it," Myrtle said as she wiped Eleanor's sweaty brow. "Your body has made no progress. It will be a long road."

"Is the baby safe?" Eleanor asked.

"I should think so. You close your eyes. I'm just going to mix some herbs."

The sun set over the low hills. Eleanor couldn't see past the nearest wooden shed. Chou appeared in the window. "Eleanor, don't fall asleep yet," he said.

"I don't think that will—" she crammed her fist into her mouth as another pain came and passed. "—happen anytime soon."

"Listen to me." His voice held none of its usual banter.

"What is it, Chou?"

"I was eavesdropping—"

"As usual."

"Let me finish!" he snapped. She blinked in surprise.

"I heard Myrtle telling Pansy you're in a worse way than she makes out. The pains shouldn't be coming this fast and this hard yet. She said your body is not ready to give the baby up, but the baby needs the water, and it's still leaking away. So you're both in danger. Myrtle said this is beyond her abilities."

Eleanor paled. "I need Mercy Leigh, Chou. She's the most skilled babycatcher at Afar Creek, and that means in all of Cartheigh."

Chou paced on the bed frame. "I could fly to Afar Creek, but it would take too long."

"I need to get word to Rosemary."

"You know Rosemary is on house arrest. No one can see her, not even the other witches. And like you said, you need a babycatcher, not a teacher."

Eleanor took a deep breath. Maybe the connection held. Eleanor had never tried to call Rosemary. She'd had no reason until now. "I need to fall asleep, Chou. Bring me some whiskey from the sitting room."

Chou looked as her like she had lost her mind along with her waistline. "It's hardly the time for a drink and a snooze!" he said.

"Just trust me. I must sleep, and I can't if I don't have something to cut the pain. Please."

Chou flew out the door and returned with a flask in his talons. She pulled out the stopper, and took a long swig, then another, wincing at the sour taste. She had never liked straight spirits.

She waited as another pain built and passed before taking another drink. Her gorge rose but she kept it down.

"Careful," said Chou.

Eleanor set the down the flask. As unaccustomed to drinking as she was, her head was fuzzy by the time another cramp came and went. "Better, Chou," she said. "Better."

Her eyes were heavy. She hadn't slept in two days, and her body was working hard. *Please let this happen. Somehow let it happen.*

"Trust me," she whispered, before drifting off.

Dorian followed Gregory across the wide lawn of Trill Castle.

"Eleanor," Gregory called. "Come out!"

Gregory opened the door of Walnut Cottage. Dorian peered over his shoulder as he stood in the hall. Gregory turned toward the broom closet.

"No," said Dorian. "No, Greg, you can't go in there. She's not in there. You can't go in!"

Gregory didn't hear him. Dorian stepped in front of the prince but Gregory walked through him and disappeared through the closed door.

Now Dorian knew Eleanor *was* inside. HighGod knew what Gregory was doing to her. He pounded on the door. "Gregory! Open the door! Eleanor! Eleanor, let me in!"

He grabbed the doorknob, but it slipped through his hands as if he were made of smoke. He tried again, and again.

The door swung open, but it wasn't Eleanor. It wasn't Gregory, either. He hardly knew Rosemary, but he recognized her at once.

"I don't have time for long explanations," she said. "Just know what I am telling you is true, and you must act on it. Eleanor needs your help. She called to me in a dream, and now I'm calling on you." She explained what Eleanor had revealed. "Mercy Leigh must go to her. If she doesn't, Eleanor and the baby will die."

"Gregory won't want me to go," said Dorian. "He hasn't let me out of his sight since she was arrested."

"Do you love her?" asked Rosemary.

"Yes, and I think you know it. I will find a way."

"You must take Mercy Leigh to Rabbit's Rest as soon as possible."

"I'll go by unicorn. It's the fastest way."

Rosemary nodded. "I will tell you, Mister Finley, I have long advised Eleanor to put aside her affection for you."

"I understand. I would do the same if I were you. You must know we've both tried. I think I've finished trying."

"Yes, and while I don't give up easily, even I can recognize futility when I see it." The door slammed shut. "Now go! There is no time!"

Dorian opened his eyes and lifted his head from his writing desk. The night had been muggy, and he had stripped off his shirt before nodding off over a letter to General Clayborne. He hadn't removed his boots, and he hopped a few times to get the blood flowing to his feet. He walked to the window, rubbing his bare arms. A light drizzle cooled the air. It must be early still. The servants were just bringing in the morning milk deliveries. He grabbed yesterday's undershirt and pulled it on over his head as he left his room. He went straight to Gregory's chambers. He ignored the guard and banged on the door.

"Greg, it's Dorian." He shook the doorknob, half expecting it to dissolve in his hand as it had in his dream.

"I'm coming." The door opened and Gregory stepped back to let him in.

"Is there some news?" Gregory asked. "I was finally getting some sleep."

"No, nothing new." It was a lie, but Dorian was beyond caring. "But I wanted to talk with you about something."

"What is it?"

"I'm worried about the baby. All this stress can't be good for Eleanor." He had already decided to leave Rosemary's nocturnal appearance out of the conversation.

"You woke me to tell me that? You think I don't know it?"

"Of course you know it," said Dorian. "But what happens if something goes wrong out there? There's no one but some country witch to help. The woman probably delivers more piglets than babies."

Gregory poured a glass of wine. The glass shook in his hands. "The baby isn't due for weeks."

"Still, don't you think it would be prudent to have someone there? We aren't talking about any baby. Regardless of Eleanor's part in this, we're talking about a Desmarais prince or princess, one of the blood."

Gregory set his glass down hard. Wine slopped over the edge. "We think it's a Desmarais baby. It could come out with a Svelyan accent."

"Is that what you believe?" asked Dorian.

"I don't know! I don't know!" Gregory sat down and covered his head with his forearms. "How could she put me in this place, that bitch! After everything I've done for her."

Dorian wanted to punch him, but he pitied him as well. It was not the first time. He knelt by his friend. Gregory looked at him, as if begging Dorian to explain it all away. His brown eyes were bloodshot, and his hair stuck together in thick clumps. Dorian could tell by the smell of sweat and booze around him he had not bathed.

"Gregory," Dorian said. He wanted to be as honest as possible. "Eleanor has always tried to be the best wife she could be, and it hasn't always been easy for her. You must give her the benefit of the doubt."

"I wish I could," Gregory said, "but…there's been something there, for a long time. I tried to ignore it, but now I can't. She stopped caring so much, Dorian, about what I did and where I was. Lately, it's like she's been somewhere else."

"She's been tired, Greg, she's never gone through this before, and after last time—"

"Who told you about last time?"

"Anne Iris." Dorian said the first name that popped into his head.

Gregory shook his head. "No, it was something else." He pounded his fist on the table. "I know it! And Roffi always sniffing around. I even asked her about him, and she lied to me. Damn them both!"

Dorian stood and tried to control his own anger. "You should have seen her before they took her to Rabbit's Rest."

"I couldn't! I couldn't go now even if I wanted to. How would it look?"

"As though you have a conscience."

"Wrong. Three hundred years ago Caleb Desmarais cut through an army of Svelyans that outnumbered his forces fourfold with no mercy. My grandfather put to death two of his own brothers for threatening his crown. My own father has never suffered one word of threat to his rule without banishing or beheading the offending party. And you expect me, the future king, to go to the comfort of someone accused of endangering the prosperity of not only my family, but the entire kingdom?"

"She's been accused on flimsy evidence and circumstance!" said Dorian. "You've chosen to believe Oliver without even hearing her story!"

"I just told you. My father puts his trust in few men, yet Oliver has served him through his entire reign without a black mark to his name. He served my grandfather. He was an apprentice under my great-grandfather. Oliver may be a blowhard, but he has never given us one reason to doubt his loyalty in nearly one hundred years!"

Gregory threw his glass into the fireplace. The bottle of wine went the same way, and the fire hissed when it shattered. He started to take up the candelabra but Dorian stopped him.

"If you can't go let me. I'll take Mercy Leigh to her." Dorian planned to go whether Gregory approved it or not, but the passage would be faster if he had the prince's support.

"I know you, Gregory. I know what you've been getting up to all this time. Your efforts at discretion were weak at best. Even if Eleanor is guilty she is not alone in her failings. Nor should the child suffer for the sins of either parent."

Gregory slid his hand to his forehead. "Go," he said. "Take the witch. Go now, before I change my mind."

Dorian ran back to his room. He grabbed a leather saddlebag and his dagger, his long bow and his quiver. He buckled his dress sword around his waist. He stopped in the kitchens and stuffed the bag with dried beef and several water flasks. He took a mount from a groom and galloped down the Paladine Road to find Senné, who had been sent to the great barns to visit the unicorn's blacksmith. As he checked the black stallion's new shoes he heard a soft rustle behind him.

"I will come with you," Teardrop said.

"No," said Dorian. "I need only one. Mercy Leigh will ride behind me."

"I will come anyway. Eleanor needs us both."

"Let her come," said Senné. "If Teardrop feels she is needed she is probably right. You'll have to keep up. I won't slow my pace."

She tossed her fine head. "Nor will I."

Dorian mounted and they cantered toward the OutCountry Road. He showed the papers Gregory had given him to the guard, who waved them through the Paladine gates.

The number of soldiers stationed around the entrance to Afar Creek Abbey surprised Dorian. He handed his orders to the lieutenant in charge. "We are to escort the witch called Mercy Leigh to Rabbit's Rest Lodge to attend the princess until the time of her trial."

The lieutenant nodded. "Everything appears to be in order."

Finally, after what seemed like an hour, a witch emerged from the dark entrance to the main building. Dorian recognized the red-haired young woman. He'd seen Mercy Leigh coming and going from Eleanor's chambers over the last few months.

"You'll ride with me." He had already warned Senné, who had grudgingly agreed.

Dorian mounted and hauled Mercy Leigh up behind him. She gripped his waist. Her bag of tools and medicines hung from her shoulders. Senné swung back a few steps as he adjusted to the increased weight, and Mercy Leigh squeezed harder. Dorian heard her soft prayers.

Dorian nudged Senné and they made their way through the gate as if there were no hurry. Dorian waved to the lieutenant, turned the corner and was about to spur Senné on when a hooded figure stepped from behind a fountain into their path.

A voice came from under the hood. "If Mercy Leigh rides with you then I will ride alone."

He caught a glimpse of dark eyes and straight white hair. "Rosemary? How did you escape?"

"They would do better to place a magician at the door when they want to contain a witch," she said with a wink. "I left Eleanor alone once, a long time ago. I won't do it again."

She stepped up to Teardrop. The mare snorted and stepped sideways. She had never carried any rider but Eleanor.

"Peace, lady." Rosemary reached out her hand. "For the love we both bear your mistress, I ask you to take me to her. I beg you to tread lightly, for I am not as strong as she."

Teardrop blew out several hard blasts of air. She lowered her head, and Rosemary stroked her nose. "Thank you," Rosemary said.

Dorian dismounted and gave Rosemary a leg up, and she gripped Teardrop's mane.

"Hold tight," Dorian said. He remounted and Mercy Leigh clutched at him again. "Teardrop, follow!"

If the anyone noticed the extra rider, he would have to catch them to discuss it.

CHAPTER 27

RABBIT'S REST

THEY MADE SURPRISINGLY GOOD time. Dorian had prepared for delays if either Rosemary or Mercy Leigh took a tumble, but both women hung on in silent determination. Dorian knew the way to Rabbit's Rest by heart. They were nearly there when Rosemary shouted through Teardrop's mane. "Look!"

Chou Chou flew over a low hill. Dorian's heart sank.

Chou landed on Senné's horn, his black tongue hanging out. "I came to find you. We must hurry. It's not going well."

He crawled into Dorian's hood and they set off. Both unicorns understood the urgency, and Dorian didn't need to encourage Senné. The stallion pushed himself.

Dorian leapt to the ground when they skidded to a halt in the courtyard. He reached for Mercy Leigh but she had already dismounted on the other side and was running into the lodge. The guards shouted and gathered around him. He thrust the orders bearing Gregory's seal at the lieutenant and ran inside after the two witches.

He heard Eleanor before he saw her. He followed the sounds of her cries to her bedroom door. The old country babycatcher stepped in front of him, blocking the doorway with her skinny arms. "Who are you?" she asked. "This is no place for a man."

"Stand aside. I don't want to hurt you."

Rosemary called from inside the room. "Let him pass, Myrtle."

Myrtle stepped aside and Dorian brushed past her. Eleanor curled on her side on the bed. Blood streaked her nightdress and sweat darkened her hair. A pile of bloody sheets lay on the floor. Rosemary tried to pull another sheet over her but she kicked it off. She gripped her knees and screamed, her eyes screwed shut.

Mercy Leigh fired questions at Myrtle as she washed her hands.

"She's not opening up," said Myrtle. "The baby is stuck."

"I have something that will help," said Mercy Leigh. "Candleroot oil, in the bag."

"I don't know it."

"It's rare. In the silver box. Hurry!"

Mercy Leigh gently lifted Eleanor's nightdress. She shifted her legs to apply the oil. Eleanor screamed again. Dorian crossed the room and knelt at her side.

"Eleanor," he said.

She opened her eyes. For a moment she looked as if she didn't recognize him. "Are you really here?" she asked.

"Yes," he said. "I'm here. I'll be right here." He took her hands and rubbed them between his own. Their clamminess frightened him.

"Stay with me, Dorian," she said.

"I will. Always."

"I don't know if I can do this."

"You can, and you will. You must. I need you." He leaned in and kissed her.

"What's this?" exclaimed Myrtle.

"Shhh," said Rosemary. "Leave them be."

Eleanor put her hands on his face and he rested his forehead against hers. Her blue and brown eyes looked into his, and they were aware again. "I need to see you," she said.

He nodded. Her brow twitched and he saw the pain coming on. She clamped down on his fingers, but she didn't close her eyes. Her mouth twisted and she cried out. It went through him like a cold wind. He gripped her hands as more contractions came and went for the next hour.

"It's working!" Mercy Leigh cried at last. "It's working, Your Highness! Push! Push now!"

Eleanor pushed, once, twice, three times. Dorian heard yelling, and realized it was his own voice, shouting her on. Her eyes suddenly widened.

"It's coming! One last push!" said Mercy Leigh.

There was a weak cry. Eleanor turned onto her back at the sound.

"She's here, Your Highness. Your daughter is here."

Mercy Leigh held up the child, then laid her on Eleanor's chest. She examined the baby's tiny fingers and kissed her stubby nose. "Angel," she whispered. "Angel."

Mercy Leigh wrapped the baby, who was getting louder by the moment as she tested her new lungs. "I'll just clean her up, but she looks wonderful."

Dorian brushed away the tears running down Eleanor's face. "She's beautiful," he said. "Thank HighGod."

"Thank you," said Eleanor.

He kissed her again. Once Mercy Leigh finished with the child she gave her to Rosemary and attended to Eleanor. Dorian stayed where he was, hunched at her side.

Dorian lifted Eleanor so Rosemary and Mercy Leigh could change the sheets. She sat on his lap in an armchair, her arms around his neck. His voice was quiet, his breath soft against her ear.

"Do you want to sleep for a bit?"

She nodded. She had already nursed her daughter. After she had changed her clothes Mercy Leigh helped her put the baby to her breast. Dorian asked if she wanted him to leave, and she told him emphatically no, but he turned away anyway. She had teased him.

"You've already seen me at far worse today."

Once she was situated and covered he came to the bed. "My mother raised me properly," he said. "I am defined by my modesty."

Now, as she curled in his lap, she recognized how tired she was. Every muscle was sore and she felt as if her insides might fall on the floor if she stood. "I would like to sleep."

"We'll take the baby to the sitting room with us for a while," said Rosemary.

"Make sure you bring her to me if she cries," said Eleanor, "even if I'm dead asleep."

Mercy Leigh smiled. "She'll be sleepy for a while, Your Highness. Take advantage of it."

Rosemary came to Eleanor and kissed her cheek. "I am so proud of you," she said.

Her next move was unexpected. She ran her fingers across Dorian's hair, then leaned down and kissed him as well, on the forehead. "And you." She left, and shut the door behind her.

Dorian carried Eleanor to the bed. He laid her on the far side, close to the wall, and pulled the covers over her. He yanked off his own boots and lay down beside her. She laughed when he covered the purple rabbit with a pillow.

"He's staring at me," he said. "Perhaps he's a spy."

Even though her body ached, it was sweet to have his arms around her. She nestled close to him, and he kissed the hollow behind her ear. "Just rest," he said.

She fell asleep immediately. After a few hours she woke, needing to know he was still there. It couldn't have been comfortable for him, but he never moved.

In the wee hours Mercy Leigh brought the baby to Eleanor to nurse. Both Eleanor and the baby were getting the idea, and she leaned into the crook of Dorian's arm as the tiny head squirmed on her breast. She didn't sleep when Rosemary came to take the child. She could tell by Dorian's breathing he was awake. After an hour or so she spoke.

"Dorian."

"Yes."

"I want to say something."

"We don't have to talk about it now," he said.

"Yes, I want to. I want to say it now."

He eased her around by her shoulder. "That's my girl. You must be feeling better."

She kissed him. "I wish I could joke, but I need to be serious."

He nodded.

"Once this is over, and I have to believe it will end well, we will return to Eclatant. We both know there is nowhere we could hide from Gregory, not in any nation, but I have to tell you I cannot consider it, even for you. I won't leave my children, and I won't try to steal them from their father and hide them away somewhere. They will be kings and queens of this country. I will do everything in my power to give them their birthright, and that includes their mother's love."

"I would never ask you to do so. I will love your children as my own, for you and for the love I have for the crown."

"Even knowing all that, I don't want to live without you. I would be your lover, in a sense, but we cannot take it to that final place. Even if we were careful…an accident…a child…"

"Eleanor, I understand—"

She put a finger over his lips. "I would ask much of you, and put you in a position of great danger, and it breaks my heart. But this is all I can give, if you will take it.

His reply was simple. "I will take whatever you have to give, and gladly. I love you, Eleanor. I always have."

She thought she might cry again, so she started babbling. "I've waited to hear you say that. I love you, Dorian. I love—"

He covered her mouth with his.

CHAPTER 28

ALWAYS ELEANOR

THE NEXT DAY ELEANOR asked for something to eat and Rosemary brought her some bread and apples. She sat up and shifted the baby. Now that she felt stronger she wanted news from home. There was no word from Gregory, and she had yet to send him a message about their daughter. His silence told her enough, and she didn't want to talk about him. She asked about the hunt for Roffi.

"The king has sent scouts throughout the country," said Dorian. "They went by unicorn, mostly to the west."

"Why west?" asked Eleanor.

"The king and Oliver determined that Roffi would most likely head west, past Harveston and into Talesse."

"Why?"

"It's the only route that makes sense. They can't go north through the Pashing Pass even if it is the most direct route; they'd have to pass Peaksend, the legion, and the unicorns of the Mines. The eastern route through the Border Pass is far too long, and the mountains are infested with colonies of tradactas. Those birds are nasty. It's possible to get past them, but you're guaranteed to lose a few men. If they go west they have to go deep into Talesse, skirt the edge of the mountains and backtrack to Nestra, but it's the only sure way of getting there."

Rosemary spoke up. "So they didn't send anyone east?"

"Someone will search the Forest of Ten-Thousand Oaks, around Harper's Crossing, but they sent the Unicorn Guard west. Why?"

"I should have said something."

"What do you mean?"

"I met with the Oracle before you came to the Abbey, Dorian. She told me she felt the Horn traveling east."

"*East?* East can only mean the Border Pass," said Dorian. "Why didn't you *tell* me?"

Rosemary threw up her hands. "I assumed scouts would be sent in all directions, and besides, there wasn't time to discuss it until now."

"Dorian, calm down," said Eleanor.

"I'm sorry, Rosemary," he said. "I'm just at a loss. It's been three days. Roffi is probably long past the Crossing by now."

"Oliver," said Eleanor. "He knew Roffi would head east, so he sent the Unicorn Guard west."

Eleanor didn't like the look on Dorian's his face as he sat beside her. She carefully laid the baby on the bed.

"Not all the Unicorn Guard are in the west," he said.

"No."

"There are five guards here, and Senné and myself. I'll take three with me, and leave the other two here with Teardrop to watch over you. I'll send word to Gregory, let him know about the baby and tell him I'm making my own search in the east."

"No," she said. "Leave Gregory out of this."

"They have to know Rosemary came here—"

"And if they see fit they can come drag me back to Maliana," said Rosemary.

"We'll wait to send word, if you insist," said Dorian. "I'll not argue with both of you, but I won't have you argue with me, either."

"I don't want you to go. It's too dangerous. Roffi left with seven men, not to mention the tradactas," Eleanor said.

"I grew up in those woods, Eleanor, I know the way. Besides, each unicorn is worth ten men—"

"Some of them are martial magicians!" she interjected.

"—and they're all on horseback."

She shook her head.

"This is the only way," he said. "I promise, if the Horn is in the east, I will find it."

She pulled him closer and spoke in his ear. "It seems I only just found you."

"I would have you vindicated and back in the palace."

After he kissed her goodbye Eleanor leaned against the pillows. She knew she couldn't go with him. She could hardly stand, the blood-flow was heavy, and the baby nursed constantly. In her frustration she threw the purple rabbit across the room. She could not stand helplessness in anyone, let alone herself.

Rosemary gave Eleanor a few minutes to compose herself after Dorian left, and then she collected the baby and handed Eleanor a tiny flask of water.

"It's from the Oracle," Rosemary said. "She said you must drink it. Only you, alone. There is a message inside, one that only you can decipher."

Eleanor looked at the flask in her hand. "What is it?" she asked, but she got no response. Rosemary had already shut the door behind her. Eleanor uncorked the flask. She sniffed the open bottle, but the dark liquid inside had no smell. She dabbed at it and put her finger to her tongue, but it had no taste. There seemed no other means to understanding, so she tipped the flask to her lips and drained it in one short gulp.

In the span of a second the cold liquid hit her belly, she blinked, and the room at Rabbit's Rest disappeared. She was not in another room, nor was she outside. It was a nothing place. Blinding white light on all sides. Nothing, save for three objects in front of her.

The first was a black and red silk bag, the colors of the Svelyan king. The second was a looking glass, backed with Fire-iron. The third item was harder to detect. It was a long white hair, wound upon itself. Its soft shimmer revealed it as a unicorn hair. It sat in the center of the mirror.

Eleanor closed her eyes and began chanting. The words were in an old language, one the magicians and witches used in the eons past when there were few divisions between them. She continued for nearly half an hour, never altering the words or the pitch.

As she spoke she sensed power lifting around her. She opened her eyes and glanced down at the mirror. Red steam rose from it. Without losing the beat of her chant, she leaned forward.

She could see into the mirror, but her own face did not stare back at her. It seemed she looked through a great reddish heap of the palace cooks' favorite gelatin dessert into a room she had never entered.

It was about the size of a country chapel, with one door, held shut with a Fire-iron beam, and no windows. At least ten armed sentries and four unicorns stood patiently around a pedestal. On the pedestal sat a nondescript lump of raw Fire-iron.

As Eleanor watched one of the unicorns threw up his head. He snorted, and his fellows joined in. They paced the room, clearly sensing something amiss. She focused her energy not on the Horn on the pedestal, but on the unicorn hair sitting on the mirror. Her chant grew louder, and her body shook as she pulled at the power swirling around her. She heard the unicorns whinnying in alarm, and the sentries shouting, but the sounds were muffled. Her eyes rolled in her head, and then snapped open.

She had a glimpse of a long white face and panicked dark eyes before the red glow blinked out and the other room disappeared from the mirror. Caleb's Horn sat on the glass, the white hair coiled around it like a constrictive snake.

"What did you see?" said a distant voice. "What did you see?"

Eleanor blinked again and the vision was gone. The white light, the mirror, the Horn; all of it. Rosemary sat in the chair beside her bed with the baby in her arms. "What did you see?" she asked again.

"The Horn, I saw...or I felt...it being stolen." Eleanor couldn't find the right words. "I was...inside the thief..."

"Then you know who stole it?"

Eleanor rubbed her forehead. "It was the thief's body, but it was my body just the same...the thief's magic...my body..." She shook her fuzzy head in frustration. "I couldn't see anything. No walls, no floor... nothing...the thief's hands were my own." She bit her lip. "There was something, though. Something familiar. Ach, I can't remember! It's like a dream...it makes sense yet I can't explain it."

Rosemary took her hand. "The Oracle believes you can decipher it. Give it some time."

"There is the problem, Rosemary." Eleanor said. She reached for her daughter. "Unfortunately time is something we are sorely lacking."

Dorian and his companions skirted the town of Harper's Crossing and followed the edges of the Forest of Ten-Thousand Oaks. They crossed from Cartheigh into Kelland, and headed north toward the Border Pass, a channel of loosely connected, narrow canyons. The path had been marked hundreds of years before with stone crosses. It was a three-day journey to the Svelyan side of the Scaled Mountains, but Dorian hoped it would not take that long to catch up with Roffi.

They reached the first cross early in the morning of the second day of travel. It had been drizzling on and off since they left the Forest. Dorian called them to a halt and dismounted. He pulled a long torch from a hook on his saddle. The soldiers looked at him curiously as he lit it and gave it to Teddy, the young guard from Solsea.

"Sorry, sir," said Teddy, "but can I ask why we'll be needing this now? It's broad morning."

"The tradactas," said Dorian. "They fear fire. Between the unicorns and the flames they will leave us alone, at least during the day. I hope so, anyway. It's very important you keep this torch lit, Teddy. I can only spare one man to carry it, and we have only this one torch. It will be black as tar up there tonight, and tradactas are night hunters."

Teddy nodded. He held the torch in front of himself as if his own breath might blow it out.

As they entered the pass the canyon walls rose up on either side of them, as tall as ten men standing on each other's shoulders. Water dripped down the granite walls, and the ground beneath the unicorn's hooves was a soggy mess. Fat worms wriggled out of the churned-up mud. Senné lifted his feet high and shook his head.

"I'm sorry, Sen," said Dorian, "but it will get worse before it gets better. The melt comes down the channel. A month ago we might not have made it through here."

"It's not just the wet," said Senné. "I feel there has been magic here."

"I'm glad to hear it. They can't be far ahead."

Dorian did not push them too fast over the slippery terrain. They plodded on through the morning and into the afternoon, eating as they rode. The dank smell seeped into their clothes and hair until Dorian no longer noticed it. Only the puff of the unicorns' breath and the mud sucking at their feet broke the silence. As they passed the third stone cross the path dipped, then widened out.

Senné balked. "I don't want to go down there."

"We have no choice. That's the way the path leads," said Dorian. Senné slid down the low hill, his hooves leaving deep trenches in the mud, and leapt the stagnant pool at the bottom. He was calling encouragement to his fellows when his ears pricked.

"What is it?" asked Dorian.

The black stallion lifted his muzzle and inhaled sharply. "I heard something. A scratch against the rock."

Dorian eyed the canyon walls. "I don't see anything."

"Maybe I am mistaken," said Senné, but his ears continued to wave.

The other two guards made it to the bottom of the hill. Only Teddy remained at the top. His unicorn was inexperienced as well. He sat back on his heels and refused to move. Teddy clucked to him, the torch waving in his hand, and finally he started forward. It looked as if they would make it until the unicorn dislodged a hidden rock, spooked, and lunged the rest of the way down the hill. Teddy was thrown onto his neck, and the torch flew from his hands. It landed in the muddy water and blinked out.

"Damn it all, you fuckin' young nimwit!" cursed one of the other guards, a crusty soldier from Maliana.

Teddy righted himself. "I'm sorry sir, I'm so sorry. I'll get it." He started to slide down but Dorian stopped him.

"We'll make do, Teddy. Don't dismount."

Teddy's apologies were cut off by a high, keening screech. Senné nickered. "The tradactas are day hunters as well, I suppose."

A rock the size of a carriage wheel crashed into the canyon and split on the boulders below it. Dorian looked up.

A tradacta stood on a rotted tree stump. It had a long white neck, and a black coat that resembled fur more than feathers covered the rest of its body. Its wings were small and useless, but each spindly gray leg ended in a horny foot whose long toes gripped the rock with claws resembling skinning knives. Dorian guessed it could look down on Senné if they stood on the same ground. Its head was tiny, but its yellow beak, as long as Dorian's sword, more than made up for it. A pointed black tongue unfurled when it hissed at him.

He drew his long bow, took aim, and shot, but it dodged. There was a frightening intelligence in its round black eyes. They seemed too large for its skull, like two meat platters crammed onto a tea table. It screamed again.

"Oh, shit," Teddy said.

More white heads on slender necks floated up from behind the rocks. Dorian took a flint from his pocket and threw it at Teddy. "Find something that will light," he said. "Anything."

Teddy jumped down. He grabbed his saddlebag and dug through it. The tradactas didn't give him long to search before they struck.

Dorian leapt from Senné's back to give the stallion more freedom to fight, and the other guards followed suit. He drew his sword and swung it wildly at one of the passing birds. The tradactas didn't fly, but they were fast. They struck with their feet and beaks and were gone almost before the men saw them. Dorian regained his balance and focused.

He swung true this time and sliced the attacking bird's head cleanly from its neck. The head sailed across the gulley, its mouth gaping at him in surprise. Senné bucked and twisted and dislodged one clinging to his withers. The bird flipped up over his head, and he pierced it neatly with his horn. He and the other unicorns fought on, felling the creatures left and right, but even with Dorian and the two guards hacking them down as well, they kept coming.

"There are too many!" Dorian screamed at Senné.

A tradacta loomed in front of him. He feinted right, and his left arm swung away from his body. The bird darted in and Dorian felt a splash of warmth. He jerked his hand away and held it up. The bird had sliced off his smallest finger.

He yelled and swung his sword, cutting off both its legs at the knee. It dropped to eye level, and he cut off its head.

"Finley! Finley!" Two tradactas pinned the soldier from Maliana against the canyon wall. He had somehow lost his sword, and he clutched a short knife. Dorian ran to him but he wasn't fast enough. One of the birds tilted its head. Dorian would not have believed anything's neck could make such an angle. It opened its beak, and snapped the soldier's head from his shoulders like a barber snipping off an errant hair. Dorian downed both of birds before they could drag the body away.

"Teddy!" he screamed. "Teddy! The fire! We need the fire!"

Teddy desperately banged the flint. "It won't go, sir! Everything is too wet!"

Dorian heaved himself onto the rocks, and leapt onto a passing tradacta. He wrested it into the mud and it collapsed on top of him. His arm disappeared to the elbow in its greasy feathers as he tried to find some way to grab hold of it. It dragged both of them a few paces through the mud. He could barely breathe through the feathers and the long-dead smell of its last meal. He finally found an angle and jabbed his sword into its belly. He pushed it off and furiously rubbed his hands in the mud, trying to dislodge the viscous blood already hardening on his skin like cooling wax. Senné's long face appeared in front of him.

"Are you hurt?" he asked.

"No." As Dorian brushed the unicorn's black mane out of his own face an idea came to him. He swung onto Senné's back.

"To Teddy," he said. "Hurry!"

Senné slid to a halt beside the frantic boy. Dorian pulled his dagger as he dismounted. "I'm sorry, Sen," he said, "but I must do this. Be still."

Senné lifted his head once and then did as his master asked.

"Teddy! Be ready with the flint." Dorian grabbed Senné's long black mane and cut it away. It drifted to the ground in thick chunks, curling as it fell. Teddy knelt down and struck the flint, once, then again.

The fire roared up. Senné reared, but Dorian reached for his bridle and tugged him down. He grabbed his forelock and hacked it off. The blaze grew, and they had to back away.

The tradactas retreated, tiny heads bouncing on their necks, their stubby wings waving. They screeched and hissed, but they didn't stay. The last one disappeared over the lip of the canyon in minutes.

"We'll stay here tonight," said Dorian. "We're tired, and we can't move this fire. We'll find something to make a new torch tomorrow."

He spoke to the other three unicorns. "You will have to give up your manes, as Senné did." They nodded and didn't complain.

"Thank you. I know it's no small thing." A stallion's mane signaled his masculinity, like broad shoulders. Dorian tried to be light. "Don't worry, I won't ask that you cut off anything else."

He applied some herbs Mercy Leigh had given him to his hand, and tied a strip of cloth around it, and but his entire left arm throbbed. He asked Teddy and Jim, the other remaining guard, to dig a grave for their fallen comrade. By the time they were finished it was dark.

"Sir," said Teddy as they passed a loaf of hard bread. "Why did the unicorn hair start the fire?"

"A unicorn's hide, and hair, are impervious to heat and cold, fire and water. When you cut the hair off, it loses that quality. It becomes brittle in seconds," Dorian said.

"It's shittin' lucky for us you remembered," said Jim. He brought out a flask, his hands shaking.

"Better put that away," said Dorian. "We need our wits about us. You two get some rest. I'll take watch. I can't sleep anyway with this hand."

The other two men propped their heads on their saddles. Senné stood over Dorian. The noise of the unicorn's breathing comforted him. He watched the fire and pictured Eleanor, asleep with the baby curled on her chest. It had not been difficult to stay awake that night as she lay in his arms. He had watched the soft pulse at her neck, her eyelashes fluttering on her cheeks. He buried his face in her hair and inhaled the scent of her. He was almost glad for her fragile condition. It would have been difficult to control himself otherwise. Even in her exhaustion and dishevelment she stirred him. He could still feel that ache now through the pain in his arm. The wound and the unrelieved pressure kept him alert.

I suppose I will have to practice self-control.

Not such a bad thought. There was more than one means to a satisfying end, and Dorian could be creative. He smiled through the pain at the idea, and let his imagination run wild for a while.

He breathed easy as he watched the fire. Peace would be fleeting when they returned to Eclatant. The great lie he would have to purport sat beside him like an uninvited houseguest, but for now he let it lie with his contempt for Gregory's cowardice. Somehow an answer seemed possible out here in the dark. For the first time in eight years he had followed his own path exactly. He enjoyed the memories, and Eleanor's love, and the calm that came with making his own decisions.

"Something is coming," said Senné, sometime after midnight. The other unicorns nickered under their breath, and Jim and Teddy stirred.

"What is it, sir?" asked Teddy, pulling out his bow. Jim did the same. "The tradactas again?"

"I don't think so," said Senné.

"Then what?" Dorian strained to hear something. He caught the sound of boots scuffling over stones, and then a few curses.

"That's no tradacta," he said. An orange light appeared on the rocks.

"Who's there?" called Teddy. He raised his bow. Dorian hushed him. The light grew, and a man appeared, carrying a torch.

It was Christopher Roffi.

"Stop!" called Teddy. "Don't come any closer!"

Roffi squinted. Dorian saw the light of recognition in his eyes, and he ran at them with his hands up.

"Put down your weapons," said Dorian, but it was too late. Jim had already let fly with an arrow. It struck Roffi in the stomach. He kept going for a few paces before falling on his knees.

"Damn!" Dorian ran to Roffi. He lifted him and dragged him toward the fire. Roffi's legs buckled again, and Dorian knelt beside him.

"I'm sorry, sir," Jim stammered. "I thought—"

"Silence," Dorian said. Roffi clutched the arrow protruding from his midsection. His hands were covered in blood.

"Chris."

"I should have known you would come." Roffi groped at the pocket of his cloak. "Here, here. Take it." He held out a small red and black bag.

Dorian peered inside. "I don't understand. Why are you returning it to me?"

Roffi spit, and beckoned Dorian closer. Dorian strained to hear his whispered reply. "I had to bring it back. I could not…I could not do it. I could not let her be taking the blame for this."

"Eleanor."

"Yes, Eleanor. Of course, always Eleanor."

Suddenly Dorian understood. He leaned toward Roffi. "You must say it," he said. "Say it out loud so we can all hear you."

Roffi nodded and raised his voice. "Eleanor is innocent. It was not her doing."

Dorian turned to the guards. "Did you hear him?"

They nodded, and Teddy ran to his saddlebag. He held up a stub of charcoal. "Perhaps if he wrote it down?"

"No paper," said Dorian. "No…wait." He took out Gregory's orders giving him permission to take Mercy Leigh to Rabbit's rest. "Here."

He held the tattered paper for Roffi, who scrawled on it, his hand trembling. *EBD Innocent. CR.*

Roffi's hand dropped. He gasped for air. The firelight turned his white hair orange and the blood on his clothes black. His voice was a ragged whisper again. "He does not deserve her."

Dorian leaned even closer, until his mouth almost touched Roffi's ear. "I hear you. I know it."

"You must take care of her." He clutched at Dorian's cloak. "I know we understand each other."

Roffi's eyes rolled and he started raving. "I did it because I love my country. For my country."

"Chris!" Now Dorian fairly shouted in his face. "Who helped you? Someone in Maliana? Who stole the Horn for you?"

Roffi's eyes focused again for a moment. "I used Margaret Easton to be close to Eleanor...I planted the Horn in her room...but there was no reason for her to steal it...so we gave her a reason in me...a love affair with me. If only that part could have been the truth. Rumors...lies... all of it." He coughed, and a gout of blood sprayed from his mouth.

"But why? Why Eleanor? Why lay the blame on her?"

"They hate her...both of them. She must be careful. Tell her, Dorian."

"Who? Who hates her? Who stole the Horn? Chris, you must say it!"

"They hate her..." His body shook, and his voice trailed off. He was gone, and he took the names with him.

As Dorian shouted his frustration to the uncaring night sky, Eleanor curled on her bed at Rabbit's Rest and watched her daughter sleep. The baby smiled, and frowned, then gave a tiny whimpering cry and the most impossibly adorable shudder. Eleanor could not join her in rest.

Will I live to see her smile a true smile?

She went back to the vision of the Horn, but still she could not identify what had made the scene familiar. She did not know the mirror. She had never seen the bag until it appeared in her music box. She'd picked hundreds of unicorn hairs from her clothes, but they were all the same. She pressed her hands to her temples in frustration, and her elbow bumped the baby's head. She let out a wail at her mother's carelessness.

"Hush, love, hush, angel girl," Eleanor said. She pulled her daughter close and the child quieted. Eleanor rested her mouth on the baby's fuzzy head and inhaled the clean, new smell of her hair.

Eleanor's eyes widened in the dim light, and suddenly the mysteriously familiar was no longer mysterious. The smell of the dream. Lemony mint.

CHAPTER 29

THE TRUTH

ELEANOR HEARD UNICORNS IN the courtyard as she prepared for bed. She hobbled to the window, telling herself it was just Teardrop, until she made out a black shape like a moving bit of darkness. When she saw Dorian dismount she nearly ran to meet him, even through the pain.

"Wait," said Rosemary. "Let him come."

Eleanor nodded, remembering she could not exactly throw herself into his arms in front of the guards. She sat on the bed. The four days he had been gone were nothing but hours of worry strung like pearls on a necklace. There was a soft knock on the door. Rosemary scooped up the baby, opened it, and slid out.

Eleanor had never seen him so worn down. She held out her arms and he came to her and rested his head in her lap.

"You're back," she said. "Thank HighGod."

"I have something for you." He reached into his pocket and held out the red and black bag.

She took it in wonder. "Only you, love," she said.

He told her his tale, and then buried his face in the silk of her nightdress. "I failed you. I did not find the name of the thief. You will never be truly safe until we know the real culprit."

She put a finger under his chin and turned his face up to hers. "You have hardly failed me, or the crown. Besides, not all wrongs are righted by a hard chase and a sharp sword."

"What do you mean?" he asked.

She explained everything, and he listened with a solemn face. "Now I must quote a wise woman," he said when she finished. "Only you, love, only you."

She fussed over his injured hand for a time before they spent a last night curled in the bed together. Neither of them slept. They took advantage of the closeness.

She faced him, and pulled his shirt over his head. She ran her hands over his back, his chest, down his thighs, wanting to memorize each muscle and bone. At first she balked when he tried to do the same. She had imagined this moment for longer than she cared to admit, but in her dreams she was lithe and strong, not swollen and exhausted. His voice in her ear told her he didn't care.

"You are so beautiful," he whispered. "My love, so beautiful."

Her tired body melted into his hands. She couldn't stop the tears from running down her face as he kissed her, and they added to the salty taste of his sweat. He reached up, again and again, to wipe them away. He rested his head on the pillow, his nose nearly touching hers. His green eyes were catlike in the candlelight.

"Don't weep," he said. "I will find a way to love you. I swear it. Do you believe me?"

"I do," she said. And it was the truth.

Eleanor's carriage was too small for four women, a baby and a parrot, but she didn't mind the close quarters. Pansy had offered to ride up top, but Eleanor insisted they all squeeze in the back. Pansy had been a staunch ally through her ordeal, and Eleanor saw no reason for her to suffer the hot sun because of her status.

They removed the doors from the coach and the breeze blew in one side and out the other. The driver was taking his time, and the gentle rocking of the wheels lulled the baby to sleep in her arms. Eleanor dozed, content that when she opened her eyes she would see Dorian and Senné riding watch around them. Some of the old distance had returned out of necessity, but his face told her it was all right.

The baby grunted and squirmed in her lap, and the coach filled with the unmistakable scent of a messy bottom. Pansy dug in the baby's bag. She moved the purple rabbit aside and handed Eleanor a new cotton diaper. Eleanor spun her daughter around for a cleanup.

"Ugh," said Chou Chou. "I think I'll stretch out a bit." He flew out the window.

Eleanor daydreamed as she wiped the baby's round legs. The new life amazed her, and she couldn't help but think of poor Roffi. He had been in the wrong, of course, but he had showed himself true. She wished Dorian could have brought his body for a proper burial, instead of a shallow grave in the Border Pass. He deserved better.

As Eleanor rewrapped her daughter Chou reappeared. He gripped the sides of the coach with his feet and beak. "Riders coming," he said.

Eleanor gave the baby to Rosemary and leaned out the doorway. Dorian was already out in front. Eleanor recognized the purple and green Desmarais banner flying above ten mounted unicorns, and picked out Vigor's proud head above the others.

It was Gregory.

His party closed the gap quickly. Gregory called Vigor to a stop when he reached Senné. He and Dorian passed words as Eleanor's carriage caught up. Dorian had sent Teddy ahead to let Eclatant know the Horn was recovered, and Eleanor delivered of a healthy child. It didn't surprise her that Gregory had come as the smoke cleared, she just wasn't sure if she was ready to see him. She looked at her daughter, awake and sucking her fist in Rosemary's arms. The driver called to the horses to stop. As Gregory dismounted and approached the carriage Eleanor made up her mind.

She stood slowly. A week after giving birth the pain lingered, but she waved away the driver's hand and took the steps herself. She reached up for the baby, and Rosemary handed her down.

She and Gregory faced each other over the dusty road. She waited for him to speak.

He cleared his throat. "It appears you are innocent of the great crime."

"Yes," she said.

"I'm glad." He took a step closer. "Is this your child?"

"Yes."

"May I see her?"

Eleanor shifted the swaddling blanket away from the baby's face. She peered up at her father with the reddish brown eyes of a fawn. The fuzz on her head was auburn.

Gregory's hands went to his hair. "May I hold her?" he asked.

Eleanor nodded. "Take care for her neck."

Gregory took the baby gingerly and rocked her. "She's beautiful." He handed her back.

"She has a name," said Eleanor.

"Oh. What have you chosen?"

"Leticia Elise, for my mother."

"Leticia Elise," he said. There was nothing Desmarais about it. He paused. "It's a fine name."

"Thank you," she said.

He turned to the people and unicorns surrounding the carriage. "Good people, loyal friends. May HighGod bless my daughter, Leticia Elise Desmarais, Princess of Cartheigh."

Gregory drew his sword. He planted it at his feet, and kissed the hilt. It was an old greeting among royalty. His subjects knelt around

Eleanor and her child, and cast their eyes to the dirt. Only Dorian looked at her. He touched his lips in salute.

Eleanor was the only woman in the Council Hall, and she knew many of the assembled advisors didn't appreciate her presence, innocent or not. She didn't care. She sat on a high stool, and shifted around the pain in her nether-regions. She crossed her arms over her flattened chest. Pansy had done her best to tie the dress up, but Eleanor wore a shawl around her shoulders to hide the loose lacing. Her breasts ached, and she willed them to stay dry until she returned to Leticia. The Council would hardly take her seriously if she leaked all over the table like a neglected milk cow.

They were discussing the Svelyan king.

"Mangolin says Roffi acted alone," said King Casper. "He denies any involvement."

"Roffi's family is as loyal to King Mangolin as any man here is to you, Your Majesty," said Dorian. "Roffi wouldn't have threatened international good will without direction from above. His reversal of loyalties can only be attributed to his respect for Your Majesty and his friendship with Prince Gregory." Eleanor and Dorian had decided it safest to omit the true reason for Roffi's change of heart.

Gregory cut in. "What I want to know is how he got the Horn in the first place. Someone had to perform the Blood Path."

It was the sort of comment Eleanor had waited for. She stood, and the room fell silent. "That is the most important question, is it not? Who stole the Horn?"

Oliver cleared his throat. "Mister Finley's account of the events in the Border Pass and the note written in Ambassador Roffi's hand have cleared you name, Your Highness. There is no need for you to further concern yourself in these matters."

"Oh, but I disagree, Mister Oliver. So great is my concern I have thought on little else, save my daughter, for over a week." Eleanor turned to the king. "As I have already informed His Majesty, I believe the answer has come to me."

The Council whispered amongst themselves but the king silenced them. "The princess asked to present her argument here, before the Council. She has explained her allegations to me, and I pray the accused can prove them unfounded. You will give her your attention."

"Thank you, Your Majesty," she said. "I will not dally, or dance around the fire. The man responsible for this crime is in this room." The Council glanced around the table, as if expecting to see a noose already around the neck of the guilty party. Eleanor took a deep breath. "Ezra Oliver."

The Council burst into a grumbly mixture of laughter, denials, and eye rolling. Gregory's fist on the table brought their commentary to an abrupt end. "My wife is speaking. Pay her the proper respect."

Oliver stood. "Princess Eleanor, I think we must clear the air. I know you and I have had disagreements, but I hope you do not think me capable of this crime."

"On the contrary, Oliver, I think you very capable, and I am about to prove it." She nodded to the two sentries at the Council Hall's entrance. They opened the door, and three butlers came in balancing a punch bowl of dark liquid between them. Another servant followed, this one carrying a tray of small crystal cups. They place the punch bowl in the center of the Council table, between two Fire-iron candelabras, and began passing cups to each man in the room.

"Gentlemen," Eleanor said. "This water comes from the Watching Pool of Afar Creek Abbey. The Oracle generously agreed to let me share with all of you that which she shared with me. You see, powerful witches and magicians can hide their spells. She could not see the thief in the water, but something told her *I* might be able to make sense of it."

Oliver pointed at the punchbowl. "A lot of nonsense, all of it. Oracles are all mist and speculation. None of it is true magic."

"Magic cannot replace memory, or observation, Mister Oliver," Eleanor said. She took a cup from the servant. "In your office you keep a potted plant. You told me it was rare, but you did not clarify how exotic it is. Gentlemen, Mister Oliver has quite the green thumb. For fifty years he has nurtured the last Blue Weathervane. A magician, and a horticulturist!"

"I'd like to know how my gardening habits are relevant," Oliver said, but his forehead was shiny with sweat.

"They are relevant because anyone who drinks this liquid will find themselves inside the crime itself. They will see the Blood Path being drawn. Watch the Horn disappear from its chamber and appear on a mirror, pulled through thin air by a spell and a unicorn hair. They will not see your hands, or your desk, or the furnishings of your office. What they will discern, however, is a smell of lemon and mint. The fragrance of the one and only Blue Weathervane."

"Dragonshit!" Oliver exclaimed, and some of the older Council members looked faint at the sound of the Chief Magician shouting profanities. "A load of bloody supposition!"

Eleanor turned on him. "You thought you hid everything, Oliver, didn't you? You live in that office. It's all so familiar you don't even notice the smell anymore, like the fishmonger who doesn't know why everyone avoids sitting beside him at chapel." She walked around the table and curtsied to the king. "I have one more request, Your Majesty. Might I hold the Horn, just for a moment?"

The king paused before taking the lump of Fire-iron from his pocket. He handed it to Eleanor, and she faced the Council once again. "May I borrow your handkerchief, Your Majesty?" The king handed her a square of white cotton. She rubbed the handkerchief over the Horn before setting the shiny rock on the table in front of her. She took a lit candle from the closest candelabra and held the handkerchief aloft. She kept talking as she touched the flame to the cloth. "If there is a trace of

Blue Weathervane pollen left on the Horn this handkerchief will show it to us."

The flames crept up the handkerchief toward Eleanor's hands. She smiled, and tossed the handkerchief into the air. Smoke swirled in front of her eyes.

The smoke was a bright, jaunty blue.

Ezra Oliver took action before the Council could recover their collective wits. Three gray fireballs left his upraised hands and soared toward the Council members across the table from him, and to Eleanor's horror two of the men tumbled out of their seats. The third one collapsed face first onto the table. The first two did not reappear, and the third did not stir. A thin line of blood ran from his ear.

Dorian shouted at the sentries, and they opened the door to a company of at least twenty martial magicians. The king had stationed the martials outside the Council Room to secure Oliver, but the Chief Magician's swift and deadly counterstrike made her fear they had underestimated their enemy. Two of the Council ran from the room, and several others took cover under the table.

As for Oliver, he had conjured a wall of gray mist around himself. Two more fireballs floated in front of his chest. His lips curled back from his teeth like a cornered badger's.

Eleanor panicked when the king stood. She hoped Oliver would not have the nerve to smite the living legacy of Caleb Desmarais in his own Council Hall.

"Ezra, have you no explanation?" the king asked, his face a contortion of grief. "I don't understand. Why would you do this?"

Oliver addressed the man whose every command he had followed for twenty-five years. "Must you ask, *Your Majesty*? Will you force me to elucidate?" When he stepped away from the table the mist went with him. "Very well, then. If your second-rate, inbred intellect prevents you from drawing your own conclusions I will have to draw them for you. HighGod knows I've done it before."

One of the martials stepped forward, but before he could strike one of Oliver's gray spheres sent him crashing to the marble floor.

"For ninety years I've killed myself for this family and this country. Now it's all going to shit in a rickety wagon. You let the witches run rampant. You let your overgrown child of a son marry this shrew, who will most likely be a king in petticoats one day. You give him—" Oliver pointed at Dorian. "—a unicorn when I've been in this family's service over three times his lifespan. Should I suffer another century of your disrespect? Should I wait for your son to force me into early retirement so he can destroy everything I've built?"

Gregory stood and leaned across the table. Dorian grabbed his shoulder from behind. "Cartheigh is the most powerful kingdom in the world, Oliver. Because of my family. Because of my father."

"You stupid boy," Oliver sneered. "You have no idea how to protect what you have. You've all gone soft, just like King Peter Mangolin, HighGod bless him and his country, says you have. The Svelyans understand what I have been seeing for years. The Desmarais dynasty has peaked. Wine and chocolate and parties have rotted what little brains you were born with."

Anger replaced the king's sadness. "We've trusted you for a century!"

"And what has it gotten me? Chained to a desk! Mangolin knew no one else could accomplish this mission. For years he's put all his magical resources into disabling the Horn. I suppose I'll be joining him sooner than I'd planned. Your pitiful attempts can't stop me. I'll have new friends, ones who appreciate my abilities."

"Friends!" Eleanor called out.

"Eleanor, sit down!" Gregory said, and Eleanor heard a king in his voice for the first time. "Sit down, now!"

Kingly or not, she ignored him. "Tell us about your other friends. Imogene Brice, for one."

Oliver's misty shield quivered. When he turned on Eleanor his eyes were nearly as fiery as his projectiles. "I have no idea what you're talking about."

"How did my stepmother help you? Roffi said someone else helped you. Don't protect her."

"With that mirror and the unicorn hair I created the strongest Blood Path ever drawn," Oliver said with absurd pride. "I allowed Roffi to pummel my face after handing the Horn over to him for the second time in that passageway. I covered my own ass and gave him ample escape time. You all believed the bruises. Every word and gesture. I hardly needed the assistance of some silly, gossiping harpy."

"Gossiping! Yes, indeed. Did you enlist her to help you spread your ridiculous claims of an affair between myself and the ambassador? What did you promise her?"

Oliver's eyes seemed to fill with his own gray magic. The whites disappeared. "You are everything that will go wrong with this country. Your loose tongue and your far flung opinions and your damnable questions. I knew any favorite strumpet of the witches would be trouble, but I thought I could set you on a useful path. I should have poisoned you myself, or better, your stepmother should have drowned you in the Clarity before you had a chance to poison the prince."

"So you and Imogene are of one mind?" Eleanor asked.

"Enough!" Oliver roared, and the gray mist trembled around him again. He shot the last fireball at another of the martials and the unlucky man crumpled. Two more misty globes replaced them.

Eleanor's chest was tight with panic. The martials were proving useless. Her eyes fell on the Horn in front of her, and a ridiculous idea leapt into her mind. So ridiculous it just might work.

She picked up the Horn. "No, Oliver, it's not enough! What did you give Imogene to make her commit treason? It couldn't have been your cock, you pitiful, impotent, sorry excuse for a man! You limp-dick, treacherous, hypocritical—"

"Shut your fucking mouth!" Oliver screamed, and both fireballs shot at Eleanor's face.

She lifted the Horn, just as she'd seen the jousting magician lift his shield last fall, and both fireballs struck the Fire-iron lump with a force that nearly knocked her off her feet. They shot back in Oliver's direction. He ducked, but not fast enough. One struck his right arm, and the wall of protective mist blinked out.

The martials surged forward, but Oliver recovered quickly. He clambered onto the Council table, clutching at his useless arm with the other one. He stumbled down the table, and the remaining Council members tipped over backwards in their seats in an effort to get out of his way. He looked frantically at the door, the windows, the ceiling. A stray fireball struck the punchbowl and it shattered. Glass and dark water spewed out over the table. Oliver's boot struck the water and shot out from under him. He seemed to float for a second, and Eleanor caught the surprise and dismay on his face. He landed on the table, or at least that's what should have happened.

There was no expected whack of man against wood. When Oliver's back touched the table the sheen of murky water bubbled and hissed. The magician screamed, and Eleanor winced at the pain in that one keening note. Gray mist whipped around Oliver's head and he sunk slowly into the thin layer of water. He disappeared, a rock thrown into a choppy sea.

Two hours later, once the carnage was cleared and the Council Hall returned to its usual pristine and polished state, Eleanor sat at the table with Gregory, Dorian, and the king. Casper held the Horn in his hand. He seemed in no hurry to return it to its pedestal in the hidden chamber.

Perhaps he will keep it under his pillow, thought Eleanor.

The king called for four glasses of whiskey and rubbed his eyes with his free hand. "I'm not sure where to begin. Eleanor, when you came to me…honestly…I assumed Oliver would easily prove you wrong. I still can't believe…"

Eleanor pitied the king, for he could not have looked more flummoxed had someone shown him irrefutable evidence that the sun would not rise tomorrow. The king lifted his whiskey glass. Dorian and Gregory started talking at once.

"Your Majesty I'm sorry I should have recommended more martials—"

"Father I had no idea—"

"Horns and fire, gentlemen. Hold your tongues, for once, both of you. My words are for my daughter-in-law, and her alone."

It seemed to Eleanor that the air had left the room with Ezra Oliver. She swallowed, and waited for his wrath.

"Oliver is gone. Alive, dead, as of now we don't know." King Casper's bushy brows came together and he jabbed one finger in Eleanor's direction. "But if not for your diligence, and your keen observations, we would never have recognized his guilt. The wolf would still be among us."

Eleanor's mouth fell open, as did her husband's and Dorian's. They resembled a school of beached fish. The king continued.

"I've lived with Oliver so long I look his loyalty and his power for granted. I've been in his office a thousand times, and I've never paid one shred of attention to his books, let alone some potted plant. And goading him with his own arrogance…and sending his own magic back in his face….limp-dick…" The king chuckled. "The Oracle's faith in you was well justified, Eleanor." The king raised his glass, and Eleanor raised hers with him. Dorian and Gregory joined them, and she drained her glass as swiftly as either.

"You will make a fine mother to my grandchildren. Let us hope for a brother for Leticia soon, shall we?" Eleanor's jaw clenched. She should have known King Casper would compliment her in one breath and cut her with the next.

"There is one last thing, and then we must all rest, for there is much work to be done," said the king, as he set his empty glass on the table. "It's about the Horn itself. I see no damage, but I wonder about this." He picked up the piece of Fire-iron and pointed at the white hair.

"It was there when Roffi handed it over," said Dorian.

"It's firmly attached. Here's the end." He gripped the unicorn hair in his thick fingers. "Perhaps if I just—" He yanked hard, and the hair unwound, spinning the Horn on the desk.

The Horn shattered with a sharp crack. It covered the Council table with shards of Fire-iron. A tiny unicorn's horn, about the size of a man's finger, lay in the middle of the sparkling pile.

For a moment no one spoke. The king put his forehead on his hands. "Oh, dear HighGod above us. What have I done?"

"Vigor," said Gregory.

He stood and left the Council Hall. Dorian and Eleanor left next, followed by the king, and made for the unicorn barn on the north side of the palace.

Eleanor did not know what she expected. Teardrop might charge her, or run from her, or worse yet, not recognize her. She only knew what her history books said, and what King Casper's terrified reaction told her. Without the Horn, the bond between the Desmarais kings and the unicorns would almost certainly be broken.

Teardrop's paddock was on the near side of the barn. Dorian, Gregory, and the king passed her and went on their own worried ways. Eleanor stopped at the gate. The mare stood at the back of the enclosure, near the stall door. Eleanor slipped under the fence rail. "Teardrop?"

Teardrop raised her head. Her liquid eyes took Eleanor in, but she said nothing. Eleanor came closer, and still the silence. "Teardrop?" she whispered.

The mare lowered her head. “Do you think me so small-minded?” she said. A fat tear slid down her muzzle.

“I—”

“No old dead thing could cleave me to you.”

“I’m so sorry,” said Eleanor, abashed. “I should have known.”

She slid her arms around the mare’s neck. When they were both composed, Eleanor asked a question. “Why, if the Horn had no power, have the unicorns protected it all these years?”

Teardrop answered as if it were obvious. “Because the kings asked us to protect it.”

CHAPTER 30

You Will Be Fortunate In Love

Eleanor sat beside the watching pool, waiting to be acknowledged. Nothing ever changed in this cavern. Even the blankets wrapped around Hazelbeth looked the same. By her third visit Eleanor's sense of urgency overcame her sense of wonder.

Rosemary, of course, was as peaceful as ever. Eleanor resisted the urge to start the conversation herself. Hazelbeth finally turned in their direction.

"Rosemary," she said, "and Eleanor Desmarais. How good to see you."

They exchanged greetings, but when Rosemary seemed inclined to linger over pleasantries Eleanor took advantage of the first pause in the conversation.

"Hazelbeth," she said. "If I may be blunt—"

"Why ask, dear?" said Rosemary.

Eleanor shushed her. "I cannot thank you enough for your assistance during the recent catastrophe—"

"Thank yourself, child," said Hazelbeth, with her usual lack of enthusiasm.

"You are too generous, and I'm afraid I must ask for your help once again. The king himself seeks your counsel. Pray, can you tell me if Ezra Oliver lives?"

The Oracle's rheumy eyes closed, and Eleanor feared she had fallen asleep. "I have known of Ezra Oliver for many years," the old witch said, "but I have never met him. He does not hold with my magic."

"Don't magicians have oracles?" Eleanor asked.

"Not many," said Hazelbeth. She opened her eyes. "I am not precise enough for them. My magic is too philosophical."

"Magicians prefer the hard and fast," added Rosemary.

"Not an uncommon trait among men," Eleanor said.

"I know he has great power. I have watched for centuries, and I have not seen his equal." The lines in Hazelbeth's brow deepened to small canyons, and she shook her head. "No matter. I cannot imagine he survived. I believe the water swallowed Oliver into his own vision. No witch or magician has ever been able to transfer a living body from one place to another. Some have tried, and all have died or disappeared forever. The pressure…the pain…if the water took him he is dead or as good as."

"Praise HighGod." Eleanor inhaled and her air-starved lungs thanked her. It seemed she'd been holding her breath since Oliver vanished into the table. "Please, one last question. I'm sure my stepmother, Imogene Brice, was party to Oliver's plan. Can the pool tell you anything about her?"

"No. I sense someone involved, but your revelation of Oliver's treachery did not destroy his protective spellwork. The identity of his accomplice is nothing but a haze."

"Oh," said Eleanor, deflating. "I cannot put their association from my mind. It must have had something to do with Sylvia…perhaps offing the poor old duke once I lost my head and position. Sylvia has certainly put herself in Gregory's path at every opportunity…but one detail bothers me. How would it benefit Imogene to be rid of me, gain a crown for Sylvia, and then have the Desmarais replaced by the Svelyan king?"

Eleanor had spent several sleepless nights concocting answers and then discarding them. She rambled on, hardly hearing herself.

"Imogene has hidden herself away in my father's house, even though she always stays with Sylvia in the duke's rooms at Eclatant. She claims ill health, but Margaret visited her and said she has no obvious ailment."

"Did Margaret ask after her opinion on Oliver's demise?" asked Rosemary.

"She did. Imogene said we were all misled by him, but nothing else." When Eleanor repeated Margaret's message something in it tickled the corner of her mind, but Hazelbeth's abrupt change of topic distracted her.

"I am sorry I disappoint you," said Hazelbeth. "Perhaps I have other news that will be heartening."

"Other news?"

"Yes. I have always watched for signs that could point to you. You are, as much as anyone can be, dear to me."

Eleanor took it as a compliment. "Thank you."

"I have seen that you will be fortunate in love."

It was the last thing Eleanor expected to hear. She chose her words carefully. "It is, I regret, difficult for me to see the truth in that prediction. Can you tell me more?"

"No. That is all. Unfortunately, I cannot offer more clarity, but keep it close to you."

"Do you—"

"Hmmm," said Hazelbeth. "Close."

Eleanor realized that was all the answer she would get.

Imogene's new maid flittered around Eleanor's head like a thirsty mosquito. She poured tea, set out cakes, and curtsied until Eleanor was certain the woman's knees would give out. Eleanor sipped her tea and glanced around the sitting room of her father's house. The past year and a half had wrought many changes. If HighGod had plunked her down in this room in a dream she would not have recognized it. She sat on a Fire-iron chair so intricately carved it would have been very much at home in King Casper's receiving room. The rest of the new furniture matched the chair's opulence, as did the elegant wallcoverings and two floor-to-ceiling tapestries. A painting of Sylvia and the Duke of Harveston hung above the fireplace, and Imogene herself glared down from opposite wall.

The Imogene in the portrait looked much livelier than the wretch sitting across from her. She had not seen Imogene since the Awakening Ball six weeks ago. The changes in her stepmother would have been alarming had Eleanor any concern for the woman's wellbeing. Her collarbones were like tree roots marring what had once been a smooth path toward her enviable cleavage, but even those treasured assets had suffered over the past month. The bodice of her golden gown sagged dejectedly. Dark circles ringed her eyes, and her hair had not seen a washing in at least a week. She looked all of her near forty years and then some.

"Missus Brice," said Eleanor. "You look like a horse that's been ridden too hard."

"How kind of you to say so, Your Highness."

Eleanor handed her teacup to the maid. "No wonder. The last few weeks have been trying for us all. Do tell, how have you been getting on without your friend Mister Oliver?"

Imogene stiffened, and Eleanor swore she noticed a tick underneath her stepmother's right eye. "He was no friend of mine."

"Leave us," Eleanor said to the maid. The startled woman dropped one last clumsy curtsy and fled with her overly sweetened tea and frilly cakes. Eleanor turned back to her stepmother and tossed all caution and niceties to the wind. "I know you were involved. Admit it."

Imogene's nostrils flared. "I'll do no such thing. You have no proof."

"Yes, you are fortunate. Both accomplices dead yet here you sit."

"I have no accomplices as I am innocent of your claims!"

Eleanor leaned back in her chair. "Banishment does provide endless hours of idle time, Mother Imogene, and you were often in my thoughts. Of course you have never born me good will, but I wondered. Would you go to such lengths, and put yourself at such risk, to satisfy an old grudge?"

Imogene's formerly glorious chest puffed out. "You can't possibly think I harbor those old feelings. I'm a woman of my own renown these days. The mother of a duchess."

"Yes! A duchess!" Eleanor said with a smile. "But have you not always truly longed for a princess? I think so! So Mister Oliver promised he'd push Sylvia on Gregory once you were rid of me. I'm sure it all made sense to you. You get a crown, and he gets an ally close to it. You lied to Margaret about Mister Roffi's intentions to get him into my rooms...easy that...the heart of one daughter is worth sacrificing for the success of the other...and then stoked a raging fire under the gossip kettles!"

"Mister Roffi lied to me—I never—"

"Bah, you gave him ample time to take the lay of the land, plant a thousand stolen trinkets, and supposedly seduce me." Eleanor propped her feet on Imogene's fancy Fire-iron table and laughed. "Besides, your own words gave you away. *We were all misled by him*. All of us."

Eleanor waited for Imogene to speak, and when she got no reply Eleanor spoke for her. "I think Oliver lied to you. You didn't know he would give the Horn to Roffi. I can imagine you, this whole time, thinking Roffi quite the fool for believing Oliver would turn it over. No, no, just a little ruse to get rid of Eleanor, then back on its pedestal it goes once Eleanor and Roffi have taken the blame. Who would believe a foreigner and a devil-eyed former chambermaid over the king's Chief Magician? Oliver used you just as he used Christopher, and me, and

King Casper's trust. All in the name of the Svelyan king's wild goose chase."

Imogene set her teacup down so hard the brown liquid leapt out of the cup and sprayed across the table. "I would never willingly endanger the Bond. I had no intention—" Her eyes widened and her mouth snapped shut in a white line. They sat in stiff silence for a while, and Eleanor was reminded of a long ago carriage ride across Maliana, and a dozen street urchins begging for the Godsmen's mercy.

"I thought so," Eleanor said. She stood up. "You're right. There's no proof. I have my suspicions and eight years of living under your roof. I have your own daughter's warnings. Your neglected daughter." She thought of her own dear Leticia, only a few weeks in the world and so adored. "I pity you, incapable of loving anyone but yourself. And Sylvia, when it suits your purposes."

Imogene's dull eyes came into sharp focus, and an old fear stirred in Eleanor's stomach.

"You'd say that to me," Imogene said. "You, who robbed me of my one true love."

Eleanor's confusion must have shown on her face, because Imogene stood. She leaned forward, until her breasts were before Eleanor's nose. With shaking hands, Imogene pulled a piece of tattered, yellowing lace from her bodice. She dangled it in front of Eleanor's widening eyes.

The pattern. Two intertwined roses. The same pattern that graced Imogene's ugly statue in the front hall. A piece of ripped lace…

Eleanor finally found her voice. "Robin."

"Yes," said Imogene. "My sweet Robin. You took him from me."

"I don't understand…how…" She shook her head. "You were so cruel to him."

"You stupid girl. I had to be cruel to him. How else could I keep him with me, in my service? Drag him from house to house for five years? No widow comes to her new husband with a groom. Could I be kind to him, sing him songs, sew him shirts…show the world how I loved him with every breath in my body? Could he speak to me outwardly of his own love…a man from Meggett Fringe who couldn't even write his own name?"

And it all made sense. Imogene rising at dawn to wake Robin…his patience at her horrendous treatment of him…his rage…no, despair, as he sliced away at her nightgown that afternoon. And here, in front of Eleanor's face, hung the remnants of that sadness. In a bit of lace and a simple, beloved carving.

"But why did he leave?"

"Your father dismissed him. After you blathered away about what you'd seen."

"No—I never meant for him to go. Father just told me to stay away from him—"

"You think Cyril would explain his plans to a ten-year-old child? He knew…when you told him…the groom, in hysterics, in the mistress's bedroom? He knew what was between us. He threw Robin out with nothing but the clothes on his back, so Robin joined the army. He said he'd come back. Earn money. We'd run away. Me and him and my girls…" Eleanor could not believe it, but tears ran down Imogene's face. "But he was killed. By a dragon, during the first transfer he worked at the Mines. His sergeant said he did it for the extra pay…"

Imogene buried her face in her hands. "And your father died a week later. I had the estate to keep us fed. A roof over our heads. I was free."

For a moment Eleanor thought of taking Imogene's hands. *I understand, Mother Imogene. I can't have the man I love, either. I know how it feels to be trapped. Oh, I do understand.*

But Imogene looked up. "You did this to me. It's your fault he's gone, you and your blabbering mouth. And still, I couldn't get rid of you. You were too much like me…a mother-killing, cursed child. A child who spoke out…like I did, when I was young. Robin loved that about me…" She paused, and seemed to wait for the pain to pass before continuing. "I couldn't send you into the streets. Even with a voice that took from me the only person who ever made me happy. But you wouldn't bend. Wouldn't become manageable. And then you stole the only dream I had left. A crown for my beautiful, exquisite daughter. I have no more pity for you, Eleanor Brice."

So the lines remained drawn. There would be no reconciliation between the two women, shared heartache or not. "I've never sought your pity, as I never sought to cause you pain," Eleanor said. "Nor will I ever, as long as I draw breath, forget your treachery against the crown."

"You can't threaten me," Imogene whispered. "My daughter is the Duchess of Harveston."

"And I'm the future queen of Cartheigh. You shaped that naïve girl who stumbled into the palace. You don't realize you also helped me put her to rest." Eleanor curtsied. "Good day, madam."

Eleanor stirred when his hand ran up her hip. She had fallen asleep quickly after Leticia finished nursing, and she was bone tired. She shifted against him, feeling his body wrap around her, and she sighed, half asleep. She felt dimly powerful that even in her body's new baby daze she could feel his arousal, hard against her back. He cupped her swollen breast and kissed her neck, just like he had at Rabbit's Rest.

"I've missed you," he said.

She rolled toward him, a sleepy smile on her face.

"And I you," she said, but when she opened her own eyes the ones that looked back at her were brown, not pale green.

She took a deep breath. Gregory leaned in and kissed her. His is tongue slid into her mouth. She turned her head.

"Gregory, I can't, not yet. It's too soon after the baby."

"I know," he said. He groped her breast again and it was no longer pleasant. He slid his hand down her flaccid belly. She grabbed it before it could go any further.

"Eleanor, please," he went on. "I promise I won't take it too far. Just let me touch you. It's been torture."

She didn't know whether to laugh, cry, or hit him. *This is part of it*, she thought, *part of returning to Eclatant.*

Maybe, but it wouldn't be the same. Not after Rabbit's Rest. Nothing would be the same. She smiled sweetly at Gregory, and kissed him back, before turning away from him and letting him continue his exploration.

"Please don't wake Ticia," she whispered. The baby slept in her cradle beside the bed. The purple rabbit watched over her.

"I'll try." She knew that gruff tone in his voice. This shouldn't take long.

Any guilt she had left floated up the chimney and dissipated into the night. She closed her eyes and thought only of Dorian's promise.

Before Ticia was a month old Gregory spoke of packing for Solsea. He suggested she leave the baby behind with a wet nurse, but Eleanor flatly refused. Just because most ladies at court abandoned their children to an army of servants didn't mean she would. Her resistance irritated Gregory, but once she promised the baby's care would not get in the way of her being on his arm he acquiesced. She would bring along the obligatory wet nurse, and a nanny, and as many of her best dresses as she could fit into. So began the delicate balance of so many mothers, the divvying of attention between children and husband. In Eleanor's case, she added a third. She and Dorian had both stepped back, afraid of giving themselves away, trying to figure out this new dynamic, but she had no doubt they would. She was more secure in his love than she had ever been in her husband's.

At least Gregory was enamored of Ticia. He held her while she napped. He made ridiculous faces at her. He even changed her diaper on one memorable occasion. Eleanor laughed until tears streamed down her face when he held the baby up to show off his efforts. The diaper promptly slid off, and Ticia just as promptly piddled on her father.

"I will give you ladies credit. There are some skills I cannot master," he said, and excused himself.

Eleanor invited Rosemary and Mercy Leigh to Eclatant for a picnic the day before they left for Solsea. Both women were visibly distressed.

"Are you sure you can't leave Ticia here?" asked Rosemary. "She'll be near grown by the time you return."

"It's so far," said Mercy Leigh. "What if she gets sick?"

"It's only for two months this year," said Eleanor, "and there are witches in Solsea, Mercy Leigh, even if they lack your skill."

"Country bumpkins," said Mercy Leigh.

"Mercy," said Eleanor, "how unlike you. Come now, you don't really want me to leave her, do you? Would you have me follow the same philosophy of mothering as Sylvia?"

"Of course not," said Rosemary. "We will miss you, that's all."

Anne Iris sat on the blanket. "Don't worry, Rosemary. Margaret and I will not let Eleanor neglect her child."

Margaret joined them. "Anne Iris will have plenty of time to watch Ticia when she's not drinking wine and chasing marriage prospects."

"You know," said Anne Iris. "Eliza wrote and said Frederick Harper is no longer engaged! Yes, he called it off. Just wait until he sees me in that blue gown..."

Eleanor laughed, anticipating the trysts her friends would get into along the cliffs. She herself looked forward to dancing off the last of her baby chubbiness. It would be good to be back at Trill Castle.

Dorian left Gregory and the other men at lawn bolls and sat beside her. Chou Chou dropped from an overhanging branch like a falling apple and lit on his head. Dorian absently put a hand to his hair and Chou crept down his arm. The parrot nibbled at the brown leather glove Dorian wore to cover his missing finger.

"It's hot," Dorian said. "I could do with some cliff breezes."

"I was just thinking the same thing."

"Indeed, the salt air does wonders for my complexion," said Chou. He hopped onto the blanket.

Dorian reached out for Ticia and Eleanor handed her over. His big hands cradled the baby's tiny head. She cooed when Dorian blew on her nose.

"Dorian!" Gregory called. "Where's the whiskey?"

Dorian gingerly returned Ticia to Eleanor. His hand brushed hers, as if by accident. She admired the length of his stride as he ambled across the playing field. He passed the whiskey to Gregory's manservant, took a ball from Brian, and gave it a lazy toss. It rolled across the lawn and gently tapped the target.

"You bastard!" said Gregory. "Everything you touch turns to gold." He draped an arm around Dorian and lifted his shot glass. "To Mister Finley, the luckiest man my kingdom." The other players laughed and joined his toast.

You will be fortunate in love.

Eleanor kissed the redheaded child in her arms. The game played on.

What happens next?

Turn the page to read the first chapters of

THE DRAGON CHOKER

CHAPTER 1

COME WHAT MAY

ELEANOR BRICE DESMARAIS DID not often pass an afternoon mucking out stalls. She had no aversion to hard work. Eight years of living under her stepmother's roof as the maid in her father's house had left her accustomed to the aches that came along with a vigorous day's labor, but all that was nearly two years behind her. It was hardly becoming for the wife of the Crown Prince of Cartheigh to haul hay bales and wield a shovel, even if her hauling and shoveling benefitted not a mere cow or horse, but a unicorn.

THE UNICORN IN QUESTION peered into the stall. Her white mane fell over the edge of the half door leading to the paddock. "This is unnecessary," Teardrop said. "Let me call the groom."

Eleanor shook her head. The grooms had lingered, embarrassed and confused, until she snapped at them to take their leave. Her own rudeness irritated her. As one who had spent much of her life in servant's shoes, she always treated the help with respect.

"I agree with Teardrop," said her parrot, Chou Chou, from his perch above her head in the rafters. "It's frightfully warm. You might expire."

"Hush, Chou," said Eleanor. "I'd rather be out here in pants than inside in a petticoat and corset."

"Why don't we take a ride?" asked Teardrop. "We could visit the beach at Porcupine Bay."

"No," said Eleanor. The thought of Porcupine Bay brought memories of his pale eyes reflecting the sky. She attacked the hay with her pitchfork.

Three festive weeks had passed in the resort town of Solsea, full of the usual summer diversions: parties, tournaments, picnics, hunts. At every event Eleanor stood beside her husband, Prince Gregory, smiling and laughing and dying inside. Only her newborn daughter, Leticia, brought her any real happiness.

Leticia was over two months old. Two months since she was accused of the theft of an enchanted national treasure and her husband abandoned her. Since she'd exposed Ezra Oliver, the king's chief magician, as the true culprit, and sent him into magical oblivion.

Two months since Dorian Finley had sworn he would find a way to love her.

Eleanor knew one false move on her part or Dorian's would send them both to the scaffold. Gregory was the heir to the throne, the keeper of the Great Bond. The living legacy of three hundred years of good fortune wrought by a mystical synergy between unicorns, dragons, and the Desmarais family. He would hardly suffer an affair between his wife and his best friend. Eleanor and Dorian had not spoken more than pleasantries since their last night together during her exile at Rabbit's Rest Lodge.

The misery of their separation in plain sight finally drove her to the physical exertion of cleaning the unicorn barn. An ocean breeze drifted over the cliffside and across the rolling grounds of the royal compound, Trill Castle, but it stopped short against the walls of Willowswatch Cottage. The modest moniker belied the mansion's heft. Its Fire-iron and granite walls blocked any hint of moving air that might have found its way to her sweaty forehead. The unicorn barn, with its stone facade and dazzlingly white interior, was cheery, but a stable is a stable. Wide un-paned windows let in both sunlight and flies, the latter of which buzzed Eleanor's face. Heat bore down on her from all sides. She ignored the headache pounding behind her eyes. She'd barely managed a full meal a day the past few weeks.

She brushed a few strands of damp blonde hair behind her ears. Sweat dripped down her face, and she wiped it away with the tears that snuck out of her mismatched eyes. One blue, one brown, both stinging with cooped-up frustration. At least the perspiration provided a disguise, let the tears flow without suspicion.

"What in the name of holy HighGod is this?"

Eleanor straightened, only to be confronted by both sources of her misery. Gregory and Dorian, in their riding clothes, stood in the barn's entrance. Gregory walked to her, but Dorian stayed framed in the passageway.

"Sweetheart," continued Gregory. "What are you doing? Let me call a groom."

"We tried to convince her, sire." Chou Chou flew down from the rafters and lit on the handle of her pitchfork. As he flapped around in an attempt to maintain his balance, a few red and blue feathers floated down amidst the hay. "Talk some sense into her before we have to call a witch to revive her."

Eleanor wiped at her face again and forced a smile for the millionth time since her return from Rabbit's Rest. "I don't mind. The exertion will help me fit into my dresses again."

"Hardly. I think you slighter than ever before. Don't disappear on me. I need something to hold onto." Gregory ran a hand down her arm and her skin crawled.

She glanced at Dorian, but he was examining a stirrup. He turned it over in his hands, and the silvery Fire-iron threw reflections of sunlight against the walls in jolly rainbows. Eleanor wished he would look at her.

"Where are you boys going?" she asked, turning back to the hay.

"Just taking Vigor and Senné for a ride down to Porcupine Bay."

Porcupine Bay, again. The hay crinkled and crackled as Eleanor flung it about Teardrop's stall.

Dorian finally spoke. "Would you and Teardrop join us?"

"I must return to Ticia." Eleanor probably would not have joined them anyway, but her breasts ached after two hours away from her daughter.

Gregory scowled, and a line appeared between his light brown eyes. "Again? What about the wet nurse?"

Dorian opened Senné's stall door. He eased the black stallion's silver horn aside and disappeared inside.

"Gregory," Eleanor said. "I can't stay away from her all day."

"Hasn't this gone on long enough?"

She swallowed her pride and sidled up to him. "Oh, stop. Don't you want me to come along to the Harper's dinner tonight?" She touched his cheek.

To her surprise he grabbed her around the waist. He spoke in her ear again. "I want you to enjoy yourself. Have a few glasses of wine. Relax."

She knew exactly what he meant. As she whispered her reply, she caught Dorian watching them over Senné's stall door. "You know I have to see a witch first, husband. The birth—I need to know all is healed."

"Well call one. Soon." It was a command, not a request. He kissed her nose and strode into Vigor's stall.

Vigor and Gregory followed Dorian and Senné into the courtyard. The grooms rushed around them, handing off bits of tack and hoof picks, happy to be allowed to do their duties. Senné and Vigor stood beside each other, black and white, like two giant chess pieces.

"Enjoy the ride," said Eleanor, as Dorian swung into the saddle.

"We'll miss you, and Teardrop," he replied. She cringed at the distance in his voice. He could have been speaking to his butler.

Gregory kissed her again. This time she felt the flick of his tongue. He mounted and she held Vigor's bridle. The unicorn nuzzled her with his velvety lips. She stroked his nose and squinted up at Gregory.

"Dorian and I have been called to Point-of-Rocks to meet with the Ports Minister," he said. "There's a shipment of raw Fire-iron coming down from the Mines. A big one."

"Bigger than usual?"

"Early summer yields are always good. The dragons burn hot in the spring months. Mating season," he said with a laugh. Eleanor ignored the reference to mating and attributed his mirth to the thought of copious amounts of money. Fire-iron, the light, wondrously versatile result of a dragon's body heat and fiery breath, was the lifeblood of her country.

"We leave the day after tomorrow."

"How long will you be gone?"

"Oh, nine, maybe ten days."

Eleanor's heart sank. It must have shown on her face, because Dorian teased her. "Don't be glum, Eleanor. With Gregory gone you can hole up with Ticia all day and night if you choose."

She tried to join him in their old banter. "I hope the Ports Minister has stored up on whiskey and wine if he's to entertain you two for ten days." It was a sorry attempt, but Gregory didn't seem to notice. He grinned.

"Don't worry, Dorian will bring me back to you with my brains intact." He leaned down. "Now go send for that witch. I don't want to wait another two weeks."

She watched them go, across the grounds toward the steep path leading from Neckbreak Cottage to Porcupine Bay. Gregory didn't look back, but Dorian did, although he didn't wave or smile. Eleanor felt warm breath on her neck and rested a hand on Teardrop's silky neck. Chou Chou lit on her shoulder. Neither spoke, but their silent understanding comforted her. She kept her face from crumpling. When Dorian and Gregory disappeared she walked up the stone path to Willowswatch to attend her daughter.

The next evening Eleanor sat on a blanket on the south lawn with her beloved stepsister, Margaret. They passed Eleanor's daughter and a basket of grapes between them. Ticia smiled and cooed and enjoyed the attention. Eleanor missed the company of her other dear friends, Anne Iris and Eliza, but with Anne Iris recently married and pregnant (under speculation that the two had not necessarily happened in that order), and Eliza busy with her second baby, neither had made the trip to Solsea this year.

"I wonder how Anne Iris is getting on," said Margaret, as if reading Eleanor's mind.

"I wonder how her husband is getting on."

"True," said Margaret. She ran a hand over her kinky brown hair, made kinkier by the summer humidity. "Perhaps pregnancy will distract Anne Iris from flirtation."

"Doubtful. She'll have more cleavage to flaunt than ever."

"Poor man, he'll be a jilted husband before he even has a chance to be a jilted father."

They laughed, and Eleanor felt a prick at the reference to jilted husbands. She'd enjoyed a brief respite from guilt in the weeks following her return to Eclatant, but lately her conscience had been hanging on her skirt like an insistent child. Although she had been a jilted wife for the entire duration of her marriage, she couldn't fully embrace her husband's comfort with deceit.

Gregory, Dorian, and Raoul Delano crossed the lawn. Raoul sat on the blanket beside Margaret and kissed her cheek. A blush lit Margaret's face, and Eleanor marveled at her friend's happy beauty. She only wished her stepmother could see it. *How Mother Imogene thinks her homely I'll never know.*

Gregory pulled Eleanor to her feet and took Ticia. He held the baby high in the air and blew on her belly. He snuffled at the fat rolls around her neck and she tried to suck on his chin. Eleanor laughed. Gregory's love for their daughter always elicited a genuine reaction from her. He rested the baby on his shoulder. She seemed no larger than a kitten against his broad chest. His auburn hair melted into the fuzz of the exact same shade on her head.

"Did you find a witch?" he whispered.

"I did, but she cannot come until Friday."

Gregory exhaled, hard. "Well, we can both think on it while I'm away." He spoke to Dorian. "I'll need something to distract me from my loneliness."

"You can drink alone," said Dorian. "You've done it before."

"Alone?" asked Eleanor.

"Dorian's sister changed the dates of her visit. She's arriving tomorrow with her family."

Dorian looked out over the cliffs. He pulled a flask of whiskey from his pocket and took a long drink. "Gregory generously gave me leave to remain at Trill with Anne Clara and Ransom and the children."

Eleanor feared her voice would shake, so she waited a moment to speak. "How kind of you, Gregory."

"Ah, Dorian only sees Anne Clara a few times a year. It was the least I could do for keeping him locked in the Council Room at Eclatant." Gregory gave Ticia to Eleanor and sat on the blanket.

Eleanor smiled casually at Dorian. "Are you anxious to see Anne Clara?"

"I am." His eyes, so light they were at once the color of the grass and the water and the washed out sky, were fixed on the Shallow Sea.

Eleanor strained for some hint, for some acknowledgement from him. He sat on the blanket beside Gregory. He tapped his fingers on the hilt of his father's Fire-iron knife, the one he always kept in a sheath along his right boot. As she looked down at his dark hair a terrible thought struck her. Dorian had changed his mind.

Gregory left the next morning with several Unicorn Guards. Anne Clara and her family arrived a few hours later. Eleanor drifted through the next two days in a fog of false happiness. She planned picnics and tea parties. She took a long nap with Ticia. She spent a floury afternoon in the kitchen making cakes with Anne Clara's children.

One of the Finley cousins hosted a dinner in honor of Anne Clara's visit, and Eleanor took an hour determining which of her gowns Dorian would find most enticing. Her choice, soft blue silk with lace trim around the bodice, emphasized her nursing-enhanced cleavage. She hovered beside Dorian throughout the party, hoping he'd ask her for a dance. She had watched with disdain for two years as countless other women desperately maneuvered around him. Her efforts were just as soundly ignored. She called for her carriage before the clockworks struck ten. Raoul and Margaret accompanied her back to Trill. She rested her head against the rocking window and closed her eyes; both to give Raoul and Margaret privacy and to avoid the passionate looks flickering between them.

One the third morning of Gregory's absence she made her way to the unicorn barn again. The grooms must have assumed her unsatisfied with their supervision of her mare's care. She could hardly detect an errant piece of straw, and could see her own reflection in the Fire-iron trough of clean water. She sat down in the scratchy straw with the pitchfork over her lap. Chou Chou and Teardrop refused to leave her alone.

"The weather is fine, is it not?" asked Chou.

"Lovely," said Teardrop. "Though I do feel thunder on the horizon."

Eleanor opened her mouth to reply; then shut it. She dropped the pitchfork and hung her head between her knees. Her stomach clenched as she held back the sobs that had been hopping around her mid-section for three days, searching for a way out. Teardrop snorted. She nibbled at Eleanor's hair and her wide hooves rustled the straw. Her mane rested on Eleanor's back like a comforting blanket on a cold night. Chou lit on Eleanor's head.

"There, there, darling," whispered Chou. "Please, don't—"

"Eleanor?"

She lifted her head. Dorian looked down at her over the stall door. She wiped her eyes and stood. Chou left her head for Teardrop's back.

"We could ride down to Porcupine Bay," Dorian said.

A few wordless minutes later and Eleanor and Teardrop were following Dorian and Senné across the grounds. They passed Margaret and Raoul as they set up a game of lawn bolls.

"Off to Porcupine Bay?" asked Raoul.

Eleanor nodded. "If only you could join us."

"If only we had unicorns we might," said Margaret. "I don't fancy hiking down that cliff in my dancing slippers."

Dorian and Eleanor waved good-bye and continued on their silent way. Eleanor did not fear the incline. She only feared what Dorian might have to say when they reached the beach. She ignored the breathtaking view around her, and the chattering of the cliff lemurs. As they descended, the wind picked up and blew the smell of salty water and damp seaweed into her face. She imagined his explanations: the danger, the immorality of lying to Gregory, the pointlessness of continuing an affair with no hope of ever being anything but just that. She heard herself trying to rationalize with him, and then screaming and crying, then agreeing with the hopelessness of it all. Her imaginary dialogue so engaged her that she lost her balance when Teardrop stopped behind Senné at the edge of the blood-colored waters of Redwine Falls.

"Let's go this way." Dorian pointed past the falls and back up the cliffside. She nodded. As they began the ascent Eleanor took hold of Teardrop's mane. She could see the falls behind them, but the path had already faded to nothing but a jagged edge along the rock. There was no beach below, only boulders reaching their scarred faces out of the tossing waves like drowning sailors gasping for air. She waved at the gulls screeching and hissing around her head. Teardrop nicked one with a swing of her horn and they retreated.

"They're protecting their nests," shouted Dorian over the wind, waves and protesting birds.

She looked down, her face blanching with dizziness, and counted no less than ten twiggy brown nests full of fat yellow eggs in the rocks around Teardrop's hooves.

"Teardrop, are you sure you can do this?" she asked.

"No," said Teardrop, "but I will try."

Eleanor gritted her teeth. "I'll leave you to it."

They climbed for half an hour. Teardrop slipped twice and dislodged several loose rocks. With each jolt Eleanor shut her eyes and muttered prayers.

Senné stopped and waited for Teardrop to catch up. Dorian pointed out a long, dark patch in the blue water. "There's a reef out there. No ships can get within half a mile, not even the villager's fishing boats."

Teardrop's footing improved with each step. Eleanor relaxed and watched the sea. She wondered how many living beings, other than the gulls and a few bats, had ever taken it in the view.

She faced forward again and her heart stopped. Dorian and Senné had disappeared. She looked down, searching for Senné's black form against the gray rock.

"Do not fear," said Teardrop. "Here we are."

Eleanor slid from Teardrop's back. The mare ducked into what at first seemed nothing more than extra darkness amidst a host of cast shadows. Eleanor just could make out the flash of Senné's horn and the light in his liquid eyes. Teardrop walked the three paces across the cave and stood beside him. He puffed in her ears and she nipped his shoulder. Both settled into quiet watchfulness. Teardrop glowed softly white against Senné's black bulk.

As Eleanor walked further into the cavern she could see her hands again. She turned toward the light, and climbed through another opening in the rock. She wondered how Dorian, with his height and breadth of shoulders, had contorted himself to fit.

He stood in a chamber made from a space between the cliff wall and a pile of boulders a hand span above his head. Sunlight streamed through the haphazard cracks between the rocks and struck the hard-packed dirt floor.

"I thought this place...we could come here..."

Eleanor threw her arms around his neck. His mouth found hers and they both tumbled to the ground.

She sat astride him and pulled his tunic over his head. Their arms collided as he repeated the favor for her. He buried his hands in her hair, then scraped them down her back. She wrapped her arms around his head and arched her back. He kissed both her breasts and his tongue flicked over her skin. He rested his head against her chest and squeezed her until she couldn't breathe.

"High God, Eleanor," he said. "How have I survived the past two months?" She hated herself for it, but she started crying. He looked up at her. "My love, what is it?"

She shook her head and bit her fist. She spoke around the sobs. "I thought—you changed your mind—you didn't want to—"

His impossibly beautiful eyes widened. "Changed my mind?"

"Yes. You've been so cold—we haven't spoken in weeks—"

He took both her hands in his. "I've been cold because I'm afraid anything I say will give me away. When Gregory told me about the trip to Point-of-Rocks I wrote Anne Clara and asked her to come right away. I've spent weeks searching this place out."

Eleanor swallowed. "I'm sorry—"

"I made my decision at Rabbit's Rest. Come what may, I'm here, in this with you."

Ten minutes later she had finally cried herself dry. She nestled in the crook of his arm as they lay in the dirt. She ran her fingers over his forearm, and lifted his hand. She kissed the knuckle that should have ended in his smallest finger, had a giant bird not snipped it off during her exile last spring. He curled his remaining fingers into a fist and then tugged at a lock of her hair. "Will you spend all of the time we have together sobbing? I'll have to store handkerchiefs up here."

Eleanor punched his arm, and rolled on top of him. "There's one more thing."

He sighed and blew her hair out of his face.

"I'm afraid this won't be enough for you. Since we can't…as we said at Rabbit's Rest…the risk of a child…"

"I told you I understand your fear. I've already considered it."

"And what conclusion have you reached?"

"Well." He laced his hands behind his head. "We can find enjoyment other ways. Not to belittle the pleasures of the most holy act, but it's not the only dance at the party."

"What do you mean?"

He could not hide his confusion. He cleared his throat. "I assumed you would be familiar with…that you had some experience with…"

She blushed. In this cave she fully planned on pretending Gregory Desmarais, Crown Prince of Cartheigh, did not exist. Unfortunately, all her experience of the intimate sort came from her association with him. For a moment it felt as if her husband had peeked through one of the cracks in the rocks above them.

"My education in this subject has been basic and…not particularly… inspired."

Dorian sat up on his elbows. "Indeed?"

"Indeed, sir."

He smiled, and looked much like an eager schoolboy about to impress his teacher with the wealth of his knowledge. "Let us get right to it."

He sat up, and once again she wrapped her legs around him. He touched her nose, then ran his fingers down to her lips. "We'll go slow."

She followed his lead and traced her own hands down his face. His fingers wound across her breasts and circled each nipple. She shivered, and stroked the smattering of dark hair covering his hard chest. She reached his belt, and then let her hands drift down further.

He sucked in his breath, and she joined him when she felt what waited for her beneath his calfskin riding leggings. She had noticed something through the fog of Rabbit's Rest, but within the span of a few days she had faced execution for treason, nearly died in childbirth, and finally heard Dorian proclaim his love for her. She'd been in no frame of mind to dwell on particulars. She'd been too overcome to fully understand his…girth.

"Dorian?"

He opened his eyes. "Yes?"

"I… Never mind. What were you saying?"

She shivered again at the color in his pale cheeks, and the shimmering dots of black in his green eyes. She had seen that look on his face before, in a broom closet, a lifetime ago.

"I said we'll start at the beginning." He loosened the buttons on her leggings. His big hand slid below the waistband and she gasped. "And we'll go to the end."

CHAPTER 2

THUNDERHEADS

TWO DAYS LATER ELEANOR sat on the edge of her bed in her nightgown. She'd asked Margaret to stay with her while the witch did a quick examination of her nether regions to determine their readiness to resume marital relations. Margaret handed her a cup of water. Eleanor always felt a bit lightheaded after such awkward sessions. Her maid, Pansy, bustled around the room, no doubt waiting to bring out the smelling salts should she keel over. Once Eleanor's head cleared she asked the witch for the verdict.

"YOUR HUSBAND MAY RETURN to your bed," said the old woman, "but I would advise you to go slowly. It must have been a difficult birth, and a difficult recovery. Excuse my familiarity, Your Highness, but have you and your husband been intimate…in other ways?"

Color rose in Eleanor's cheeks as she thought of Dorian's gentle explorations. "I've experienced some intimacy, but it hasn't been painful."

"It may take some time to readjust to true relations."

As the witch gathered her tools, Eleanor asked if she might have a few words alone. After Margaret and Pansy left the room Eleanor called the old woman to the chair beside the bed. "Are you sure I'm ready?" she whispered.

The witch nodded. "It may indeed take a few tries, but with care you'll be fine."

Eleanor took the woman's hand. "I think myself not healed. I think I'm not ready."

Comprehension dawned on the witch's face. "Your Highness—"

"Please. Can't you just say—"

The witch shook her head. "Lady, I understand your plight, and your fears. Others have said the same to me—"

Hope leapt into Eleanor's chest. "And you helped them."

"I have, in the past, stretched the truth—"

Eleanor squeezed her hand again.

"—but in this case I cannot. I cannot lie to the prince."

Eleanor let go and hid her face in her hands. The witch made more excuses but Eleanor did not hear them. She had three days until Gregory's return. She dismissed the witch and called for Chou Chou. She sent him to Dorian's room with a message.

Dorian tugged at Eleanor's leggings.

"Lift your seat. They're stuck," he said. She giggled and did as he asked. She lay on her back, watching the sunlight flicker through the cracks between the boulders. She caught sight of a gull or two flashing past. Her heart was light, the witch's visit blissfully out of her mind.

Dorian kissed her navel. "Are you ready for lesson number two?"

She ran her fingers through his wavy hair. "I'm always prepared for any lesson, at any time."

"We'll see." His kisses trailed down her belly. He pushed her right leg to a gentle bend. His hand wrapped around her thigh, and he bit the inside of her leg. She exhaled hard as his mouth crept lower. She looked down at him.

"Dorian, what are you doing?"

"Shhh."

She felt his tongue and gasped. "Oh! What are you—"

"For once, Eleanor, please, don't ask me questions."

She didn't ask him anything else, but a few minutes later all her questions were answered. She cried out, with such gusto she heard Teardrop whinny in alarm from the exterior cavern.

She stared up at the rocky ceiling, her chest rising and falling. "HighGod above," she finally said. "It's no wonder you have to beat the women off with a stick."

He collapsed against her, laughing. She reached for his shoulders and pulled him toward her face. "Thank you," she said. "That was quite enlightening. However, I don't see what was in it for you."

"On the contrary, your pleasure is mine."

She touched his lips. "How can I reciprocate?"

His mouth curled at the corners and her pulse quickened again. "There is a way, if you're keen."

She kissed him and pushed him onto his back. "I have a notion of how to proceed, but I may need some direction."

He murmured his agreement. She unbuttoned his leggings and took his quiet instructions. As always, Eleanor was a quick study.

Eleanor counted Margaret Easton her dearest friend. As for her other stepsister, Sylvia Easton Fleetwood, Duchess of Harveston, there was no love lost between them. Margaret and Sylvia's mother had married Eleanor's father when all three girls were in the realm of ten years old. Within a month Cyril Brice had unexpectedly gone on to HighGod. Imogene Brice had wasted no time dismissing Rosemary, the witch who had been Eleanor's tutor for as long as she could remember. Imogene promptly designated Eleanor as the maid in her own father's house, and generally harassed and abused her for the next eight years. Thankfully, Rosemary provided Eleanor with clandestine tutoring, for Eleanor was unsure if she would have survived life under Imogene's harsh rule without the solace of learning and letters. Sylvia followed her mother's lead in all things, from her hatred of Eleanor to her scrambling up the social ladder. While Eleanor had softened to Margaret long before her unexpected elevation, the enmity between herself and Sylvia only deepened with time and good fortune.

Regardless of her personal opinions, Eleanor knew Sylvia was not the most famous hostess in Cartheigh for nothing. Never had a lady taken the social calendar by storm so quickly. No other hostess was so beautiful or gracious. No one else provided such lavish food and drink or music so lively. No one else could attract quite the caliber of guests, or boast such a fabulous setting as The Falls, the most magnificent estate on the Solsea cliffs. When Sylvia offered to host the Waxing Ball the other ladies agreed it was a fine idea, although it was unheard of for a hostess in her second season to take responsibility for the climax of the weeklong Waxing Fest.

Eleanor wondered if some of the smiling, simpering women secretly hoped the party would fall as flat as the chest of a six-year-old girl. They did not realize that Sylvia was never without a plan. According to Margaret, she'd come up with this one last winter, over several long, hopelessly boring months in Harveston with her mother, her baby son, and her ancient, doddering husband. She'd planned at least ten parties' worth of themes, many of which she'd already unveiled this summer. She had saved her greatest vision, however, for the Waxing Ball.

Throughout the ball Eleanor watched Sylvia with begrudging respect. Her stepsister stood on the outskirts of the party all night, directing the magicians. She swept past Eleanor and Margaret as the servants passed morsels of shrimp and sweet cheeses.

"Sister, here. Take this." Sylvia thrust her wine glass at Margaret. She pushed her dark hair off her shoulders. "Where are the damn servants?"

"Passing the shrimp, Your Grace," Eleanor said to the top of Sylvia's head.

Sylvia's eyes were the same shade as her hair. She squinted up at Eleanor, but ignored the comment. She seemed to have bigger shrimp to skewer. "That damn apprentice set off a drizzle beside the chocolate fountain. He'll never conjure at a party in Solsea again."

Eleanor watched a young magician frantically waving his arms in an attempt to dissipate what appeared to be a miniature rain cloud. "A bit harsh, perhaps?" asked Eleanor.

"Hardly. Better to make an example of one magician and keep the attention of the others on their spells and their pay." Sylvia pranced off in the direction of the hapless apprentice.

By the end of the meal, the temperature in the ballroom had dropped, and a light breeze picked up. Leaves on the enchanted pear trees dotting the room showed their pale undersides. The willow trees shed a profusion of enchanted pink petals. The petals drifted amongst the dancers, never seeming to feel the need to meet the floor. People pointed at the thick clouds swirling against the ceiling. The unmistakable scent of impending rain filled the air. Eleanor saw Sylvia wave at the magician in charge, and the storm broke.

The candles dimmed to a faint glow. Everyone gasped as the first fingers of lightning shot through the clouds. Rain pelted from the sky, but it disappeared above the tallest guests' heads. On cue, the musicians started in with a boisterous reel, and the flashing lightning kept perfect time to the music. The dancers stampeded the floor.

Gregory appeared at Eleanor's side. They joined the swirl of faces and colors leaping out from the darkness. He pulled her embarrassingly close, but she supposed it didn't matter, as no one could see her properly anyway. Sylvia had draped herself across one of the handsome Fleetwood boys, a cousin of her own decrepit husband.

She deserves a bit of a lark after so much effort, thought Eleanor.

The energy in the room seemed to flow not only from the lightning, but the dancers themselves. Eleanor would have lost herself with the rest of them had she not been so preoccupied. She looked for Dorian in the jostling, sweaty mob.

"Amazing, isn't it?" Gregory yelled. "Leave it to your stepsister to reinvent the Waxing Fest!"

She abandoned her search and smiled at him. "Yes, it's—"

He interrupted her, but she couldn't hear his words over the thunder, or read his lips through the flashing lightning.

"Pardon?"

He shouted into her ear. "Tonight you return to me. A most wonderful night!"

Eleanor joined Margaret and Chou Chou in her stiflingly warm carriage. Gregory and Dorian had brought Vigor and Senné, as they often did on summer nights. Eleanor opened the windows and tugged at the bodice of her gown. As she wiped her sweaty neck, she silently blessed Pansy for suggesting an upswept coiffure. She envied her husband and her lover their pants and their cooling breeze. Eleanor and Margaret chatted about the ball.

"Astounding," Eleanor said. "A monsoon, in the Duke of Harveston's ballroom."

"Sylvia's always loved storms," said Margaret. "When we were very small she'd strip off all her clothes and run naked through the rain. You can imagine it drove Mother mad."

Eleanor laughed. "She would have liked to do so tonight."

"The male guests would have approved, if not the ladies."

Chou Chou joined the conversation. "Sylvia was particularly interested in the opinion of one male guest."

Eleanor pinched Chou's beak. "Not her husband, I assume."

"No, yours."

"That's nothing new. Sylvia thought herself halfway to the crown last spring during my exile. She needs to keep herself in Gregory's sights in case I'm accused of treason again, or choke on a chicken bone."

Chou landed in Eleanor's lap. His round yellow eyes fairly bulged from his head. "Don't you want to know what she said to him?"

Margaret leaned toward him. "Chou, were you spying on my sister?"

He nodded.

"Well, tell us what you heard!" she said.

Chou's scaly toes curled and uncurled. "I took a few turns around the ceiling while we waited for the carriage. As soon as you ladies left Sylvia made a line for Gregory. I clung to the tapestry behind them for a listen." He cleared his throat, and the voice of Sylvia at her most coyly charming slipped from his beak.

"Are you having a nice time, Your Highness? Can I get you anything?"

Gregory, with a hint of impatience: *"Lovely time, yes. I'm afraid I must be going."*

Sylvia again: *"So soon? Why? If you leave the party might as well end. I'll just call off the storm and send everyone home."*

Margaret scowled. "Must she be so obvious?"

"Shhh," said Chou in his own warble. Gregory returned. *"If it were up to me we would be the last to go, but I'm afraid Eleanor must return to our daughter."*

Sylvia again: *"You could send them on and stay. I'd love the company."*

"Gregory obviously wanted to follow you. He started to walk away but Sylvia grabbed his hand. *"It must be difficult for you, Your Highness, with the princess so dedicated to your daughter."*

Gregory: *"Of course she's dedicated to our daughter. As any mother should be."*

Sylvia: *"Oh, don't I know it, as I'm also dedicated to my own dear son. I've heard nothing but praise for the princess's mothering."* At this kind sentiment Margaret coughed into her hand. *"But I think some women forget. We must remember the needs of our husbands, lest we never become mothers again."*

Chou laughed Gregory's rumbling chuckle and ducked his head under his wing, in what Eleanor assumed was a reference to Gregory's habit of swiping his hands through his hair. *"Indeed, Your Grace, I think you're correct."*

Chou paused. "Now this next, I hope I can do it justice. Sylvia sounded...unlike herself. Like...an old friend offering advice. *"In all seriousness, Your Highness, Princess Leticia is young. I'm sure Eleanor will learn. Just give it some time."*

Gregory again. *"I appreciate your concern. Now I really must be going. Thank you for another memorable night."* Chou pecked Margaret's hand, in a birdie goodbye kiss. "Once he left Imogene appeared out of nowhere, like one of those enchanted lightning bolts. She grabbed Sylvia's arm and whispered a lot of somethings in her ear. I couldn't catch a word, but it didn't appear to be a pleasant conversation. Sylvia stormed off, and I had to make a swoop for the carriage."

"I must get a parrot," said Margaret.

"Thank you, Chou," said Eleanor. "How comforting to know of Sylvia's concern for my marital felicity."

Margaret put a hand on Eleanor's knee. "Don't worry, darling. I'm sure Gregory has no interest in my sister."

Eleanor squeezed her hand and smiled. She rested her chin on the window ledge and inhaled the salty Solsea air. Let Margaret think what she would, but Eleanor's disquiet had nothing to do with jealousy or concern for Gregory's fidelity. She'd lost interest in both subjects long ago. The same could not be said of the topics of her stepmother and Sylvia. Eleanor remained convinced of Imogene's involvement in Ezra Oliver's ill-fated plot to bring her down, although she'd never uncovered any proof. Imogene's discouragement of her daughter's solicitation of Gregory's affections could mean only one thing. Imogene had heeded the warning Eleanor had given last spring. *I'm the future queen of Cartheigh...I won't forget.*

She must not want to draw attention to herself, Eleanor thought.

Apparently Sylvia did not share her mother's newfound modesty.

Eleanor had chosen Letitia's nursery herself. The spare bedroom, connected to Eleanor's own chamber in the south tower of Willowswatch cottage by a narrow passageway, had a lovely picture window overlooking the gardens surrounding Speck Cottage. She thought someday Ticia would enjoy looking out at the wood-planked cottage with its pink shutters and cozy front porch. Speck had always reminded Eleanor of a doll's house.

Darkness hid the soft yellow rugs and the carved silver suns the servants had hung from the ceiling. She couldn't see the heirloom Fire-iron cradle with its rabbit fur dragon robe, or the embroidered purple rabbit stationed beside Ticia's silk pillow. She dared not light a candle, as experience had taught her the flickering lights would rouse the baby from her milk-induced sleep. Eleanor would have a time getting her back into the cradle, however, after Sylvia's outlandish Waxing Ball that did not seem such an awful prospect. The more time she spent in the nursery, the more likely her husband would give up and returned to his own chamber.

She'd lifted Leticia from her cradle, sat in the rocker, and put the baby to her breast. Leticia responded with sleepy obedience and set about nursing in her sleep. Eleanor tickled her chin and her feet to keep her going, but after half an hour the poor child was so full and tired her head flopped to one side and her lips locked. Eleanor held her upright for a few minutes to give the air a chance to escape her belly, and laid her in her cradle.

She pulled the straps of her nightdress back over her shoulders. She waited in the dark for a while, listening to Ticia's soft breathing and the distant crash of waves through the propped windows. Sweat beaded on her forehead. She might have stood there all night had she not heard a voice calling her from beyond the closed door.

"Eleanor? Are you not finished?"

She found her husband sitting on her writing desk, a glass of wine in one hand and a wooden jewelry case in the other. She assumed Gregory must have dismissed Chou. Last summer he'd usually stayed with Teardrop on such nights, but tonight she wondered if he'd gone to Dorian.

A voice in her head screamed at her to go to Gregory, but she couldn't. She sat on the dainty pink coverlet. He crossed the room and slid the strap of her nightdress over her shoulder.

"I had the witch's report. I'm glad you're well again. I brought you something from Point-of-Rocks."

She opened the box. A necklace, one the likes of which Eleanor had never seen, lay on a velvet pillow. The chain itself, Fire-iron links interspersed with tiny diamonds, was a wonder, but the large center stone captivated her.

It was about the size and shape of a chicken's egg. Tiny lights shifted and flickered inside it, like handfuls of sand lit ablaze and come to life. As Eleanor watched the stone turned from midnight blue to canary yellow to a deep blood red. The red remained for a while, before giving way to rose petal pink, then a bright lizardy green. The green must have been satisfactory, because the color held as she lifted the necklace.

"Fascinating," she said. "What is it?"

"It's called spectite. I picked it up in the Point-of-Rocks bazaar. Some traveling Mendaens found the stone in abundance on the southernmost islands. Where men and women go naked day in and day out, even magicians and witches, and they know nothing of learning or true magic."

"I've heard of those places," Eleanor said, as the green became a snowy white. She forced herself to look at Gregory. It was hard to believe that less than two years ago his very presence had been enough to fix a smile on her face. "Thank you."

Gregory sat beside her on the bed, and she lifted her hair. "I thought of you when I saw it." He hooked the clasp. "It's been so long. I've ached for this day."

"As have I." The fewer words out of her mouth the less likelihood of her bursting into tears.

He pushed her back on the bed and lifted her nightdress. She grabbed at his hand. "Gregory, the witch said we must be careful. Go slowly, because the birth was so difficult. She said it might take several—"

"Yes, sweetheart, I understand. She said something about it."

"Gregory, I'm—"

His mouth cut her off. He unbuttoned his leggings. She turned her head when he pushed against her. It started out slowly enough, but then his pace quickened. She gasped.

"Gregory!"

He must have misread her meaning. He bore down hard, once, twice, three times, and groaned. There was no mistaking the meaning in her cry this time. She rolled away from him before he had a chance to do so first, as he always did. She curled on her side and tucked her hands between her legs.

"Eleanor?" He shook her shoulder.

She pressed her face into the coverlet. Every fiber of her being wanted to hit him. Scratch his eyes out. Rip every auburn hair from his head.

Ticia, Dorian, Ticia, Dorian. The names formed a protective circle around her temper and her sanity. She faced him. The tears on her cheeks showed him her opinion of their reunion. She had assumed him drunk, but his eyes were surprisingly clear.

"Maybe a few attempts would have been a good idea," he said with an awkward laugh. He stood, and tucked himself back into his leggings. He stood at the end of the bed with his back to her.

"I'm sure next time will be better." He walked to her side of the bed and kissed her forehead. "I'll leave you to get some sleep. I'm sure Ticia will have you up with the sun. Goodnight, sweetheart."

When he was gone she took up two pillows and dragged the pink coverlet from her bed. She crept into her daughter's room and spread the blanket on the floor. She rested her head on one pillow and put the other one over her head, but try as she might she could not sleep. She finally gave up and sat in the rocker until the sun crept over Neckbreak and Walnut Cottages on the eastern side of Trill Castle, and the bitterbits began screaming their morning wake-up songs.

Chou Chou returned with the dawn. He flew into Leticia's open window. "Darling," he whispered as he lit on the back of the rocker. "What are you doing in here? And awake?"

"Where were you?"

"I stayed with Dorian."

"I see."

"I told him of the return to...the former state of affairs," Chou said, his voice even lower. "He was quite disturbed."

Eleanor felt as if she were listening to her own voice from outside her head. "Disturbed. Yes, aren't we all."

CHAPTER 3

WHAT IT'S LIKE FOR A MAN

"DAMN."

"What is it?" asked Gregory.

"Damn, damn, damn!" Dorian threw a few extra damns in for good measure. "My bow. It's cracked."

Gregory took the bow from Dorian and ran his fingers along the polished wood. He flexed it and it bent at a decidedly sharp angle. "Damn is right, man. It's done in." Gregory turned on the two stable boys they had brought from Trill, and his own manservant, Melfin. More servants came and went across the dirt and grass courtyard, if it could be so called, of the Egg Camp. They loaded pack animals with food and drink to sustain Gregory and his friends during their long day's hunt. The Egg itself cringed behind them, a three-story oblong stone house embarrassed by its own architectural awkwardness. "Which one of you fools cracked Mister Finley's bow?" Gregory asked. "Fess up, now!"

Dorian dropped the bow and fixed a look of supreme irritation on his face. The stable boys, each of whom clenched the bridle of a skittish hunter, exchanged panicked glances. Dorian thought the younger of the two might hide behind the horse if only he could convince the animal to stand still.

Dorian took hold of the feistier horse and swatted the animal's neck. "Stand, you bloody fool."

The horse threw up his head and chewed his bit. "Sorry, sir," the horse said.

"Now boys," Dorian said. "Did either of you damage that bow and fail to inform me?"

The younger boy looked at him with damp brown eyes and let his older friend answer. "No, sir. We didn't, I swear—"

"I forgive you. It must have been a sad accident." Dorian hardly wanted to torture these poor children, since he had in fact broken the bow himself before they left Trill. A pity to sacrifice such a fine weapon. The older boy started to thank him but he turned back to Gregory. "Looks like I made the ride out here for nothing."

"I'd say use one of mine, but they're all too short for you. So are Raoul's. Too bad Brian's not here."

"Ah, Smithy. He got more than he bargained for when your father made him Duke of the Northcountry."

Gregory laughed. "He has a castle and a fortune and a title to make the Smithwick family proud—"

"But he won't be enjoying life on the edge of the Dragon Mines like he enjoyed Solsea summers. More rain, fewer beautiful women."

"He'll be back next year, once he's settled into his responsibilities. He'll need to find a wife. But we could certainly use his long arms right now."

Both men fell silent, and Dorian could see solutions rolling through Gregory's mind and being dismissed. "I'll ride back to Trill for a spare," said Dorian. "I should have brought one in the first place."

"It does seem the only option. Senné can get you there in a few hours."

"You and Raoul go on without me." Dorian held up his left hand. "Between the ride and a meal and stringing a bow with nine fingers, I won't be back until this evening."

"Too bad, friend."

Dorian clapped Gregory on the back. "Ah, you know Senné and I always enjoy a long ride. Besides, I'd rather have two days of good hunting than three sitting on my ass in the Egg."

"I have some feminine entertainment joining us after dinner."

Dorian doubted Gregory meant women of musical persuasion. "All the more reason to hurry back," he said.

"I told Melfin to make sure they're lively." Gregory tugged at the back of his neck. "I enjoy lively women…enthusiasm…" He muttered to himself as he wandered to his mount.

Dorian waited around the courtyard with a cheerful, aching smile plastered on his face. He called out wishes for a pleasant weather and slow quarry. He waited until Gregory, Raoul and their attendants disappeared over a low hill. He'd never seen fine Desmarais hunting horses move so slowly. If he pushed Senné they could make it back to Trill Castle in under two hours.

"Bring Senné," he said to the older of the two stable boys. The boy did not dally.

Just over three hours later, in the cave above Redwine Falls, Dorian wrapped his arms around Eleanor's shoulders. She sat between his bent knees, chattering about this and that, but he scarcely heard her. He grunted answers to her questions. He ground his teeth, all the while cursing himself for the anger that simmered beneath his monotone responses.

Excitement had turned to anxiety as he picked up the bow he'd strung two days ago, left Trill, and backtracked up the cliff to their cave. To his surprise, once he started the ascent towards a seemingly successful rendezvous, tendrils of irritation wrapped sneaky fingers around his mind.

Dorian pulled Eleanor closer, like a selfish toddler hiding a favorite toy in his lap. He buried his face in the flaxen thickness of her hair, and then bit the side of her neck. Another childish gesture. Next he would stand up, stomp his foot and shout *mine!*

"What's wrong?" she finally asked.

"Nothing." He pulled her around to face him and kissed her.

"Maybe we should talk about—"

He kissed her again, and snipped off her words before they could spread through the cave like the roots of a stubborn weed. She returned his kiss, but for the first time he sensed her holding something back.

Her reluctance added to his frustration. His hands chased themselves over her body, trying to wipe the past two weeks away and take them back to that last meeting, before Gregory returned from Point-of-Rocks. His need for her, the need that sat in his groin and in his heart as if his blood had turned to hot Fire-iron, made him reach a hand under her tunic, then thrust it down the front of her leggings.

She did not respond as she had before. There was no gasp of delight, no exhale of hot sweet breath on his neck. She grabbed his hand. "Dorian, please."

He turned away from the sorrow in her mismatched eyes, like bits of earth and sky trapped in her face. "I'm sorry. You don't want…you don't want me to…I understand."

"No, that's not it… I just…I'd hoped to avoid this topic."

"Say it." He walked to the wall and leaned his forehead against the cool stone.

He closed his eyes as her halting words floated over his shoulder. "Gregory…he's been very...attentive…" The noise of his teeth scraping together in his own head sent chills down his back. "…and not very patient. I have some…pain."

Dorian's lungs seized in his chest. The breath he finally drew in fairly sucked all the air out of the cave. "Motherfucker! Mother—motherfucker—"

Dorian rarely swore, but even the shock on her pale face did not silence him. Senné's silver horn poke through the cave opening. "Is something wrong?" he asked, with the calmness of a servant asking after an undercooked steak.

"No! Everything is just fucking perfect!"

Eleanor climbed through the hole. Dorian waited a few minutes, and then followed her. She stood between Senné and Teardrop, her face hidden behind the swirling black and white silk curtains of their manes.

Dorian spoke to Senné first. "Peace, old friend. No anger justifies my rudeness. Pray, forgive me."

"I have never known you to speak so," said Senné, "and I feel only worry at the pain that would bring forth such words from your mouth. You have my forgiveness."

Teardrop eyed him with less understanding. He spoke to Eleanor through a protective layer of shiny white hair. "Eleanor, come back. Please, I pray you will also forgive me."

She stepped out from behind Teardrop. Teardrop snorted her concern but Eleanor silenced her with a few quiet words of reassurance and a squeeze around her arched neck. She wiped her wet face on the mare's mane. Teardrop muttered to Senné and kicked the rock wall behind her. The sound of her agitation followed Dorian and Eleanor into the chamber.

Eleanor sat on the dirt floor. He sat before her, as if in preparation for an imaginary game of poker. She broke the silence. "I understand your anger."

"What if we were careful, Eleanor? I've never, not in all these years, had one woman lay a claim of a child on me. You know I can control—"

"Is that what this is about?" Her face went from white to fiery red.

"Of course not, but it…you don't know what it's like for a man… for me…knowing he can have you whenever—"

He knew as soon as he said it he'd crossed an un-crossable line. Her anger made his seem kitten-like in comparison.

"For a *man*? For you? *You don't have to bed him!* You don't have to feel him jabbing and scraping away at you—feel your pride and heart and your soul shriveling up like a…a bunch of grapes left out in the sun!"

Teardrop whickered from the other chamber, but both unicorns must have assumed there would be no peace in the cave this afternoon.

"So the fact that you've gone ten or twelve or however many years without spawning any *bastards* with the *hundreds* of women you've bedded is supposed to make me risk my daughter and any poor child we might beget and even your own stupid neck?"

He grabbed her arms. "Eleanor, please—"

"I won't. I'm leaving—"

"I'm so sorry." An unfamiliar burning ran from his eyes to his nose. "I'm afraid I might very well kill Gregory with my own two hands for causing you pain. I'm so jealous and angry I don't know if I can live with it."

She swallowed with a small chuffing breath. He let her pull him into her lap, as much of him as would fit without squashing her. He rested his head against her chest. "I'm sorry. I'm sorry," he whispered.

"Shhh, dearest. Don't. I love you, Dorian. I forgive you."

As she stroked his hair some of the anger ran out of him. He could not say all, but it relieved some of the pressure.

"We always knew this would come," she said.

"I didn't imagine he would hurt you."

"Darling, we must speak freely, or every one of our meetings will end like this. We return to Maliana in less that two weeks. It's unlikely we will be able to meet here again, and we have no safe haven such as this at Eclatant."

The impending return to the capital city and the shining Fire-iron monolith of Eclatant Palace had loomed in Dorian's mind for weeks. He spoke from the vicinity of Eleanor's breast. The weight of his head pulled the collar of her tunic low, and his breath bounced off her skin and back into his face. "If we can find a hideaway we may have an easier time of it. There are so many people about and our duties keep us from much leisure. More excuses to come and go. You have your charity work—"

"—and your Council duties and unicorn training."

Dorian nodded. "With the Paladins adding Senné to the breeding program we'll be spending even more time in the stables. Perhaps if I was put out to stud it would ease this ache in my poor neglected personals and I'd not be such a mouthy ass."

She flicked the end of his nose and kissed his forehead. "In that vein I must address another dragon in this cave. It brings me the same pain you must feel in relation to my...my marital arrangements. You cannot go on leading a seemingly celibate life, darling. You were hardly thus before. It will only raise suspicions."

Dorian sat up from her lap. "Gregory is full of questions. I said I've been bedding a girl from the village, but I don't know if he believed me. With honesty, in this regard my past history is not serving me well."

"Please...believe me," she said as she wrung her hands. "I would not expect you to live like a magician for the rest of your life. If you must take your pleasure elsewhere I won't begrudge you." He started to rebuff her, and then stopped himself. He wanted no one else, yet he could not deny the need to keep his reputation as a wonton womanizer somewhat alive, if only for the sake of their secret. Nor could he ignore the tiny hated voice in his mind, the one that asked a simple question. *Never again?*

He flinched at the pain in her furrowed brow and downcast eyes, but when he squeezed her hand she squeezed back. He put a finger under her chin made her look at his face. "I love you Eleanor. I'll never lie to you. If anything I do causes you pain you must tell me, and I will cease and desist. Soldier's honor."

She gave him a weak smile. "So it's come to this, that I would tell the man I love to bed another woman." Before he could respond she cupped his face in her hands. "Enough, all of it. We've spent most of this beautiful afternoon screaming at each other."

"I must return to the Egg. It will be nigh dark before I get back."

"Then make me forget, Dorian Finley. Give me something to take from this cave and hold onto in my bed when the sun goes down."

So he did just that.

Find out what happens next in book 2 of *The Cracked Slipper Series*

THE DRAGON CHOKER

ALSO BY STEPHANIE ALEXANDER

The Cracked Slipper

The Cracked Slipper Series, Book 2: *The Dragon Choker*

Coming Soon: The Cracked Slipper Series,
Book 3: *The Glass Rainbow*

Coming in 2020: *Charleston Green*, set in Charleston, South Carolina, the story of a clairvoyant mom of three, who uses her paranormal talents to solve a century-old murder mystery while rebuilding her life after a devastating divorce.

ACKNOWLEDGEMENTS

The Cracked Slipper Series has been a ten-year labor of love. Since I began the first book in 2009, my life has changed immeasurably. I've been through the hardest times in my life, and come out the other side with an outcome that is beautiful beyond anything I thought it could be. Too many people have been a part of this process to name them all, but a few require special recognition. First, to my sister-cousin, Haley Telling, thank you for always cheering me on, and coming up with wonderful ideas for ways to get my work out into the world, and helping me keep my chin up when the process beat me down. This is a hard business, and your eternal optimism helped me remember that the stories are the heart of it.

Thank you to my mother, Dianne Wicklein, who I admire above all other women, and who is a testament to the redemptive power of tenacity and faith. Thank you to my three wonderful children, who have gone from babies to teenagers while I labored on this project and rebuilt my life. They are my reason for pushing myself on good days, and my reason for getting out of bed on bad ones.

Lastly, thank you to my husband, Jeffrey Cluver. I would call you my Prince Charming, but as this book has tried to illustrate, Prince Charming is overrated. Instead, I will call you my best friend, my closest confidante, the rock I cling to when I'm floundering in a sea of writer-ly self doubt. You read my first drafts; you give me feedback I didn't know I needed; you spark my imagination when it's feeling about as combustible as a wet match. Thank you for being you.

There are so many others, but I will have to thank them all in person, lest I risk running on for another hundred thousand words. But lastly, thank you to my readers, who fell in love with Eleanor, her journey, and the enchanted universe she inhabits. I hope I've done justice to her story, and your imaginations.

—Stephanie

About the Author

Stephanie Alexander grew up in the suburbs of Washington, DC. Drawing, writing stories, and harassing her parents for a pony consumed much of her childhood. After graduating from high school in 1995 she earned a Bachelor of Arts in Communications from the College of Charleston, South Carolina. She returned to Washington, DC, where she followed a long-time fascination with sociopolitical structures and women's issues to a Master of Arts in Sociology from the American University. She spent several years as a Policy Associate at the International Center for Research on Women (ICRW), a think-tank focused on women's health and economic advancement.

Stephanie embraced full-time motherhood after the birth of the first of her three children in 2003. Her family put down permanent southern roots in Charleston in 2011. She published her first novel, *The Cracked Slipper*, in February 2012. Along with two sequels (*The Red Choker* and *A Ring in Blue*), the series has sold over 40,000 copies. *The Cracked Slipper* has made multiple appearances on Amazon's fantasy bestseller lists, and peaked at #11 in all genres. Stephanie has appeared on local and national media, been a contributor on many writing blogs and in writing magazines, and regularly joins with book clubs for discussions of her work.

In addition to her personal writing, Stephanie returned to the College of Charleston as an Adjunct Professor of Sociology and Women's Studies, and launched her freelance ghostwriting and editing business, Wordarcher, LLC. She has ghostwritten dozens of books, from novels to memoirs to academic theses. Beginning in the Fall of 2015, as a single working mother, she attended law school on a full academic scholarship, earning her juris doctor with honors from the Charleston School of Law in December, 2017.

She currently practices family law in Mount Pleasant, South Carolina, the Charleston suburb that is the setting of her latest novel, *Charleston Green*. Her personal experience rebuilding her life after divorce inspires both her legal work and her fiction.

CPSIA information can be obtained
at www.ICGtesting.com
Printed in the USA
LVHW011647150520
655693LV00003B/523

9 781647 040215